THE TIGER
MOM'S TALE

THE TIGER
MOM'S TALE

Lyn Liao Butler

BERKLEY

New York

BERKLEY
An imprint of Penguin Random House LLC
penguinrandomhouse.com

Copyright © 2021 by Lyn Liao Butler
Readers Guide copyright © 2021 by Lyn Liao Butler
Excerpt from *Red Thread of Fate* copyright © 2021 by Lyn Liao Butler
Penguin Random House supports copyright. Copyright fuels creativity,
encourages diverse voices, promotes free speech, and creates a vibrant culture.
Thank you for buying an authorized edition of this book and for complying
with copyright laws by not reproducing, scanning, or distributing any part of it
in any form without permission. You are supporting writers and allowing
Penguin Random House to continue to publish books for every reader.

BERKLEY and the BERKLEY & B colophon
are registered trademarks of Penguin Random House LLC.

Library of Congress Cataloging-in-Publication Data

Names: Butler, Lyn Liao, author.
Title: The tiger mom's tale / Lyn Liao Butler.
Description: First edition. | New York: Berkley, 2021.
Identifiers: LCCN 2021002706 (print) | LCCN 2021002707 (ebook) |
ISBN 9780593198728 (trade paperback) | ISBN 9780593198735 (ebook)
Subjects: LCSH: Racially mixed women—Fiction. | Taiwanese
Americans—Fiction. | Families—Fiction. | Inheritance and
succession—Fiction. | Taiwan—Fiction.
Classification: LCC PS3602.U8757 T54 2021 (print) |
LCC PS3602.U8757 (ebook) | DDC 813/.6—dc23
LC record available at https://lccn.loc.gov/2021002706
LC ebook record available at https://lccn.loc.gov/2021002707

First Edition: July 2021

Printed in the United States of America
1st Printing

Book design by Elke Sigal

To Pinot and Lokie, my heart and soul

1

Alexa Thomas had just bitten into a sesame ball when her mother told her she was in love with a woman.

Lexa wasn't really listening. She was absorbed in the Chinese pastry, her eyes closed and her elbows propped on the marble countertop in her sister's kitchen. Her teeth sank into the crispy exterior coated with sesame seeds, and just like the first time she'd eaten one in Taichung when she was eight, her taste buds exploded with the sweetness of the red bean paste in the center. Back then, her delighted exclamation caused her Taiwanese father to beam a smile on her so full of warmth she could still feel it all these years later.

"Did you hear me? Are you upset?"

Lexa's eyes opened at her mother's question. Sunlight streamed through the window, and she squinted, trying to see her mom's expression. It took her a moment to focus. She didn't have many pleasant recollections of her father and was reluctant to let go of the nostalgia caused by the memory of his smile and the scent of sandalwood she associated with him.

"I'm leaving Greg," Susan said.

Lexa froze, her teeth clamped around the chewy treat. "Hmpf?"

"There's someone else." Susan cleared her throat. "It's . . . she's a woman."

Caught off guard, Lexa inhaled sharply and choked. *Brilliant.* But really, what was the proper response when your sixty-one-year-old mom told you she was leaving your stepfather for a woman? She coughed and spat the sticky rice into her hand. "Who? How?"

"Phoenix. My acupuncturist. She's half-Asian like you," Susan said with false cheer, as if that made everything okay.

"Cool." *Cool?* Lexa's brain had stopped working. And boy, was Maddie going to flip out when she got back to her apartment.

"I'm happy. But I feel terrible about Greg." Susan sighed. "He's upset."

"You think?" Lexa's stomach twisted. "Sorry, it's just . . . poor Dad." Greg had adopted her when he married her mom soon after Lexa's first birthday.

"There's more." Susan took a deep breath. "I also quit my job to get my yoga teacher certification. I thought you'd understand, being a personal trainer."

"What?" Lexa's jaw dropped, and her hands flew up; she forgot about the morsel in her hand until it stuck to her hair. She cursed, just as her sister burst into the apartment.

"Sorry I had to leave." Maddie was breathless as she plopped onto the stool between Lexa and their mom at the breakfast bar, her face flushed from the early June heat. She pulled at the collar of her bright pink hoodie. "What did I miss?"

"Well . . . uh . . ." Lexa glanced at their mom.

"Corey get to school okay?" Susan asked, her voice still not quite right. Maddie had run out soon after they arrived at her apartment to take her three-year-old to afternoon preschool.

"Yes." Maddie stared at the side of Lexa's head. "What's that in your hair?"

"Um . . . sesame ball." Lexa waved a hand in the air as Maddie's gaze darted between Lexa and their mom. When Maddie narrowed her eyes, Lexa looked away. She concentrated instead on extricating the gelatinous mess from her long black hair, which she'd always lamented wasn't blond like the rest of her family's.

"Okay, what's going on here?" Maddie asked, and poked Lexa in the side.

Lexa gave her sister a don't-look-at-me face.

"Why don't you eat something? I brought your favorite. The wrap is gluten-free." Susan handed Maddie a chicken Caesar wrap and then reached behind Maddie to pluck the mess out of Lexa's hair.

"Thanks," Maddie and Lexa both said at the same time.

"So what's the occasion? Are you trying to bribe us or something?" Maddie gestured to the sesame balls, Lexa's favorite, and the other goodies spread out on her counter.

Lexa averted her gaze, tracing the veins in the white marble countertop as her brain scrambled to compute that her mom was leaving Greg . . . for a woman. As their mom told Maddie the news, Lexa hunched her shoulders, braced for her drama queen sister's reaction.

"What?" Maddie dropped the wrap, her mouth open like Lexa's had been a while earlier.

For a few seconds no one spoke, and the only sound in Maddie's apartment was the muffled traffic noise from Third Avenue, seventeen floors below.

Then Maddie found her voice. "So first you had a fling with Lexa's father all those years ago, and now you're leaving Dad for *another* Asian? Is it because he's white and you're, like, totally obsessed with anyone who's Asian? You don't even care if it's a pussy or a dick."

"Maddie!" Lexa gasped. "What's wrong with you?" She'd known Maddie would lash out, but this was a new one.

"Don't be crass, Madison." Susan rubbed her temple. "It's not about ethnicity. I would love Phoenix even if she was from Mars and had purple skin." She put a hand on Maddie's arm, but Maddie shook her off and moved her stool closer to Lexa's. Lexa bumped her shoulder against Maddie's, something she'd always done when her younger sister needed her.

"But she's, like . . . she's . . . a female," Maddie sputtered.

"It's not about gender or ethnicity. Sometimes you just connect with someone." Susan sighed and shifted out of the beam of sunlight, and suddenly Lexa could see her face clearly. She was startled at the intensity in her mother's eyes.

"So, what, it just happened?" Lexa was still struggling to understand. Her mom and Greg had been married for over thirty years, and before that, she'd had that fling with Lexa's Taiwanese father. She'd never mentioned being attracted to women.

"Yes. It's about the soul. She gets me on a level that no one ever has." Susan looked at Lexa. "Except maybe your father, all those years ago."

"Oh my God!" Maddie clapped a hand to her mouth. "You've been carrying a torch for Lexa's father all these years? You never really loved Dad?"

"Yes, I mean, no . . . I mean, yes! I love Greg." Lexa was surprised to see how flustered their normally unflappable mother was. "It's just a different kind of love."

"You really felt like that for my father?" Lexa could hear a touch of longing in her own voice and mentally shook herself. She wasn't that naïve little girl anymore, yearning for any news about her birth father, who lived so far away in Taiwan.

"Hello?" Maddie rapped the counter with her knuckles. "We're talking about Mom leaving Dad for a *woman*. Not about your father, who couldn't care less about you."

Lexa stood, her hands on her hips. "That's not true." But actually, Maddie was right.

"It's not like you care either." Maddie turned back to their mom. "I can't believe you'd do that to Dad. How did you just suddenly turn gay?"

"Leave her alone." Lexa was curious too, but she couldn't help defending their mom. "It's her life, and she deserves to be happy."

Maddie turned on Lexa. "Are you saying she wasn't happy with Dad? You *would* side with her. Dad isn't your real dad, so it's fine if Mom leaves him heartbroken and all alone."

Lexa drew herself up to her full height of five three and glared at Maddie. She was four years older, but Maddie had two inches on her.

"There are no sides. And Greg is my real dad. He's the one who raised me."

"Girls, stop. I'm sorry. I didn't want to break up our family." Susan slumped over the forgotten feast she'd brought. "Please don't fight about this."

"What happens now?" Lexa couldn't bear the defeated look on her mom's face and went to her, placing a hand on her shoulder.

"We're putting the house on the market. I'm moving in with Phoenix, and Greg is moving to the apartment in the city." Susan reached back and laid a hand over Lexa's.

Maddie let out a cry and jumped off her stool. Lexa swallowed hard. This was really happening. If she was this shocked, she couldn't imagine what the news was doing to Greg.

"I invited Phoenix to our dim sum brunch next Saturday. I want you to meet her."

Lexa's hand slipped off her mom's shoulder. Meet her mom's new lover? Already?

"No way. I'm not going." Maddie stamped her foot like she was a child having a tantrum, rather than the thirty-one-year-old mother of two that she was. She glared at them and stormed out her front door, leaving Lexa and her mom to stare at each other.

A moment later, Maddie slammed back in. "No. You get out."

Lexa picked up her purse and sidled toward the door.

"Not you," Maddie said. "Her."

"I have to go." Lexa eyed the door. She could go back to the gym early. She needed to think, to process this. She hated family drama. Maybe that was why she'd never wanted kids.

"What, you have a client?" Maddie asked. "They're more important than family?"

"They're not more important, but they need me."

Maddie stood in front of Lexa, blocking her way. "*I* need you. You're always so busy, with your clients and your friends and dating. I'm surprised you made time for us today."

Lexa shrugged. She did have a busy life. She'd worked hard over the years and had an impressive list of personal training clients. "Mom said it was important."

Maddie pointed to their mom and said, "You. I want you to leave."

"Maddie, don't be like this." Susan pressed a hand to her heart, and Lexa's resolve to leave cracked. As much as Lexa wanted to get out of there, she realized she had to stay and take control. She'd always been the one to smooth things between her mom and Maddie. Lexa figured that was why their mom had told her first.

"Mom." The look that passed between them spoke volumes.

"What?" Maddie looked back and forth between them. "What are you saying to each other? You always leave me out."

Susan turned to Maddie. "I'm sorry." She picked up her purse. "I love you."

Maddie didn't answer, and their mom left, after one last look at Lexa. When they were alone, Maddie sank onto her stool and stared at her counter. "I can't believe she's doing this to Dad." Gone were the anger and bravado she'd shown just moments before.

"I know, but it's not like she did it on purpose. Don't be so hard on her."

Maddie suddenly sat up straight. "Did you know? Did she tell you first?"

"Uh . . ." Lexa plucked the sesame ball off the counter to give her hands something to do. "She told me literally a minute before you came back."

Maddie pursed her lips. "You guys always have secrets from me."

"Maddie, we don't . . ." Lexa stopped because she *had* kept a secret from Maddie—a big one. "Anyways, this is Mom. How can she be gay? Or is it bisexual?" She frowned, thinking. "And I can't believe she quit her job to be a yoga teacher. She hates to exercise." Too late, Lexa realized her mom hadn't told Maddie that last part yet.

"What? She quit her job too?" Maddie's iPhone rang, and she looked down at the display. "Oh, no. It's the nurse from Connor's school."

While Maddie was on the phone, Lexa paced her sister's two-bedroom apartment, which was filled with real furniture from Ethan Allen, unlike Lexa's own studio, which was furnished with castaways. How could she help Maddie accept their mom's situation when she herself was still reeling? *Get a grip, Lexa. It's not as if someone died.*

Maddie ended the call and stood to grab her keys off the counter. "I have to get Connor. He's sick." She pointed a finger at Lexa. "And just for the record, Mom's making a big mistake."

"Give her a break. I'm as upset as you are. But we need to support her and Dad."

"No, we don't. I'm never speaking to Mom again."

Great. Maddie wasn't going to make this easy for their mom. Lexa already had a dysfunctional relationship with her Taiwanese father. She wasn't going to let her American family fall apart too. "You can't do that."

"Watch me." And Maddie slammed out her front door for the second time, leaving Lexa alone with the half-eaten sesame ball in her hand, wondering what had just happened to their family.

2

A week later, Lexa's client Andi Versacci handed her a bag of sesame balls before hopping on a treadmill in the crowded gym. Andi jabbed at the start button as if it had offended her.

"Where did you get sesame balls at eight in the morning on the Upper East Side?" Lexa held the bag away from her with two fingers, eyeing it with apprehension.

"Don't ask," Andi said. "And go easy on me today. My head is killing me."

Lexa tore her gaze off the bag and studied her client. Manhattan's newest celebrity chef was in old sweats and wore no makeup, her curly dark hair shoved into a messy bun. Lexa didn't comment, knowing Andi would tell her eventually. Her clients always told her everything.

It took only three minutes. "I got them in Chinatown this morning."

"And what were you doing in Chinatown on a Tuesday morning when you live up here?"

"I had a hankering for Chinese food?"

Lexa raised her eyebrows and placed the bag on top of her clipboard.

"Okay, fine. I hooked up with a guy last night. He lives down there and I stayed over."

"How was it?" Lexa asked with interest. They'd recently joined a dating site together.

Andi glowered. "I don't want to talk about it."

Lexa stopped the treadmill. "That bad, huh?" She wasn't having much luck either. Although there was that guy from San Francisco she'd met at the gym the previous month . . .

"So I treated myself to those paper-wrapped sponge cakes you got me once." Andi gave Lexa a sidelong look as they walked onto the weight floor. Weights clanged and machines whirled, competing with the buzz of conversation and the music pumping from the speakers.

"How many cakes did you eat?" Lexa could read each of her clients like an open book.

"Um . . . ," Andi mumbled. "Only six, but they're small. So it's like one big one, right?"

Lexa sighed. "All right, don't worry. We'll do a HIIT workout."

Andi grimaced at the mention of high-intensity interval training. Within ten minutes, her cheeks were red and she was gasping for breath as she jumped from a squat into a push-up.

"I hate burpees," Andi panted when she'd finished the set.

"Don't stop. Do bridge pulses and then get into a plank." Just then, Lexa's phone dinged.

"Why don't you check that while I rest?"

"No rest for you." Lexa smiled to take the sting out of it. She loved being a trainer. Better to be the one in charge than to have things happen that you had no control over.

Andi pouted but got into bridge pose by planting her feet

firmly on the floor, knees bent, and lifting her butt off the ground. "I fucking hate you."

"Hey, you're a celebrity now. You shouldn't curse in public." Andi's popular Food Network show followed her life as the executive chef of Bisque on the Upper East Side.

Andi shot her the finger and counted out loud, something she did because she claimed Lexa couldn't count and always made her do extra. Lexa checked her phone, and the smile slipped from her face.

It was from her half sister in Taiwan.

CALL ME ASAP. Something's happened to Baba.

A feeling of dread ran down Lexa's spine. She and her father rarely spoke these days, but she'd once cared for him. She'd thought he was so handsome in all his . . . *Asianness*, with the same black hair and square jaw she had. Lexa was the black sheep of her blond family with her Asian features. But in Taiwan, she looked like her Taiwanese family, and no one asked if she was adopted. Although there were some who thought she wasn't Asian enough . . .

"Earth to Lexa? Can I stop?" Andi had gotten into plank when she'd finished her bridges.

Lexa started, her heart beating fast, and blinked until Andi swam back into focus.

Andi collapsed out of her plank. "Are you okay?"

"I'm sorry. I need to call my sister in Taiwan. It sounds like an emergency."

"Of course. I'll just use the elliptical while you're gone." Andi wagged her eyebrows, and Lexa rolled her eyes. She knew Andi would sit and check her phone until she got back. Scooping her clipboard off the floor, Lexa headed to the employee lounge.

Hsu-Ling didn't pick up, and Lexa sent her a text. She drummed her fingers on the table in the empty lounge, frustrated that her sister hadn't answered. She reached for the bag of sesame balls and ripped it open, taking one out and biting into it just as her phone rang.

She swallowed, trying to get the sticky mass down her throat before she picked up.

"ChiChi?" Hsu-Ling called Lexa by her Taiwanese nickname.

"What's the matter? What happened to Baba?" Lexa managed to get out.

"He was in an accident." Hsu-Ling paused. "He's gone. He didn't make it."

Lexa's heart stopped, and a ringing sounded in her ears, drowning out the gym's music. The bite she'd swallowed lodged itself in her throat.

"So much has happened. There's more—a lot more. Can you come to Taiwan?"

Lexa shook her head hard. "No, I . . . I can't."

"Then I'm coming to New York. After the funeral."

"Really? Why?" Lexa's forehead crinkled. Hsu-Ling was afraid to fly and had never been on a plane.

"I need to talk to you about that last summer."

"What?" Lexa was suddenly sweating. "I'm at work. Can I call you back in a bit?"

"I'm so tired. I'll call you tomorrow morning, nine thirty my time? I have a lot to tell you. Would be better when I can think clearly."

"Oh. Okay." They said good-bye, and Lexa hung up, her thoughts in a jumble as she stared at the sesame balls.

To the Chinese, they symbolized happiness and good fortune. Yet when she'd eaten one last week, her family had been broken up by her mom's news. And now her father, whom she hadn't seen in twenty-two years, was dead, and her sister was flying to New York to talk about the summer she'd spent her whole life trying to forget.

She stood suddenly and threw the bag into the garbage. Damn those stupid sesame balls. They were bad luck. If she hadn't taken a bite, maybe her father would still be alive. As tears welled in her eyes, she realized she'd always thought there'd be time to reclaim her Taiwanese heritage and get to know her father again one day. Now, it was never going to happen.

. . .

Just as she predicted, Andi was sitting on a bench texting away when Lexa returned to the gym floor. She tapped her on the shoulder, and Andi looked up, startled.

"Oh, hey. I just got off the elliptical." She wiped a hand over her brow. "Whew, I went hard on that thing."

"Yeah, right. Come on, let's go. I'm sorry I was gone so long."

"No worries. What did your sister say?"

Lexa opened her mouth to answer, but instead, to her surprise, a sob escaped.

Andi pulled her down on the bench next to her. "What happened?"

"It's my Taiwanese father. He was in an accident. He didn't make it."

"Oh, no." Andi put an arm around her. "I'm so sorry."

Lexa inhaled and breathed in the familiar smell of disinfectant, sweat, and the rubbery odor of the mats in the gym. She was determined not to cry at work, and it took a few minutes to get her emotions under control. "It's okay. I didn't really know him. We should finish your session."

"Absolutely not." Andi squeezed her arm. "And it's not me being lazy. I don't care if you weren't close. You just found out your father died."

Lexa blew out a breath. "Okay. But let me at least stretch you. I need to move."

They made their way to a massage table. On autopilot, Lexa lifted Andi's leg to stretch her hamstrings.

"You don't talk much about your Taiwanese father and sister." Andi shot her a questioning look. "Why is that?"

"I haven't seen him since I was fourteen. We used to alternate traveling—I'd go there one summer, and he'd come to New York to see me the next time. But then . . ." Lexa fell silent.

Andi waited, and when Lexa didn't continue, she asked, "Taiwan is part of China, right?"

"Well." Lexa let out a short laugh. "If you ask my father's family, Taiwan is a separate country. They've been in Taiwan for many, many generations. My father always said, 'We're Taiwanese, not Chinese.'"

"I didn't know that. What about your sister?"

"We don't really know each other. I haven't seen her since she was ten and a half and I was fourteen. We keep in touch mostly through social media and the occasional emails or texts." Lexa bent Andi's leg to stretch her hips.

Andi waited a beat, and when Lexa didn't add more, she said, "Tell me about your father."

"What's to tell?" Lexa snapped.

Andi looked taken aback by Lexa's sharp tone, and Lexa winced. It wasn't Andi's fault that Lexa's father had died, bringing back all those memories.

"I'm sorry." Lexa closed her eyes for a moment before opening them to find Andi staring at her with sympathy.

"It's okay." Andi reached up and touched Lexa on the arm. "You don't have to tell me."

Lexa bit her lip, glad for the reprieve, but then a memory came to her. Before she could stop herself, she said, "My mom thought I was half-Japanese for the first two years of my life."

"What?"

"She taught English in Japan for a year. Right before she came back to New York, she and her Japanese friends took a trip to Thailand, and she met my father there. She thought he was Japanese because he was with a group of Japanese men." Lexa focused back on the stretch and took Andi's leg across her body into a spinal twist. "She didn't know she was pregnant until she came home. Her friends tried to find him, but no one knew who he was."

"Really?"

"She kept me, even though some people told her she should have had an abortion." Lexa made a face. "I'm glad she didn't."

"Me too. And now she's moved in with a woman." Lexa had told Andi about Phoenix. "I love it. She's such a free spirit."

"My father resurfaced two years later, when my mom's friend Kiko ran into him at a party in Tokyo. She's the one who told him about me. Turns out he was Taiwanese. He used to live in Japan and had kept in touch with his friends there."

Andi laughed. "That must have thrown her for a loop."

Lexa nodded. "She was so nervous when Kiko called her and said she ran into the man my mom had a fling with. But Mom really wanted me to know my father, so she asked Kiko to tell him. Kiko showed him a picture of me, and he said I had the Chang jaw." He'd claimed her as a daughter and started writing to her with the help of a friend who could read English.

"I don't get it. Why haven't you seen him in all this time?"

Lexa switched the stretch to Andi's other leg. "It's . . . a long story."

Andi stared up at her, and Lexa suddenly didn't want to talk about her father anymore. "So what's with the guy from last night? Is he Chinese?"

"No."

"Was it good?" Lexa wiggled her brows.

"Ugh." Andi shuddered. "I don't know what I was thinking. He only went out with me because he found out I had a show on the Food Network. I thought he liked me. I guess turning forty has somehow dimmed my bullshit detector."

"You're not forty for another few months."

"Which is an old hag to my mom." Andi wrinkled her nose. "She pointed out at lunch the other day that my eggs are getting older by the minute. Not that I need the reminder. I do want kids."

"People are getting married later, especially here in the city." Lexa finished stretching Andi and gave her leg a pat.

"I know. But she got married when she was twenty-three. I'm a dinosaur as far as she's concerned." Andi hopped off the table. "Anyways, I've got to go. I need a nap."

"I'll make up the missed time with you another day."

"Don't worry about it." Andi reached over and gave Lexa a hug. "You know I love you, even though I say I hate you every session, right? I couldn't have lost those thirty pounds without you."

Lexa nodded against Andi's shoulder, taking comfort from her friend's concern. "I know. Thanks for being here." She pulled away and studied Andi. "And you know you look great." Andi was curvy with a big chest and butt, but she was healthy and toned, thanks to the workouts. And she looked great on camera.

Andi smiled and waved. "See you later."

After Andi left, Lexa dropped onto an empty bench and dialed her mom's cell. She still had ten minutes before she had to teach a group fitness class.

When Phoenix picked up, Lexa's spine straightened. They were answering each other's phones already?

"Hi, Lexa," Phoenix said. "Susan is at her yoga training. She forgot her phone."

"Oh." Lexa's eyebrows lifted. So her mom really *had* quit her job of thirty-six years in the office of her daughters' old Catholic school in Queens.

"Is everything okay?" Phoenix had a low, soothing voice.

"Yes."

"I'm looking forward to meeting you."

Lexa had agreed to meet Phoenix that Saturday at the monthly dim sum brunch that Lexa and Maddie had started with their mom a few years earlier. Maddie was still refusing to go.

"Right." Lexa couldn't bring herself to say she was looking forward to meeting Phoenix too. Not after speaking to her dad and hearing the sadness in his voice. "Can you have her call me back?"

Phoenix said she would, and they hung up. Before Lexa could get off the bench, a group of women approached her. The brunette with her hair in a high ponytail called out, "Lexa, hi!"

"Can't wait to take your cardio sculpt class," said the woman wearing a bright orange top. "I ate a huge plate of pasta last night." After a pause, she added, "With cream sauce and a lot of bread." She fidgeted, as if her clothes were itching her. "And I had two glasses of wine." She dropped her gaze to the floor. "Okay, it was more than two glasses, but I didn't finish the bottle."

The brunette hit her on the arm. "Why do you always confess to Lexa exactly what you ate? Now she's going to make us suffer."

The confessor hung her head. "I can't help it. Every time she looks at me, the truth falls out."

Lexa gave an evil grin. "Don't worry, we'll burn it off. Let's go."

They groaned but followed her into the studio like docile lambs. For the next hour, Lexa led her class through a series of high-intensity exercises. She channeled her shock over her father's death into the workout, pushing her students relentlessly with no breaks and yelling more than she usually did. By the end of class, she was as sweaty as everyone else, but her mood had lifted. There was nothing like a good workout to take her mind off her problems. Her students shot her dirty looks and muttered about sadistic instructors as they left the studio.

After a quick shower and change, she headed toward Sixty-Fifth Street and Fifth Avenue, about a ten-minute walk from the gym. She had an eleven-o'clock appointment with her private client Priscilla Lockwood. Lexa's phone rang as she crossed Lexington Avenue.

"Hi, Mom. You're done already?"

"No, I realized I forgot my phone and came back." Her mom had moved into Phoenix's apartment on the Upper West Side this past weekend. Their house in Whitestone really was being put on the market—just another reason for Maddie to hate Phoenix. "What's up?"

Lexa told her about Hsu-Ling's phone call.

"Oh, no. How did it happen?" Her mom's voice was raspy.

"I don't know. I was in the middle of a session. She's supposed to call me back later, around nine thirty tonight. And she's coming to New York."

"I thought she was afraid to fly? And that it's inconvenient because of her leg. Why's she coming?"

Lexa's half sister had been born missing part of a leg, the result of something called amniotic band syndrome. The stringlike amniotic bands in Hsu-Ling's mother's womb had wrapped tightly around the baby's right limb, causing an amputation below the knee.

"She said she wanted to talk about that last summer . . ." Lexa's voice trailed off.

"What? Are you going to Taiwan for the funeral?"

"No." Lexa could feel the high from her class wearing off and frowned. "Do you think I should?"

"Maybe."

"I don't know." Deep in thought about actually returning to Taiwan after all this time, Lexa ran across Park Avenue without looking. A yellow cab screeched to a stop in front of her, narrowly missing her. The driver laid on his horn, yelling and making an obscene gesture. Her heart beating wildly, Lexa waved in apology and ran onto the divider in the middle of the street.

"Are you okay?" Her mom's concerned voice came through the phone.

"Yes." She forced herself to take a deep breath and waited until the light changed before crossing the rest of the street.

"I'm sorry about your father. You should take the rest of the day off."

"I can't. My clients are counting on me."

"But your father just died. They'd understand."

"I didn't know him. I haven't seen him in almost twenty-two years. All I got from him was the occasional email or card."

"He's still your father."

Lexa was silent as she dodged around a dog walker leading a pack of well-groomed purebreds down the sidewalk, and then ran across Madison Avenue after carefully looking both ways.

Her mom spoke before Lexa could answer. "You might think you're okay, but your father's death is going to bring back all those memories."

"I've been fine all these years without him. I didn't need him. I made my own life here." So then why was her heart aching?

"Call me after you speak to Hsu-Ling, no matter what time it is, okay?"

"Okay."

"Honey? I know I've been distracted with Phoenix, but I'm always here for you."

"I'm fine." Lexa probed at her feelings like a sore tooth. Was she upset at her father's death? Or was she upset because she *wasn't* more upset about it?

"Maybe you should take a Kung Fu class. That always made you feel better."

"I should." Lexa had found Kung Fu when she was fourteen, studying with Shifu, who was a Shaolin Temple monk. But it'd been a while since she'd gone to class. The more clients she'd taken on, the less time she had for her own interests.

"Maddie's not going to like it that Hsu-Ling is coming."

"I know. I've got to go. I'm at Mrs. Lockwood's."

They said good-bye, and Lexa sighed as she rounded the corner at Sixty-Fifth and Fifth. Her past and her present were about to collide, and she had a feeling it wasn't going to be pretty.

3

June, Twenty-Eight Years Ago
Whitestone, Queens

Maddie stood in the doorway, hugging her beloved bunny, NoNo, to her chest. She surveyed the wreckage of their room. Clothes were flung everywhere: on the two beds over their Laura Ashley comforters, on the floor in front of the closet, and heaped into an open suitcase sitting on the floor. New Kids on the Block's song "Step by Step" was playing on the portable radio, and Lexa sang along as she pulled clothes out of her dresser and held them up to her body.

Lexa and Mommy were leaving the next day for somewhere far away, and they weren't taking Maddie with them. She had to stay home with Daddy.

"Lexa, why are you going away? I want to come."

Lexa looked over her shoulder. "We told you already. I'm going to meet my father."

"Daddy's your father."

"Maddie." Lexa blew her hair out of her face in exasperation and turned to face her sister. "Daddy is my dad, but I have another father, my real one." Lexa jiggled from one foot to another, looking nervous, like she had when Daddy was teaching her how to swim.

Maddie walked to her sister's side. "I want to go with you." She reached out and wound a hand through Lexa's long black hair. Lexa always let her play with it. Maddie loved Lexa's hair, because it was so straight and soft and so much darker than her own blond curls.

But that day, Lexa pulled her hair out of Maddie's hand. "You can't. You're too little. And I'm *finally* meeting my father. I'm so excited."

Maddie's bottom lip quivered. "I'm not too little. I'm almost four."

"That's too little." Lexa puffed out her chest with pride. "Mommy said it's my eighth birthday present. I'm finally old enough to go all that way to meet him."

"Oh." Maddie looked down and caught sight of her sister's favorite pink sundress, the one with strawberries on the pockets, lying on the floor. "You're taking that dress?"

"Yes. I hope he likes it." Lexa picked it up and folded it carefully before tucking it into a corner of the suitcase. Maddie wasn't allowed to touch the dress "for any reason at all!" This must be a big deal if Lexa was taking it with her. Then Maddie noticed something else.

"What's that?" Maddie pointed to a bunny that looked exactly like her NoNo.

"I got it for Hsu-Ling. You love your bunny so much I thought she'd like one too."

"Sue who?" Maddie asked.

"My other little sister. Her name is pronounced 'Sue-ling.'"

"*I'm* your sister!" Maddie stamped her foot and pulled the bunny out of the suitcase.

"Give me that!" Lexa grabbed the stuffed animal out of Maddie's hands and put it back in the suitcase. "You are my sister, but I have another one. A Taiwanese one."

Maddie stared at her in surprise. Lexa had always given in to her. Maddie waited for Lexa to say she was sorry. But Lexa ignored her. When she turned back to the dresser, Maddie grabbed the bunny again and ran down the stairs into the living room.

She wedged herself and the two bunnies between the couch and the wall. There was just enough space for a small girl to hide. She would leave the new bunny here. She didn't like that her big sister and Mommy were going away without her. She didn't like that Lexa had another little sister, and she didn't want her to have a bunny just like hers. She whispered in No-No's ears, reverting to baby talk, "Me no like it."

Taichung, Taiwan

Almost eight thousand miles away, another little girl crawled as fast as she could out of her apartment and into the small courtyard at the front of their building. Her mama was on the phone, and Hsu-Ling took the opportunity to escape. She headed to the tree that grew next to the big red gate. Using the stool she kept at the bottom of the tree, she climbed into the low branches. She was almost four and a half now and could pull herself up with her arms.

She could hear her mama's voice in her head, Aiya! *You're going to kill yourself!* Her mama wanted Hsu-Ling to wear her leg, but Hsu-Ling hated it. She'd be walking along fine, and then bam, she was on the floor. Mama always made a fuss, but Baba would wave her away and tell her to stop hovering.

The red gate opened, and she held still as her baba and his best friend, Pong, walked into the courtyard. Their building was on a quiet side street, but she could hear the roar of traffic from the busy section of the city in the distance when they opened the metal gate. She giggled.

They heard her and looked up. "Hey, little monkey." Her baba spoke in Taiwanese instead of Mandarin. "What are you doing up in that tree again? Your mama will have a heart attack if she sees you."

He walked over, and she launched herself at him, causing him to grunt as he caught her.

"What did you bring for me?" she asked.

"Your favorite—*tian bu la*." Pong handed her a paper cup filled with fish paste that had been molded into balls and other shapes, deep-fried, and smothered in a brown sauce.

Hsu-Ling's eyes lit up, and she used her fingers to pop a piece into her mouth.

"What do you say?" her baba chided, taking the paper cup from her and handing it back to Pong. "Let's save the rest for dinner, huh?"

She swallowed and said, "*Xie xie*, Uncle Pong."

Pong held up a white box. "Let's get this inside before the icing melts."

"Oooh, the cake with the fresh cream and fruit? For my sister's birthday?" Hsu-Ling asked.

Uncle Pong nodded. "In honor of your American sister coming tomorrow."

Hsu-Ling clapped her hands. "I can't wait to meet my *jie jie*." She'd been hearing about her older sister who lived in America all her life.

"We'll have to speak only Mandarin when she's here, since she doesn't understand Taiwanese," her baba said.

"All right."

Baba carried her to their front door. He called up the

stairs, "Ma! Ba! I'm home. Come down for dinner when you're ready."

"*Hao!*" Hsu-Ling's ah-ma called down in answer. All of Baba's family lived in this building. Baba's parents were on the second floor (and often left their front door open), and his younger sister and brother lived with their families on the third and fourth floors. They gave the ground floor to Hsu-Ling's family because of her leg.

Baba put Hsu-Ling down in the foyer to take off his shoes. He placed a hand for balance on the giant blue-and-white porcelain vase at the entrance that someone had given her parents as a wedding gift. Mama always complained it was too big, but Baba said he liked it.

Hsu-Ling waited as the two men lined their shoes neatly in the foyer, and then she crawled with them into the apartment. Baba went first to the small shrine in their living room. He didn't light an incense stick; instead, he brought his hands together in front of him and bowed three times to the photos of his grandparents and the statue of the goddess of mercy, Guan Yin.

Pong greeted her mama, who was stirring *dua mee gee* on the stove. Hsu-Ling's mouth watered at the aroma of the big noodles simmered in a thick soup with chives and roasted garlic that was a Taichung specialty. It was such a local dish it didn't even have a name in Mandarin, only Taiwanese.

"You'll have to wear your leg when they're here," Mama said. Hsu-Ling looked up at her sharp tone.

"She doesn't have to wear it if it bothers her," Baba said without turning away from the shrine. "They know about her leg."

Mama stopped stirring. "I don't want them to treat her different."

"They won't." Baba blew out a breath in exasperation. "Why do you always point out her disability?"

Hsu-Ling looked back and forth between her parents. She hated it when they fought about her.

Pong stood at her mama's side. "Our little one is beautiful with or without her leg. Right, *xiao mei*?" He called her little sister, the family's nickname for her.

She smiled at him but then looked at her baba, who was still standing in the living room. Why didn't he greet Mama like Uncle Pong did? Why were her parents staring at each other like that, as if something smelled bad? She'd heard Baba and Mama whispering late the night before, their voices rising. What were they talking about?

"Is everything ready for my American grandchild's visit?" They all looked up as Ah-Ma walked into the apartment. She was a petite woman, smaller than Hsu-Ling's mother, but she commanded any room she entered.

Mama rushed out of the kitchen to Ah-Ma's side and guided her to a dining room chair.

"Pin-Yen, is the spare room ready?" Ah-Ma shook off Pin-Yen's hands with impatience and sat herself down.

Mama's mouth hardened, but she nodded her head.

"Jing Tao, you picked up the birthday cake I ordered?"

"Yes, Ma."

"Good." Ah-Ma nodded in satisfaction. "I want everything to be perfect. Ah-Gong should be here soon. Pin-Yen, can you get the bowls ready?"

"Yes, Ah-Ma." Mama lowered her eyes and went back to the kitchen.

Uncle Pong placed a hand at Mama's waist and whispered something into her ear. She smiled as she ladled noodle soup into the bowls lined up on the counter. But her voice was stern when she turned to Hsu-Ling. "Go wash your hands. I know you've been climbing that tree."

Hsu-Ling hesitated, but when Baba walked into the kitchen and kissed Mama on the cheek, she relaxed. Everything was fine. There was nothing to worry about. They were finally going to welcome her American sister into the Chang family the next day.

4

Lexa had just finished with her six-thirty client, Jason, when she heard someone calling her name. She looked up to see her personal training manager, Bryson, hailing her from the edge of the stretch area, where he stood with a young Asian woman.

"Lexa, come meet Christy Sung when you're done. She's looking for a trainer."

Jason sat up on the massage table and mopped his face with a towel. "We're done. I can't take any more."

Bryson grinned at Jason. "She made you beg for mercy again, huh?"

Jason nodded. "Yup. And I'm not ashamed to admit it." He was a big man, well over six feet tall, and weighed more than twice what Lexa did. "I don't know what got into her, but she was brutal today." He turned to Lexa. "See you next Monday night."

"Bye, Jason. Good work."

He limped toward the men's locker room as Bryson handed Lexa the training request form. She glanced at it: twenty-three, healthy, no injuries, wanted to lose twenty pounds, preferred six thirty in the morning.

"Christy, this is one of our trainers, Lexa Thomas. Lexa, Christy."

Christy peered at her from under her bangs. "I really want to lose weight, but my father doesn't believe in personal trainers. He said if I had more self-control, I wouldn't be this fat."

Lexa studied Christy, who was a little overweight but wasn't fat. "He says that to you?"

Christy nodded.

Lexa clucked her tongue. "Asian fathers, huh? They think they're being helpful."

Christy's eyes widened. "Yes! That's why I wanted an Asian woman for a trainer. I knew you'd understand."

"Oh, but I don't know Asian fathers. I mean, I have one, but my dad is white."

Christy looked confused. "What?"

"It's . . . I have two fathers."

"Oh." Her eyebrows rose, and Lexa realized she must think she had two fathers who were married to each other. "Are you Korean like me? Or maybe Japanese?" Christy asked.

"I'm half-Taiwanese," Lexa said. "But my mom thought I was half-Japanese at first." Christy blinked at her. "She thought my father was Japanese. Actually, she met him in Thailand, but she was with Japanese people and . . ." She trailed off as Christy gaped at her.

"Never mind." Why was she telling a stranger something she'd only told her friend that morning? Lexa rubbed the side of her head. It'd been a long day.

Bryson hid a smile and gestured to one of the floor trainers. "Jennifer, can you show Christy how to work the cardio machines while I talk to Lexa?" Once Jennifer led Christy to the cardio area, he turned to Lexa.

"Can you take her? I know your schedule is full, but she really wants an Asian woman, and you're the only one we have." He smirked. "Plus, she needs you. Since you understand about strict Asian parents and all."

Lexa gave him a dirty look. "Yeah, I'll take her."

When Jennifer brought Christy back, Lexa made an appointment with her for the next morning. After saying goodbye, Lexa headed for the front door. She was deep in thought about her upcoming phone call with Hsu-Ling and didn't see her group fitness manager, Elise, until she ran into her.

"Hey, sorry." Lexa reached out to steady Elise. "You're here late." She'd known Elise for years, since Lexa had first started working at the gym. Elise was of Jamaican, Puerto Rican, and German descent and had the smoothest light brown skin, which Lexa envied.

"I had to put in the summer schedule. I'm starving. Want to grab some Thai food?"

Lexa hesitated. She was starving too, but she didn't want to miss Hsu-Ling's call. Yet on the other hand, she didn't want to sit home by herself, obsessing about what had happened to her father. She looked at her phone and saw it was a quarter to eight. If she was quick, she could make it home in plenty of time for Hsu-Ling's call.

"Sure. Thai sounds perfect." Her parents had met in Thailand. She was suddenly craving Thai food.

. . .

When she got home from dinner, she saw she had just missed a FaceTime request. Shit. It was only a quarter after nine. Hsu-Ling wasn't supposed to call until nine thirty.

Lexa sent Hsu-Ling a message.

Can you talk?

Can't. They just called a meeting. My first day back at work since Baba died. I'll call you as soon as I'm done.

Lexa poured herself a glass of water and placed it on the coffee table someone in her building had put out on the curb. The rustic wood was beat-up, but Lexa liked it, drawn to the chunky legs and the wide surface, which was perfect for all the books she piled on it. She clicked on the TV while she waited and sank onto the beige couch she'd rescued from her parents' basement. Her Rottweiler, Zeus, jumped up next to her. He turned in a circle and settled down, pressing his body against hers and laying his giant head on her leg.

She leaned down and gave him a kiss on the top of his head. Sure, he was probably ten times the size of the miniature dachshund she'd envisioned adopting two years earlier when she'd broken up with her last boyfriend. But she'd taken one look at the Rottweiler puppy in the shelter and knew that he was her dog.

"It was love at first sight, wasn't it, Zeus?" She took his head between her hands and nuzzled his nose. He licked her face in agreement when she scratched him behind the ears. "I haven't seen Hsu-Ling since she was ten. Why's she coming to New York?"

Zeus cocked his head. She was positive he understood and even talked back. Right then, he was asking, "How do you feel about that?"

"I feel like my past is about to come back and bite me in the ass." She leaned down to hug him and gave a dry laugh. "Hsu-Ling and I don't know each other. It'll be weird to see her after all this time."

She and Hsu-Ling had bonded the first time they met, when Lexa was eight and Hsu-Ling four and a half. Even though Hsu-Ling hadn't known English then, they'd understood each other with Lexa's limited Mandarin. Lexa still remembered the way Hsu-Ling had grabbed her around the middle and wouldn't let go when Lexa had to go back to New York. "*Buyao zou.*" Don't go.

But then that last summer happened and they'd lost each other. Even though they'd reconnected a few years later, it wasn't the same.

Lexa's phone rang, and she grabbed it, accepting the FaceTime request.

"What happened? How did Baba die?" Lexa asked as soon as Hsu-Ling's image appeared.

Hsu-Ling stared at her. "I don't even know where to start. It's not just Baba," she said in near-perfect English. "Uncle Pong also died. The same day as Baba's accident two days ago."

Lexa sucked in a breath.

"It was the lung cancer for Uncle Pong. It came back about a month ago, and the doctor said he only had a few weeks left. He was admitted to the ICU last week." Hsu-Ling stopped and bit her bottom lip. Lexa's mind raced, a jumble of images swimming before her eyes and a roaring sound inside her head. When Hsu-Ling spoke again, it took a few seconds for Lexa to clear her head enough to hear her. "He was having trouble breathing on his own, and the doctors wanted to put him on life support, on mechanical ventilation."

"That's awful."

"Baba and I were with him when they told him. You know how close they were." Lexa nodded. Pong was more than her father's best friend. Her baba had loved him like a brother and would have stood by him no matter what. "After the doctor left, Pong told Baba he had something to tell him."

"What did he say?"

"I don't know. He could barely talk, and I didn't catch

most of it, but Baba did. Something about being in love with someone and how he'd lied. And that you didn't take the necklace?"

Lexa's mouth opened when she heard that. No words came out, but it didn't matter. Hsu-Ling wasn't done.

"Pong said some things about my mother and that you were just an innocent child. Said he didn't want to lose face. He kept saying he was sorry. I don't know what any of that means." Hsu-Ling ran a hand over her face. "Then all these machines went off, and doctors and nurses rushed in and they made us leave his room."

"Oh, no." Lexa laid a hand on Zeus's back for support.

Hsu-Ling took a breath. "Baba was so upset. We were standing outside Pong's room, waiting to see what had happened, and he kept saying, 'ChiChi, I'm so sorry.' He said the two of us had to go to New York right away and find you, apologize to you." She swallowed, and Lexa watched, fascinated at the way her throat moved.

"Then what happened?" Lexa whispered.

"He ran out of the hospital before I could stop him. I guess he wasn't paying attention and drove his scooter down the wrong way on a street he's been on a million times before." Hsu-Ling's eyes filled. "How could he do that? He knew those roads like the back of his hand!" Hsu-Ling's face scrunched up as the tears overflowed. "He hit a car head-on and died at the scene."

Lexa put a hand to her mouth and felt a tear trickle down her cheek.

Hsu-Ling wiped her own eyes. "I'm so sorry to be the one to tell you. And that it took me so long. There was so much going on, and then Uncle Pong died a couple of hours later."

"On the same day."

"Yes. I knew I needed to see you in person. Find out what's going on. And also there's Baba's will . . ." Hsu-Ling stopped and dropped her face into her hands. "I can't believe he's gone."

Lexa pressed her lips together, thinking about the father she barely knew. Her mom had forbidden her to go back and see him after that summer, and then she'd found Kung Fu and grown up and no longer cared. So why was her heart pounding so hard because her father had finally said the words she'd longed to hear for so long? *ChiChi, I'm so sorry.*

"Lexa?"

She looked up and realized she'd been quiet too long. She said the first thing that came to mind.

"I guess all that smoking finally caught up with Uncle Pong."

5

June, Twenty-Eight Years Ago
Taichung, Taiwan

There was a flurry of excitement when Lexa and her mom arrived at her birth father's home at last. She was overwhelmed by the amount of people crowding her father's apartment; her father's parents (her ah-ma and ah-gong!), aunts, uncles, cousins. She stood next to her mother, not saying much, as Ah-Ma studied her face. She said something in Taiwanese that Lexa couldn't understand, but from the smile on Ah-Ma's face, it must have been good.

Hsu-Ling threw her arms around Lexa and beamed up at her with a delighted smile. "My *jie jie*! You're finally here!"

Lexa smiled at her younger half sister, even as she couldn't believe she was really standing in front of her father, Chang Jing Tao, who was as handsome as a movie star. He was tall for an Asian man, probably just shy of six feet, with a square jaw and jet-black hair that was long in the front. They exchanged shy smiles until his wife, Pin-Yen, a stern-looking woman with a wary look in her eyes, finally cleared her throat loudly, forcing them to look away from each other.

Once everyone had had a chance to greet Lexa, her father shooed them all out of the apartment, except for Ah-Ma and Ah-Gong. Ah-Ma gestured to Pin-Yen, and Pin-Yen rushed to the kitchen and took out a beautiful cake, covered in white cream and decorated with luscious pieces of fruit.

Ah-Ma spoke in Taiwanese, and her father translated: "To welcome you to our family. And to celebrate your eighth birthday."

Lexa stared in delight at the cake, her heart about to burst out of her chest. As Pin-Yen cut slices, she looked around at her new family and found Hsu-Ling studying her.

"You look so Taiwanese," Hsu-Ling said. "I thought you'd look more American."

Her father translated, and Lexa's mom smiled. "I know. I always thought children take after their mother, but Lexa definitely looks more Taiwanese than she does like me."

Lexa's father laughed. "Ha! Guess my sperm very strong." Pin-Yen, who spoke English, made a strangled noise, and Lexa's mom had a coughing fit. Lexa looked suspiciously at her mom. It sounded like she was trying not to laugh.

"She's not really Taiwanese though." Pin-Yen spoke for the first time. "She's half-white, so not Asian enough."

An awkward silence followed. Pin-Yen had spoken in Mandarin, so Lexa wasn't sure if she'd heard her right, and she knew her mom didn't understand.

Her father cleared his throat. "My good friend Pong, he be here soon. He speak perfect English, will translate." Lexa looked up at the name. Pong had been the one who'd helped her father write to her.

The group fell into stilted conversation, so when Pong arrived, it was as if a ray of light had entered the room. They all turned toward Pong like sunflowers toward the sun. He was a jolly man with a big laugh. Barrel-chested with a full head of shiny black hair, he was shorter than her father. He made Lexa think of an Asian Santa without the beard.

"Welcome, American sister," Pong said, pulling her in for a brief hug. Her father hadn't hugged her; he'd only patted her on the back and smiled when they first met. Lexa's mom had told her it wasn't an Asian custom to hug and kiss on greeting, like it was in America.

Pong had rented a van and took them sightseeing once her baba had helped his own mother and father back to their apartment. They went to Taichung Park (which Uncle Pong told them was the oldest park in Taichung) in the North District, to the hospital where her father worked as an X-ray technician and where Hsu-Ling met with the various members of her medical team for physical therapy and to get fitted for new prosthetics, and to Hsu-Ling's school.

When they were at the park, Hsu-Ling tripped on her prosthetic leg and fell flat on her face. Lexa stared, horrified to see her sister sprawled facedown on the sidewalk. Just when she moved to help her, Hsu-Ling rolled to her side, laughing, and their baba pulled her up. Meanwhile, Hsu-Ling's mother hovered, clucking her tongue and dabbing at Hsu-Ling's hands and knees with a tissue.

"Stop it." Hsu-Ling swatted away her mother's hands. "I'm fine." She studied her prosthetic, made of a soft white plastic, her round cheeks flushed from the exertion of walking. "I didn't break it." She smiled up at Lexa, and Lexa smiled back, even though she wasn't sure what Hsu-Ling had said. Lexa had been going to Chinese school since she was five, but her Mandarin was basic at best.

Hsu-Ling fell many more times that afternoon, and Lexa was impressed by her determination. By the fifth fall, Lexa had gotten used to it and no longer reacted when her sister tripped.

They had a late lunch of *niurou mien* at a noodle shop. Lexa slurped up the noodles, savoring the braised beef and the broth flavored with star anise, five-spice, peppercorns, garlic, and ginger.

Her mom sat next to her on the rickety stool. "Good, huh?"

Lexa nodded, her mouth too full to speak.

"Don't eat too much." Hsu-Ling leaned around her mother to look at Lexa, her chin-length hair swinging around her face. "We're going to the night market, and there's so much good food!"

On the van ride to the night market, Lexa's mom whispered in Lexa's ear, "Is it just me, or does your father's wife look like she's about to have a heart attack, having me around?"

Lexa turned to look at Pin-Yen. The woman was always hovering around Hsu-Ling, fussing at her daughter. She'd barely spoken to Lexa or her mom all afternoon.

Lexa turned to her mom, her forehead creased. "You think she doesn't like me?"

Her mom hugged an arm around her. "I think it's me she doesn't like."

A half hour later, they stood at the FengJia University gate, the entrance of the FengJia Night Market. Pong had managed to wedge the van into a spot that Lexa was pretty sure wasn't for parking. She looked dubiously at the back of the van, which was sticking out into traffic. But Pong just laughed and pulled out a cigarette, lighting up.

He'd taken only a few puffs when Hsu-Ling said in Mandarin, "No smoking, Uncle Pong!" She waved her hand in front of her nose. "Smoking is bad for you. People die from it!"

Uncle Pong laughed and put out his cigarette. "You're the smoking police now, huh, *xiao mei*?" He gave Lexa a wink.

"Yes." Hsu-Ling put her hands on her hips and almost toppled over. Her mom pulled open the stroller stashed in the back of the van and pointed to it.

"I'm not a baby. I'm four and a half!" Hsu-Ling stuck out her bottom lip in a pout.

"Sit. You've been on that leg all day."

Hsu-Ling glared at her mom, but common sense won out, and she plopped into the stroller. "Fine. Let's go!"

There were people everywhere, and both sides of the street were lined with food stalls; shops selling clothes, bags, and other knickknacks; and arcades where children darted in and out. A hum of excitement hung in the air, and Lexa could make out the smell of barbecued meats mixed with aromas she wasn't familiar with. One stall they passed had grilled squid stuck on a stick. Another stall featured giant vats of boiling water where different colored fish balls floated, ready to be scooped out and skewered.

Her father stopped at a stall and handed her what looked like a hot dog.

"This is a sausage, tucked into a rice sausage." He pointed to the white part. "Hsu-Ling, do you want your own, or do you want to share with Lexa?"

Hsu-Ling smiled at her older sister. "Share."

Lexa took a bite and closed her eyes. It was so good. The slightly sweet sausage had a smoky flavor that was balanced by the seasoned rice. Being here in this place, surrounded by all this new food, with the euphoria of finally meeting her real father and other half sister, heightened her senses.

"*Gei wo!*" Hsu-Ling reached out, and Lexa understood enough to know she wanted the sausage. She watched Hsu-Ling take a bite as Pin-Yen fluttered around her with a plastic knife.

"*Aiya*, Hsu-Ling. I was going to cut that. You don't want to get germs." Pin-Yen gave Lexa a sidelong glance.

While Lexa was trying to figure out if she'd heard correctly, Hsu-Ling handed the sausage back to Lexa. Lexa held it in her hands, looking at Hsu-Ling's mother with uncertainty until her father walked up next to her.

"We're all family here." He patted Lexa on her arm. "We share the same germs."

Hsu-Ling giggled. "I just gave you my germs." She waited until Lexa took another bite. As the flavors bombarded Lexa's mouth, she forgot about Hsu-Ling's mother.

Her father continued to buy food from different stalls. "Stinky tofu," he said, and handed over a paper bowl of fried cubes of tofu, from which a sour and pungent odor emanated. Lexa and her mom both wrinkled their noses, but at her father's urging, she tried a bite and found she liked it. It tasted better than it smelled.

"And this," her father said, pointing to another bowl, "is *tian bu la*, Hsu-Ling's favorite."

Pong walked back from another stall and handed Lexa an ear of corn on a stick, coated in something brown. "Roast corn. Very special sauce." He stepped away, and Lexa saw him sneaking a cigarette. He caught her eyes and put a finger to his lips, pointing to Hsu-Ling. Lexa giggled. She liked Uncle Pong.

Her baba and Pong took turns bringing her food, each dish better than the last. The flavors were rich and strange, yet comforting in her mouth. She'd never seen or tasted most of what was put in front of her, but she fell in love with every bite. It was like a dream, seeing all the Taiwanese people around her and even being able to understand some of the Mandarin. When she saw a group of blond tourists standing lost in the middle of the night market, she felt a moment of recognition. But for once, she wasn't the one who stood out. She looked like everyone else around her. She was Taiwanese.

"Are you having fun?" Uncle Pong asked her. He handed her a bubble tea.

She nodded as she sucked up a tapioca ball through the thick straw. "I've never seen so much food in my life." Lexa smiled widely, and she looked at her family. They were smiling back at her, all except Hsu-Ling's mother, who had stopped at a shoe store and was examining a pair of high-heeled sandals.

"Baba!" Hsu-Ling pointed to a jewelry store. "We have to get ChiChi one of these bracelets!" She held up her arm and showed Lexa the green circular jade around her wrist.

Lexa looked up from her bubble tea. "ChiChi? Who's that?"

Uncle Pong laughed. "You. It means beautiful, or adorable."

Pin-Yen gave an unladylike snort, and they all turned to look at her. She waved a hand in front of her face. "Sorry, something caught in my throat."

Lexa's father came to her side. "When your mother's friend in Japan showed me a picture of you, that was the word that popped into my head." He spoke in Mandarin. "This character." And he drew the character in the air. "I've thought of you as Chi ever since."

Uncle Pong translated, and Lexa ducked her head, a big smile spreading over her face.

"Hsu-Ling's been calling you ChiChi," said Uncle Pong. "In Taiwan, doubling up on a name is a form of affection. She has trouble saying your American name." It was true. Lexa had noticed that Hsu-Ling had been calling her "Re-xa."

Hsu-Ling pointed to the jewelry store from her stroller. "Baba, let's go in."

"Good idea." Their baba turned to Lexa. "We'll pick one for you."

Lexa's mom came to her side after Pong translated. "You don't have to do that. I'll buy it for her."

"No, please." Lexa's father addressed her mother in English. "Her eighth birthday tomorrow. Will be my present to her." Lexa's heart swelled when she heard that. Her father switched to Mandarin and said, "Parents often give this bracelet to their daughters as a symbol of their love and protection. The jade will protect and heal her body and spirit."

"Mommy, please?" Lexa turned beseeching eyes to her mother.

Her mom turned up her hands in defeat. Together, they trooped into the store, and once she was wearing a bracelet, Lexa couldn't stop looking at it. The jade was cool yet heavy on her wrist. She held her arm carefully, afraid she'd bang it against something and break it.

Hsu-Ling's yell startled her. "Look! *Bao bing!* You have to try shaved ice, ChiChi. It's so good. Uncle Pong, hurry!"

Lexa's stomach groaned in protest. She'd already eaten far more than she usually did. But Hsu-Ling's enthusiasm was contagious. Her father came to her side and slipped his hand into hers while her mother took her other hand. She smiled at them, and they ran after Hsu-Ling, who was egging Uncle Pong to push her stroller faster and faster.

6

⌒

"They're both dead?"

Lexa called her mom as soon as she hung up with Hsu-Ling. She could tell by her mom's voice that she'd woken her up, even though it was just after ten thirty at night.

"Yes. She said Baba wanted to come to New York." Lexa's voice broke. "To apologize."

"What?" Her mom's voice rose. "He knew the truth?"

"I think so. But he died before Hsu-Ling could find out what he was talking about."

Her mom didn't say anything for a moment. "Okay. We can deal with this."

"Can I come over after my one-o'clock client tomorrow? I don't have anyone until six after that."

"Yes. I'll leave my teacher training early. I'll tell them I have a family emergency."

Lexa exhaled. "Thanks, Mom."

. . .

Lexa tossed and turned in bed, sitting up to plump her pillow and find a cool spot. She was usually a good sleeper, but now she couldn't shut her mind off. She'd tried to go to bed after talking to her mom because she had to be up so early the next day for her appointment with Christy Sung. But after two hours, she gave up.

Turning on the bedside lamp, she picked up her phone and scrolled through it, looking at pictures on Instagram, checking Twitter and Facebook. One of her Taiwanese cousins, Li-Chung, had posted pictures of Lexa's father on her Facebook page, and Lexa stared at his face. How had so many years gone by already? She'd turned her back on her father and her heritage without a thought, concentrating on her Western life. But now a stab of regret went through her.

She scrolled through the pictures, reading the translated captions and comments.

"Beloved father, my uncle has passed away."

"So sorry for your loss!"

"Tell Hsu-Ling we love her."

"What a loss. He was a wonderful husband and father. The best!"

Lexa made a noise in her throat at that last comment, and Zeus picked up his head.

"It's okay, buddy. Everything's fine." Zeus pressed his warm body against her as she thought about her father. He'd been a wonderful father to Hsu-Ling, but not to Lexa.

Zeus nudged her with his nose, and Lexa stroked his head. "I need to talk to someone. My mind is going crazy." But who'd be up at this hour? Maddie went to bed early because of her kids. Andi got out late from work at the restaurant, but even she was probably in bed by now.

Then she thought of Jake Wagner, the guy from San Francisco she'd met a month earlier. Even though she knew they had no future together, she smiled thinking about him. They'd been texting back and forth since he went home, and he'd mentioned in the last text that he was coming back to New York again soon for work.

She sent him a text. **Hey, are you up?**

He answered right away. **Hi, pretty lady. What are you doing up? Isn't it late in NYC?**

Couldn't sleep.

Sorry about that. But glad you texted. Was going to let you know tomorrow. I have to be in NYC in about ten days. I'll be there for your birthday.

That's great! She followed that with the emoji blowing a kiss.

I'll give you more details tomorrow after I book a flight. Can't wait.

Me either!

I think I hear Sophia—need to check. Are you going to bed?

Not yet.

Okay, be right back. And he blew a kiss back at her.

Lexa smiled as she snuggled deeper into bed. Her head knew she and Jake had no future, but the rest of her body was stubborn and didn't care. She thought about the day they met as she waited for him to come back from checking on his little daughter.

She had just finished with a client at the gym and was leaning on a portable massage table, looking over her notes, when the table legs collapsed, taking her with it. Stunned and slightly bruised from the fall, she'd lain there in a heap until Jake had come to her rescue. One look into his kind green eyes, shining above a slightly crooked nose and a strong jaw with a dimple in the chin, and she was lost. He'd asked her to dinner, telling her he lived in San Francisco and was in town for business. She'd been smitten, despite the fact that he was in the middle of a divorce and had a three-year-old daughter named Sophia.

She'd spent as much time as she could with him for the

week he was in town. He took her to an art class on the Lower East Side with a well-known graffiti artist and organized a picnic in Central Park. They also spent many hours entwined together in the heavenly bed in his hotel room.

He was perfect for her in every way except one. Lexa hugged her pillow, remembering how taken aback he'd been when she told him she didn't want kids. She'd never had the maternal instinct or heard her biological clock ticking. In fact, her biological clock seemed to have died years earlier.

She knew they had no future. He was the first guy in a long time who got her heart pumping as much as a good workout. But he lived in San Francisco, had a child he had joint custody of, and wanted more kids. It was never going to work.

Despite this, she was convinced she was half in love with him by the time he left. *No future, Lexa.*

Now, she looked at her phone when her text alert sounded.

I'm back. So where were we?

You're taking me out for my birthday.

Yes, definitely.

They continued to text back and forth until Lexa's eyes grew heavy.

I need to go to bed. I have a six thirty client tomorrow.

Ouch. And you know I get up at three thirty. He worked in investment banking and operated on Eastern Standard Time.

You should be in bed! Good night!

He sent the emoji of the smiley face with hearts for eyes.

She sent back the red heart emoji and the one waving its hands.

And he followed that with the champagne glasses clinking together, along with the birthday hat and cake.

She sent him the thumbs-up emoji.

A laugh bubbled from inside her. In this day and age, they could have a whole conversation using only emojis. How technological of them. And the added bonus was, she hadn't thought about her father for a whole hour. Jake was fun, and he made her laugh. That was enough for now.

7

She slept through her alarm and woke at six in a panic. After throwing on a pair of black lululemon leggings and her trainer T-shirt, she brushed her teeth and dragged a brush through her hair, not bothering with makeup. She took Zeus for the quickest pee possible and then ran for the gym, arriving on the gym floor one minute late. Christy Sung was already on a treadmill warming up.

"Morning, Christy." Lexa panted slightly from her mad dash. "Ready to get started?"

Christy looked at her like a deer caught in headlights, and Lexa reached over to stop the treadmill before she fell off the end.

Christy stepped onto the outer edges, straddling the belt. "I didn't realize there would be so many people. It wasn't this crowded when I came yesterday."

Lexa looked around at the early-morning work crowd. Almost every cardio machine was occupied, and men and women lifted weights on the gym floor as if their life depended on it. From the group cycling studio, the instructor's voice, amplified by her microphone, yelled, "Come on, I want more. Pump those legs!"

She turned to Christy. "You came at the end-of-the-night peak time yesterday."

Christy beckoned to her, and Lexa leaned closer. "I don't know if I can work out in front of all these people," Christy whispered. "They're all going to stare at me."

"No one is paying attention to us. They're all too busy trying to get their exercise in before work, or else they're admiring themselves in the mirror." Lexa gestured with her chin toward a couple. They had weights in their hands but were too busy making muscles and admiring their arms and backsides to be doing much exercise.

Christy giggled and hid her mouth with her hands.

"Come on." Lexa gently took Christy by the arm. "I'll be here with you the whole time. The fact that you came here and signed up for sessions is a big step. Some people are so scared of the gym and afraid other people are judging them that they never make it here. So you've already taken the biggest, scariest step."

"I have?" Christy asked in a small voice.

"Yes." Lexa guided her to a bench. "We'll start slow and work your way up. Okay?"

"Okay." Christy looked around, still fearful. "But what if someone makes fun of me? I feel stupid."

"If anyone says anything, they'll have to deal with me." Lexa made a mean face and struck a Kung Fu pose.

Christy smiled. "You look like that girl from *Crouching Tiger, Hidden Dragon*."

"Oh, yeah?" Lexa relaxed her stance and pulled a low step over. "I studied Kung Fu."

"No way, that's so cool," Christy breathed. "I'm so glad I got you as a trainer."

Lexa ran her through a set of simple exercises to assess her form, and when they stopped, Christy wiped a hand over her brow. "I'm sweating," she said in surprise. "I hate sweating."

Lexa cracked a smile. "You're going to sweat more once we pick up the pace."

Before Christy could answer, the guy with the over-developed shoulders next to them dropped his massive weights to the floor with a thud.

Lexa gave him a squinty-eyed stare. *Dude, if the weights are so heavy that you can't place them down with respect, maybe you shouldn't be using such heavy weights.*

She turned back to Christy, whose shoulders were hunched. "My father called me last night. He said I was an ungrateful, selfish daughter who should not have moved so far away from them."

Lexa made a face in sympathy. "Does he say stuff like that a lot?"

"Yes." Christy looked down. "He's really strict. And he puts me down all the time. That's why I started eating, to feel better."

"That's tough." Lexa showed Christy the proper way to do a squat, and Christy copied her. "As your body gets stronger, you'll feel stronger emotionally too. You may not be able to change what your father says to you, but you can change how you react to it." People tended to tell their trainers their innermost thoughts. Sometimes she felt like a therapist.

"I want that. That's why I decided to move out. I knew if I stayed in his house, I'd never feel good about myself." She looked down. "Sometimes I wish I had a different father."

"Oh, Christy. No matter how much he hurts your feelings, he's still your father. You'd miss him if he were gone." *And I would know.*

"See, this is why I wanted an Asian woman trainer. I knew you would understand. I feel better already."

"Well, I don't exactly understand . . ."

"Oh, that's right. Your parents are white."

Lexa could tell Christy was about to ask more questions. She really didn't want to talk about her family right then, so deflected her with a question of her own. "What about your mother? What's she like?"

"She defers to my father all the time. She never speaks up for me. She wouldn't dare go against his wishes."

They resumed the workout as Christy talked about her mother, and Lexa found herself tuning out, her mind on her own problems. Even just the day before, she would have thrilled at helping a new client and thrown herself 100 percent into this first session. And while she still wanted to help Christy, her head wasn't all there. Finding out her father had died was making her question why she'd always put her job first. Why hadn't she reconciled with him in all these years? Why hadn't she gone back to Taiwan and claimed her rightful place in the Chang family? Why had she let that woman drive her away from her heritage?

"I'm sorry about your father," Susan said. She handed Lexa a bottle of water and sat on the couch, folding her legs into a lotus position. She was wearing black yoga pants with a pink floral top.

"Thanks." Lexa couldn't get over the change in her. A few months earlier, she'd never have pictured her mom, who'd always claimed to be allergic to exercise, doing yoga. Who was this woman?

Lexa fingered a hand-drawn Malaysian batik shawl that

was flung over the back of the couch, marveling at the bright colors and intricate design. She shifted uncomfortably, thinking it was strange to be in Phoenix's apartment when she hadn't met the woman yet. And even stranger to think this was where her mom lived now, as of this past weekend. Lexa couldn't wrap her mind around seeing the lopsided green ceramic vase she'd made for her mom years earlier sitting on an unfamiliar shelf, or the gray place mats her mom had made during her sewing phase on the dining table. They didn't belong there. They belonged in their home in Whitestone.

"What did Hsu-Ling say?" Her mom leaned back on the couch and fixed her eyes on Lexa.

Lexa relayed the conversation she'd had with her sister and then took a gulp of water to soothe her dry throat. Only then did she notice the label on the bottle. "When did you start drinking Evian?"

Susan shrugged. "Phoenix likes it. I bought some Poland Spring, but they're still in the pantry."

Lexa gave her mom a look, because Susan had always said people who bought Evian were stupid. Evian was "naïve" spelled backward.

Susan ignored her. "When's the funeral?"

"There's a seven-day mourning period, and then his body will be cremated and transferred to a columbarium. They have to wait for the right day to bury him." Lexa found the Taiwanese funeral customs confusing. "Hsu-Ling said he wouldn't be buried for a few months."

"But there will be a funeral after the cremation? Shouldn't you go back for that?"

"Probably." Lexa turned to her mom. "But would that be for the best? The family is grieving. I haven't been a part of

their family in twenty-two years. My presence would probably cause chaos. Especially for you-know-who."

They stared at each other. "You're probably right," Susan
said.

"As much as I hate her, I don't think this is the time to
confront her." Lexa dropped her head to the back of the couch,
feeling the unfamiliar nubby texture of the tweed fabric against
her skin. "I've made my peace with the past. I hate that it's
all coming back again."

She could feel her mom studying her. "Are you sure you've
made your peace with it? You've kept it a secret. I know I was
the one who wouldn't let you go back to Taiwan when you
were a child, but I thought you'd reach out to your father
once you were grown. But you've kept him at a distance."

"I know. I just . . ." Lexa closed her eyes. "I didn't trust
him anymore."

"But he was your father. He did reach out to you. He
wanted to come visit you."

"But not right away. By the time he said he wanted to see
me, I didn't care anymore. I had my life here." Lexa breathed
in, and even the lemongrass scent in Phoenix's apartment was
unfamiliar. What was her mom doing there? She should be at
home with Greg.

"Are you happy, Lexa?"

Lexa's eyes popped open. "Yes, of course. I love my job
and my life in the city."

"Maddie's married with two kids. You're about to turn
thirty-six and still single. All you do is work." Susan looked
down. "Sometimes I think your clients mean everything to
you."

"They are important to me. It's my job."

"But it shouldn't be your life. Don't you want to get married, have a family?"

"I have Zeus. And I've been doing online dating with Andi."

"How's that going?"

Lexa shrugged. "Not well, but not for lack of trying."

"I worry, because you keep saying you don't want kids. I don't want what happened with your father to keep you from having your own family."

"Not everyone wants kids," Lexa retorted.

Susan shifted on the couch, tucking her legs under. "I hate that you don't know your Taiwanese family. That you've basically cut all traces of your Asian heritage from your life."

"It doesn't matter anymore." Lexa suddenly felt overwhelmingly tired and slouched down so that her feet rested on the wooden coffee table.

"Don't put your feet on that." Susan swatted Lexa's leg.

"What?" Lexa swung her feet to the ground with a thump. They always put their feet up on the coffee table at home.

"Phoenix got that the last time she was in Southeast Asia. It's very expensive."

Lexa stared at her. "Seriously?"

"I want to respect her things." Susan lifted a shoulder and then sighed. "It's only been a few days since I moved in. We're still getting used to each other." When Lexa didn't reply, her mom asked, "Has Maddie said anything about me? She won't take my calls."

"I know. She's acting like a brat."

"What about you? Are you okay with me and Phoenix?"

"I don't know. It's hard seeing your things in her apartment." Lexa grimaced. "I'm trying to understand, but I feel so bad for Dad. He called yesterday and asked if I could help him move tomorrow . . ." She broke off. "He sounded so sad."

Susan's shoulders drooped. "I thought about not acting on my feelings for Phoenix. I didn't want to break up our family. But the more I denied my feelings, the more I felt I was living a lie." She turned unhappy eyes to Lexa. "I couldn't do that to Greg. Or to Phoenix."

Lexa laid a hand on her mom's arm. "I know. I just had no idea you weren't happy. Or that you felt that way about women." She'd wracked her brains trying to see if she'd missed a clue over the years. But there was nothing.

Susan gave a dry laugh. "Believe me, I didn't either. It surprised the heck out of me too."

"So, um, the way you feel about Phoenix. That was really how you felt about my father?"

"Yes and no." Susan gazed off into space. "With your father, it was instant connection and chemistry. We met on that beach in Phuket, when my Japanese friends convinced me to go with them to Thailand before I came back to New York." She sighed. "It was so romantic. We only had a week together, but we were in love. It was so intense and so exciting. We just got each other."

Lexa smiled, swept away by the emotion on her mother's face. She loved hearing about how her parents had met and was consoled to know she'd been conceived out of love. "It sounds magical."

"It was. He told me to call him Alex, his American name." Susan looked at Lexa, her eyes full of love. "I named you after him."

"What about Dad? Did you love him like that?"

"It was different. With Greg, it was more gradual, based

on trust and respect. He was my best friend. I was five months pregnant with you when we met, and he still wanted to go out with me." She smiled at Lexa. "And with Phoenix, it's a combination of the two. We connected, not just physically but also on an emotional level."

"Oh." Lexa squirmed, not wanting to think about her mom and Phoenix being physical. Really, what did they do together? They were in their sixties!

"Does talking about Phoenix make you uncomfortable?"

"No!" Lexa said, too fast. And then, "Yes. Maybe."

"I want to be able to talk to you about her."

"I know. It's just so much. You and Phoenix, and now my father dying."

"I know." Susan reached out and stroked a hand down Lexa's hair. "You've had quite a shock this week."

Lexa was quiet, and then turned to her mom. "Do you think he ever loved me?"

"Oh, honey, of course he did. He was so smitten with you." Susan paused, and her expression hardened. "But I lost all respect for him that last summer. I know he wasn't perfect." Susan laid a hand on Lexa's cheek. "But he made a big mistake, and he lost you."

8

June, Twenty-Eight Years Ago
Taichung, Taiwan

Susan stood at the front of the traditional Chinese medicine store breathing in the pungent, slightly musty, and bitter odor coming from the shelves and bins of herbs, roots, and flowers. Along one side, a glass countertop ran the length of the shop, where a woman wearing a giant tan apron stood helping Lexa and her father. Behind her, row upon row of small wooden drawers held the more mysterious and expensive items, such as dried insects and parts of animals used to cure or help any kind of ailment imaginable.

It was their last full day in Taiwan before they returned to New York the next day. It had been a whirlwind ten days, filled with so much sightseeing and getting to know the family that Susan's head was spinning. She'd been nervous to see Jing Tao again, and knew Greg was afraid she was still attracted to Lexa's father. But to her relief, that spark of attraction they'd had in Phuket had simmered to a mutual respect and understanding. Susan truly loved Greg. Their relationship had started out as a friendship for her, but she'd fallen in love with him over the years. She and Jing Tao were different people now, grown-up and each with their own families.

Pong and Jing Tao had taken Susan and Lexa shopping on their last day. Hsu-Ling had wanted to come, but her leg was red and irritated from walking so much this week and a half. Pin-Yen had ordered her to stay home and practice her Chinese characters. Susan had been surprised that a four-and-a-half-year-old could already write so many characters.

Jing Tao was discussing herbal remedies and teas with the shopkeeper for Lexa to take back to New York. Lexa stared up at her father, her adoration clear on her face.

"They look happy together," Pong said.

"Yes." Susan nodded in agreement with Jing Tao's best friend. Pong had been their translator the entire trip, and she'd been grateful to have someone who could speak English to converse with. He didn't have a wife or family and had told her Jing Tao's family had adopted him as an honorary uncle.

"He loves her." Pong was staring at Lexa and Jing Tao, a wistful look on his face. "From the moment he heard about her, I think she stole his heart." He turned to Susan. "You have no idea how happy he is to finally meet her and get to spend time with her."

Susan smiled. "And she loves him. I've never seen her so happy. I can't tell you how glad I am that the two of them have bonded. It's wonderful to see her get to know her Taiwanese family and heritage."

They made their way to the counter and watched the shopkeeper bag the herbs. Susan peered over Lexa's shoulder. "What's all this?"

Jing Tao pointed to a clear plastic bag. "This is four-spirits soup. All the herbs are in the packet: lotus seed, barley, gor-

gon fruit, Chinese yam, and poria cocos. It helps the diges-
tive system. Pong will write the directions for you, but very
easy to make."

"And what's that?" Susan pointed to another bag.

Pong translated. "Astragalus. It boosts the immune system
and fights disease. Keeps you healthy."

"That's ginseng, right?" She pointed to slices of a dried
brown root. It was the only thing she recognized.

Pong nodded. "Good for boosting energy and reducing
stress, among other benefits. Just drop a few pieces into a cup
and pour hot water over it to make a tea."

Jing Tao paid, and then spoke in English. "You hungry?
Maybe a snack next before we go to bookstore?"

Lexa nodded eagerly, and they all followed him out of the
store. Lexa and her father walked ahead, holding hands. Jing
Tao was talking, gesturing with his free hand. Susan knew he
was trying to make up for the past eight years, trying to cram
as much as he could into their visit. As for herself, she was relieved to be away from Pin-Yen. She was getting tired of the
woman's cold stares, as if she could somehow make Susan and
Lexa disappear. It was so tiresome. Pin-Yen needed to get a life.

Jing Tao pointed through the window of a bakery. "Look,
sesame balls. My favorite. I can't believe I didn't get you one
yet." They trooped into the bakery, and Jing Tao bought them
each a sesame ball. Susan watched as Lexa bit into the crispy,
chewy ball. When the unfamiliar flavors burst in her mouth,
a look of surprised pleasure crossed Lexa's face, and she let out
a squeal of delight. Jing Tao gave Lexa the biggest smile
Susan had ever seen, and Pong laughed. Lexa was too busy
devouring her first sesame ball to notice anyone else.

"Sesame balls are now my new favorite dessert," she said,
to a round of laughter.

Her father looked at her, his face soft with indulgence and something Susan recognized as pure love. "Hsu-Ling likes them, but she could do without them. It's nice to see one of my daughters loves them as much as I do," he said.

Lexa turned to Susan. "Can we get these in New York?"

Susan nodded. "I've seen them in Chinatown."

"Oh, good!" Lexa clapped her hands. "Then every time I eat one, I'll think of you, Baba."

Jing Tao beamed another smile at Lexa so full of warmth that Susan could feel the love radiating from him. "Do you want a bubble tea to go with it?" Jing Tao asked.

Lexa nodded. "*Wo yao yibei zhenzhu naicha.*"

Susan felt sad all of a sudden, listening to Lexa ask for a bubble tea in Mandarin. In just over a week, she looked and sounded more like a Taiwanese girl than Susan had thought possible. She was so happy Lexa was getting to know her other family. But a part of her couldn't help feeling as if she was losing her daughter. Lexa would soon be fluent in a language Susan couldn't even begin to understand.

They went back out into the crowded street when Lexa had her bubble tea, and once again, Jing Tao and Lexa led the way to the bookstore. Suddenly, Pong reached out and grabbed Susan by the elbow when a man on a scooter roared past them on the sidewalk. Susan jumped, her hand on her heart. "Thanks," she said. "I still can't get used to people driving on the sidewalks as if it's normal."

"Ah," Pong said, with a twinkle in his eye, "anything goes here in Taiwan when it comes to traffic rules."

She smiled at him, this man who had been so kind to them. "Thanks for being so good to Lexa and helping Jing Tao make her feel welcome."

"I'd do anything for Jing Tao and his family." He nodded to Lexa. "She's a special girl."

Gladness replaced the sadness in Susan's heart. All she'd ever wanted was for Lexa to know where she came from. It hadn't been easy bringing up an Asian daughter in a white world. People asked all the time if Lexa was adopted. She knew Lexa hated how she stood out in their family, so it was nice to see her fitting in so well with her new family, to know they loved her as much as she did. Watching Lexa and Jing Tao together, Susan couldn't imagine anything breaking the bond that was forming between father and daughter.

9

When Lexa opened her eyes, it took her a moment to realize she was still in Phoenix's apartment. She must have fallen asleep on the couch. She rubbed her eyes and sat up, Phoenix's shawl falling off her body. Remnants of the dream she'd been having about her father floated in her mind, but before she could grasp them, they evaporated.

"Mom?" She sniffed, the lemongrass scent of Phoenix's apartment strong in her nose. She pulled out her phone and saw it was almost five o'clock. She had to be back on the Upper East Side for a six-o'clock client. Standing up, she saw a note on the coffee table.

I went to take a yoga class. Have to get in a certain number of classes for my certification. You fell asleep and I didn't want to wake you. Love you.

Lexa picked up her purse and was about to leave when she stopped. She was alone in Phoenix's apartment. She'd be meeting her in three days, but curiosity about this woman who had broken up her family overwhelmed her now. Looking around furtively, Lexa made her way to the bedroom. Her mom had given her a tour when she first got there, but now she wanted a closer look. Who was this Phoenix?

The bedroom was gorgeous. It was filled with teak furniture from Malaysia, simple and basic in the old kampong tradition. The room was done in shades of greens and browns, as found in nature, and there was a serenity that was so different from the hectic city life outside the windows. Lexa stared at the bed, trying to imagine her mom sleeping with a strange woman.

She wandered over to the bedside table on what she knew was Phoenix's side and opened the drawer. She'd seen her mom's glasses on the other table. Feeling like a thief, she held her breath and peered in, hoping like hell she didn't find a vibrator or something. She saw notebooks, pens, bobby pins, and a tube of hand cream. Pushing a book aside, she found a small laminated picture and pulled it out.

A much-younger Phoenix looked back at her, her long dark hair falling in waves around her shoulders and one arm wrapped around the arm of an older Asian man. Lexa assumed it was Phoenix's father. Lexa's mom had told her Phoenix was half-Malaysian and half-French. She studied Phoenix's face, marveling at how beautiful she was. She was laughing and turned slightly toward the man.

A car horn honked repeatedly outside the window, and Lexa jumped. The picture slipped from her fingers and slid under the bed. She dropped to her hands and knees to retrieve it as beads of sweat popped out on her forehead. Placing the picture back in the drawer and closing it with a bang, she ran out of the room and grabbed her purse from the couch. She shouldn't have been snooping. She slammed out of the apartment, her face burning.

. . .

By the time Lexa made it back to the gym for her six-o'clock client, she had a pounding headache. The lack of sleep combined with everything going on in her life made her bleary-eyed and slightly nauseated. She was glad this was her last client of the day.

She walked onto the gym floor and saw her client Kiley McGuire talking to Bryson, the personal training manager. Bryson waved her over and said, "Kiley was just about to tell me her big news. But why don't you tell Lexa instead?"

He walked away as Lexa stifled a yawn.

"You'll never guess what happened!" Kiley was practically vibrating with excitement.

"You met someone?" Even to her own ears, Lexa could hear the sarcasm dripping from her voice. They were the same age, but Kiley's main focus in life was to find a rich husband.

"Yes." Kiley's eyes rounded with hurt, and her mouth parted.

Lexa felt like she'd just kicked a kitten. "I'm sorry. What happened?"

The injured look cleared from Kiley's blue eyes. "I met the most amazing man!" Kiley had a high voice that squeaked when she was excited.

"That's great, Kiley." Lexa took a medicine ball off a rack and handed it to her. It slipped from Kiley's grasp and rolled away.

Kiley leaned over to chase after the ball, her butt up in the air. Lexa heard a low whistle behind them and turned to find a guy staring appreciatively at Kiley's backside.

"Kiley," Lexa said in a loud whisper. "Put your butt

down!" Lexa saw the guy walking toward them and fanned the air in front of her. "Oh, sorry. I just let one rip. Must have been those beans I ate last night." The guy froze, uncertain. She flipped up a hand in apology. "Hey, man. Sorry. I wouldn't get any closer if I were you."

He turned and practically ran back to the weights he'd left by a bench.

"Did you really fart?" Kiley finally grabbed the ball and stood up.

Lexa crossed her arms over her chest and rolled her eyes. "Of course not."

"Oh." Kiley's voice was small, and she shrank away from Lexa.

Lexa pinched the bridge of her nose. What was wrong with her? Why was she taking things out on Kiley? It wasn't Kiley's fault she was kind of ditzy. Okay, stop. She was being unkind now. She took a deep breath and forced herself to give Kiley a smile.

To Lexa's relief, Kiley smiled back and her session sped by. Kiley talked while Lexa tuned out. Was Lexa's mom right? Did she need to get a life outside her job?

All of a sudden, she realized Kiley had stopped talking and was staring at her.

"I'm sorry. Did you ask me something?"

Kiley blew out a breath, ruffling her bangs. "I wanted to know if you've ever had regrets. Like, maybe you'd always believed you wanted a rich husband, but then you meet this incredible man and he doesn't have a lot of money. But he's so amazing, and if you blow him off just because he has no money, will you regret it?"

Lexa's face softened as she listened to Kiley. "So this amazing man isn't rich?"

Kiley shook her head so hard that her ponytail whipped back and forth.

"Well, is money the most important thing to you?"

Kiley shrugged. "I don't know. Maybe." Kiley studied her. "I bet you never have regrets about anything. You're so sure of yourself."

"Oh, believe me, I have my regrets."

Kiley contemplated that in silence. And then she said, "It's not good to keep things inside. You have to face the past in order to confront your future."

Lexa stared at her, her mouth slightly open. Where had that insight come from? It shamed her to think she'd been judging Kiley unfairly. But she realized Kiley was right. Lexa's father's death was bringing back the past whether she liked it or not. Maybe it was time to put on her big-girl pants and deal with it, instead of pushing it out of mind like she had all her life.

"Thanks. I needed to hear that. Let's get you stretched out."

Kiley beamed and said, "I got that from a fortune cookie." She turned to walk to the stretching area and promptly tripped over a weight on the floor. She sprawled butt-up on the mats. Lexa couldn't suppress her laugher, but then saw the same man who'd shown so much interest in Kiley's backside earlier walking toward them again.

"Dude." Lexa waved the air in front of her. "Remember those beans."

And he sailed on without stopping, as if he'd meant to walk by all along.

10

The next afternoon, Lexa took the 6 train to her dad's apartment after she finished training the Shapiros. The cash she made from the private clients she trained in their homes nicely supplemented her gym salary. It meant a lot of running back and forth, but some of her private clients, like Beth and David Shapiro, had become close to her and told her they couldn't live without her. Even though they were in a stratosphere of wealth that she couldn't even imagine with their massive apartment on Fifth Avenue, waterfront house in Southampton, and palatial vacation home in Florida, they treated her like family (albeit a lowly member).

The train bumped along underground, each jolt fraying her nerves because she knew she was going to have to tell Greg and Maddie the truth about what had really happened that summer. She was seeing them both that day. She knew it was time to come clean, before Hsu-Ling came to New York.

When the subway jerked to a stop at Thirty-Third Street station, Lexa jumped out, rehearsing in her mind what she'd tell Greg and Maddie. She was on her way to help Greg move into the studio apartment he'd bought before he met her mother, the one he'd been renting out all these years since he'd moved into the Whitestone house. He still worked as an accountant in Manhattan, and the studio was convenient to his office.

Maddie had refused to help but would meet them later for dinner. Should she tell Greg now? Or wait and tell them both together at dinner? She'd have preferred to tell Greg first and then rely on his support to tell Maddie, but the thought of having to tell it twice made her head hurt. Maybe it'd be better to wait and tell them both together at dinner.

"Dad, did you know about Phoenix?" Lexa asked, once they'd gotten the boxes from his car inside. She'd been wondering if he'd been shocked to find out about her mom's affair. Her mom claimed they hadn't done anything until she'd told Greg about Phoenix a month earlier, but Lexa wasn't sure if she was only saying that to assuage her guilt.

"Maybe. I didn't know Susan had fallen in love with a woman, just that she was talking about Phoenix a lot."

"You're lucky this apartment was empty when Mom told you the news last month."

"I know." Greg stopped in the middle of the studio with a box in hand. "We thought about selling it for years, but now I'm glad I didn't."

Greg brought the box to the tiny kitchen, and Lexa started unloading cups and plates into the cabinets. "I just don't get it. You guys always seemed so happy."

"We were, in a way." He ran a hand through his hair, which wasn't as full as it used to be and was more gray than blond these days. "I always thought I loved her more than she loved me."

Lexa stared at him, noticing the deep lines on his face and the defeated stoop of his shoulders. "You thought you loved Mom more?"

He made a face. "You were her number one priority. She told me as much when I asked her to marry me. Said you guys were a package deal. But I loved her and you, and I thought that would be enough."

"Oh." Maddie always said Lexa and their mom left her out. Now she wondered if their dad felt the same way. "She did love you." Lexa wasn't sure whom she was trying to convince.

"She did." He put the books he'd taken out of a box onto a small bookshelf. At home in Whitestone, they had a whole wall with built-in shelves dedicated to books, since they all loved to read. It gave Lexa a pang to see only his books there on this small portable shelf. His shoulders slumped forward, and Lexa could suddenly see what he'd look like when he became an old man.

She walked over to him and put her arms around him from the back.

"Love you, Dad. You'll always be my dad." He half turned to hug her and gave her a smile before turning quickly away, but not before she saw the tears shining in his eyes.

.   .   .

"What do you mean she's coming to New York?" Maddie asked, competing with the mariachi music playing loudly over the speakers. They were seated at a bright green table in the Mexican restaurant around the corner from their dad's apartment. Maddie had joined them for dinner, after all the moving was done.

"That's what she said," Lexa said. "And why are you focusing on my sister when my father died?" She'd told them on the phone about her father, but this was the first time she'd seen them since she got the news.

"I'm sorry," Maddie said. "I really am. But you haven't seen him in over twenty years. It's not like you'll miss him."

"Maddie." There was a warning in Greg's voice. He reached out and laid a hand on top of Lexa's, giving it a squeeze.

Lexa smiled at him before turning to Maddie. "Nice of you to help us move Dad."

"I couldn't." Maddie pushed her hair off her face. "Then it'd be real."

They sat in silence until their waiter came to get their drink order.

Once he left, Maddie asked, "So why's your sister coming to New York? Doesn't she have to plan the funeral or something?"

"She's coming after the funeral. She has some legal stuff to go over with me. And she wants to talk about something our father said to her before he died." Lexa studied the menu, working up the nerve to tell Maddie and Greg the truth. But before she could, Greg spoke.

"I don't like it." Lexa looked up at the intense tone in Greg's voice. His forehead was creased, and he was frowning fiercely, as if facing down an enemy.

"I don't like that he's dead either." Lexa was taken aback by the way he was scowling.

"That's not what—" He broke off and muttered something under his breath.

"So I finally get to meet your other sister?" Maddie's voice had a sneer in it.

"Madison." Greg gave her another look. "Be nice."

"I am nice." Maddie pulled the basket of corn chips in front of her and dipped one into the salsa. "But don't you think it's weird that they've ignored Lexa for all these years and now suddenly her sister is coming to see her?"

"They haven't ignored me. We keep in touch." Lexa gritted her teeth, determined not to let Maddie get under her skin.

"But neither of them has made an effort to see you. And I don't understand why you haven't wanted to go back to Taiwan. I thought you loved it." Maddie worked her way through the chips as the waiter placed their margaritas in front of them. Lexa knew her sister would finish the basket and then complain that they let her eat too much.

Lexa could feel Greg staring at her. *What is wrong with him?*

"I do love Taiwan. It's just . . . it's complicated." *Spit it out, Lexa.* Why was she finding it so hard to tell them?

"What's so complicated?" Maddie took a sip of her frozen margarita.

Greg caught Lexa's eyes. He seemed to be trying to tell her something.

What? she mouthed at him, but his glance skated away, and he changed the subject.

"Looking forward to your birthday dinner next weekend?" Andi was throwing a party for her at her restaurant.

Lexa nodded. "You're both coming, right?"

"Are Mom and that woman going to be there?" Maddie asked, at the same time Greg said, "Of course we'll be there."

"Yes, Mom and *Phoenix* will be there. If Dad doesn't mind, why should you?"

Maddie sniffed. "What kind of name is Phoenix anyways? It sounds made-up. I bet her real name is Prudence, or something like that." Neither Lexa nor Greg replied because Maddie knew as well as they did that Phoenix was her real name.

"You are going to show up at dim sum on Saturday to meet her, right?" Lexa asked.

Maddie narrowed her eyes. "I told you I'm not going."

Lexa let out a sigh and turned to Greg. "Are you okay with seeing Mom with Phoenix?" She was suddenly worried Greg had only agreed to come for her sake.

"I, um . . ." He shook his head. "It'll be fine. I want to be there for you."

"Wait, is your other sister going to be here for your birthday dinner?" Maddie asked.

"No, she doesn't get in 'til two days after my birthday."

"I don't get why she's coming. What does she want?" Maddie's eyes lit up. "Hey, maybe your sister is sick and needs a kidney. Or maybe your father left you something and she's upset and wants to contest the will?"

"Maddie! Really?" Lexa glared at her. "You better be nice to her. I don't know why you dislike someone you've never met."

"I just don't like the whole situation, that's all. Families keep in touch and help each other, yet your Taiwanese family hasn't seen you in over twenty years."

"You're one to talk about family. You haven't talked to Mom since she told you about Phoenix."

"I hate that woman. She broke up our family. She's a home wrecker."

Greg's hand slammed down on the table. "Madison Louise Thomas. That's enough."

"You always blurt out what you're feeling without thinking of the consequences first." Lexa shook her head in disgust at Maddie. "When are you going to learn to control your tongue? It's going to get you in trouble one of these days."

Maddie lifted her chin. "I just don't like that woman. And my last name isn't Thomas anymore. It's Brennan."

"Phoenix didn't break up our family, Maddie. But you're

doing a damn good job of it yourself." Greg took a long drink of his margarita. "I told you Susan and I had our problems long before Phoenix even came into the picture."

"But how can you stand to see them together?"

"Because I still love your mother, as a friend." He paused and forced a smile, but Lexa could see the effort it was taking him to look cheerful. The lines around his eyes were more pronounced, and his smile didn't quite reach to the corners of his mouth. "I want her to be happy, and she's happy with Phoenix. You need to accept that. And you need to accept that Lexa has another family. Whatever her reason for coming to New York, you're going to welcome her sister."

Maddie looked down and noticed the chips basket was empty. "I don't know how you're so accepting of Lexa's other family. If it were me, I'd have freaked when Mom's friend called to tell her Lexa's father had resurfaced. Weren't you afraid he'd take Lexa away?"

Lexa looked at Greg. She'd never thought about how he'd felt when her father was found.

Greg let out a breath. "I was happy for Lexa to know her birth father. So let's be nice to her sister, okay?"

"Whatever," Maddie muttered. "You can't make me."

"You're acting like a two-year-old," Lexa said.

Maddie kicked her under the table, making Lexa yelp.

"Girls." Greg gave a defeated sigh. Lexa caught his eyes and grew still. Had he been afraid that Lexa's father would try to take her away? And had he been relieved by the estrangement between Lexa and her father? She'd always taken Greg's love for her for granted, but now she wondered what he'd thought when she'd refused to see her birth father after that last summer. As Maddie continued to argue with their dad, Lexa sat in silence, wondering how to bring the conversation back to tell them the truth. In the end, she decided that night wasn't the right time. She ignored the voice in her head that was saying, *Coward. Just tell them now!* She would, before Hsu-Ling got to New York.

11

Her phone rang with a FaceTime request as she was putting the key in her front door. Lexa rushed inside, dumped her bag on the floor, and accepted the call. Zeus pushed his nose into her leg, and she reached down to pet him as Hsu-Ling's image filled the screen.

"Hi, Hsu-Ling. Everything okay?"

"Yes, everything's fine. Are you busy?"

"No. I just got home from dinner with my dad and Maddie. What's up?" Lexa kicked off her sneakers and plopped on her couch, thinking this was the most she'd talked to Hsu-Ling on the phone in almost two decades.

"I met with the lawyer yesterday. Baba and Uncle Pong used the same man."

"Oh." Lexa patted the spot next to her, and Zeus jumped up. She leaned against his side, grateful for his company and his loyal presence as her nerves jumped at the mention of lawyers.

"I know I was a bit vague the other day when I talked to you," Hsu-Ling said. "I'm sorry. I was still in shock."

"It's okay." Lexa scratched Zeus behind his ear, and he panted happily.

"So, Baba left most of his money to Mama. But he left his property to us both equally."

"What? Really?" Lexa's hand stilled on Zeus's fur. "Why would he do that? You're his real daughter."

"Don't say that. You're his daughter too."

"I know, but that's not fair to you." Lexa ran her hand down Zeus's back. She was afraid Hsu-Ling was going to accuse her of manipulating their father into leaving her something, just like Maddie had predicted at dinner.

"Chi, stop. It is fair. You deserve half of whatever he had."

"I bet your mother's upset . . ." Lexa chewed on her bottom lip.

"She is." Hsu-Ling stared at her. "How did you know?"

Lexa shrugged.

Hsu-Ling ran a hand through her hair. "Anyways, it's all kind of complicated."

"What do you mean?"

"I assumed when the will said his property that it meant the building my family lives in. When our grandfather passed away a few years ago, everyone thought the building went to our father, since he's the oldest son."

"It didn't?"

"Apparently not. The lawyer was being really cryptic about it. He said maybe our father owned it. But that it depended on you."

"What?" Lexa wrinkled her brow in confusion. What did she have to do with the building her Taiwanese family lived in?

"I don't know what's going on." Hsu-Ling twisted a finger around the bottom of her hair. "And the lawyer said Pong left you a letter that has to be hand delivered to you. He actually left money in his will for someone to fly to New York and personally deliver the letter."

"That's ridiculous!" Lexa's face screwed up as she tried to make sense of what Hsu-Ling was telling her. "Why would Pong leave me a letter that has to be hand delivered? I haven't seen him since I was fourteen."

"I know. I was just as confused. But the lawyer was adamant. I told him I was going to New York, and he said I could give it to you. And he said our father's will depends a lot on what you do about the letter."

"I don't understand." Lexa fell back against the cushions.

"Me either. I asked the lawyer if I could open it and read it to you, and he said no. Pong left specific instructions that only you were to open it."

"Just open it and read it. I don't want to wait until you get here."

Hsu-Ling looked back at her, not blinking. "I want nothing more than to rip it open and see what's going on. But I can't. He won't even give me the letter until right before I leave for New York."

"This is so stupid." Hsu-Ling frowned, and Lexa backed off. "I'm sorry. I know it's not your fault. I can't imagine what Pong could possibly have to say to me."

"I know. My whole family is confused. I asked Ah-Ma, but she has no idea what's going on. If Baba didn't own the building, then who does? And what does Pong have to do with it?"

Lexa rubbed her head. "This is making my head hurt."

"Me too. You have no idea." Hsu-Ling paused, a mix of emotions passing over her face. "Mama is going crazy. I keep catching her ranting and raving about something, but when I ask her what's going on, she snaps at me that it's nothing." Hsu-Ling lowered her voice. "I heard her cursing our father once. She said some bad things about him."

"That's terrible." Lexa really didn't want to ask, but she had to know. "Did your mother curse me too?"

Hsu-Ling stared at her, indecision on her face. "Um."

Lexa let out a short laugh. "I'll take that as a yes."

"Why would she do that? She wouldn't tell me anything. I think she's losing her mind."

Lexa sighed. "Your mother hates me, Hsu-Ling."

"What? Why?"

"It's a long story. I didn't realize it until the summer I was twelve." Lexa rubbed the side of her head.

"What happened that summer?"

Lexa huffed out a breath before speaking, reluctant to bring up the past. "I don't know. She wasn't exactly warm toward me on that first trip when I was eight, but she was okay. That second time I visited, when I was twelve, something changed. She did *not* want me there."

"Are you sure?"

Lexa nodded. "She said as much, and the way she looked at me . . ."

"I . . . I don't know what to say." Conflicting emotions flitted across Hsu-Ling's face.

Not wanting to alienate her sister before she saw her, Lexa quickly added, "We can talk more when you get here."

"I wish I was coming earlier." Hsu-Ling had booked her flight the day before and sent Lexa the itinerary.

"You'll be here in less than two weeks."

"I've missed you." Hsu-Ling's glance skittered away. "You disappeared without a word. I thought you hated me."

"No! I wrote to you, and you didn't write back until I was going to college."

Hsu-Ling's eyes flew to Lexa's face. "So you did write," she said slowly. "I knew it."

"What?" Lexa cocked her head. "Of course I did. I thought you said you got my letters when you finally wrote me back?"

"My mother," Hsu-Ling muttered. Then she changed the subject, asking about Lexa's dinner with her dad and Maddie.

They talked for a few minutes more before Hsu-Ling had to get back to her work as an editor on a Taiwanese TV show. After disconnecting, Lexa stayed on the couch with Zeus, thinking about all the years that had gone by since she'd last seen Hsu-Ling. She wondered what she was like as an adult. She really only knew her half sister from Facebook.

Hsu-Ling loved Facebook and posted often, usually cheerful, self-deprecating posts like, *Bet you didn't think I could balance so well! Lol!* with a picture of her on a paddleboard.

From her page, she seemed like a positive, happy person, the exact opposite of Maddie. But who knew what Hsu-Ling was really like after all these years? People tended to post the most flattering photos, boasting of amazing vacations or children for their hundreds of "friends" to like and comment.

Her two sisters would meet for the very first time soon. Lexa could only pray that Maddie would be on her best behavior. She knew Maddie saw Hsu-Ling as competition, but maybe a miracle would happen and they would hit it off. But deep in her gut, she had a feeling it wasn't going to be that easy.

12

〜

July, Twenty-Four Years Ago
Taichung, Taiwan

I don't want to practice the piano. I want to make tea eggs with ChiChi and Ah-Ma." Hsu-Ling stamped her prosthetic leg and crossed her arms over her chest, her face screwed up in a scowl.

Pin-Yen scowled back at her daughter and pointed at Ah-Ma's piano. "Stop arguing with me and practice." She refused to back down, directing her laser-focused eyes on Hsu-Ling. She knew what was best for her daughter, and right then, making tea eggs wasn't it.

"No, no, no, no!" Each "no" out of Hsu-Ling's mouth got louder and louder until she screamed the final "no."

Pin-Yen could feel steam coming out of her ears. Why was her daughter acting like this? And in front of her half sister? She stalked over to Hsu-Ling and grabbed her by the upper arm, intending to haul her over to the piano and make her sit. But before she could, a quiet voice stopped her.

"Pin-Yen. You've already signed her up for all those *buxi-*

ban classes all summer. She practices the piano every day even though she hates it. Let her have some fun with her sister, huh?" Ah-Ma's voice was mild, but Pin-Yen heard the steel beneath the words.

Pin-Yen let go of Hsu-Ling's arm and turned to confront Ah-Ma. But one look into the older woman's eyes and Pin-Yen knew she had to back down. She didn't say anything, just nodded, and Hsu-Ling cheered, rushing to Lexa's side in the kitchen.

Ah-Ma gave a brief nod in return. "Good," she said before turning to the two girls.

Pin-Yen dropped down heavily into a dining chair and watched with resentment as Ah-Ma taught her granddaughters how to make tea eggs.

"We need the biggest pot I have so that we can fit two dozen eggs." Ah-Ma spoke in Mandarin so Lexa could understand. Pin-Yen would never admit it out loud, but she was impressed by how much Mandarin Lexa understood this trip.

Ah-Ma gestured for Lexa and Hsu-Ling to gently place all the eggs into the pot. "Then we fill it with enough cold water to cover the eggs." With Lexa's help, Ah-Ma carried the heavy pot onto the stove.

"What kind of tea do you use?" Lexa picked up the box of tea bags and sniffed it.

"You can use any kind, but I like this black tea." Ah-Ma handed the tea bags to Hsu-Ling, who was now perched on a high stool next to the stove. "Put fifteen of these into the water."

Pin-Yen watched her daughter carefully count out fifteen bags. She frowned, tapping one foot impatiently. Hsu-Ling needed to do her homework. How long was this going to take?

"Now we add the star anise, rock sugar, soy sauce, salt,

and my secret ingredient." Ah-Ma pulled out a box of herbs and handed it to Lexa.

"*Angelica sinensis.*" Lexa sounded out the English spelling.

"Can I stir now?" Hsu-Ling picked up a wooden spoon from the counter.

Pin-Yen made a move to help, because it looked like Hsu-Ling was going to fall off the stool. But Ah-Ma stopped Pin-Yen with a pointed stare, and Pin-Yen sank back into her chair. She hated having to acquiesce to Ah-Ma's every wish. But Ah-Ma was the real head of the family, and everyone listened to her. Pin-Yen had always bent over backward to please the older woman. Not that it made a difference; she was convinced she'd never get Ah-Ma's approval.

"Here, let me help you." Ah-Ma covered Hsu-Ling's hand with her own, and together, they stirred the mixture in the pot. "We want to mix it up gently before I turn on the heat."

"And that's it?" Lexa looked dubiously in the pot.

Ah-Ma laughed and let go of Hsu-Ling's hand. "No. We'll let it come to a boil and then turn it down to simmer for an hour. Then we have to take each egg and crack the shell without peeling it and then let it simmer for a few more hours."

"We break the eggs?" Lexa looked even more unconvinced.

"Just enough so that the tea mixture will get inside the shells and create a marble effect."

Hsu-Ling paused in her stirring to address Lexa. "It makes the eggs look so pretty, like they have a design on them."

"So we won't be able to eat them for a while." Lexa sounded disappointed, and Pin-Yen had to agree with her. It was a long process just to eat an egg; so much easier to buy them from a cart on the street. But Ah-Ma wanted to teach

Lexa as many of their family's traditions as she could. Pin-Yen crossed her arms over her chest and pursed her lips, not sure why it bothered her that Ah-Ma was showing so much interest in Lexa.

"Hsu-Ling, give it one more good stir and then we'll turn on the flame."

Hsu-Ling stuck out her tongue and, holding tightly to the pot with one hand, directed all her attention on her task.

Gently, gently, Pin-Yen said to Hsu-Ling in her head when she saw her daughter's motions getting bigger and bigger. Ah-Ma and Lexa were talking and not watching Hsu-Ling. Pin-Yen stood, about to yell out a warning, but then she bit her tongue. Ah-Ma was always telling Pin-Yen she was too hard on Hsu-Ling. Fine, she wouldn't step in this time.

Hsu-Ling gave one final stir, letting go of the pot to use both hands. Her foot slipped on the stool and she pitched forward, falling heavily against the pot. The contents spilled out, showering Hsu-Ling with the dark liquid.

Hsu-Ling shrieked, and Pin-Yen jumped up. "*Aiya,* look what you've done. You made a big mess."

Lexa grabbed a towel and used it to dab at her little sister while Pin-Yen scolded her daughter for being clumsy.

"I'm sorry, Ah-Ma." Hsu-Ling's voice trembled, and Pin-Yen could see the worry in her daughter's eyes. "I just wanted to make sure it was all mixed together."

Ah-Ma smiled. "Don't worry, *xiao mei.* Accidents happen." She peered into the pot. "It doesn't look like you broke any eggs. Why don't you go change and I'll start boiling them?"

Pin-Yen reached to take her daughter's hand, but before she could, Lexa stepped in front of Hsu-Ling. "Hop on. I'll give you a ride down."

"You don't have to." Pin-Yen crossed to Hsu-Ling to prevent her from getting on Lexa's back. "She's all wet. She'll get you dirty."

Lexa turned and looked at Pin-Yen. "It's okay. I can change too. Come on, Hsu-Ling."

Hsu-Ling climbed onto Lexa's back with a happy laugh just as Jing Tao and Ah-Gong came in the front door.

"There you all are." Jing Tao reached out to tweak Hsu-Ling's nose.

"Baba!" Hsu-Ling called from Lexa's back. "We're making tea eggs, but I spilled it all over myself and Lexa is going to help me change."

Ah-Gong laughed and patted Hsu-Ling on the head as they headed past him to the door.

Pin-Yen trailed after them. "I'll just go with them and make sure everything is okay."

She touched Jing Tao briefly on the arm and then rushed out after the girls. They were already on the first floor by the time she caught up with them.

"I can help her myself if you want to go back." Lexa looked back at Pin-Yen.

"Are you sure?" Pin-Yen stopped on the stairs. She would like to see how Jing Tao's day was. But Hsu-Ling was her responsibility.

"It's no problem. We'll come up when we've both changed." Lexa smiled up at Pin-Yen.

"If you're sure . . . thanks." Pin-Yen stayed on the step until Lexa and Hsu-Ling had disappeared through the door of their apartment. She knew she hadn't exactly been welcoming toward Lexa, and definitely not to her American mother. But really, the girl wasn't so bad. She was kind, and her love for Hsu-Ling was obvious. Maybe Pin-Yen should get to know her better on this trip.

She turned and went back up the stairs to Ah-Ma and Ah-Gong's apartment. The door wasn't shut all the way, and just as she was about to push it open, she heard her name.

Pin-Yen froze for a second before leaning her ear toward the opening. Why were they talking about her? Was Ah-Ma telling Jing Tao again that she thought Pin-Yen was too strict with Hsu-Ling? Ah-Ma murmured something, and Pin-Yen strained to catch her words. Then her husband answered, and she heard every word clearly.

"I want to provide for her. It's only right. She's my daughter too. I don't agree with you. I think Pin-Yen would understand." Pin-Yen's eyes widened with alarm. Was Jing Tao talking about Lexa? What did he mean by "provide"?

"Son, I know that woman. She will not be pleased that you want to include Lexa in your will." Ah-Gong spoke up, and Pin-Yen nodded in agreement, glad that someone was on her side. But then her heart rate picked up as the words sunk in. Jing Tao wanted to put Lexa in his will? No!

She almost spoke the word out loud and clapped a hand to her mouth. They couldn't know she was eavesdropping. She needed to hear more.

"But she's my daughter. It's only right."

Ah-Ma spoke again, and Pin-Yen's ear was practically glued to the door by then, eager to catch every word.

". . . she is very smart. Maybe we'll finally have a doctor in the family, eh, Jing Tao?" Ah-Ma's voice was teasing, but Pin-Yen's mouth hardened. It was no secret Ah-Ma wanted Jing Tao, her firstborn son, to be a doctor, but instead, he'd become only an X-ray technician. Jing Tao hated the sight of blood. He was always good-natured about failing to fulfill his mother's dreams, but Pin-Yen didn't appreciate it. There was nothing wrong with being an X-ray technician.

As if reading her thoughts, Jing Tao laughed. "Yes, Ma, maybe you'll finally get that doctor you wanted. She does excel at sciences, and you're right, she's quite clever."

Hearing the pride in her husband's voice, Pin-Yen bristled. Hsu-Ling was just as smart. Why didn't Ah-Ma assume Hsu-Ling would be the doctor of the family? Why her—the girl who wasn't even really Taiwanese or a part of the Chang family?

Pin-Yen pulled away from the door, taking a deep breath. It wouldn't do to let them know she'd heard their talk. But Jing Tao's words struck fear in her heart. Hsu-Ling was his rightful daughter, not that girl, even if Pin-Yen had been softening toward her. Pin-Yen just had to make sure Hsu-Ling became a doctor and made Ah-Ma proud.

She was about to open the door when a voice said from behind her, "Are you okay?"

Pin-Yen gasped and whirled around to face Lexa, her hands flying to her chest. "What are you doing?"

Lexa gave her a strange look. "Coming back to help Ah-Ma with the eggs."

"Where's Hsu-Ling?"

"She had to use the bathroom."

"You left her alone in the apartment?" Pin-Yen's voice rose, all charitable thoughts toward Lexa chased away by Jing Tao's words.

"I . . . She's . . . We're all right here . . . ," Lexa stammered.

Pin-Yen narrowed her eyes at her. "I'll get my daughter." She brushed past Lexa to go down the stairs, but then turned back, unable to let it go. "Don't think I don't know what you're up to. You don't belong here."

Lexa's eyes widened, and her mouth opened. Pin-Yen locked eyes with her, staring as if she could see deep into her soul. And if what she saw was only an innocent twelve-year-old girl, Pin-Yen brushed the thought aside. This girl was a threat to her own daughter. She wasn't going to let her worm her way into the hearts and finances of the Chang family. With one last look, she turned and went down the stairs to get her daughter.

13

⌁

The next morning, Lexa spoke to her mom on her cell while she took Zeus for a walk before going to the gym. She'd called her mom after hanging up with Hsu-Ling the night before, but her mom hadn't answered. She'd gone to bed early again. When her mom and dad were together, they used to stay up late, sometimes past midnight. Lexa thought she was dealing well with her mom's lifestyle change, but it was the small things like this that were throwing her off. She was used to being able to call home whenever she needed her parents.

Lexa had just finished telling her mom about her father's will when she heard someone calling her name.

"Lexa. Lexa! Yoo-hoo, Lexa!"

Lexa stopped in the middle of the morning rush-hour crowd on Second Avenue heading to subways and buses and looked over her shoulder. A smartly dressed woman wearing a gray skirt suit with a cream silk blouse hurried up to her. It took Lexa a moment to place her as someone who took her classes religiously.

"Hi, Carla." Lexa marveled at how some women could look so put together that early in the morning. She herself was still in the big T-shirt she'd slept in, with shorts thrown on, and she hadn't had time to put in her contacts. She made a gesture to indicate that she was on the phone.

Carla ignored her and held up an arm to jiggle the skin under it. She was super thin, with long legs that Lexa envied, but Carla always complained she was fat. The few times Lexa had told Carla she looked great, Carla had nearly taken her head off.

Now Carla asked, "How do I get rid of this? Do you think I'm starting to get bingo arms?" She waved her arm to demonstrate.

At the same time, Lexa's mom was saying on the phone, "Oh, boy. Pin-Yen must be spitting mad. I don't like the sound of this."

Lexa spoke into the phone. "I don't either. Can you hold on a sec, Mom? I just ran into someone I know."

She turned back to Carla. "I'm on the phone with my mom. Can we talk about this at the gym?"

"Can't you just show me some exercises I can do? My arms are so flabby!" Carla shuddered.

"You look great—"

Carla cut her off. "Oh, shut up, I do not. You're the one with the perfect body. I hate you."

"Oh, grow up, Carla. Can't you take a compliment?" As soon as she barked this out, Lexa wanted to take it back. Carla's face froze in confused shock, and Zeus took that moment to take a giant crap by Carla's foot.

"Oh!" Carla jumped back, and Lexa reached down to pick up the poop with a plastic bag while juggling her cell phone against her shoulder.

"I'm sorry." Lexa was saying sorry a lot lately. "Look, you know you can't spot train one area of your body. You look fine." Lexa tied the bag shut and let it dangle from her hand.

Carla caught a whiff and backed away. She pulled out her phone. "Will you look at the time? Got to go!" And she hurried down the sidewalk.

Wave a bag of poop at a well-dressed woman and she goes running in the opposite direction. "High-five, Zeus." Zeus sat and raised a paw for her to slap. She'd taught him that one night when she had no plans and had stayed home, drinking almost a whole bottle of wine by herself.

Watching Carla's retreating back, Lexa felt a wave of remorse. She hated when someone accosted her for advice when she wasn't at work. But she shouldn't have been so mean. What was wrong with her? Why couldn't she control her emotions lately?

"Lexa? Are you still there?" Susan's voice floated out from her cell, and Lexa started. She'd forgotten her mom was on the phone.

"I'm sorry, Mom. Someone wanted fitness advice on the street." Lexa threw out the bag in the nearest garbage can.

"Hm." Lexa could hear the disapproval in her mom's voice. "And you think you don't need a life outside of your job."

"Yeah, yeah." Lexa and Zeus started walking again. "Anyways, I guess we'll have to wait until Hsu-Ling gets here to find out what's going on. But I wanted to ask you something else. Did you ever tell Dad what happened?"

"About . . . Oh."

"He was acting weird at dinner last night. Almost as if he knew."

"Yeah, that." Susan cleared her throat. "I might have told him when we broke up."

"Might?" Lexa's voice rose in question.

"We got in an argument when I told him I was leaving.

And somehow it came around to you and how he always felt I was hiding something from him about that summer." Susan cleared her throat again. "Since I'd told Phoenix what happened, it was only right that I tell Greg the truth."

"What?" The word exploded out of Lexa's mouth. "You told Phoenix? Why?"

"I'm sorry. Don't be mad. I needed to talk to someone. I've felt so bad about you not knowing your Taiwanese family. It was always my intention that they be a part of your life. I could talk to Phoenix about anything. Somehow, the story just came out."

"Okay." Lexa placed a hand on her heart, willing it to slow down. Wasn't she too young to have a heart attack? "I'm not mad. But I can't believe Dad and Phoenix both know. Was he . . . Did he . . ." Lexa stopped and bit her lip, not wanting to voice her fears out loud. Zeus halted on the sidewalk and looked up at her in concern.

"No, he didn't believe it, if that's what you're asking. He loves you. He thinks of you as his own, as much as Maddie. You know he proposed to me the day you were born. He took one look at you and said to me, 'I don't want to be just some man in her life. I don't even want to be her stepfather. I want to be her father. Marry me and let me adopt her.'"

Lexa smiled, her face softening as it always did when she heard about how Greg proposed to her mother because of her.

"I know. But this all sucks."

"What sucks?" Susan asked. "Your father dying and the business with the will? Or Greg and I breaking up?"

"Both." Lexa tugged gently on the leash and turned around to head back to her apartment.

"How's he doing?"

"Who, Dad? You haven't talked to him?" Lexa's brows wrinkled. From the way Greg was talking at dinner, she thought her parents were still speaking.

"No." Susan's voice dropped. "He asked that I not call him for a while."

"Oh, God. And I just assumed he'd be fine with seeing the two of you at my birthday dinner next week." She smacked the side of her head with the heel of her hand. "What was I thinking? What do I do?"

"Lexa, he loves you. He wants to be there for your birthday, like he has been for every one of them that he could since you were born."

"But if it's going to hurt him to see the two of you together . . ." Lexa tried to keep the accusation out of her voice. She regretted telling her mom she could bring Phoenix. She should have thought about her dad's feelings. It was too soon to be inviting Phoenix to family functions.

Susan sighed. "I'm sorry, Lexa. I just want you guys to get to know Phoenix like I do. Your dad will be fine."

"Mom?" Lexa was thinking about the look on Greg's face when Maddie had asked if he'd been afraid Lexa's father would take her away. "Did Dad ever feel, I don't know, threatened by my relationship with my father?"

"No, never." Susan's voice was firm. "He was always in favor of finding your father because he felt it was important for you to know where you come from. He couldn't understand why you stopped seeing him after you were fourteen. But I kept my promise to you. I didn't tell him until recently."

"Okay." Lexa had reached her building. "I've got to go."

"See you tomorrow at dim sum. I can't wait for you to meet Phoenix."

Lexa made a face, glad her mom couldn't see. They hung

up, and she let herself into the front door of her building. She leaned against the wall in the hallway, Zeus waiting patiently at her side. She should have told Greg herself what had happened in Taiwan that last summer. But she'd been fourteen, only a child still, and so terrified by what had happened. She'd lost her father and couldn't bear the thought of possibly losing Greg. But she should have known he would have stood by her no matter what, because in every way that mattered, Greg had been her real father throughout her entire life.

14

Lexa checked on the brownies in her tiny oven, waiting for Maddie to bring over her kids. She was babysitting for three-year-old Corey and her brother, Connor, who'd just turned six, while Maddie and her husband, Mike, went out to dinner. She checked the time. Perfect. The brownies would be ready in five minutes, right when she was expecting the kids. Her phone rang.

"Hey, I don't need you to babysit." Maddie's words were rushed.

"What's the matter?"

"Mike and I got into a fight, and I told him there was no way in hell I was going out with him tonight."

"What happened?"

"Nothing. He's being a dick."

"You guys should still go out, make up."

"No. I kicked him out."

"Oh, Maddie." Lexa was used to Maddie's temper tantrums and felt sorry for Mike.

"Do you know what he said to me?" Lexa could tell Maddie was spitting mad. "He told me I was selfish for not wanting to meet Phoenix tomorrow. He said I was being a bitch. That I should get over myself and support Mom."

"You're really not going tomorrow?"

"No! I told you a million times. Who does he think he is, telling me I'm being selfish for not wanting to meet the woman who broke up our family? That would be like betraying Dad."

"Maddie, it's not really—"

"Don't you start!" Maddie's words tumbled over one another. "I'm not going, and neither of you can make me. I can't stand it. I can never again call our home number and know that Mom or Dad will pick up." Lexa could tell Maddie was crying. "God, I hate her so much. And I hate Mike too. I hope he doesn't come home tonight."

"Maddie, you don't mean that."

"Yes, I do. The kids and I are going to watch a movie together and I'll make brownies and we'll eat every single one."

"I thought you were doing gluten-free?"

"Fuck gluten-free. I'll eat whatever the hell I want tonight." And with that, she hung up, leaving Lexa staring at her phone.

"Okay, now what?" Lexa said out loud. She turned off the oven and pulled out the brownies. They smelled so good. If she stayed home, she'd probably eat most of them by herself. Her clients seemed to think she was born motivated and with iron willpower, but the truth was, she could succumb to cravings with the best of them. It was just that she worked out for a living. And was blessed with a fast metabolism.

She cut a piece even though it was still too hot and picked up her phone. Taking bites of the gooey brownie, she contemplated what to do. She really didn't want to be alone that night. Then she thought of what her mom had said that morning about telling Greg the truth and decided to call him.

"Hey, Dad. Got a minute?" Lexa leaned against the kitchen counter.

"Sure, what's up? The kids there yet?"

"No. Maddie just called. She canceled her date with Mike. They got in a fight."

Greg made a sympathetic noise.

"Mom told me this morning that she told you the truth about what happened in Taiwan."

There was a pause, and Lexa could hear rustling from Greg's end. "Yeah. I wish you'd told me yourself. Why didn't you?"

"No one enjoys speaking of things they're ashamed of."

"It's not your shame."

"It doesn't matter anymore." Lexa popped the last bite of brownie in her mouth and eyed the pan.

"It does matter, Lexa. It's kept you from your Taiwanese heritage."

She swallowed before speaking. "Can I come over?"

"Oh, um . . ."

"Wait, do you have a date?" Lexa pushed off the counter. Was her dad dating already?

"No, nothing like that. But I'm meeting some friends for dinner. I can cancel . . ."

"No, don't. I'm glad you're going out. We can talk this weekend or next week." Lexa let out a laugh. "After all, I've waited this long."

"You sure?"

"Yes. Have a good time. Bye."

She hung up and scrolled through her phone again. She and Andi had set up Bumble accounts. Lexa had swiped right to like some of the men and had gotten a few instant connections. There was one guy in particular who'd caught her eye, and they'd messaged back and forth. He'd asked her out for drinks that night, but she'd said no since she was supposed to be babysitting. Would it seem desperate if she messaged him now, asking to meet up?

Hey, so plans changed and I don't have to watch my niece and nephew. Any chance of meeting for that drink tonight?

To her relief, he answered right away. Sure, I'm free. Where do you want to meet?

She suggested a restaurant where she knew the bartender, and he said he'd meet her there in an hour. After putting down the phone, she sat for a moment thinking about Jake. Was it wrong of her to go out on this date? She wasn't in a relationship with Jake. And as much as she liked him and was looking forward to seeing him again, she knew he wasn't right for her. So wasn't it in her best interest to keep dating to find the right guy?

Springing up, she headed for her closet to find something to wear. With all the chaos in her life right then, she was glad she didn't have to spend Friday night by herself.

.   .   .

The restaurant wasn't crowded when she got there. Her friend Rob, a skinny man who usually had a cigarette dangling out of his mouth when he wasn't working, acknowledged her from behind the bar and nodded in the direction of a man sitting at the far end.

"Lexa?" The man with thick dark hair and chiseled cheekbones stood when she reached him.

"Nice to meet you . . . uh." She suddenly couldn't remember his name. Was it Paul? No, it was Peter. She'd been so drawn by how good-looking he was in his profile picture that she'd barely glanced at his name. Yes, she could be shallow sometimes.

They shook hands, and he held a barstool out for her.

"You're as beautiful in person as your photos."

"Thanks. You look like you too." They smiled, even as their eyes appraised each other.

She ordered a Cosmo, and they chatted easily, talking about their jobs. Her eyes widened when he said he used to be an underwear model, and she couldn't resist checking him out. Smoking body. He was easy to talk to, and she relaxed, glad she'd decided to contact him rather than stay home in her apartment.

Out of the corners of her eyes, she saw Rob hovering, his brows furrowed together. She wagged her eyebrows at him, trying to signal that she liked the guy.

"Are you okay?" Peter asked. "Something wrong?"

"It's all good." She turned back to him, and he moved his barstool closer.

"Can I tell you something?" His whisper caused shivers of anticipation to go down her spine.

She nodded.

"Asian women are like lotus flowers, ready to blossom under the right guy's touch, and I think I'm that guy for you." He reached out to caress her cheek. "I love the subservient manner of Asian women. You're all so dainty."

Lexa drew back sharply. Oh, dear Lord, no. He was one of *those*—a guy with yellow fever, who loved Asian women unconditionally. She cast about frantically in her mind for an excuse to end the date right now. A sudden case of stomach virus? A sick aunt?

Unaware of Lexa's inner thoughts, Peter continued to whisper. "I've always wanted to drive down the FDR Drive in my convertible on a hot summer night with the top down and a beautiful Asian woman in the passenger seat next to me." He paused and leaned even closer, causing Lexa to lean far enough away from him that she almost fell off her stool. "While giving me a blow job. What do you say? I have my car out front. Want to get out of here and go for a drive?" And with that, while her mouth was hanging open, he took the opportunity to ram his tongue inside her mouth, where it darted around like a serpent ready to strike.

She pulled back and made a choking sound, trying to catch her breath. Peter mistook this for passion and whispered, "Got you all hot and bothered, didn't I? I knew you were going to be the right girl for this fantasy, being Asian and all. I can't wait to feel your mouth on my hard cock while the wind blows through the car as I'm driving down the FDR." And then he licked her ear.

That did it. She jerked her head away and waited until he looked at her. "Do you want to know what I think?"

He smirked and leaned back, thinking he had her. "Tell me."

"I think," she said, and leaned in so he'd be sure to catch each word, "that you need to cool off." And she upended the rest of her drink over his crotch and hopped off her stool.

He reached for a napkin to blot his lap but gave her a sly smile and narrowed his eyes at her. "Oh, you so feisty," he said in a fake Asian accent. Bringing his hands up in prayer, he bowed to her. "*Konichiwa*."

"*Konichiwa* is Japanese, you, you . . ." Lexa sputtered, unable to think of a word insulting enough to hurl at him. "I'm half-Taiwanese."

His eyes lit up. "I love Thai food!"

Lexa's mouth dropped open in disbelief. "Taiwan! Not Thailand. Listen. I'm not subservient, and I'll never blossom, so this date is over."

"Oh, so sorry," he said in that fake Asian accent, which

drove her crazy. He wagged a finger in front of her face. "You, my lotus flower, are playing hard to get. I know your games."

Rob walked up to them and studied Peter like he was a diseased piece of fruit. "Lotus flower? Lexa is *not* a lotus flower. Is there a problem here?"

Peter held up his hands. "No problem. The lady and I were just getting acquainted."

"No, we're not. And I'm not playing hard to get. Let me make it clear." Lexa enunciated each word clearly. "I'm. Not. Interested."

Peter stood and made a move toward Lexa. Rob stepped between them. "I'd leave her alone, buster. Lexa knows Kung Fu."

Peter raised an eyebrow at Lexa. "Oooh. You play rough. I love it. You look so delicate on the outside, but you're a tiger on the inside." And he made claws with his hands and growled.

"Okay, that's it. You're out of here." Rob grabbed Peter by the back of the shirt at the same time that Lexa reached for Peter's drink and threw it in his face. She knew it was immature, but oh, it was so satisfying. Peter sputtered and started to protest, but the other bartender came over, and he and Rob escorted Peter out the front door.

By the time Rob returned, Lexa was fuming. She was mad at the man who thought it was okay to ask for a blow job within minutes of meeting her, and mad at men who had an Asian girl fetish. Did he think just because she was Asian, she would give him a blow job on the first date?

"I was trying to get your attention and tell you I think he's married," Rob said. "He kept doing the ring finger rub, like he's touching a ring that's usually there."

Lexa smacked her forehead. "He probably has a wife and kids stashed somewhere."

"Scumbag," Rob growled.

"I'm out of here. I'm going to go visit Andi at Bisque." It was still early, and she didn't want to go home yet, where the pan of brownies was sitting in her kitchen and the ghosts from her past threatened to resurface. She knew Andi was going to die laughing when she told her.

"Go, go," Rob said, giving her a hug. "Sorry your date didn't work out."

Lexa grabbed her purse and was about to leave when Rob cocked his head to the side and asked, "Why the FDR? Why not the West Side Highway?"

15

‿‿

Lexa sat at a round table covered in a long white tablecloth in her favorite dim sum restaurant in Chinatown. She shifted on the gold fabric–covered chair as she waited for her mom and Phoenix to arrive. She couldn't believe Maddie wasn't coming. She'd called her one more time that morning, but Maddie hung up on her as soon as she mentioned Phoenix's name.

Lexa was a nervous wreck. She'd accepted her mom's change in sexual orientation well, she'd thought, at least better than Maddie. But actually meeting her mom's new lover was another thing. She was afraid she'd blurt out something inappropriate like, "So what do you two do in bed?"

Before she could obsess more, Susan and Phoenix arrived.

"Sorry we're late. The subway was so slow this morning." Susan studied Lexa's face. "You look terrible. Are you not sleeping?"

Lexa glared at her mom and swatted her hand away when her mom reached for her face. Probably to point out the bags under her eyes.

Susan gave Lexa a look but then turned to introduce Phoenix. Phoenix was a slim woman with short, fashionably styled salt-and-pepper hair, and she wasn't much taller than Lexa. She was dressed in a flowing tunic printed with large bright flowers over white leggings and gold strappy sandals. It might have looked garish on someone else, but on Phoenix, it looked elegant. There was a serenity about her that matched her bedroom, and Lexa felt a rush of heat to her face when she remembered how she'd snooped through this woman's drawer.

Susan did most of the talking while they waited for the dim sum carts in the cavernous restaurant, which was beginning to fill with the late Saturday morning diners. "I told you Lexa's a personal trainer and fitness instructor, right?" Phoenix nodded. Susan turned to Lexa. "And you know Phoenix is an acupuncturist?"

"I know, Mom."

Susan turned back to Phoenix. "Lexa inspired me to go for my yoga teacher training. She's the one who told me to try yoga and acupuncture when my migraines got so bad." She looked at Lexa. "I guess we have you to thank that we met."

Phoenix gave Lexa a small smile.

"So you've known each other, what, two years now?" Lexa asked.

"Yes. But we didn't become, um, intimate until after I told Greg about Phoenix." Before Lexa could respond, Susan changed the subject. "Phoenix, did I tell you Lexa used to do Kung Fu? That's why she got interested in training." She turned back to Lexa. "And you and Phoenix have a lot in common! She's half-Asian too."

Lexa had never seen her mother so unhinged. She bordered on hysteria, and Lexa couldn't help thinking she'd get whiplash from the way she was looking back and forth between Phoenix and Lexa.

"Susan." Phoenix laid a hand on Lexa's mom's arm. "You've told both of us about each other already. Don't worry so much."

Susan blew out a breath. "Sorry. I'm a little nervous."

Just then, a waitress rolled a metal dim sum cart to their table. Phoenix reached over and picked out a bamboo basket of crystal shrimp dumplings and another of roast pork buns. "You've told me so much about the food here, and I can't wait to try it."

Lexa waited for the next cart and chose a basket of steamed beef short ribs with black bean sauce and one of the pan-fried turnip cakes. Her mouth watered as more carts came by, and soon their table was full of food.

As they ate, Lexa could see her mom visibly relax. The conversation remained light, focusing on the food they were eating. Susan told Phoenix they had started this monthly dim sum tradition soon after Maddie got married. Lexa was sorry her sister wasn't there with them.

When the cart with sesame balls rolled by, Phoenix reached for one. "Susan said these are your favorite."

"No!" Lexa shouted so loud that Phoenix dropped the plate back on the cart with a thud, causing the waitress to let loose a stream of rapid Cantonese, none of which they understood. "Sorry." She could feel her cheeks burn as eyes turned to look at them from surrounding tables. "I don't like them anymore. They're too . . . They bring bad luck."

"What?" Susan looked startled. "I thought you didn't believe in Chinese superstitions and ghosts?"

"I don't." Lexa stabbed her chopsticks into the sticky rice wrapped in a lotus leaf on her plate, remembering too late that chopsticks sticking up indicated bad luck. "But, you know, I was reading about Taiwanese funeral customs, and it said that the Chinese believe the soul of a deceased could become stuck somewhere between here and the afterlife. It got me wondering if my father's soul is stuck."

Phoenix tilted her head in interest. "Because of the way he died?"

"Yes."

"Maybe you need to go back to Taiwan . . ." Her mom stopped when Lexa leveled her with a stare. After a moment, she changed the subject. "I thought sesame balls were considered good luck?"

"They are. But I was eating one when you told me you were leaving Dad. And I had taken a bite of one when Hsu-Ling called to tell me my father died. So my brain kind of decided sesame balls equal bad news."

"Oh, no." Susan looked stricken. "I brought those sesame balls with me because I thought they would help soften the news."

Lexa made a face. "You turned me off them."

"I'm so sorry."

"It's okay." Lexa suddenly realized what she said and turned to Phoenix. "I'm sorry. I didn't mean to imply that you and my mom are bad news. But it was bad news for my dad, and then Maddie flipped out . . ."

"Lexa, don't apologize," Phoenix said. "I know what you mean."

Lexa nodded and looked down at her food. She thought of Greg, all alone in his tiny studio, and suddenly felt guilty for sitting there, making nice with the woman who broke up his marriage. Maybe it was too soon to be meeting Phoenix. Maybe Maddie had the right idea. She should be with her dad that day. But she wanted to support her mom. It was all so confusing.

"Susan told me about your father. I'm sorry, Lexa." Phoenix's comment jolted her back to the conversation at the table.

"Thanks."

"My father died when I was twenty-two," Phoenix said, her voice low.

Lexa looked up. "He did?"

"It was an accident, like your father. One day, he was just gone."

"Oh, no. I'm sorry."

Phoenix waved a hand. "It's okay. That was a long time ago. I just wanted you to know I know what it's like to lose a father."

Susan's phone rang. She looked at the display and said, "I'll be right back. It's the real estate agent about the house."

Lexa studied her plate as her mom left the table. She hadn't lived in that house in over ten years, but it was always waiting for her when she needed to go home. Now there would be either Phoenix's apartment or Greg's tiny studio. Those weren't home.

"Lexa." She looked up to find Phoenix studying her intently. "Your mom told me about what happened all those years ago in Taiwan. I felt I should tell you that I know."

Lexa picked up the teapot and poured herself a cup. "I know. Mom told me yesterday that she told you."

"She did?"

"Yes. I'm surprised she told you before she told Dad."

Phoenix held out her cup, and Lexa refilled it. "She told me before we became lovers."

Lexa made a face. It was hard enough picturing her mom having sex with her dad. She really didn't want to picture her mom and Phoenix together. Maybe she wasn't as accepting of her mom's news as she'd thought.

Lexa took a sip of her tea. "You mean when she was going to you for acupuncture?"

"Yes. For those bad migraines."

"How did you get from migraines to talking about me? Don't you just put the needles in and then leave the patient?"

"I do. But we'd talk before and after the session. I asked her if there was anything going on in her life that might be causing her stress."

"And she just told you?"

"No, not right away. It came out slowly, over the two years I was treating her. She was really worried about you. She needed to tell someone." Phoenix reached out and placed a hand over Lexa's. Her hand was smooth and surprisingly cool. "I'm sorry that happened to you. And that your father died before you could make amends with him."

"Yeah." She couldn't believe she was having this conversation with Phoenix. She hadn't even talked about it with her dad yet, and this woman she'd just met knew her long-held secret.

"If you ever want to talk, I'm here. Sometimes it's easier to talk to someone not involved."

Lexa pulled her hand away. "I don't want to talk about it." She couldn't believe this woman was trying to work her way into Lexa's life by bringing up the one thing she didn't want to talk about.

Phoenix didn't reply. Lexa looked away from Phoenix's gaze, angry. Yet she felt something building within her, a pressure in her chest fighting to come out. She bit her bottom lip when a thought came unbidden into her mind. She tried to push it away, but the more she tried, the more it forced its away to the front of her mind. She didn't want to bond with this woman who'd broken up their family. But she found herself turning to Phoenix, and before she could stop herself, the words came out.

"Don't tell Mom," Lexa said, her voice barely above a whisper, "but I wish *that woman* had died instead of my father."

16

Pin-Yen took a broom and swiped at the cobwebs hanging off the ceiling of the spare room, attacking them with a force that would have scared Hsu-Ling if she'd been in the room. Pin-Yen was filled with anger at having to prepare this room for Jing Tao's other daughter. She'd managed to use Hsu-Ling and her various appointments with doctors, the physiatrist, the physical therapist, and the prosthetist as an excuse so the girl had only visited them twice, once when she was eight and again at twelve. But now that girl was coming the next day because she had just turned fourteen, and Jing Tao thought she was old enough to stay with them for the whole summer.

Pin-Yen knew she couldn't condemn the girl outright. Jing Tao adored his American daughter. But how she wished the girl didn't exist. Once upon a time, she'd thought maybe she could accept her husband's other daughter, but now she knew the girl was a threat to Hsu-Ling. Pin-Yen had to be smart and bide her time to find the right way to get rid of that girl once and for all.

Because Jing Tao had told Pin-Yen recently that he had finally changed his will to include *her*. Pin-Yen had been horrified. He hadn't done anything after that conversation she'd overheard between Jing Tao and his mother two years earlier. Pin-Yen had relaxed, sure her husband knew Hsu-Ling was his true daughter. But now he was acknowledging Lexa? The Chang legacy belonged to Hsu-Ling, Jing Tao's legitimate daughter. How did he even know Lexa was his? They'd never done a paternity test. He'd taken one look at her picture and said she had the Chang jaw, and that was it. No amount of persuasion on Pin-Yen's part had convinced him that he needed to be sure. What a fool he was. He was too blinded by his fling with that American woman to even consider the baby might not be his.

Pin-Yen fumed as she cleaned, fueled also by her anger at Hsu-Ling's poor school performance. Hsu-Ling had missed a problem on a math exam. She should have gotten a perfect score. They'd gone over and over the homework, Pin-Yen drilling Hsu-Ling after she came home from *buxiban*, the supplementary learning classes that Hsu-Ling took after school and in the summer. There was no reason Hsu-Ling should have come home with a less than perfect score. They'd just have to work harder. Hsu-Ling was ten and a half already and needed to focus on her studies if she wanted to get into the medical school at National Taiwan University. Pin-Yen decided right then that Hsu-Ling needed a private tutor. Hsu-Ling was already doing *buxiban* for music, math, science, and art, but her poor performance on this test proved she needed extra help.

Pin-Yen took the thin padding stuffed with dried grass off

the top of the woven bamboo bed and beat at it with her hands until dust swirled in the air, imagining it was her husband's other daughter she was beating. Of course she'd never lay a hand on the child. But she'd watch the girl carefully, and she'd figure out a way to protect Hsu-Ling, Jing Tao's true daughter. She'd worked too hard on Hsu-Ling to let *that* girl steal her daughter's future.

Pin-Yen looked at her watch. Hsu-Ling should be almost done with her piano lesson. And then one hour for homework before dinner, then an hour of reading followed by character-writing practice. Hsu-Ling complained she never got to play with her friends, but there was no time for friends. Friends were a distraction that Hsu-Ling didn't need.

She gave the mattress one last beating. Throwing it on the bed, she watched as it sank, lifeless, back into place. She sniffed in satisfaction. Her daughter would be a doctor and the true heir of the Chang family. And Lexa would spend no more than a few nights on this bed. Pin-Yen would make sure of it.

17

〜

"Are you sure Phoenix doesn't mind having Zeus here all weekend?" Lexa stood in the doorway of her mom and Phoenix's apartment. When Lexa had mentioned to her mom that Jake was in town for a few days, Susan had offered to take Zeus for the weekend. Lexa had walked Zeus through Central Park to the Upper West Side, and now she eyed Phoenix's immaculate apartment with uncertainty. Zeus's paws were dirty, and he shed a lot.

"Don't be silly. Phoenix loves dogs." Susan gestured them inside. "At least one grandchild is allowed to stay with me."

"What do you mean?" Lexa's brows rose. What had Maddie done now?

Her mom unclipped Zeus's leash, and he walked into the apartment, sniffing with his nose to the ground. "I offered to take Corey and Connor next weekend so Maddie and Mike could have time together. She didn't text me back."

"She wouldn't keep her kids from you."

Susan's shoulders drooped. "I think she might, just to make a point." She put a smile on her face. "Anyways, have fun with Jake. Don't worry about Zeus. We'll take good care of him."

Lexa reached out to hug her mom. "Thanks. I'll pick him up before my birthday dinner on Sunday. And don't worry. I don't think Maddie would use Corey and Connor against you. She knows they love you."

Susan gave a sad smile. "I hope you're right."

. . .

Lexa wound her way through the hotel bar until she was standing in front of Jake.

"Hi." She couldn't stop a smile from spreading over her face.

"Hi, yourself." He pulled her in for a hug. She leaned into him, the feel of his strong body against hers sending sparks through her. It'd been more than a month since she'd last seen him, and pleasure spread in her body like warm soup on a cold day.

"I'm glad you're here." Lexa slipped onto the barstool next to Jake, her heart rate quickening just by being in his presence.

"Me too." He got the bartender's attention, and once Lexa had ordered a drink, he asked, "So how are you? Tell me everything."

"So much is going on. You won't believe it." It'd been almost a week since Lexa had met Phoenix.

"Try me." He looked into her eyes, and she wanted to tell him about her mother's news and her father and Hsu-Ling, but she decided to start with something lighter.

"Work is great. One of my clients, who's also a close friend, has a Food Network show that's getting really popular."

"What's the name of the show? I'll look for it."

Lexa told him about Andi and her show as the bartender placed her glass of wine in front of her.

"And I have another client whose whole goal in life is to find a rich husband. But she recently met and fell in love with a starving artist, and now she doesn't know what to do."

"Ah. Marry for love or money. That's the age-old question."

Lexa took a sip of her wine. "I'm only telling you because Kiley has asked me before if I told my boyfriend about her." She stopped, embarrassed. "I don't mean I think of you as my boyfriend." She stopped again because Jake was now smirking at her. "Anyways, she . . . um." Flustered, Lexa lost her train of thought and took another gulp of the very excellent Viognier.

"You were telling me about Kiley?"

"Oh, right. So this morning, she tells me this man is the love of her life." Kiley had shown up for her session brimming with news about the artist she'd met a couple of weeks earlier. "Apparently, the sex is amazing and they're soul mates."

Jake's smile took over his face. "But she can't get over the no-money thing and wants your advice on whether to dump him and find a richer man?"

Lexa nodded. "Basically. But she's not the gold digger this is making her out to sound like. There's something kind of sweet and innocent about her. I think she just had a rough childhood and grew up thinking money was the answer to happiness."

"How does she pay for her training sessions, then?"

"Her mom. She married a rich man, hence the belief that marrying for money is the way to happiness. She'll do anything to help Kiley find one for herself."

"Huh." Jake looked thoughtful. "What's she going to do, then, if she's in love with this guy?"

"I don't know." Lexa shrugged. "Kiley really wants kids and thinks this guy would make a wonderful father, but how's he going to support them when he's a struggling artist?"

"Your clients really do tell you everything."

"Pretty much."

Jake leaned in then and kissed her, erasing all thoughts of Kiley and her poor boyfriend from her mind. What was it about Jake's kisses that had such an effect on her? She clung to him, wanting to get closer even as she was aware of being in public with the noise of the Friday night crowd around them. She could kiss him all day.

He pulled away and studied her for so long that she grew uncomfortable. Did she have something in her teeth? Or a booger hanging out of her nose?

"What?" Lexa gave him a questioning look while bringing up a hand to shield her face.

"Just . . ." Jake broke their gaze and looked down at the bar for a moment before raising his eyes back to meet hers. "So. You really don't want kids?"

Lexa started, still thinking about whatever unsightly thing was sticking to her face. It took a moment for her brain to understand what he'd said. She made a noncommittal gesture with her hand, relieved it wasn't anything gross that had caused him to look at her like that.

"No. And you want more kids?"

He shrugged. "I guess I always thought I'd have at least two. It'd be nice to give Sophia a sister or brother. If I ever meet the right person."

Lexa looked away, not wanting him to see how much she wanted to be his person, yet at the same time, how much she didn't want to be his person if he wanted kids.

There was a pause as they both took sips of their drinks and looked around the bar. "What else is going on?" It was obvious Jake was trying to change the subject. "You said so much is happening."

"Well." She looked down at their hands, which were entwined together. "My mom left my stepfather for a woman a few weeks ago, and my Taiwanese father died."

His jaw dropped, and he squeezed her hand. "I'm so sorry. Why didn't you tell me?"

"It didn't feel like something I could write in a text. Plus, I don't really know you."

He squeezed her hand again. "You can call me anytime. I know we've only seen each other once before, but I feel like I know you."

"Thanks. I don't really want to get into it right now. It's all kind of confusing. And my half sister from Taiwan is coming to see me. She'll be here next week."

"You're not going over there for the funeral?"

She paused, knowing it sounded strange that Hsu-Ling was coming here instead of her going back to Taiwan. "No." She didn't elaborate.

His eyebrows rose, but he didn't say anything.

"I just can't go back there."

He held up a hand. "It's okay. You don't have to explain. Even if you weren't close to him, I know it must be hard for you to lose him. I'm sorry. I really am."

"Thank you."

"Do you want to talk about him?"

"What's there to say?" Lexa lifted a shoulder. "He lived across the world, and I only saw him a few times in my life."

"He didn't want to see you?"

"He did. When he first found out about me, I was only two. He was getting married, so he couldn't come to New York, and my mom thought I was too young to go to Taiwan. I didn't meet him until I was eight."

She stopped, not willing to go further. Jake sensed this

and changed the subject. "What about your mom's news? Did you have any idea?" He kept her hand firmly in his.

"Nope. Completely out of the blue. My sister isn't speaking to Mom."

Jake's eyes shone with sympathy. "Family drama. That's tough."

"Yes." She gave a small smile. "But let's not talk about it. I want to enjoy my time with you and forget all that for a night." He didn't have to be at work until Monday morning, so they had the whole weekend to look forward to.

"Okay. You ready for dinner?" He gazed into her eyes, and a spark jolted through her body. She was so tempted to suggest they skip dinner and go right to his hotel room when something about his features made her tip her head to the side and study him closer.

"What?" Now it was his turn to look uncomfortable.

"Are you part Asian, by chance?"

He smiled. "Actually, yes. My father is half-Japanese and half-German. And my mom is Jewish. You can imagine the teasing I used to get."

"I bet." She shook her head. "I did too, for different reasons." The bullies in her class had chanted at her, "Ching, Chong, Chinaman!" and pulled at their eyes until they were mere slits. She'd go home and cry to her mom, who wasn't Asian at all.

Jake tilted his head. "Growing up, I never knew where I fit in. I wasn't really Asian, but I wasn't fully Jewish either."

"Me too!" Lexa's eyes widened at their shared feelings of not belonging. "I grew up with my white family, and I stuck out. And when I was in Taiwan, I wasn't Asian enough." A look of understanding passed between them.

Jake opened his mouth, but before he could say anything,

the waiter put their bill in front of them, breaking the spell. Jake slipped his hand out of hers and reached for his wallet to pay for the drinks. "I forgot to tell you. I got us tickets to that underground concert, for after dinner."

"The one in a secret location?" Jake had told her about the concerts where the location wasn't revealed until the day before.

"Yes. It's in Chelsea tonight."

She jumped off the barstool. "That sounds like fun." She loved that he'd found them something unusual to do, instead of the standard dinner and drinks.

They linked hands again and walked two blocks to the Asian fusion restaurant Lexa had picked for the night. Before they went in, Jake stopped at an isolated part of the street and pulled her close against him. He kissed her with so much passion that her senses overflowed. All she could think about was his lips on hers and how divine it felt to be in his arms. When he finally let her go, she swore she saw stars and smiled at him dreamily.

"Let's go in before I do something I'll regret." Jake leaned his forehead against hers before pulling away.

She turned and floated toward the door of the restaurant and promptly walked into the wall. Clutching her nose, she stumbled back against Jake, and he wrapped his arms around her. After making sure she was okay, he laughed, hugging her close to him. Even though her nose was burning, she laughed along with him, and they locked eyes. For just one moment, Lexa forgot she'd decided there was no potential with him. She almost invited him to her birthday dinner in two days, but at the last minute she bit back the invitation.

Be careful, Lexa. Don't fall in love with him.

18

⌒

Happy birthday!" Andi gave her a hug when Lexa walked into Bisque that Sunday afternoon. A section of the bar had been roped off for Lexa's birthday dinner. Gardenias floating in clear bowls graced every table, and tiny white lights strung along the walls and tables made the place sparkle like fireflies in the night.

"Happy birthday, my sweet girl." Lexa's mom came up behind her and gave her a squeeze.

Lexa smiled and looked around. Her mom and Phoenix were there, as well as her dad with Maddie hovering near him, shooting death stares at their mom and her new . . . girlfriend? Is that what you called a woman in her sixties? Maddie's husband, Mike, had Corey in his arms, and Connor ran up to Lexa and threw his arms around her legs.

She realized it was the first time her entire family plus Phoenix was in the same room together. She was still glowing in the aftermath of her weekend with Jake, and even the awkwardness of her family situation couldn't dampen her spirits.

"Happy birthday, Aunt Lexa. Do you want to see my new dinosaur?" Connor made it roar at her, and she jumped back in mock terror.

Elise, Lexa's group fitness manager, walked over and, after greeting Lexa, admired Connor's dinosaur.

Lexa's mom picked him up. "Connor, you're a really scary dinosaur, you know that?"

Connor nodded at his grandma. "I know. *Roar!*"

Lexa's mom laughed. She drifted off to the bar with Connor to get him a drink. Andi looked after her and said, "I can't believe your mom quit her job to be a yogi. And that she has a girlfriend. She's my hero."

"I know." Lexa couldn't stop smiling. "I'm still getting used to it. But she seems happy."

"Why are you smiling like that?" Andi eyed her with suspicion.

"It's my birthday, and you're all here. Why shouldn't I be happy?"

Andi squinted at her. "It's more than that. It's Jake, isn't it?"

Lexa didn't say anything, just smiled even wider.

"Someone had sex," Elise said.

Lexa nodded in agreement. "Really good sex."

"Oh my God. Tell me more. I have not had really good sex in a while." Andi leaned closer, her eyes glimmering.

"He's amazing," Lexa said. "Everything we do is so natural and right. Even when we're not in bed." She blushed when she thought of all the things Jake had done to her that weekend, all the places he'd kissed with his mouth.

"I'm so jealous." Andi hit her on the shoulder.

"Guess what he gave me for my birthday?"

"Jewelry?" Andi guessed.

"Flowers? Lingerie?" This from Elise.

Lexa shook her head. "No. Last time he was here, we talked about wanting to visit every state in the United States before the age of fifty. We were trying to figure out how many states each of us had been to." She stopped and smiled, thinking about Jake's gift.

"Tell us! What did he get you?" Andi jabbed her in the side with her elbow.

"He got me a map of the United States that you can put a wine cork in for every state that you've visited. Isn't that the most unique and thoughtful gift ever? He knows I like wine, and I can hang it up as wall decoration."

"Okay." Elise crossed her arms over her chest. "That's pretty impressive. He needs to give men lessons on how to give women thoughtful gifts."

"I know, right?" Lexa hugged her arms around herself, giddy at the thought that her friends thought he was as great as she did.

"So he was just like you remembered?" Elise asked.

Lexa nodded.

"Guess Yellow Fever Guy doesn't stand a chance, then." Andi wiggled her brows at her.

"Who?" Elise's forehead wrinkled in confusion.

"I met this guy from Bumble for a drink last week. Before Jake got here." Lexa made a face, thinking about the unpleasant experience.

"You didn't tell me about this," Elise said. "How was it?"

"The guy was nuts. Seriously. Obsessed."

"What do you mean? Obsessed how?"

"Obsessed with Asian women. He had the worst case of yellow fever I've ever seen."

Elise was still confused. "What's that?"

Lexa and Andi exchanged a look, and then Lexa explained. "It's when a guy is completely obsessed with Asian women. They only date women who are Asian. They don't even care if she's smart or interesting or pretty. As long as she's Asian, they're hooked. We call it yellow fever."

Elise snorted out a laugh. "I've never heard of that. So was he at least cute or funny?"

"At first I thought he was hot. But then he just got creepy. I told him I was Taiwanese, and he told me he loves Thai food. He was talking in this fake Asian accent, and it drove me nuts."

"What kind of fake accent?"

"You know, like, 'You so beautiful!' I wanted to scream that I speak English."

Andi guffawed, making Elise laugh.

"But the best was when he told me Asian women are like lotus flowers, ready to blossom under the right guy's touch, and he was that guy for me." Lexa saw Elise smile as she reached up to touch the lotus flower necklace she was wearing.

"I bet that went over well." Andi had a smirk on her face.

Lexa shuddered. "I was so creeped out, and then he told me he loves the subservient manner of Asian women. Do I look like the subservient type to you?" She looked around, daring her friends to agree.

They shook their heads with straight faces.

"And then he had the audacity to tell me he wanted a blow job while driving down the FDR in his convertible!"

"Oh my God! What did you do?" Elise asked.

"I dumped my drink in his lap and told him I wasn't subservient and I'd never blossom, at least not in his presence. My friend Rob and another bartender escorted him out after I threw his drink in his face."

"You didn't!" Elise clapped her hands. "Good for you. I've always wanted to do that when guys get fresh at bars, but I've never had the nerve. Does he have your phone number? I hope he doesn't turn out to be a stalker."

"We only communicated through the app, and I blocked him as soon as I left the restaurant."

"That's good. But if you like Jake so much, why did you go out with this guy in the first place?" Andi looked at her with curiosity.

"Because Jake isn't forever potential." Lexa pretended not to see the skeptical looks her friends were sending her way.

"So where's Jake, by the way?" Andi asked. "Why didn't you invite him tonight?"

Maddie walked up before Lexa could answer. "What are you guys whispering about? Andi, the food is so good." Waiters were circulating through their party with appetizers while everyone had drinks before sitting down to dinner.

"Thanks. We're just talking about your sister's amazing sex life."

Maddie looked wistful for a moment and took a sip of her apple martini. "Where is he? I want to meet him."

"You guys," Lexa said. "It's not like I'm dating him. I didn't want him to get the wrong idea, so I didn't invite him. Anyways, he's seeing friends tonight."

"He didn't celebrate your birthday with you?" Maddie asked.

"He did. He took me out to brunch this morning." Lexa smiled again, feeling a tingle run through her body just thinking of the time they'd spent in his hotel room before brunch.

"When's he going home?" Andi asked.

"Not 'til Thursday morning. I hope I get to see him at some point this week, but Hsu-Ling's coming on Tuesday, so I'm not sure."

"You seem to like him a lot," Andi said. "This is the most you've talked about a guy in a long time."

Lexa nodded. "I do. And I could stay in bed with him all day." She laughed when Andi poked her in the side.

"But doesn't he live in San Francisco?" Maddie asked. "And has a kid he can't leave?"

"Yes." Lexa sighed. "I know. There's no way we have a future together."

Maddie studied her for a moment. "Well, you do always pick men that you can't have a long-term relationship with."

"I do not." She would have argued further, but Maddie cut her off.

"Hey, can you tell Mom that Connor and Corey can't sleep over next weekend? I'm not letting my children spend the night in that woman's apartment."

"Tell her yourself. It's Mom's apartment now too." Lexa's forehead crinkled in annoyance. "She's standing right there. And why are you punishing your kids? You know they'd love to spend the weekend with Mom."

Maddie tossed her head but then froze when she saw Phoenix picking up Corey in her arms. "Oh, no, she doesn't." And she stomped off toward their mom and Phoenix and snatched Corey out of Phoenix's arms before taking Connor by the hand and dragging him away from the two women. Lexa ran after her, hoping to stop a scene, but Maddie had already disappeared into the bathroom with her kids by the time Lexa reached her mom's side.

A waiter walked by with a tray of mini short rib tacos, offering one to Lexa before she could say anything. But she saw the glance her mom and Phoenix exchanged and noticed the sad droop of her mom's mouth.

Lexa took a taco and turned to Phoenix. "Thanks for

coming," she said, hoping to make up for Maddie's rudeness. She looked to her friends for backup, but they'd all abandoned her. Andi had turned to talk to other people when Lexa had run after Maddie, and Lexa saw Elise talking to her dad on the other side of the bar. Her mom excused herself, and Lexa hoped she wasn't going to follow Maddie into the bathroom.

"How're you holding up?" Phoenix asked.

"Okay." Lexa's eyes tracked her mom's progress, and she was relieved when her mom went over to talk to some of Lexa's friends from the gym.

"That's good."

Lexa nodded and put the taco in her mouth as a distraction. It was delicious, and she chewed slowly, trying to think of what to say. She didn't know how to act around Phoenix, after the terrible confession she'd made to her the other day.

"Well, happy birthday." Phoenix reached over and gave her a brief hug when Lexa had finished her bite. Lexa stiffened in her unfamiliar embrace, and Phoenix pulled back.

"Thank you." Lexa knew the smile she gave Phoenix didn't reach her eyes. She looked over at her dad to see if he'd seen Phoenix hug her, and she was relieved he had his back to her.

"Thanks for inviting me. I know it's not easy for you and your sister to accept me." She spoke softly, looking away from Lexa. She coughed, and Lexa suddenly felt bad for being so distant with her.

"Maddie will come around."

"And you?" Phoenix raised her eyebrows in question.

"I just want my mom to be happy. If she's happy with you, then I'm okay with it. It'll take some time to get used to, but I'll come around too."

Phoenix smiled, and Lexa found herself smiling back.

"By the way, I didn't mean it the other day when I said I wished Hsu-Ling's mother had died instead of my father." It'd been eating at Lexa, that she'd told Phoenix something so personal. She had no idea why she'd blurted that out.

"Lexa, it's fine. I know what you meant. We all say things we don't mean in the heat of the moment. She hurt you when you were fourteen. Of course you feel animosity toward her."

Lexa stared at Phoenix. Maybe the older woman really did understand how she felt. Before she could respond, Lexa's mom called to Phoenix from across the bar. Phoenix touched Lexa on the arm lightly, and then headed toward Susan. Lexa stood still for a moment, watching Phoenix and her mom together. Then she shook her head and walked over to her dad and Elise.

"I'm glad to see you talking to my friends." She put an arm around Greg and turned to Elise. "Where's Bryson?" Elise had gotten divorced five years earlier and had a son who'd just graduated from college. She'd been seeing Bryson, the personal training manager, for a while.

"Oh, we broke up. Months ago."

"What?" Lexa was surprised. "I didn't know that."

"It's no big deal," Elise said. "We're better as friends. Plus, it was getting old sneaking around, since the gym doesn't like it when employees date each other."

"I'm sorry."

Elise waved a hand. "It's fine."

"Well, my dad isn't here with anyone either. You can be her date, right, Dad?" She smiled at him. "Even though she's too young for you."

Greg turned red and drained his glass of beer before setting it down on the bar. "I need to ask your mom something," he said, and left abruptly.

Lexa was embarrassed. "I'm sorry. I don't know what's wrong with him. He usually has a better sense of humor than that."

Elise shook her head, a small smile on her face. "Don't worry about it."

Lexa watched Greg as he walked over to her mom and Phoenix. He reached out a hand as if to place it on her mom's back before withdrawing it and scratched his neck instead. Even from here, Lexa could see the blush on his face. He looked so uncomfortable.

She shouldn't have invited Phoenix. She'd done so to show her mom she supported her decision, without thinking how it would affect her dad. *Poor Dad*, she thought, realizing it was becoming a familiar refrain. She vowed to be more sensitive to his feelings. He'd been there for her all her life, always ready to back her up, proud of her no matter what. He'd been a father to her in the truest sense of the word, unlike her real father.

Before she could brood any more about her two fathers, Andi clapped her hands and announced that dinner was ready. As the guests moved toward the dining tables reserved for their party, Lexa found herself surrounded by her friends and family. She allowed them to sweep her into their midst and plastered a smile on her face. But inside, the glow she'd felt from her weekend with Jake was fading, overshadowed by her worry for her family.

19

⁓

Hsu-Ling? What's the matter?"

"*Aiyo*, ChiChi. You're not going to believe what's going on here." Hsu-Ling's voice burst out over the phone, and Lexa's heart picked up speed.

"What happened?"

"It's my mother. I'm so mad!"

"Your mother?" Lexa had Hsu-Ling on speakerphone and gripped the edges of the phone hard when her fingers threatened to drop it. She'd just come home from her birthday party and was more than a little tipsy. Her head swam as she squinted at the wall clock above her kitchen sink. It was one thirty in the morning, technically Monday morning now.

"Baba said right before he died that it was all Mama's fault, but he didn't say *what* was her fault. I didn't tell you because I didn't know what he was talking about. I asked her, but she wouldn't tell me. Until today."

"Hsu-Ling. You're not making sense." Lexa's head was fuzzy from all the cocktails she'd consumed. She opened the fridge and grabbed a small bottle of Poland Spring, guzzling half of it in one gulp.

Lexa heard her sister take a big breath. "I'm sorry," Hsu-Ling said. "I'm just so upset."

"Start at the beginning."

"Whatever Pong said to Baba, Baba was angry. He said he was so mad at Mama that he could strangle her. Mama and I had a big fight today. She's been against me going to see you, keeps telling me I'm making a big mistake. I asked her why Baba was so mad at her, and it finally came out."

"So now you know how much your mother hates me."

"No! She doesn't hate you."

"Trust me, Hsu-Ling." Lexa's voice was quiet. "She despises me. I bet she wished I'd died instead of our father."

"Lexa!"

"It's the truth."

"She told me she did something to make sure you went away that summer and never came back. But she wouldn't tell me what she did. Why didn't you tell me?"

"I didn't know if you'd believe me." Lexa set down her phone on the coffee table, suddenly too tired to hold it up.

"She took all the letters you ever wrote me and threw them away."

"I'm not surprised." Lexa had suspected, but it was still a shock to have her suspicions confirmed.

"I only found out because when I was fourteen, I came home sick from school one day and found a letter you'd just sent on her desk. She claimed it was the first one. That's when I started writing to you."

"Why didn't you tell me you never read any of my letters before you were fourteen? You made it sound as if it was your choice not to write to me until then."

Hsu-Ling sighed, a long, heavy sound. "I guess I was protecting my mother. Plus, she was always so negative about you. Didn't want me to contact you, said you didn't like me and wanted nothing to do with me, so why should I want to stay in touch with you? I guess maybe I believed some of that."

"She said that? It's the furthest from the truth."

"I know now . . ." Hsu-Ling stopped, and Lexa could hear her breathing rapidly.

"Are you okay?"

"I don't know. I have so many questions. We have so much to talk about."

"We do." Lexa closed her eyes, resigned to the fact that the past was coming back, no matter how much she wished it wouldn't. "I'm sorry, Hsu-Ling. I would have told you sooner, but I didn't want to put you in the middle."

"My flight's tonight, in a few hours. I'm leaving for the airport soon." Hsu-Ling paused. "I want to know everything. With Baba and Uncle Pong dead, you're the only one left who can tell me, since my mother won't."

Lexa didn't answer right away. She stared at her hands, and the old humiliation washed over her even after all these years. But then she remembered what Greg had said, about it not being her shame. She raised her chin. She wasn't a child anymore. She'd done nothing wrong, and it was time Hsu-Ling knew the truth.

"Okay. I'll tell you everything when you get here."

20

Tuesday morning, Lexa wove behind a row of treadmills at the gym and headed for Christy. Hsu-Ling would be landing at JFK Airport in a few hours, and Lexa was jittery with nerves.

She drew up next to Christy's treadmill. "Look at you! You're walking so fast."

Christy's cheeks were red. "That's because I'm mad. My father is such a jerk." She pressed the speed button until she broke into a jog.

"What did he do?"

Sweat dotted Christy's hairline. "He told me my consulting job was stupid even though I'm making so much money now. He said it wasn't as important as being a lawyer. Why does he always have to compare me to my sister?"

"That sucks." Lexa reached out to slow the treadmill. Christy was getting all worked up, and she didn't want her to trip.

"I hung up on him." Christy turned to Lexa, her eyes wide with shock. "I can't believe I did that." She turned back to the treadmill and jabbed at the incline button. "A few weeks ago, I'd never have imagined I could defy my father. But ever since I started working out with you, I feel braver."

Christy continued to talk about her father, stabbing the incline button with every word, but Lexa listened with only one ear. She was thinking about Hsu-Ling's arrival, nervous to see her sister for the first time in twenty-two years.

"Lexa!"

She looked up to see Bryson waving at her from the edge of the cardio section. He gestured to Christy, and Lexa turned back just in time to see Christy, whose treadmill was almost vertical by then, go flying off the back of the machine.

Lexa's mouth opened in shock, but before she could react, Jennifer, a floor trainer who happened to be standing behind Christy's treadmill, put her hands up to stop Christy's fall and somehow pushed Christy back upright. Lexa finally sprang into motion, her hands fumbling on the decline button before remembering to yank out the red emergency cord.

Bryson came running up. "Are you okay, Christy?"

The treadmill belt came to a halt and returned to its original flat position. "I'm so sorry," Lexa said, as she reached out to steady her client.

Christy placed a hand over her heart. "Oh my goodness. I almost fell."

"It was my fault. I wasn't keeping my eyes on you." Lexa felt heat flood her face as people all around the gym turned to stare at them. Her heart pounded out of control. She'd almost let her client go flying off the back of a treadmill. This wasn't like her. She was usually so vigilant.

"It's okay." Christy turned to Lexa. "It was my own fault. I was so mad at my father, and I wasn't paying attention."

"Are you sure you're okay?" Bryson asked.

Christy nodded. "I'm fine." She ducked her head and whispered to Lexa, "People are staring at me."

Lexa realized her hands were shaking, and she felt like

she'd just run a marathon. Bryson looked at her hard and turned to Christy.

"Why don't we have Jennifer finish your session today?"

"Oh, but I want Lexa." Christy turned worried eyes to Lexa.

"I think Lexa needs to go home. She doesn't look good." Bryson cocked his head in question at Lexa.

"I'm sorry, Christy," Lexa said. "I think Bryson's right. My head isn't here right now."

"We'll comp this session," Bryson said. "Okay?"

After one more worried look at Lexa, Christy allowed Jennifer to lead her onto the training floor. Lexa was afraid to meet Bryson's eyes. But his voice was gentle when he spoke.

"This isn't like you, Lexa. Are you okay?"

She nodded, since she couldn't form words over the lump that was growing in her throat.

"Do you want me to reschedule the rest of your morning?"

She nodded again, and when Bryson patted her on the shoulder, she had to bite her lips to keep from crying at his kindness when he should have been yelling at her for her negligence.

Lexa paced her apartment, waiting for Hsu-Ling, who was taking a taxi from JFK Airport. She'd spent the morning cleaning her apartment in an effort to work off her nervous energy, berating herself for allowing her personal life to put a client in jeopardy. Zeus followed faithfully at her heels.

Lexa threw herself onto the couch, and Zeus jumped on top of her and licked her face until she succumbed and laughed out loud.

"Get off me, you big goof! What do you think you are, a ten-pound dog?" Zeus paused in his licking and panted at her, his tongue sticking out and his head cocked to the side.

Her buzzer sounded, startling her, and her laughter died as she pushed Zeus aside gently. Running to the intercom, she pressed the button.

"I'm here!" Hsu-Ling's voice was staticky.

"Stay there, I'm coming down."

Lexa slipped her feet into flip-flops and flew down the four flights of stairs and out the front door. And there she was. Hsu-Ling, all grown up, slightly shorter than Lexa, but with the same wide smile she remembered from when she was ten and a half and Lexa was fourteen. Her hair was cut to graze her shoulders, and despite the hours of traveling, her eyes sparkled. Hsu-Ling had inherited her mother's sturdy build while Lexa had gotten their father's long limbs. But they had the same square jaw and cheekbones and looked more like sisters than Maddie and Lexa did.

"How was the flight?"

"Good, thanks to the drugs." Hsu-Ling laughed and dropped the bag she was holding to throw her arms around Lexa.

Lexa hugged her back and then picked up Hsu-Ling's suitcase and dragged it inside the front door.

"What do you have in here? This thing weighs a ton."

Her sister grinned. "I didn't know what to pack. I've never been this far from home."

"I live on the fourth floor and there's no elevator. Are you okay?" She glanced at Hsu-Ling's right leg, but her sister was wearing pants, so Lexa couldn't tell she had a prosthetic leg.

"I'm fine." Hsu-Ling waved Lexa up the stairs before her.

By the time they made it to Lexa's apartment door, both of them were gasping for breath. Zeus was waiting, and it wasn't until then that Lexa thought to ask, "Are you afraid of dogs?" There was so much they didn't know about each other.

"No," Hsu-Ling said, holding out a hand for Zeus to sniff.

"He's so big. Much bigger in person." She rubbed his head, and he licked her arm in approval.

Zeus herded them inside, and Lexa threw out her arms. "Welcome to my home."

Hsu-Ling dropped her bag to the floor. "I'm so glad to see you."

They gazed at each other without a word, each taking note of all the changes the past twenty-two years had brought. Lexa walked to Hsu-Ling. "I'm glad you're here too. And I'm so sorry about Baba." She put her arms around her sister, and they held each other for a moment, until Hsu-Ling pulled away.

"Where's the bathroom? I really have to pee." She wiggled her hips and bounced on her heels.

"Is that the Taiwanese version of a pee-pee dance?"

"A what?"

"When someone has to go to the bathroom badly, they dance around."

"Oh, yes." Hsu-Ling laughed, and Lexa pointed to the bathroom. As she waited for Hsu-Ling, Lexa tried to catch her breath. Her sister was really here. The little girl she remembered was all grown up.

Hsu-Ling came out of the bathroom. "Much better." She looked around Lexa's studio. It was small but cozy, and filled with pictures of her family and friends. Hsu-Ling's eyes studied the wood-and-cork map of the United States that Jake had given her, which was hanging on the wall over the couch. Then her eyes settled on a picture Lexa had placed on the windowsill. It was of Lexa and Hsu-Ling with their father, from the last summer she'd been in Taiwan. Hsu-Ling walked over and picked it up. "I can't believe this was the last time we saw each other."

"I know."

"I was so mad at you. I came back from Ah-Ma's that day and you were gone. I didn't know why you never came back to see me again." There was a hitch in Hsu-Ling's voice.

"I couldn't."

They looked at each other in silence until Lexa asked, "Are you hungry? I know we have a lot to talk about, but why don't we get something to eat before we check you into the hotel?" Hsu-Ling was staying at a hotel on Lexington Avenue, a fifteen-minute walk from Lexa's apartment.

"Yes. I'm starving." Hsu-Ling gave a visible shake of her head. "I want pizza. Or maybe a bagel—you were telling me how amazing the bagels in New York are. Or a pastrami sandwich? I've never had one."

Lexa laughed, and the tension dissipated. "You're here for a week, so we'll have plenty of time to eat all that. How about pizza for now? Maddie's going to meet us at your hotel later, and we'll go out to dinner. I can't wait for you to finally meet her."

"Sounds good. I can't wait to meet her either."

"Do you want to shower first?"

"No. I'll just wait until I get to the hotel. It'd be too much trouble taking my leg off and then putting it back on."

"Okay, let's go."

They walked to the pizzeria around the corner and found stools facing out the front window so Hsu-Ling could people watch. Hsu-Ling took a bite of her giant slice of pizza and moaned in pleasure.

"Sorry," she said, speaking in Mandarin, trying to separate the long string of cheese from her pizza. Lexa had told her she wanted to practice her Chinese. "This is the best pizza I've ever had."

Lexa smiled at the expression on her sister's face. She reminded Lexa of herself on her first trip to Taiwan, when they'd taken her to the night market.

They talked about what Hsu-Ling wanted to see and do while she was in New York, making a list while Hsu-Ling chowed down on her pizza with gusto. When they'd finished eating, Lexa turned on her stool to face her sister.

"So where's that letter from Pong? I'm dying to read it and see what the heck is going on."

"It's in my purse. You want it now?"

Lexa scrunched up her nose, looking around the noisy and crowded pizzeria. There was a long line at the counter, and people were looking for available seats. "I guess not here. Why don't we go back and get your bags and check you into the hotel? We can talk there."

"Sounds good."

They threw out their garbage and made their way back to Lexa's apartment to get Hsu-Ling's luggage. Lexa hailed a cab to take them to the hotel. Sitting in the cab next to the sister she hadn't seen in twenty-two years, Lexa realized she was nervous. Her palms were clammy, and her heart was racing the closer they got to the hotel. She knew the truth was finally going to come out. She'd never talked about it with Hsu-Ling because she was sure her half sister would side with her mother. After all, Lexa would stand by her own mother no matter what. But as she'd always hoped her father would one day believe her, she'd also held out hope that Hsu-Ling would also believe her.

Taking big breaths in through her nose and then slowly exhaling out through her mouth to ward off anxiety, Lexa knew she was about to find out if there was anything left to that bond that she and Hsu-Ling had forged all those years earlier.

21

Lexa sat on the bed in Hsu-Ling's hotel room and watched her pull out a bottle of Johnnie Walker Black from a bag.

"Duty-free, baby." Hsu-Ling waved the bottle, making Lexa laugh. Hsu-Ling had told Lexa she wanted to learn more American slang and phrases on this trip. Lexa marveled at how comfortable they were with each other, as if they'd only seen each other the day before.

Hsu-Ling said in Mandarin, "Our relatives drink like fish. Whenever we have family dinners, someone inevitably breaks out the scotch and then everyone turns red from all the alcohol." Hsu-Ling poured a shot into a plastic cup, toasted Lexa, and threw it back.

"I'm impressed." Lexa accepted the cup Hsu-Ling poured for her but added ice cubes from the bucket of ice they'd gotten from the machine in the hall.

Hsu-Ling made herself another drink, with ice this time, and sat on the green brocade lounge chair across from the bed. "So."

Lexa swirled the scotch around in her cup and decided to cut to the chase. "Can you tell me more about the day Baba died? I know you told me, but I want details."

Hsu-Ling turned her head away from Lexa. "It was the cancer." Her voice came out funny.

Lexa looked at her with curiosity. "You mean Pong? I know that. But what exactly happened? When Baba ran out?"

Hsu-Ling took a big gulp of scotch. "Oh, right. Baba." Her head fell back on the lounge chair as if she was too tired to hold her neck up. "I was afraid he was going to have a heart attack or something because his face had gotten so red when Pong was talking to him. When we were waiting outside Pong's hospital room after all those machines started beeping, I was holding on to Baba's arms. He said he had to go, and he spun around so suddenly that I went flying in the opposite direction and slammed into some chairs. He didn't even know what he did; that's how intent he was to get to you."

"Oh my God." Lexa covered her mouth with her hands. "Were you hurt?"

Hsu-Ling closed her eyes. "Not really. Just had the wind knocked out of me, and I landed on my right side, so it hurt to walk. By the time a nurse helped me up and let me go, Baba was long gone." Hsu-Ling's eyes opened, and she looked right into Lexa's. "And you know the rest."

"Did you . . ." Lexa swallowed and tried again, even as her stomach clenched at the image of Hsu-Ling lying helpless on the ground while their father drove his scooter to his death. "Did you see him?"

"Yes." Hsu-Ling's voice came out barely above a whisper. "I ran out of the hospital as fast as I could, just as an ambulance was pulling out of the emergency area. I knew it was for him. I ran after it . . ."

"Oh, Hsu-Ling." Lexa slipped off the bed and went to kneel next to her sister's chair, grasping her hands in hers.

"At first I blamed myself. If only I'd managed to keep him

from running out of the hospital." Hsu-Ling looked down at Lexa. "But then I was so angry at Uncle Pong." She lifted her chin, a hard glint in her eyes. "He killed Baba."

"He didn't kill him . . ." Lexa trailed off, because maybe a small part of her also blamed Pong for upsetting their father and sending him to his death.

"When Ah-Ma heard how Baba died, she was convinced our father's soul is stuck and not able to travel to the after-life."

Lexa looked up at Hsu-Ling. "I read about that. Ah-Ma really believes it? Why?"

"In Taiwan, we believe if someone dies with unfinished business or of a violent death, their soul can't rest and move on until they resolve the issue." Hsu-Ling pointed to Lexa. "Ah-Ma believes you're Baba's unfinished business."

"I'm responsible for Baba's lingering soul?"

"In a way. Ah-Ma thinks it's important that you come back to Taiwan and say good-bye to Baba."

"How does she know his ghost is lingering?" Lexa didn't believe in ghosts, but a sudden shivery feeling had her rubbing her upper arms as if she'd gotten a chill.

"She said she feels him." Hsu-Ling let that statement sink in and then leaned toward Lexa. "But more important, I want to know what my mother did to you."

"How much did she tell you?"

"Not much. When we got into that argument before I left to catch my flight, I asked her what Baba was talking about, why he'd be mad at her. And what Pong meant when he said he'd been in love with you all these years."

"Pong wasn't in love with me." Lexa wrinkled her nose. "I haven't seen him since that summer."

"I know. My mother told me he was in love with her."

"Your mother?" It all suddenly made sense. Why Pong had taken Pin-Yen's side, why he'd lied.

"Yes." Hsu-Ling's hands fisted in her lap. "She was so smug, I wanted to slap her. She said Pong had been in love with her for years, since before I was born. He'd do anything for her."

"Did Baba know?"

"I don't think so. He seemed genuinely shocked when Pong told him."

"Oh, God." Bits and pieces of the summers Lexa had spent in Taiwan flashed through her mind.

"I told her Baba seemed more concerned about you than he did that his best friend was in love with his wife. She almost spit in my face." Hsu-Ling ducked her head, as if avoiding her mother's spite. "She said some nasty things about you."

"I can imagine." Lexa's voice shook.

"She said a woman has to protect what is hers. That this isn't like the old days, when women had no power and had to do whatever their husbands wanted. She said I'm Baba's real daughter, not you, and you had no right to worm your way into our family." Hsu-Ling stopped to gauge Lexa's reaction. "I'm sorry, ChiChi."

"It's not your fault."

Hsu-Ling stared off into space. "She's been hard on me all my life. Always pushing, pushing. She felt I had to be better than everyone else to make up for only having one leg. I had to be smarter, a better pianist. I was supposed to be a doctor." Hsu-Ling let out a bitter laugh. "Too bad I couldn't play the piano to save my life. And I did go to medical school, but I dropped out. It wasn't what I wanted. I can barely stand the sight of blood."

Lexa watched her sister. She'd always suspected Pin-Yen of being a Tiger Mom, but this was the first time Hsu-Ling had acknowledged it. "I always thought your mother pushed you too hard."

"I finally grew a backbone when I realized I wasn't cut out to be a doctor. I wanted to work in entertainment." Hsu-Ling laughed again. "You should have heard the yelling when I told her I was dropping out and getting a job as an unpaid intern on a TV show." Hsu-Ling turned her gaze on Lexa. "But enough about that. I want to know what my mother did to you."

Lexa drank the contents of her cup in one swallow, feeling the scotch burn its way down her throat and warm her belly. "Your mother." Lexa swallowed back the bitterness in her throat. "She accused me of all sorts of things. Remember the gold necklace Ah-Ma gave you?"

"Yes. She was going to buy one for you, but then you disappeared and never came back." Hsu-Ling's left eye twitched slightly, much like Lexa's own did when she was upset.

"That's because your mother made sure I would go away and never come back."

22

July, Twenty-Two Years Ago
Taichung, Taiwan

They'd warned her that Taiwan would be really hot in July. And she remembered the heat from the past two summers she was there. But she didn't remember it being *this* hot. Every time she stepped outside, out of the air-conditioning, she literally felt like she was being roasted alive. The air was so stifling it was as if someone had stuffed hot cotton balls in her nose and down her throat. Sweat formed immediately and soaked her shirt.

She'd only been there for three days, and she was miserable. Hsu-Ling had a list of activities planned, but after the first day, Lexa had begged to stay in the air-conditioning. At least indoors, she could think. When she was outside in the heat, it felt like her brain had turned to mush.

"ChiChi, don't you want to go to Taichung Park?" Hsu-Ling scooted into the room on her bottom and stared at Lexa sprawled on the bed. "I want to go to the playground with you." She spoke in Mandarin, and Lexa was happy she understood it all. She'd been keeping up with Chinese school, and her spoken Mandarin had gotten really good over the years.

"Hsu-Ling, I'm so hot." Lexa hated the whine in her voice. "I don't know how you guys stand it. I'd die if I lived here."

Hsu-Ling looked at her with worried eyes. "You get used to it. What if we go get shaved ice?"

"Do we have to go outside?" Lexa was only half joking. She'd been looking forward to this trip for so long. But she couldn't make her body sit up.

Hsu-Ling didn't answer, and Lexa heard her crawl out of the room. Lexa closed her eyes, hoping the cool air would revive her. She couldn't spend the whole summer lying down like this. There was so much she wanted to see and eat and do with her Taiwanese family.

She heard someone walk into her room, and even before she opened her eyes, she knew it was her baba. He always smelled like sandalwood, a fresh-cut woodsy scent. "Poor Chi," he said. "You're melting, aren't you?"

Lexa struggled to sit up. "I'm sorry. I don't know what's wrong with me."

"It takes getting used to," he said. "And we're having a heat wave right now. Plus you're jet-lagged. You'll feel better in a few days."

She nodded, hoping he was right. Her mom had left that morning for Japan. She was going to visit her friends in Tokyo for the next few weeks before flying home from there. They'd decided Lexa was going to fly home by herself at the end of summer now that she was fourteen. She was excited to be on her own for the first time, but there it was, her mom not even gone a day, and she was miserable.

"I tell you what," Baba said. "Why don't we visit Uncle Pong in his new ice-cream store? It's air-conditioned, and the ice cream will cool you off."

"Yes!" Hsu-Ling said from the doorway. "Uncle Pong has the best ice cream."

"Okay." Lexa nodded.

Pin-Yen poked her head into the room. "Ah-Ma is here. She wants to show Lexa the necklace they gave Hsu-Ling when she was born." Something in Pin-Yen's voice made Lexa look up, but Pin-Yen was looking at Hsu-Ling. "Hsu-Ling, you should be at *buxiban*. You have to do well on the next math exam to make up for that bad test score."

"That wasn't a bad score. She only missed one question." Baba gave his wife an exasperated look. "And besides, her sister is here. She can miss *buxiban* for a few days."

Pin-Yen placed her hands on her hips. "It wasn't perfect. Go study while Ah-Ma visits with Lexa."

"No." Hsu-Ling stuck out her bottom lip.

Pin-Yen stared at her without answering, and after a moment, Hsu-Ling caved and, with a loud huff, went to her room.

Lexa walked into the living room. Ah-Ma sat on the blue couch, a red velvet bag in her hand. "Chi-ah, sit here." Ah-Ma touched Lexa's arm. "*Aiya*, you're so tan," she said in Mandarin. "You should stay out of the sun."

"My friends are all tan," Lexa said.

"In Taiwan, we value pale complexions." Pin-Yen spoke from the doorway of her daughter's room. "Like Hsu-Ling's skin. She's got the perfect skin."

"Hsu-Ling does have pretty skin." Lexa nodded her head in agreement. She looked down at her tanned arms and legs and gave a laugh. "Not me."

Pin-Yen muttered as she headed to the kitchen, and Lexa

flushed. She was pretty sure Pin-Yen had just said Lexa wasn't really Taiwanese. Lexa thought she looked like everyone else here, but Pin-Yen kept pointing out she wasn't Asian enough.

Ah-Ma distracted her by handing her a gold necklace.

"It's so pretty." Lexa admired the delicate gold chain with small charms dangling from it, ending in a ruby surrounded by small diamonds.

"It's real gold and gemstones." Hsu-Ling poked her head out of her room.

Ah-Ma nodded. "We gave one to all our granddaughters when they were born."

"Ah-Ma is keeping it for me until I'm fourteen; then I get to wear it for special occasions," Hsu-Ling said.

Lexa handed the necklace back to Ah-Ma. "Thank you. It's beautiful."

"Good. I'll pick something like this for you." Ah-Ma patted Lexa on the cheek and stood. "I have to get back to Ah-Gong. He's not feeling well."

"Can I keep the necklace for today?" Hsu-Ling came out of her room. "We're going to Uncle Pong's for ice cream, but I want to wear it when I come back."

"You're not going for ice cream, Hsu-Ling," her mother called from the kitchen. "You have to study."

Ah-Ma's brows rose at Pin-Yen's tone, but she nodded at Hsu-Ling. "I'll get it from you later."

Hsu-Ling crawled forward and took the necklace from Ah-Ma before taking it into her room and putting it on her nightstand.

"Come on, let me put your leg on so we can go." Baba held out Hsu-Ling's leg.

Pin-Yen came out of the kitchen. "She's not going."

Hsu-Ling crawled back into the living room. "I want to

go. Please?" When Pin-Yen just shook her head, Hsu-Ling turned to her father and Ah-Ma. "Baba? Ah-Ma?"

"Pin-Yen, her sister is here. Give her a break, huh?" Ah-Ma spoke in a soft voice, but even Lexa heard the steel in her words.

Pin-Yen stared at her mother-in-law. After a moment, she said, "Yes, Ah-Ma. But as soon as she gets back, she needs to study."

Hsu-Ling cheered, and their father asked, "Are you coming, Pin-Yen?"

Pin-Yen shook her head. "No, you go. I have to go to the market."

Lexa watched as Hsu-Ling's parents exchanged a look, and then her baba turned to her with a smile. "Help me get this leg on Hsu-Ling."

Pin-Yen stood in the foyer and leaned against the large blue-and-white porcelain vase that had been there since she married Jing Tao. She wished Jing Tao would let her give it away. It was ugly and too big, but it had been a present from his grandparents, and he refused to part with it. She watched her husband leave the apartment with his two daughters. Her lips pressed together, she narrowed her eyes as a plan took shape in her mind.

"ChiChi, you live!" Uncle Pong was behind the counter. "I thought the Taiwan heat wave knocked you out for good." He smiled at her. "You look stunning." Lexa blushed, looking down at the sundress she wore. It was white and gauzy with flowers along the bottom and made her feel pretty and grown-up.

Hsu-Ling hopped up and down at Lexa's side. "What flavor do you want? My favorite is the bubble gum."

"They all look so good." Lexa scanned the ice creams in the case. "What's that one over there?" She couldn't read or write Chinese as well as she could speak it.

"Good taste." Uncle Pong nodded in approval. "That's my new special. It's coffee ice cream swirled with sweet cream and pieces of white chocolate."

"Ew." Hsu-Ling screwed up her face.

"Cone or cup?" Pong asked.

"Cup, please." She looked around the empty store. "Do you work here all the time?"

"No, I have college kids who work for me. I usually have two on at a time—one at the front and one in back making ice-cream cakes. The girl who was supposed to work up front right now quit on me without warning." He raised his voice and called out, "Hey, Yung! Come out here."

Lexa looked up and saw a boy, probably seventeen or eighteen, emerge from the back. He was astonishingly good-looking, with high cheekbones and a flop of hair falling over one eye. He wore a large white apron over his ripped jeans and was holding a spatula in one hand.

"This is Chi, Hsu-Ling's American sister. She's visiting from New York."

The boy raised a hand and said, "Yo." He studied her from under hooded eyes, and Lexa dropped her gaze, but not before she noted the earring in his left ear.

"Yung just finished his first year at National Taiwan University," Pong said proudly. "He's home for the summer." Lexa knew Taiwan University in Taipei was the top-ranked university in Taiwan, because Hsu-Ling had told her Pin-Yen expected Hsu-Ling to go to medical school there. Lexa had stared because Hsu-Ling wasn't even eleven yet.

Uncle Pong handed the ice cream to Lexa. She watched as he scooped bubble gum ice cream onto a cone for Hsu-Ling, aware that Yung was watching her.

Self-conscious, she took a spoonful of her ice cream and forgot about the older boy. "This is the best ice cream I've ever had."

Uncle Pong's chest puffed up with pride. "Jing Tao, your daughter has good taste."

Lexa looked up to find Yung staring at her. She and her friends talked about boys at school all the time, but she felt as if she were going to wet her pants now that a boy was actually looking at her. For the first time since she'd gotten to Taiwan three days earlier, Lexa wasn't miserable and hot. The ice cream was cool and delicious, and she loved the vibe of the store, with its candy-colored walls and Chinese pop music playing from the speakers. Plus, there were cute boys who stared at her.

"Hey, I just had a great idea." Uncle Pong came out from behind the counter. "How would you like to work here in the afternoons when it's the hottest out?"

"What would I have to do?" Lexa asked, excited. She'd get to work with Yung.

"Serve the customers. Mostly scoop ice cream and ring up sales. Maybe help Yung or me decorate cakes if there aren't any customers in the store."

Lexa looked at the intricate flowers and borders on the cakes. "I don't know how."

Pong waved a hand. "Don't worry, I'll show you."

"What do you think, Chi?" her baba asked. "Do you want Pong to put you to work?"

"No!" Hsu-Ling wailed. "I don't want her working here! She's supposed to be visiting us, not working for Uncle Pong."

"It'd only be for a few hours, *xiao mei*," Uncle Pong said. "The rest of the time, she's all yours."

Lexa smiled at him. "I'd love to work here."

"I'd pay you, of course."

Lexa shook her head. "I don't care. I could work for ice cream. I love ice cream."

Uncle Pong raised a hand, and Lexa gave him a high five; then he pulled her in for a hug. She grinned up at him and, on impulse, gave him a kiss on the cheek. Seeing the scowl on Hsu-Ling's face, Lexa went to her sister. She wanted to reassure Hsu-Ling they'd still have plenty of time together that summer. She had no idea that these were some of the last moments she'd spend with her sister.

23

Lexa stopped talking when the phone suddenly rang, making them both jump. Lexa had been so focused on the story that it took her a moment to remember she was in New York in Hsu-Ling's hotel room, and not back in Taiwan.

Hsu-Ling reached over to answer the phone.

"Yes. Okay. Send her up. Thank you." Hsu-Ling hung up and turned to Lexa. "Maddie's here."

"She's early," Lexa said in surprise. She got off the bed and walked to the door, opening it to wait for Maddie to arrive.

Lexa felt the air change the minute Maddie stepped into the hotel room. She introduced them, but neither spoke; instead, they sized up each other with their eyes.

Maddie was the first to speak. "What happened? What did you say to upset Lexa?"

"Maddie." Lexa rolled her eyes at her. "Don't be rude."

"Fine. Nice to meet you." Maddie's chilly tone indicated it was anything but nice.

Hsu-Ling had stood as soon as Maddie came in, and now she nodded at Maddie. "Nice to meet you too." Gone was the warmth and enthusiasm she'd shown around Lexa. Her tone matched Maddie's. The tension in the hotel room was so thick Lexa could almost taste it.

Lexa closed her eyes. This wasn't how she'd pictured her two sisters meeting for the first time. Praying for strength, she opened her eyes and injected cheer into her voice. "Come on, guys. Lighten up. My two sisters are meeting for the first time. This is big!"

"You look awful." Maddie scowled at Lexa.

"Thanks." Lexa made a face at her.

"Are you okay?" Maddie asked.

Lexa sat at the edge of the bed. "We were just talking about what happened the last time we saw each other."

"What happened?"

When Lexa didn't answer, Maddie said, "Jesus Christ. I'm so sick of all this secrecy." Maddie turned to Hsu-Ling. "Tell me what the hell happened in Taiwan all those years ago. What did you and your family do to Lexa to make her not want to go back there?"

"Maddie." Lexa reached out a hand to stop Maddie. "She had nothing to do with it. She was only ten at the time."

"I didn't know what happened," Hsu-Ling said. "Lexa was just telling me."

Maddie snorted. "Yeah, right. You didn't know what happened."

"What's your problem?" Hsu-Ling threw up her hands. "You don't know me. You don't know anything about me."

"I know enough to know that you all did something to Lexa to make her not want to even talk about what happened that summer."

Hsu-Ling placed her hands on her hips and glared at Maddie. "You don't know shit about anything." Lexa was taken aback. She'd never heard Hsu-Ling curse in English. It sounded like "sheet" when she said it. "Just like I don't know what happened that summer either."

Lexa dropped her head into her hands. She'd always known Maddie was jealous of Hsu-Ling, but she'd thought Hsu-Ling had been looking forward to meeting Maddie. Why did they sound like they hated each other?

"Guys. Stop it." Lexa stood and moved so that she was directly between her sisters. "If you two would calm down, I'll tell you everything."

Maddie turned to Lexa. "Ever since you came back from Taiwan that summer, you haven't been the same. You used to include me in everything, but you stopped doing that." She sounded wistful. "It felt like you and Mom had a secret you didn't want me to know."

"Maddie, we didn't keep a secret from you on purpose."

"Hsu-Ling knows."

"I don't," Hsu-Ling shot back.

"It's not a competition," Lexa said.

"You're my sister." Maddie sat next to Lexa. "I should be the one to help you."

"Hsu-Ling is my sister too."

"Did someone abuse you? Were you molested?" Maddie blurted.

There was a stunned silence before Lexa found her voice. "No! Why would you think that?"

Hsu-Ling spoke up. "It was my mom. She was the one who hurt Lexa."

Maddie turned to Hsu-Ling. "Your mom? What does she have to do with anything? I thought it was your father who did something to Lexa."

"No." Hsu-Ling reached over and grabbed Lexa's hands. "Why does my mother hate you so much? What did she do to you?"

24

⌒

July, Twenty-Two Years Ago
Taichung, Taiwan

Lexa wiped the counter and sighed with happiness. She loved working in the ice-cream store. That day was her first day, and it was turning out to be the best job ever. She got to taste the ice cream, and Yung had spoken five words to her. He'd said in Mandarin, "*Ni hao, mei guo ren.*"

Uncle Pong had laughed. "Don't call her an American. She's Taiwanese too."

Yung studied Lexa. "Are you part white? You don't look completely Asian."

Lexa looked down and could feel her cheeks turning red. She'd thought she looked like everyone else around there. Why did people keep pointing out that she didn't really fit in?

Uncle Pong had showed her how to use the soft-serve machine and how much ice cream to scoop for each size. She'd gotten the hang of the cash register right away, and he'd said, "You're smarter than some of the college kids who apply here." He'd stayed at the front with her for the first hour, but now he'd gone back into his office. She was proud to be trusted with his whole store. She couldn't wait to email her mom and dad and tell them about her job.

"Chi, is there anyone in the store?" Uncle Pong called from the back.

"No."

"Come on back. Yung and I can show you how to decorate the cakes. We'll hear the bell if anyone comes in."

"Okay." She put down the cloth.

Decorating cakes was easier than she thought. They showed her how to fill the pastry bags with the frosting and then how to twist the end shut.

"You need a steady hand," Uncle Pong said. They watched Yung pipe a border on a cake.

"Here, you try it." Yung handed her the bag.

Her first border wasn't as smooth as Yung's, but it was passable.

"Nice." Yung nodded in approval.

"Thanks." She snuck a peek at him, and he smiled at her.

She finished the white border, and then Uncle Pong said, "Why don't you get the tub of pink icing from the walk-in freezer? You can pipe that while Yung finishes the rest of the white."

"Sure," Lexa said.

Yung looked up from the cake he was working on. "You got it? It's really heavy."

"I can do it." Lexa headed for the freezer. Uncle Pong had showed it to her the day before. It was gigantic and filled with tubs of ice cream, icing of all colors, and all sorts of other supplies. She left the door cracked so the light would stay on, just like Uncle Pong had shown her.

She found the pink icing at the front of the freezer. She

had just picked it up when the door opened behind her. She caught her breath and turned to find Yung standing at the door. He let the door close partway so it felt like they were alone in the icy coldness.

She let out a nervous giggle, and before she could move, he walked to her and put his arms around the tub of icing so that their arms touched. *Ohmigod*, she thought to herself. *Yung and I are hugging the same tub.*

"I'll get that for you," Yung said. With reluctance, she let go and followed him to the door. He turned back and winked at Lexa before he pushed it open with his hip.

She didn't move for a moment, stunned with happiness that he'd *winked* at her, but then her chattering teeth made her rush out. Yung handed her a fresh pastry bag. "Fill this, and then you can start on this cake."

She spent the next hour helping Yung while Uncle Pong went back to his office. She ran to the front to ring up sales when she heard the bell but spent most of her time with Yung. They didn't talk much, but he complimented her work, and once they'd finished decorating all the cakes, he stood and stretched.

"Want some ice cream? I think we earned it."

"Sure." She followed him to the front of the store and pointed at the vanilla soft serve when he asked what she wanted. She watched as he made a perfect cone, and ate it while he made himself a cone of the vanilla and chocolate swirled together.

He hopped onto the counter and sat there, grinning down at her as she licked her ice-cream cone. She'd had sex ed at school and her mom had talked to her, so she had a general understanding of how sex worked. But she'd never even kissed a boy, and something about the way Yung was staring at her made her self-conscious. She was focused on the creamy texture of the ice cream when Yung reached over and touched her nose.

"You got some ice cream on your nose," he said.

"Oh. *Xie xie.*" She thanked him, her face turning hot, and wiped her nose with a napkin.

"No problem." He withdrew his hand and took a bite of his ice cream. "You know, you're pretty cool. For a kid."

The smile she aimed at him dimmed when he said the last part. She was trying to come up with a clever comeback to show him she was older than she looked when Uncle Pong called from the back.

"ChiChi, your baba's on the phone. He says it's important."

Lexa pushed away from the counter and turned to go into the back, but not before she caught the way Yung was smiling at her, as if he knew she had a crush on him. Her face flaming, she walked away. Years later, when she thought back to that moment, she'd always remember the taste of the vanilla ice cream in her mouth and the burning humiliation at the back of her throat that the older boy she liked thought she was only a cute kid.

. . .

"Want some pineapple ice?" Hsu-Ling asked. She was sprawled on the floor of the living room with a pot of ice that her mother had made. Hsu-Ling scraped her spoon across the top, scooping up chunks of pineapple-flavored ice along with bits of pineapple. She held it out to Lexa, who leaned in and took the mouthful. It tasted like Italian ice, only with more texture.

"That's good," Lexa said, even though her stomach was

still in knots from the way her father had sounded on the phone. He'd asked her to come home right away. Something had happened, and he needed to speak to her. His voice was wrong, as if he was talking to a stranger. The ice cream Lexa had eaten soured in her stomach at his tone. Now, she glanced at him, searching for a clue as to what was wrong, but his face remained closed and blank. She'd never seen him look so stern before.

Pin-Yen took the pot out of Hsu-Ling's hands. "Go to Ah-Ma's. You need to practice the piano. Your teacher said you were horrible last week."

"No." Hsu-Ling glared at her mother. "I hate the piano. I'm so bad at it."

It was true. Pin-Yen had made Hsu-Ling play for Lexa and her mom on their first day there. They'd sat in Ah-Ma and Ah-Gong's living room, where the piano was, and suffered through ten minutes of wrong notes and chords clashing before their father had shut down the impromptu performance.

"Don't argue with me." Pin-Yen pointed at the door. "You wouldn't be bad if you practiced every day. You need to be well rounded to get into Taiwan University."

"Why?" Hsu-Ling wailed. "I'm only ten and a half! And ChiChi just got home."

"You've already missed *buxiban* all week because of her. Go! Practice, practice, practice." Pin-Yen clapped her hands with each word.

Hsu-Ling scowled but crawled out of the apartment. When Pin-Yen shut the door with a loud click, Lexa's heart jumped.

"What's going on?" she asked, sitting on the couch. "What happened?"

Pin-Yen crossed her arms over her chest. "Hsu-Ling's

necklace is missing. Ah-Ma came to get it this afternoon and Hsu-Ling couldn't find it."

"Oh, no," Lexa said. "Maybe it fell on the floor?"

"No. We looked everywhere." Her baba shook his head. "Do you know where it is, Chi?"

"I haven't seen it since Ah-Ma showed us yesterday."

Her baba ran a hand through his hair. "Chi, you can tell me the truth. It's okay."

"I am telling you the truth." Lexa stared at him, wondering what he was talking about.

"Pin-Yen said she saw you playing with it last night, after we came back from the park."

Lexa shook her head. "No, I didn't." She looked at Hsu-Ling's mother. Why would she say Lexa had been playing with it when she hadn't been anywhere near it? "I swear."

Her baba came and sat next to her on the couch. "Did you take it, maybe to keep it safe, and then you were going to give it back to Hsu-Ling? Maybe you forgot?"

"I don't know what you're talking about." Lexa had a bad feeling in the pit of her stomach, like she felt right before a test she hadn't studied for.

Jing Tao looked at Pin-Yen, a helpless look on his face. Pin-Yen stepped forward. "I think you took it. I think you're jealous of Hsu-Ling and took her necklace."

Lexa's mouth dropped open, and she thought for a moment maybe her Mandarin wasn't good enough to understand properly. Was Pin-Yen accusing her of stealing the necklace? "No! I'm not jealous of Hsu-Ling. Why would I be? Ah-Ma said she was getting one for me. Why would I take Hsu-Ling's?"

"Prove it." Pin-Yen loomed over her, her mouth set in a hard line, and Lexa felt the beginnings of anger.

"I can prove it. I don't have it. You can search my stuff if you want." She stood, not wanting Pin-Yen to have the advantage over her. She walked into her room and over to her suitcase, which still held her clothes, as there was no closet in that room. "See for yourself. I don't have it."

Her baba walked to her side. "It's okay, Chi. If you say you didn't take it, I believe you."

Pin-Yen pushed him out of the way and crouched over the suitcase. She pushed Lexa's clothes aside and held up a red jewelry bag. "What's this?"

Lexa stared at it. "I have no idea."

Pin-Yen opened it and spilled Hsu-Ling's necklace into her hand. "I told you she took it." Her voice was triumphant.

Lexa turned to her baba, speaking in English. She couldn't think fast enough in Mandarin. "I didn't take it, I swear. I don't know how that got in my suitcase."

He looked at her, disappointment on his face. Then something in the suitcase caught his eyes, and he reached down. "What's this?"

He picked up a few photos, and Lexa watched as his face changed from puzzlement to disbelief, and then to sorrow.

"What is that?" Lexa asked. "That's not mine."

Her baba looked at her. "Did you do this, Chi? Why?"

She looked at the photos in his hands and slowly took them from him. They were pictures of her and Hsu-Ling with their baba between them, taken on the first day she was here. But Hsu-Ling's face had been x-ed out with a black marker, and one of the pictures had been slashed with a knife right over Hsu-Ling's face and torso.

Lexa looked up in shock. "Who did this? Why are they in my suitcase?"

Her baba sat on the bed heavily. "Chi, is it true? You're jealous of Hsu-Ling?"

"No! I'm not. I didn't do this. Someone put them in my suitcase."

"Who would do such a thing?" Her baba looked at her, his eyes beseeching. "I've done everything I can to make you feel welcome. To let you know I love you as much as Hsu-Ling, that you are my daughter too. Why would you do this? Why would you want to hurt Hsu-Ling?"

"I didn't, Baba. I'd never hurt Hsu-Ling. She's my little sister." Lexa's heart was pounding so hard she could feel every heartbeat in her fingers.

"I saw you trip her last night at the park." Pin-Yen crossed her arms over her chest. "When she got that nasty scrape."

Lexa whipped around to face Pin-Yen. "What are you talking about? Hsu-Ling tripped. I didn't make her fall."

"That's what Hsu-Ling said, but I saw with my own eyes. You deliberately stuck your foot out as Hsu-Ling ran by."

"Baba, she's lying. I'd never do that." Lexa pressed her fingers to her eyes. She couldn't believe this was happening. Why was Pin-Yen lying about her?

"Jing Tao, there's more." Lexa looked up at the hiss in Pin-Yen's voice. The older woman had a self-righteous, almost smug look on her face. "She's been flaunting her body, throwing herself at the men."

"What?" Lexa cried. "I haven't." Tears sprang to her eyes. "Why are you saying this?"

Pin-Yen locked eyes with Lexa. "He told me. He told me about your little crush."

25

I thought she was talking about Yung," Lexa said, her voice low.

Maddie put her hands on her hips. "There is absolutely nothing wrong with flirting with an older boy. It's not like you did anything." She stopped and looked at Lexa. "Did you?"

"Of course not!" Lexa was aghast. "I'd never even kissed a boy at that point."

"There's nothing wrong with flirting," Maddie said again.

Lexa glanced at Hsu-Ling, who hadn't said a word. "Pin-Yen wasn't talking about Yung."

Maddie shot Lexa a look. "Who else were you flirting with?"

"No one." Lexa tried to catch Hsu-Ling's eyes, but her sister was looking the other way. "Hsu-Ling?"

At the sound of her name, Hsu-Ling turned toward Lexa. She didn't say anything, but her eyes were full of sorrow.

"Do you want me to stop?" Lexa couldn't tell how Hsu-Ling was feeling. Was she upset with Lexa, thinking she was exaggerating and telling lies like their father had? Or did she believe Lexa that her mother had lied?

"No." Hsu-Ling's voice was firm. "Tell me the rest. I need to know why my mother tore our family apart."

26

July, Twenty-Two Years Ago
Tokyo, Japan

At first, all Susan heard was static. Kiko had said the call was for her, and she'd picked up, expecting to hear Lexa's voice.

"Hello?"

Nothing, and then she heard a catch of breath.

"Lexa? Is that you?"

"Mom . . ." The sound of sobbing filled the phone. It tore at Susan's heart.

"What's the matter, baby?" Susan asked, alarms going off throughout her body. "Take a deep breath. Whatever it is, we'll fix it."

She heard Lexa's breath shudder out as she tried to control her breathing. "Mom . . . I want to go home. Please. Come get me. Please . . ." And she started crying again. Her plea was so sad and heart-wrenching that Susan felt as if someone had reached into her chest and ripped out her heart.

"Lexa, calm down. Tell me what happened." But she couldn't get a coherent answer. Finally, she said, "Put your father on the phone."

"*Wei*," Jing Tao said when he picked up.

"What's going on? Why's she crying like that?" Susan's voice was fierce, and she felt the adrenaline running through her body.

"We have problem. You should come back to Taiwan." His voice was stiff, no trace of the warmth that was usually present when he spoke with her.

"Put her back on the phone." Susan matched his tone with her own curt response.

"Mom." Lexa's voice was barely above a whisper.

"What happened? Tell me." Susan softened her voice.

"Can you come? Please, Mommy. I just want to go home."

Lexa only called her Mommy when she thought she was in trouble. Susan was instantly on alert. "Yes. I'll get on the first flight. I'll be there as soon as I can."

Taichung, Taiwan

"What did you do to my daughter?" Susan's voice trembled with anger. "Why is she crying like this?" She stood on one side of Jing Tao's living room in front of the intricately carved lacquer chairs inlaid with mother-of-pearl dragons, her arm around Lexa. Jing Tao stood on the other side of the room, next to Pin-Yen and Pong.

"You should ask Lexa what she did to *my* daughter." Pin-Yen's voice was high-pitched, and she spoke in a mix of Mandarin and English. "Lexa is a danger to Hsu-Ling, and I won't have her living under my roof."

"Pin-Yen." Jing Tao spoke her name like a warning, his

voice low but commanding. He placed a hand on her arm. "This is my house too, and my daughters, both of them, are welcome."

Pin-Yen flicked him a disdainful look. "If you let that *mei guo ren*"—she waved a hand in Lexa's direction when she said "American"—"stay here, I'm taking our daughter away."

Jing Tao lowered his voice even more and spoke directly to his wife. Susan strained to catch his words even though he spoke in Mandarin. She looked at Pong, who only stared back at her.

Jing Tao turned to Susan and switched to English. "We think Lexa might have accidently hurt Hsu-Ling." His eyes pleaded with Susan to understand, and in that moment, she couldn't see why she'd ever thought he was attractive.

Susan crossed her own arms over her chest. "No way. Lexa would never hurt Hsu-Ling. What exactly do you think she did?"

Pong spoke up and told Susan in English about the necklace and the photos while Lexa clung to her mother's side. When Pong got to the part about tripping Hsu-Ling, Lexa spoke.

"I would never hurt Hsu-Ling! I didn't do any of that. They're lying." Her eyes reddened, and Susan tightened her grip on her.

"I know my daughter, and she would never steal a necklace or slash Hsu-Ling's picture, let alone harm her. Lexa adores Hsu-Ling. Something's going on, and I intend to get to the bottom of it." Susan looked directly at Jing Tao, wondering if he was buying into his wife's act. Susan knew the woman was lying.

Jing Tao crossed the room and stood in front of Lexa. "Maybe you make mistake? You didn't mean to hurt Hsu-Ling? If you just apologize to Hsu-Ling and Pin-Yen, we can forget this." He took Lexa's arms in his hands, and she flinched. His eyes widened in surprise, and he dropped his hands to his sides.

Lexa lifted her chin and looked her father in the eyes. "I can't apologize because I didn't do it. I would never hurt Hsu-Ling. And why would I steal her necklace when Ah-Ma told me she was buying one for me?"

"Because you're a greedy little half-breed who's trying to worm your way into our lives and take what is rightfully Hsu-Ling's." Pin-Yen spat the hateful words in a mixture of English and Mandarin, but Susan got the gist of it. Susan shoved Lexa behind her and jabbed a finger in Pin-Yen's face.

"You better step back, or I swear I'm going to punch you. Do not speak of my daughter like that. Lexa is a kind, sweet girl, and all she wants is to get to know her father and her Taiwanese heritage." Susan put up both hands, and when Pin-Yen kept advancing, Susan shoved her.

Jing Tao and Pong both sprang forward when Pin-Yen screeched and let loose a string of rapid Mandarin, her arms flailing. Jing Tao grabbed Pin-Yen around the waist and hauled her away from Susan, while Pong held Susan back by placing his hands on her shoulders. Susan shook off Pong and put her arms around her daughter. Lexa's face was drained of all color, and she was shaking violently, as if she'd been caught in a blizzard without a coat.

Pong held up his hands. "Please. Everyone, calm down."

"Calm down?!" Pin-Yen shouted from behind Jing Tao. She turned to her husband and said something to him in Mandarin, her arms gesturing and pointing to Susan.

Susan looked at Pong. "What did she say?" But he stared at her, at a loss for words.

Pin-Yen looked right at Susan and said in English, "I said,

I want your American whore to take her bastard child out of our home, now."

"Mommy! She called us bad words."

Susan looked at her daughter, her mouth open in shock. But then she found her voice. It trembled with anger when she addressed Jing Tao. "I know this is your house, but I will not allow your wife to say these things about my daughter. I don't know what's going on, why your wife is so jealous of an innocent little girl that she has to invent lies, but I will not stand for it."

Before Jing Tao could respond, Pin-Yen pushed him out of the way and sneered at Susan, "Innocent? Ha!" She turned to Pong. "Tell them what Lexa did to you."

Pong's mouth opened and closed, and he looked helplessly at Pin-Yen. "I . . . Pin-Yen. Please." His eyes pleaded with Pin-Yen, and Susan could sense his reluctance.

"Tell them, Pong," Pin-Yen said, her voice as hard as nails. "Or I will."

27

Maddie spied the bottle of Johnnie Walker on the desk in Hsu-Ling's hotel room and poured a shot into a plastic cup. "I need a drink." She leaned a hip against the desk. "This is like a soap opera."

"No. Just my life," Lexa joked from her spot on the bed, but neither Maddie nor Hsu-Ling laughed.

Hsu-Ling stood at the end of the bed. "What did Pong say?"

Lexa put down her cup on the night table and rubbed her face with both hands. "He told them that I'd come on to him. That I tried to get him to kiss me and that I rubbed my 'nubile' body all over him every time I hugged him." Lexa buried her face in her hands. "It was disgusting."

"You were fourteen years old!" The words burst out of Maddie like bullets spraying the room. She flung out a hand and directed her glare at Hsu-Ling. "She hadn't even kissed a boy. How could they possibly believe she'd do that to a grown man?"

Hsu-Ling held up her hands, as if to ward off Maddie. "Hey, I'm just as shocked as you are. There's no way Lexa did any of that. I was there."

"I feel gross just talking about it again." Lexa picked up her head and shivered, rubbing her hands over her upper arms. She looked at Hsu-Ling. "Your mother hates my guts. She wanted to get rid of me so bad, she would have done anything to turn Baba against me." Lexa's mouth turned down at the corners. "She succeeded. Baba and I never saw each other again."

"That's horrible!" Hsu-Ling's voice was hoarse, and her hands were clenched in fists. "No wonder she was so upset when Baba's will was read."

Lexa let out a short laugh. "She must have about died when she found out he left me the same amount he left you." She swung her legs over the side of the bed and sprang up so suddenly that Hsu-Ling took a step back in surprise. "I have to go home. I'm sorry. I wanted to take both of you out for dinner, but my head is killing me. I need to lie down. Maybe we can get together later tonight if I feel better?"

"Okay." Hsu-Ling blinked rapidly. "I'm sorry. Sorry for what my mother did to you."

"It's not your fault." Lexa reached out and touched her sister on the shoulder. "This is just so much for me to remember. All I wanted was for Baba to believe me, but he didn't. He chose your mother and Pong over me, and there was nothing I could do."

The two sisters looked at each other, and then Hsu-Ling reached out and pulled her into her arms. Lexa felt, rather than saw, Maddie get off the bed.

"I'll take you home," Maddie said.

Lexa pulled away from Hsu-Ling and gave Maddie a small nod. "Thanks." To Hsu-Ling, she said, "I'll call you later."

Lexa and Maddie walked out the door, but Hsu-Ling placed a hand on Lexa's arm, stopping her before she could close the door. "Baba did love you. He was so distraught after you left." They stared at each other, and then Lexa nodded and left with Maddie.

28

July, Twenty-Two Years Ago
Taichung, Taiwan

Jing Tao sat in the courtyard by himself, smoking a cigarette. He'd quit years earlier, when Hsu-Ling was a baby,
but Pong had left a pack behind. He lit up without thinking,
drawing in a lungful of smoke as if he'd never stopped. He
ran a hand through his hair, which he still kept long in the
front like it had been when he met Susan in Thailand.

He didn't know what to think. He loved his daughter, but
he couldn't ignore his wife's accusations. She was so adamant,
and she'd never lied to him about anything before, so why
would she start now? Maybe the truth lay somewhere between
Pin-Yen's version and Lexa's. Maybe Lexa had been jealous
that Hsu-Ling was his full-time daughter. But he couldn't
imagine Lexa mutilating the pictures of Hsu-Ling with the
kind of vicious strokes evident in the photos found in Lexa's
suitcase. If Lexa hadn't done that, then who had? It was pre-
posterous to think Pin-Yen had done it to frame Lexa, as
Susan had suggested. His wife would never do that.

Yet if Pong hadn't corroborated Pin-Yen's story, he didn't know if he'd have fully believed her. Chi was a well-behaved girl. Her mother and stepfather had raised her well. She was smart and had a good sense of humor. She was respectful to adults and her family, and he couldn't imagine that she would harm Hsu-Ling. He'd seen the way the two sisters had bonded, and it had warmed his heart. But Pong, his brother, the person closest to him, who knew him inside and out, had said Chi had come on to him. And that he'd seen Chi try to hurt Hsu-Ling.

Jing Tao might doubt Pin-Yen, but he trusted Pong with his whole heart. Pong, who'd never married and who'd said he didn't need a wife. (Jing Tao had often wondered if Pong was gay, but Pong always denied it.) "I have you and your family," Pong said. "That's enough for me. I'm too much of a bachelor to live with anyone. I'd rather enjoy your family and be able to go home where no one is nagging me and where my things stay in the same spot unless I move them."

Jing Tao rubbed a fist over his eye. Hsu-Ling was going to be so upset to find ChiChi gone when she got back from Ah-Ma's. He could already hear her wails and her questions. What was he going to tell her? Pin-Yen wanted to tell her the truth, but Jing Tao refused. He would not tell his ten-year-old daughter what they were accusing Chi of.

Inhaling deeply from the cigarette, he let the smoke fill his lungs. He couldn't get the image of Chi staring at him, willing him to believe her, to come to her defense, out of his mind. The last words he and his older daughter had exchanged echoed in his mind.

Let's try to work it out. I love you. Hsu-Ling loves you. Please don't go.

I can't stay, Baba. You don't believe me.

I do believe you. But Pong and Pin-Yen wouldn't lie. Maybe you were jealous but didn't mean any harm?

I'm not jealous of Hsu-Ling, and I didn't lie. I want to go home.

And he'd stood by, the tiniest little bit of doubt in his heart, as she'd packed her bags and Susan had hustled her out of his apartment and out of his life without a backward glance.

He dropped his cigarette to the floor and ground it out with his shoe. In the next breath, he slammed his fist into the red metal gate, over and over, ignoring the pain in his knuckles, until they bled and the bright red blood ran down his arm and spattered onto the concrete floor of the courtyard.

· · ·

Inside the apartment, Pin-Yen had seen Jing Tao grab the pack of cigarettes before slamming out the front door. She knew he'd probably sneak one, but she let him go. Let him have his little guilty pleasure. She'd gotten what she wanted.

He'd sat in stunned silence right after Lexa and her American mother had stormed out of the apartment, not even a half hour earlier. Pin-Yen hadn't said anything, knowing she needed to play the part of the supportive wife now. Instead, she'd rubbed his back and brought him a shot of scotch, which he'd tossed down before burying his face in his hands. She'd sat next to him for a few minutes, her physical presence a reminder that she was his wife and would always stand by his side. When at last he'd looked at her, she'd seen the resignation in his eyes.

Taking his face between her hands, she'd said in a gentle voice, "It's better to know now the true nature of that girl."

He'd nodded, his mouth turned downward, but hadn't replied.

"You'll see, it's for the best," Pin-Yen had cooed, stroking her husband's hair, loving the silky feel of it and proud that he still had a full head of black, black hair. "When you feel better, you'll see this was a blessing. You can take her out of your will, and the Chang money will stay in our family, where it belongs."

He hadn't replied, but she'd seen from the stoop of his shoulders that he knew she was right.

Now, with a small, satisfied smile, she turned to the room where Lexa had stayed. She would get rid of all evidence of Jing Tao's other daughter. Her plan had worked. She'd gotten rid of that girl.

Stripping the bed of the sheets and the quilted comforter that Ah-Ma had made when Hsu-Ling was born, Pin-Yen considered burning it but knew Hsu-Ling would be upset. She'd insisted her *jie jie* use her prized comforter for the summer. Pin-Yen's mouth twisted in displeasure when she caught a whiff of the fruity scent from the shampoo Lexa used. Pin-Yen couldn't wait to get everything in the wash and erase all traces of that girl. Her baby was the only daughter who counted in their family.

Her Hsu-Ling, the most perfect daughter. It had been Pin-Yen's fault that she'd been born with only one leg. Pin-Yen had worried herself to death, knowing something she'd done while she was pregnant had caused Hsu-Ling's amniotic band syndrome. Even though the doctor had told her it hadn't been her fault, she knew he was wrong. It had been her fault. She'd devoted her life to getting the best for her daughter.

And now, she'd made sure Hsu-Ling would inherit this building from her father, the eldest son of the Chang family. Since Jing Tao didn't have any sons, the building should rightfully go to the eldest son of the next brother in line. But Jing Tao's brother had two daughters, so Hsu-Ling would inherit.

Not Lexa, that bastard daughter, even though technically she was the eldest daughter.

She crumpled the bedding together and lugged it to the laundry machine in the enclosed porch at the back of the apartment. She stuffed it all in and loaded the soap. She'd hang up everything when it was done, on the lines crisscrossing the balcony. Like most Taiwanese families, they didn't own a dryer.

While she waited for the wash, she thought of what to tell Hsu-Ling. She knew her daughter was going to be upset that Lexa had disappeared without saying good-bye. She had no idea why Hsu-Ling had developed such an attachment to the girl, despite her best efforts to persuade her daughter that Lexa wasn't to be trusted. Hsu-Ling would sulk and pout, but she'd get over it and forget she ever had a sister. They were well rid of that girl. Pong had helped to make sure of that. Jing Tao may not have believed her, but she knew he'd never doubt Pong.

Good thing she had Pong wrapped around her finger, and had since they were teenagers. Allowing herself another smile, she went into the kitchen and pulled out a box of Tai Yang Bing, sun biscuits. The delicate, flaky pastries filled with condensed malt sugar were her favorite. She usually rationed them out because she didn't want to gain weight. But she deserved a treat for a job well done, for ensuring her daughter's legacy. She took a bite and closed her eyes, savoring the taste of victory on her tongue.

29

Mom's just getting out of her teacher training and said to order dinner for her." Lexa hung up with their mom as she and Maddie walked into Lexa's apartment.

Maddie scratched her neck and looked back at the front door. "Maybe I should go."

"Please stay." Lexa looked up from the drawer where she kept the takeout menus and gave Maddie a beseeching look.

"It'll just be awkward."

"I need you, Maddie. I need both you and Mom tonight. Can't you put your anger at her aside? For me?"

Maddie scowled but threw herself on the couch. "Fine. But only because you've had a shitty day and I feel bad for you." She patted the cushion, and Zeus jumped up next to her, turning in a circle until he sat half on Maddie and half on the couch. "Oof. You weigh a ton, Zeus."

"What do you want to order?"

Maddie looked up, an evil smile spreading over her face. "Indian. Lots and lots of Indian food." Their mom wasn't a fan of the smell of curry. Lexa rolled her eyes and picked up the Indian menu, as well as the one for her favorite sushi restaurant.

. . .

Susan wrinkled her nose as soon as she walked in. "You can smell the curry all the way from downstairs." She gave Lexa a hug and headed for a window, opening it to let in the hot summer air. "Hello, Madison. I'm assuming you're the one who ordered Indian to irk me."

Maddie smirked but didn't reply. Lexa massaged her temple with one hand.

"So what happened?" Susan asked as they opened the takeout containers from the Indian and sushi restaurants.

Lexa told her everything Hsu-Ling had told them while they ate. By the time she was done, tears were running down her cheeks, and she swiped an angry hand over them.

Susan rubbed her back. "You've kept all this inside all these years. It's time you let it out."

"I hadn't seen him in so long, and I'd accepted that he wasn't a part of my life. So when he died, I think I felt shame that I *wasn't* more upset, more than any real grief." She rubbed a hand over her eyes, knowing she was smudging her eye makeup. "But when Hsu-Ling told us how she'd run after him and found him in the road . . ."

She stopped and tried to swallow past the lump in her throat. The sushi she'd just eaten sat like a rock in her stomach. Maddie stood and grabbed a bottle of water from the fridge and handed it to her. Lexa gave her sister a grateful look and drank the cold water.

When she could speak again, she said, "I can't believe Pong lied because he was in love with Pin-Yen."

"I knew there was something going on." Susan shook her head. "I could see why Pin-Yen wanted you gone, but Pong? He was so nice and seemed to like you so much."

Lexa let out a sigh. "I wonder if Baba would have believed Pin-Yen if Pong hadn't backed her up. All this time wasted, because Pong was in love with her."

"It wasn't all on Pong though," Maddie said. "Hsu-Ling's mother was the one who made up all those lies, who planted the pictures. She's the one to blame."

Susan nodded. "I could kill her. She did all this to keep you out of the family. And yet, your father still left you half." She couldn't keep the satisfaction out of her voice. "God, I wish I could have seen her face when she heard about the will."

"Me too." Maddie grinned at their mom.

"Wait." They both looked up at Lexa when she spoke. "You're talking to Mom again."

Susan smiled slowly. "You are."

"Oops." Maddie closed her eyes. She took a big breath as if filling her body with air, and then held it for a moment before slowly exhaling out through her mouth.

"You're doing a yogic three-part breath," Susan said, surprise in her voice.

"Yes." Maddie continued to breathe.

"Where'd you learn yogic three-part breath?" Lexa asked. "You hate yoga."

Maddie opened her eyes. "I just started. I wanted to see what the hype was all about."

Lexa caught her mom's eyes and raised an eyebrow. Maddie had been very vocal in her derision of yoga when their mom told her she was getting her certification.

"That's great. I'm glad you're giving it a try," Susan said. "Do you like it?"

"It's not bad." Maddie closed her eyes again. And then she said, "Oh, and by the way, I think Mike and I are getting a divorce."

"Oh, Maddie." Lexa and her mom exchanged a glance.

"Hey." Susan gently shook Maddie on the shoulder until she opened her eyes. "This is a hard year for our family."

Maddie shrugged, a gesture that was meant to convey her usual "whatever," but Lexa could see the pain in her eyes.

"Are you sure?" Lexa reached out to brush one of Maddie's blond curls away from her cheek.

Maddie gave her a smile filled with sadness and resignation. "I don't know."

"How long have you been thinking about this?"

Before Maddie could answer their mom, a phone rang, and each of the three checked to see if it was hers.

It was their mom's. "It's Phoenix. Hold that thought."

While their mom talked to Phoenix, Lexa sat quietly at Maddie's side. They both heard their mom say, "I'll be right there."

She ended the call and looked at them. "I'm sorry, girls. I have to get Phoenix. She's stuck on a Metro-North train." She walked to where she'd dropped her purse and took out a hair elastic. "She took a train to Westchester for a client, and the train she's on hit someone. She's stuck at the Scarsdale station indefinitely. And she has to be back in the city for a client in about an hour."

Both Lexa and Maddie watched as their mom gathered her hair into a quick ponytail and then stood in front of them, awkwardly twisting her fingers together.

"I'm really sorry. I know this is the worst timing. For both of you." She stopped and stared at her daughters. "Maybe I should stay and tell Phoenix to call a cab. I'm being insensitive. What was I thinking? And, Lexa, what about the letter from Pong? What did it say?"

"Oh, no. I totally forgot about it." Lexa's mouth opened.

She couldn't believe she had forgotten to get the letter from Hsu-Ling. She'd been dying to read it, and yet they'd gotten sidetracked when they started talking.

"You don't have it?" Susan's forehead creased. "I thought that would have been the first thing you asked for as soon as you saw Hsu-Ling."

"It was, but we got distracted."

"Let me call Phoenix back. You girls need me more." Susan stopped and twisted her fingers again. "But she said there's a huge line for the taxi and she really needs to get back into the city . . ."

Lexa stood and went to their mom. "Mom, go. Don't worry."

Maddie turned to Lexa. "But . . ." Lexa could see the indecision in Maddie's eyes and knew she was battling between wanting their mom to stay and acting like she didn't need her.

Susan looked at them. "Are you sure? Just say the word and I'll tell Phoenix I can't come."

"We'll be fine. Maybe I'll go and get the letter from Hsu-Ling and then we can catch up once you get Phoenix."

Susan stood for another moment, her eyes darting between Lexa and Maddie. "Okay. Thanks." She flashed a last look of apology and was gone.

Lexa and Maddie both plopped onto the couch at the same time. Lexa bumped her shoulder against her sister's. "I guess this is the way things are going to be now. Mom's got someone new to worry about."

"Yeah." Maddie leaned into Lexa's shoulder, her hair falling forward to hide her face.

"Hey," Lexa said, reaching over to brush back Maddie's hair. "I'm here for you."

Maddie turned toward Lexa, her eyes shiny with unshed tears. "I'm here for you too."

. . .

A beam of sunlight across her face woke Lexa the next morning. She'd forgotten to pull the shades before they went to bed. She turned her head and saw only the top of Maddie's blond head peeking out of the comforter. She'd never understood how Maddie could sleep with her face covered.

Maddie had stayed with her the night before, and they'd talked long into the night. Lexa had really wanted to go back to Hsu-Ling's hotel and get Pong's letter, but in the end, she hadn't. She was too tired, and she honestly didn't think her system could take any more shock that day. Instead, she and Maddie had their first honest talk in a long time.

Maddie told her about her growing dislike for Mike. Everything he did drove her crazy. She wasn't sure if she even loved him anymore. No, he didn't cheat on her, and she didn't cheat either. She was too tired from taking care of the kids and their life to even think about an affair. She wanted something but didn't know what. She only knew she couldn't live with Mike anymore.

Lexa studied Maddie's face, thinking about Maddie's words from the night before. She flushed as she realized she'd been so wrapped up in her own problems, she hadn't seen that Maddie's marriage was in trouble. She'd just assumed Maddie was being her dramatic self when she complained about Mike. As if sensing Lexa's scrutiny, Maddie's eyes opened.

"Hey, sleepyhead. Good morning."

"What time is it?" Maddie struggled to sit up in Lexa's

queen-sized bed. She dragged Lexa's light blue down comforter up with her.

"It's seven." Lexa pushed back the comforter and got out of bed. "You want coffee, or do you want to go back to sleep?"

Maddie yawned without bothering to cover her mouth. "Coffee. I'm up already."

Lexa crossed to the tiny kitchen and prepped the coffeemaker. Once she had two cups, she brought one back to Maddie in bed.

"Mmm." Maddie took a sip and closed her eyes. "I can't remember the last time someone brought me coffee in bed."

Lexa settled herself on the couch next to the bed. "Mike doesn't do that for you?"

Maddie opened her eyes and glared at Lexa. "I don't want to talk about him."

"Fine. What do you want to talk about?"

"I can't believe Hsu-Ling's mother is the one who kept you away from Taiwan. Where's the Lexa I know, the Kung Fu warrior who'd fight anyone who gets in her way?"

Now it was Lexa's turn to glare at Maddie. "I don't want to talk about it." They'd talked the subject to death the night before.

"I just don't get why you didn't tell Dad and me."

Lexa clenched her jaw. She could still remember pleading with her mom on the plane ride back from Taiwan that summer not to tell Greg or Maddie. "I was embarrassed and ashamed. I felt so . . . gross. I didn't want Dad to think I could have possibly done any of that."

"Are you kidding me? Dad would have never believed that."

"I was fourteen. I was humiliated. I thought I was so grown-up, and then to have that happen . . ." Lexa looked at

Maddie. "Besides, you hated my Taiwanese family. I didn't want you to know that they hated me too."

"I didn't hate your Taiwanese family." Maddie's eyes were full of remorse. "I just hated that they took you away from me."

Lexa gave her a small smile. They drank their coffee in silence, until Maddie put her mug on the night table and reached for her phone. "Guess what Mom's up to these days?"

"What?"

"I was on Instagram yesterday. Guess who popped up?"

"No!" Lexa drew out the word. "Mom's on Instagram?"

"Yup. She's posted five photos so far and has over two hundred followers already." Maddie clicked on the Instagram icon on her phone. "They're all yoga poses."

She held out her phone, and Lexa grabbed it from her.

"She looks good." Lexa stared at a photo of their mom in reverse warrior pose. She was wearing formfitting yoga clothes in a pretty shade of purple and looked relaxed and happy.

"But she's not wearing a bra!" Maddie said, taking the phone out of Lexa's hands. "You can see her nipples! She's over sixty. She should not be posting half-naked pictures of herself on social media."

"She's not half-naked, you prude." Lexa snatched the phone back to take a closer look. "She's wearing a yoga top with a built-in bra."

"Whatever." Maddie took her phone back again and studied the picture.

"So did you follow her?" Lexa asked. She hadn't been very active on Instagram lately, so she had missed that their mom had gotten an account.

"Maybe."

"You did, didn't you? Why can't you just admit you miss Mom? Don't you want her to be happy?"

"You're not dealing any better with Mom's new life."

"Yeah, but at least I'm making an effort. I met Phoenix, and I'm talking to her." Lexa took a sip of her coffee and let the flavor linger in her mouth. "Tell me why you're so mad at Mom."

"Because I always thought Mom and Dad had such a great relationship. They liked each other. They were friends. I wanted Mike and me to have what they had." Maddie picked at her fingernails as she talked, an old habit she hadn't quite kicked. "They were equal partners. They both worked. They both looked after us. They took turns cooking dinner and doing laundry."

"I didn't know they were having problems either."

"I was going to tell you and Mom about Mike that day when she asked if we could all meet for lunch. That's why I suggested my place. I thought it was the perfect time to ask for her advice, since it had been a while since the three of us got together. You canceled our dim sum the month before." Maddie shot Lexa a look full of accusation.

"Oh." Lexa thought back and remembered that a client had asked for an emergency session because she had to face an ex that night at a wedding. At the time, it had seemed important. But now, looking back, Lexa wondered why she'd let a client's desire to look good win out over her own family.

"Anyways, Mom told me her news before I could tell her about Mike."

"Ouch." Lexa's face screwed up in sympathy. "No wonder you were so upset."

"When she said she was leaving Dad, something just snapped. All this time, I thought they had such a great relationship. It was what was giving me hope that maybe Mike and

I could get past this." Maddie hunched her shoulder. "I couldn't take it. If they broke up, then what chance do Mike and I have?"

"I'm sorry. I've been so involved in my own life that I didn't know you were unhappy."

"It's okay." Maddie picked up her coffee mug again and wrapped her hands around it, as if trying to warm them. "You had good reason."

"Are things really that bad?"

"I don't know. All I know is that I've been so mean to him lately, but I can't seem to stop. Everything he does is wrong. Everything he says irritates the hell out of me. He's miserable, I'm miserable, and if we keep this up, the kids are going to be miserable too."

Lexa looked at Maddie. She didn't have any advice for her sister. She'd never been married. Their mom was the one who'd know what to say. But she wasn't here.

"I wish Mom was here." Maddie voiced Lexa's thought.

"Are you mad she didn't come back last night?"

Maddie's sigh was resigned. "Yes. She'd rather go to a fund-raiser for abused women with Phoenix than be with her daughters, who need her."

"It's not like that. She was going to come back. She just forgot they had tickets already." Even to her own ears, the excuse sounded lame to Lexa. "Besides, I told her I wasn't going to get the letter from Hsu-Ling until today."

"But what about me?" Maddie turned her blue eyes on Lexa.

Lexa crawled back into the bed with Maddie. She put an arm around her sister, and Maddie laid her head on Lexa's shoulder. "I know, Mads. But she's always put us first her whole life. Maybe it's her turn to be first."

Maddie's voice was small. "I wish she hadn't decided to get a life right when I need her."

"Yeah. Her timing sucks."

Maddie was quiet for a moment. Then she turned her head to look at Lexa. "You always came first with her. Ever since you got back from Taiwan that summer. I was so jealous."

"Oh, Maddie." Lexa wanted to protest, but she knew Maddie was right. She'd made her mom pinky swear on that plane ride back from Taiwan to keep her secret from Greg and Maddie. Now she wondered if it had been unfair of her to make her mom choose between Lexa and the rest of the family.

30

Hsu-Ling handed a sealed white legal-sized envelope to Lexa, who stood just inside Hsu-Ling's hotel room. Lexa had stopped by to get the letter after saying good-bye to Maddie. She'd canceled her Wednesday morning clients the night before after her mom had left to get Phoenix, knowing she needed to spend time with her sister. She never canceled last minute on her clients and had felt guilty doing so. But after Christy's near-accident the previous morning (had that only been the day before? It felt like so long ago, after everything that had happened in the past twenty-four hours), she knew it was better to take the personal time off.

"Open it," Hsu-Ling said. "I want to know what it says."

Lexa grimaced and took the letter from her. "For some reason, I'm scared."

"It can't be that bad."

Lexa slipped a finger under the flap and opened the letter. Taking a deep breath, she unfolded it and looked at it. It was written in English and dated almost two years earlier.

Dear ChiChi,

If you're reading this, then I'm gone. Most likely from the lung cancer that I just found out I have. Hsu-Ling was right, smoking is bad for me. I should be afraid of dying, but I'm not. I feel as if it's what I deserve. Chinese karma?

First of all, I need you to know how sorry I am for what I did to you. I know you won't believe me, but I never meant to hurt you. I was so in love with Pin-Yen back then, drunk on her, even as I was so miserable and hated myself that I was in love with my best friend's wife. But you were an innocent child, you trusted me, and I broke that trust when I lied for Pin-Yen. And even more, I broke the bond between you and your father, and for that I am so sorry. There are not enough apologies in the world to make it right to you.

I tried so many times to tell Jing Tao the truth. When I saw how much he suffered over the years after you left, I wanted so badly to tell him I lied for Pin-Yen. A few times, I even started telling him about how Pin-Yen asked me to lie for her. But I never did. I'm a coward. He's the only family I have. I was an orphan and grew up in orphanages and foster homes. I met Jing Tao when we were ten. He rescued me from a gang of older kids who were beating me up. He was almost as big as them, and he wasn't afraid. He's the only person who's ever stood up for me. Ever since then, he's been the brother I'd wanted all my life. I couldn't imagine telling him that I was in love with his wife and lied for her, driving you away. I couldn't lose his trust and his love.

I'm not telling you this to make you feel sorry for me. I just want you to understand, even a little bit. ChiChi, he loves you. You have no idea how happy he was when he found out he'd fathered you. I think he loved you from the minute he saw your picture. He's so proud of you, his American daughter, and had such big plans for you. His only fault is that he chose to believe his wife because I backed her up. I know if I had told him Pin-Yen was lying, he'd never have believed her.

The doctor says the cancer is advanced. We may be able to beat it, or we may not. I may have six months left, or a few years. It doesn't matter to me. I'm ready to go. But before I go, I have to try to make things right between you and your father.

I may not have known you for long, but I know you would never take money from me, not after the lies I told about you. But I think you may take it to save your father. His family fell into financial difficulties about ten years ago. You know his whole family lives in that building. When his father died, Jing Tao thought he'd inherit the building, as the eldest son. But he soon found out that his father, your ah-gong, was living in debt. He was borrowing against the building in order to keep the façade of their lives. Jing Tao was shocked. The bank owned the building, and unless he could come up with the debt plus interest, the bank was going to take back the building, and three families plus their widowed mother would be homeless.

That's when I stepped in. I started buying buildings when I was young, investing in them and turning them into apartments or shopping centers. I saved the money I made from the ice-cream shop, and since I don't have a family, I took risks and bought buildings no one else would have. They paid off, and I ended up making a lot of money. I bought the Changs' building, allowing the entire family to continue living there. I only charged Jing Tao a pittance in rent and told him I'd leave the building to him if I should die first. Jing Tao decided not to tell his siblings and the rest of the family that his father had lost the building. Even his mother doesn't know. I was the only one he told.

When I found out I had cancer, I changed the will slightly. Jing Tao will still get the building, but only if you accept my gift of some money and a brand-new apartment in one of the buildings I recently acquired. I'm hoping you will use the money and apartment to come back to Taiwan and get to know your father again. It's my fault you've been apart all these years. This is the only way I know of to make sure you come back to Taiwan. If you don't accept my gift and come back by my final prayer ceremony, then the building will be sold after my death, and your father and his whole family will lose their home.

I'm sorry if this seems harsh to you, but I had to make sure you'd return once I was gone. Please see this as my last effort to make things right by you, a way to help you come back to Taiwan, to your heritage, and to know the father who grieves for you every day.

Like I said, I am a coward. I saw Pin-Yen for who she really is years ago, a manipulative woman who enjoyed having me at her beck and call, and held it over me that I was in love with my best friend's wife. I should have told Jing Tao, but I couldn't face him. His respect means everything to me, and I couldn't lose face in front of him and admit I'd lied and accused his innocent daughter, all because I was in love with his wife. I will never forget the look of anguish on his face that last day when your mother came and took you away. I will go to my grave knowing I

was the one responsible for his pain. I hope in my death, I
can help the two of you become father and daughter again.
   With my deepest apologies,
   Pong

Lexa looked up from the letter, and the room spun. She
was filled with so many emotions, she couldn't even begin to
articulate them. There was anger, along with shock and disbelief that he had had the audacity to place her in the position to decide the financial ruin of her estranged Taiwanese
family.

Hsu-Ling stared at her, her eyes filled with questions.
Without a word, Lexa handed the letter to her sister. Her ears
rang, and a strange chill went down her back, causing her to
shiver. She watched Hsu-Ling's face as she read the letter
change from polite interest to affection, and finally to confusion and horror when her mouth opened and her brows knit-
ted together.

Pong's words echoed in Lexa's head as Hsu-Ling looked
up and caught her eyes. They stared at each other, the full
meaning of Pong's letter sinking in.

Coward . . . ChiChi, he loves you . . . so proud of you . . .
come back to Taiwan . . . if you don't accept . . . building will be
sold . . . lose their home . . . look of anguish on his face that last
day . . . coward, coward, coward.

31

You can show yourself out." With a nod, Mrs. Lockwood dismissed Lexa and disappeared into her bedroom. Lexa was left standing alone in the lavish bathroom, complete with gold fixtures and a crystal chandelier hanging from the high ceiling. Mrs. Lockwood liked to work out here instead of their fully equipped gym whenever she was in a bad mood.

Lexa let out a breath of relief and rolled her shoulders to release some of the tension that had accumulated after training her most difficult client a few hours after reading Pong's words. It was like pulling teeth trying to get Mrs. Lockwood to do anything.

Lexa had gone home after getting the letter from Hsu-Ling and curled up on her couch with Zeus nestled at her side, stunned into immobility for two hours. She kept glancing at her phone, waiting for Mrs. Lockwood's personal assistant, Olivia, to text, canceling Mrs. Lockwood's noon appointment. Lexa hadn't canceled it herself because eight times out of ten, Mrs. Lockwood canceled at the last minute but still paid her as per her twenty-four-hour cancellation agreement. But wouldn't you know it, the one day Lexa needed her to cancel, she hadn't.

So Lexa had dragged herself off the couch and gritted her

teeth through the appointment, wondering all the while why she kept difficult clients like this, ones who drained her so completely in each session. But then she thought of the money Mrs. Lockwood paid her even when she canceled, and she knew she couldn't afford to give her up as a client.

Unless you accept Pong's conditions and take the money he left you.

The thought came unbidden into Lexa's mind as she went toward the connecting dressing room to let herself into the hall from that door. She halted.

Could she take the money from Pong? Deep in thought, she walked into the dressing room, forgetting about the extra moving racks of evening gowns one of the maids had wheeled in during their session, until an Oscar de la Renta smacked her in the face. Swatting the black dress aside, she tripped over the leg of the rack, falling face first into a sea of designer clothing. Grabbing at a Valentino (or maybe it was a Christian Dior), she tried to right herself without impaling her leg on an over-turned red-soled Louboutin heel. But her arms flailed, and she found herself in a heap on the floor with a piece of lace ripped off a gown in her hand. Sweating profusely from the attack of the designer labels, she tried desperately to get off the floor while looking toward the door to Mrs. Lockwood's bedroom. She was relieved to see it was still closed, and Mrs. Lockwood hadn't seen the assault on her beloved clothing.

She finally managed to get to her feet and eyed the clothing rack as if it was her enemy. Instinct took over, and she did a series of kicks and swipes, spinning around to defend herself. She dropped into the final stance and heard clapping behind her.

Whirling around, she found Olivia standing at the door leading to the hallway. "That was beautiful," she said.

Lexa patted the clothing on the rack, trying to hide the piece of lace in her hand. She bowed to the clothes as she backed away slowly toward Olivia. "Sorry," Lexa mumbled. "But Mrs. Lockwood's dresses attacked me."

Olivia laughed. "Don't worry, I won't tell her." Olivia winked at Lexa as they went out into the hall. Lexa jabbed at the elevator button, willing it to hurry up and whisk her away.

Fleeing from the Lockwoods' lavish Fifth Avenue apartment filled with important French period furniture, Lexa felt like a little kid who had escaped from a disapproving parent. She dropped the piece of lace into a garbage can and pulled out her cell phone. She knew her mom was at her teacher training, so she called Greg, since they'd yet to discuss what had happened in Taiwan. And now, with finding out what Pong had done, she really needed a parent's advice.

"Dad. Can I come over?" She knew he was working from home that day.

Greg must have heard the urgency in her voice, because he didn't question her. "Of course. Did you eat yet? I'll make us lunch."

"Thanks, Dad."

She put her phone back in her purse and picked up her pace, deciding to walk the thirty or so blocks plus five avenues to Greg's apartment. She needed to work off this nervous energy, which was threatening to bubble out of her. As she walked, she thought of actually accepting Pong's money.

The whole purpose of his gesture was to make her go back to Taiwan and reconcile with her father. Her father was dead. If she went back there, she'd have to see Hsu-Ling's mother.

She stopped dead in the middle of the sidewalk, causing the man who was walking behind her to slam into her.

"Watch it." The man gave her an irritated look before stepping around her. But Lexa didn't hear.

Could she face Pin-Yen again just to save her Taiwanese family? And more importantly, what was Pin-Yen going to do when she found out what Pong had done?

32

Wow, your apartment is so clean." Lexa looked around her dad's place and couldn't believe her eyes. He wasn't the neatest person. He usually left clothes in piles all over the floor and let the dishes pile up in the sink until her mom yelled. But now, his studio was spotless.

"I finally put everything away."

Lexa sniffed the air. "It smells good too, like lemon cleaner. What happened?"

"Really? I'm that big of a slob that you're surprised when my apartment smells good?"

She grinned at him but didn't answer. Walking into his kitchen, she opened the small refrigerator and poured herself a glass of sparkling water. She was sweaty and thirsty from the long walk.

Greg swatted Lexa on the shoulder when she walked by him toward his dining table. "I made turkey pita pockets with hummus and sprouts."

"Did you put cucumbers in there?" Lexa lifted one end of a pocket to peek in. She and her dad had invented this sandwich one afternoon when she was sick and stayed home from school. They'd tried to stuff as much as they could into a pita pocket.

"What do you think?"

"Thanks." She reached out, meaning to give him a quick hug, but she ended up wrapping her arms around his neck and squeezing tight for more than a moment.

"Are you finally going to tell me what happened?"

"Let's talk while we eat." She walked to the couch to drop her purse and was making her way back to the dining table when something on the coffee table caught her eye. It was a silver necklace in the shape of a lotus flower. It looked familiar, but she couldn't place where she'd seen it before. Her dad's eyes followed her gaze.

Lexa cocked her head in her dad's direction. "Did you have a woman over?"

His face reddened, and he looked away. "Um."

"Dad, it's fine," she said, sitting at the table and picking up her sandwich. "I'm glad you're going out. Anyone special?"

"Maybe." He shrugged and sat across from her.

She took a bite and waited, but he didn't explain. "You're not going to tell me?"

He shrugged again and scratched his arm. "There's nothing to tell. I want to know what's going on with you."

"Well, you know Hsu-Ling's mom accused me of being jealous of Hsu-Ling and trying to hurt her. And that Pong said I'd come on to him." She looked down, unable to meet his eyes.

"I wanted to throttle them when I heard. That woman. How could she make up lies like that? And Pong!" Greg stood up and paced in front of Lexa. "I could kill him."

"Dad, he's already dead."

He stopped pacing, and they looked at each other. For some reason, Lexa got the urge to laugh. This wasn't funny; keeping this secret from him all these years wasn't funny, but she couldn't stop the giggle that escaped as she dropped her sandwich back on the plate.

"You think this is funny?" He stared at her, his eyes practically bulging out of his head. "Your father's friend accused you of coming on to him. You! At fourteen! And his wife basically drove you away!"

"No, I'm sorry," she said, trying hard to stop. "It's just that I cried so much already. Laughing is better."

His face stony, he waited until her hysterical laughter had died down. Then he sat across from her at the small round table. "I wish I'd been there. I would have set that woman straight. No one accuses my daughter of something she didn't do and gets away with it." His eyes gleamed with anger, and the last bubble of laughter faded from Lexa.

She reached across the table and grabbed his hand. "Thanks, Dad."

"I can't believe your father didn't stick up for you. I know he didn't know you like I do, but still. He's your father. He let that woman drive you away." He shook his head and clamped his lips together.

Lexa let go of his hand and picked up her sandwich again. She took a bite and used the time it took her to chew to gather her thoughts. When she'd swallowed, she said, "There's more. Do you want to hear it?"

"Of course."

So while her dad ate his sandwich, she told him about Pong's letter. And watched as he almost choked when she told him the fate of her Taiwanese family's home now rested on her.

"He what?" Her dad picked up his water and took a big sip. "He made it your responsibility? If that man wasn't already dead, I'd kill him."

Lexa sat back and looked at her dad, her throat clogging

up. This man believed in her, in a way her birth father hadn't. She knew without a doubt if it had been him, Greg would have backed her up no matter what.

"I love you, Dad," she said quietly.

He looked up, and his face softened when he looked at her. "I love you too. That's never going to change. I will always believe you."

"I know. You brought me up. He didn't. My father barely knew me." She bit her lip. "And now he never will."

Greg didn't answer, instead giving a grunt before focusing back on his lunch. They finished eating in silence. Then Greg got up and walked to his desk. He opened the top drawer and pulled something out and came back to the table. He placed two small objects in front of her, and Lexa looked at him in surprise.

"You still have these?" she asked. "I thought we threw them away." She picked up one of the small round jade bracelets and ran her fingers over the smooth surface.

It was the jade bracelet her father had bought her the first time she met him, when she was eight. The other was the one he'd gotten her that last summer when she was fourteen, to replace the first one, which had gotten too small.

"I picked them out of the garbage after you went to bed that day."

Lexa held up the bigger of the two bracelets. "You helped me get this one off my wrist the day I came home from Taiwan." Lexa gave a wry smile as she remembered how frantic she was to remove the piece of jade from her wrist. It had been weighing her down, as much as her father's betrayal had weighed down her heart.

"You couldn't get it off. I had to use soap and water to slide it off." Greg sat back down in his seat. "And you wouldn't tell me what happened. Even when I asked if your father had done something to you, hit you or worse."

"He didn't."

"Not physically. But he broke your heart."

Lexa played with the bracelets in her hands, listening to the delicate clink when they hit against each other. "Why did you keep these for me?"

"Because I knew you'd want them again one day. Maybe not right away, but I thought one day you'd reconcile and you'd regret throwing them away." Greg looked down at his hands and clasped them together on the table. "And there was a part of me, deep, deep down, that was secretly glad you hadn't come back with stars in your eyes like you did every time you saw your father."

"You were jealous?"

Greg gave a small nod. "I knew it was petty, and I knew it was wrong. So I saved these jade pieces for you in case you'd ever want them back. Your father did love you in his own way, no matter what happened."

He cleared his throat, and she looked up. She stood and went around the table to stand behind him and wrapped her arms around him.

"It wasn't petty, and it wasn't wrong. You're human. Thanks for saving them. You're right, I'm glad to have them now." And she hugged her dad tight, even as she clasped the symbol of her birth father's love in her hands.

33

*

"What time is it?" Lexa let out a loud yawn and covered her mouth, too late. Her body tingled, and her toes brushed against Jake's leg, sending a thrill down her spine.

"It's almost eleven," Jake said.

"I have to go." She sat up in the hotel bed, where Jake had just made love to her. She stretched her arms over her head, luxuriating in the smooth white sheets, and let out a long sigh. "I have to let Zeus out."

Jake pulled a gray T-shirt over his head. Lexa watched with regret as his torso disappeared. He was still in town for work, and he'd called after she got home from her dad's that afternoon. When she said she had plans for dinner with Hsu-Ling, he'd offered to take them both out. They'd gone to Anassa Taverna at Sixtieth and Third Avenue, and Lexa had been relieved that Hsu-Ling and Jake had gotten along so well. Both she and Hsu-Ling had needed a night out to not think about Pong's letter or the state of their family.

"Thanks for taking Hsu-Ling out too," Lexa said.

He smiled over his shoulder. "It was nice to meet her. Although I thought she was going to deck me when I said she was hip and cool."

Lexa laughed. Hsu-Ling had thought Jake was talking about her hips and had gotten offended.

"If you have to leave, I'm coming with you. You're not walking home by yourself."

"It's fine." Lexa found her clothes and got dressed. "I walk around by myself at night all the time."

He gave her a look. "What's that supposed to mean?"

She laughed. "It means I'm a New Yorker. This is my neighborhood. And I know how to take care of myself." She got into horse stance, her legs bent in a squat with her elbows close to her side and her hands fisted and turned up.

"Lexa." She turned at the serious note in his voice. "I had a great time with you tonight," he said. "But what's wrong?"

"What do you mean?"

"You seemed so, I don't know, angry when I first saw you. I couldn't tell if it was directed at me or not."

"I'm sorry. I'm not angry at you," she said. "Not at all." She relaxed her stance and walked over to him. "Something happened earlier today."

He pulled her in, giving her a gentle kiss on the lips. "Want to tell me about it?"

"I don't think you really want to hear this," she said. "I wasn't going to say anything. I didn't want to ruin our night."

"Nothing can ruin this night."

So she told him what Hsu-Ling had told her about her father and Pong's death, and about the letter Pong had left her.

"I have to go back for his final prayer ceremony." She sat on the edge of the bed and leaned forward, her hair hiding her face.

"What's the final prayer ceremony?"

"It takes place a hundred days after someone's death. It's kind of the first big ceremony following the death. Hsu-Ling said a nun comes to the house and chants blessings and prayers, and the family gathers to remember the dead."

"So if you don't go back to Taiwan by then and claim his inheritance, your family will lose their home?"

She nodded. She could see by the way Jake's eyes narrowed and his mouth parted slightly that he was appalled. "That's blackmail."

She blew out a breath. "I know." It helped that he was just as taken aback by Pong's letter as she was. "But the funny part is, he had no idea our father was going to die before him. I'm not sure what happens to the building now that my father isn't alive to inherit it."

Hsu-Ling had thought it would come to both of them, but she had to check with the lawyer. She hadn't known about the debt and that Pong had actually owned the building and not her family. It was a big mess.

Jake sat down next to her and put an arm around her. She leaned into him, drawing warmth from his body. With all the old memories and buried emotions surfacing in the past couple of weeks, and now with this bombshell Pong had dropped, she suddenly longed to tell Jake everything. She wanted him to know her, know what she was feeling. But she didn't normally let down her guard like this around men, and she pinched herself on the arm instead, so hard it hurt. *Careful, Lexa. You've only known the man for a few weeks.*

"What are you going to do?" Jake asked.

"I don't know," she said. "My first instinct is to say screw it and not accept it. But there are other people involved, my Taiwanese family. I guess I'll wait to see what the lawyer says first. Then we'll see."

"That's an awful position to be put in."

"I know. And he acknowledged that in the letter. But he

said it was the only way he knew of to make sure I'd go back to Taiwan and make up with my father." She let out a hard laugh.

Jake reached out and took her hand in his. "Why haven't you gone back to Taiwan in all this time?"

Lexa sighed. "It's a long story. I'll tell you another time." She ducked her head, embarrassed that she'd just assumed there would be another time with Jake. "I've missed Taiwan. I loved it so much when I was young. But I have to think of my clients. I can't just take off and leave them hanging. They need me."

He rubbed her back, slow circles one way, before he switched and did circles the other way. "Your clients will survive without you."

"Yeah." She knew he was right. She was using her job as an excuse.

She closed her eyes when his mouth settled on hers again. She sighed against him, loving the way his lips felt and the way his tongue touched hers, claiming her mouth in a way that made her want to stay melded to him forever.

"I think I'm falling in love with you, my Kung Fu girl," Jake whispered against her lips.

Lexa froze. Her eyes opened, and she stared into Jake's kind eyes, her thoughts in a jumble. And instead of telling him she was falling for him too, a strangled laugh came out of her.

He continued to gaze at her, and, uncomfortable, Lexa pulled away and stood. And as she always had in the past when faced with emotions she didn't know how to deal with, she fell back on her Kung Fu training. She sailed through a Kung Fu form for him, her body remembering the familiar movements she'd done a million times before.

Jake clapped when she was done. "Tell me about your Kung Fu training."

Lexa looked at him and knew he was giving her a way out of answering his proclamation of love. Grateful for the reprieve, she said, "I started going when I was fourteen. Something . . . happened that summer, and Kung Fu was my way to forget about it. I could focus on the physical training, pushing my body hard, kicking faster, higher, working on my stretching and not having to think."

She stared off into space, Shifu's commands echoing in her mind. *Chest up, Lexa. Go harder, more chi, faster!*

The first time he'd said "chi," she'd looked up, startled. She thought he'd been calling her by her Taiwanese nickname. But she soon realized he meant the word energy. He'd singled her out, and when he learned Chi was her nickname, he had taken to calling her that when he was pleased with her, and Lexa when he wasn't happy with her. She'd thrived under Shifu's teaching, gaining back her confidence and healing her heart.

Jake touched her on the arm, bringing her back to the hotel room. She turned to look at him. "Shifu believed in me. He was always telling me to believe in myself, trust myself. Train harder and be honest with myself." She smiled, her eyes gazing off into space, remembering his words. "I was so proud when he asked me to move to the adult classes when I was sixteen. I got to wear the blue uniforms that the adults wore. And I was finally able to get past what happened . . ." She trailed off.

"What happened, Lexa?" Jake's voice was so gentle it almost brought tears to her eyes. Instead of answering, she leaned over and kissed him, pressing her lips firmly to his, as if she could keep the answers inside only by stopping her mouth from talking.

And when he kissed her back with as much passion, she longed to tell him that she was falling in love with him too, and that she was going to miss him so much when he flew home to San Francisco the next day. But she said nothing.

34

The next day, images from her night with Jake flitted through her mind as she trained Andi. She berated herself for acting like an idiot. He'd told her he was falling in love with her, and she hadn't been able to answer. What was wrong with her that she couldn't let go and tell him how she felt? Why did the thought of falling in love with Jake terrify her so much?

"Okay. Stop moping and tell me what's wrong." Lexa was jolted back to the gym by Andi's command. She focused her eyes on Andi, who had stopped doing standing rows with twelve-pound weights to stare at her.

"You mean besides that my whole life has turned upside down?" Lexa tried for a flip tone, but it didn't quite work.

"Yeah. It's Jake, isn't it?"

Lexa picked up her cell phone and stopped the stopwatch she was timing Andi with. "I don't want to talk about it. Tell me about you. Anything new?"

"I had a date last night. It did not go well."

"Another one?" Lexa arched her eyebrows, about to say something snide. But then she remembered her remorse at snapping at her clients lately and vowed to rein in her snark. "Let's do a four-minute tabata round, and then you can tell me about it."

Andi frowned. "No tabata! Who invented this twenty-second-on, ten-second-off bullshit?"

Lexa smiled but started the timer and gestured for Andi to start with mountain climbers. For all her complaining, Andi worked hard and was able to finish the round without too much effort. Lexa handed her a water bottle. "Okay, tell me about your date."

"The guy seemed great. He looked like his picture, said he wants to get married and have kids." Andi sat on a bench to take a gulp of water. "We met for drinks on the Upper West Side. You won't believe what he said to me."

"What?"

"He took my hand and was like, 'I think we have good chemistry. But before this goes any further, I have to ask you a question.'"

Lexa smiled. "What, he wanted to know about your pot-smoking ex-boyfriends?"

"No." Andi scowled. "He asked, 'Are you willing to convert to Judaism?'"

"What?"

"Exactly! All I could think was, 'Huh?'"

"What did you say?"

"I stammered something incoherent." Andi screwed the cap back on her water bottle. "He told me he wants to raise his children in the Jewish faith, and the mother has to be Jewish or willing to convert. Since he's forty already, he didn't want to waste time getting to know someone for months only to find out she won't convert."

"But that's great he knows what he wants. I think that's smart."

"Then you date him."

"Maybe I will." Lexa lifted her eyebrows at Andi. "What's his profile name?"

Andi looked incredulous. "Are you kidding me? No. You're not going out with him. I have nothing against the Jewish religion. I'd totally convert if I were in love with the guy. But I don't know him!"

Lexa burst out in laughter at Andi's reaction. "What did you say to him?"

"I said no." Andi stood up with her hands on her waist, her workout forgotten. "So he says, 'Thank you for being so honest. I really had hopes for us. I think we would have made beautiful babies.'"

"OMG." Lexa collapsed to the ground, holding her sides.

Andi wasn't done. "Who says that?" She grabbed a mat and slammed it on the floor. "And then you know what he did? He left some money and walked out, leaving me sitting there with my mouth open. He dumped me on the first date!"

"Oh, no. What did you do?"

"I sat there like an idiot. I asked the waiter for the check, and you know what *he* said? He asked if the gentleman was in the restroom."

"And?"

"I had to tell him the gentleman was not in the restroom. In fact, the gentleman had left the premises. And instead of just getting me the check like a nice waiter would do, he leaned down and whispered to me, 'A lover's spat? Don't worry, the makeup sex is always the best.' And then he winked at me. He. Winked. At. Me." She said the last with so much derision Lexa couldn't help laughing again.

"I don't even want to know what you said to him."

"I told him the truth. And he blinked and said, 'Honey,

I've never heard that one before!' And he sashayed off to get my bill and to tell the rest of the staff about the poor dear seated outside who just got dumped because she wouldn't convert."

"Andi, stop," Lexa said between fits of laughter. "You're killing me."

Andi finally got down on the mat and did a set of push-ups. "I'm about ready to give up on this online dating thing. It's so much work, and I get more dick pics than I do actual nice guys who want to date a nice, semi-normal, successful woman."

"I'm surprised guys aren't lining up to date you. You look great."

"I wish." Andi grimaced. "I always feel like a side of meat on display when I'm out at bars, waiting for someone to look me over and decide if I'm worthy. Or else they recognize me from TV and only want to go out with me because they think I can help them with their acting careers. I cook. I don't act." Andi flipped over on the mat. "Enough about me. How are you?"

"Okay. Taking it one day at a time."

She was about to elaborate when she looked up and saw Kiley walking toward them. Lexa was meeting with Kiley after Andi's session, but she was ten minutes early. Kiley looked nervous, and Lexa noticed she wasn't wearing her workout clothes. She was dressed in a sleeveless black sheath that hugged her body, with a pair of snakeskin high-heeled sandals. Her hair was down and blown out to float around her face. She threw her arms around Lexa. Lexa met Andi's eyes over Kiley's head, and Andi sat up on the mat.

Lexa pulled away after a moment and saw tears in Kiley's eyes.

"What's the matter?"

Kiley released a breath and said, "I came to say good-bye. I'm leaving."

"Where're you going?"

"I decided I didn't care if John has no money. I love him so much. He's moving to San Francisco because a gallery there has agreed to show his work, and I'm going with him." She suddenly seemed to notice Andi for the first time. "I'm sorry, Andi. I'm cutting into your time." She hiccupped the last word.

Andi stood and waved a hand. "It's okay. We're basically done. You look like you need Lexa more than me."

"You don't even know me, and you're so nice." And at that, Kiley burst into tears. Elise, who was walking by at the moment, took in the scene and beckoned to Lexa to take Kiley into her office. Andi gave Lexa a hug and said, "I'll catch you later."

"I'm sorry. I keep cutting your sessions short." Lexa returned the hug.

"Trust me, you gave me my money's worth already." Andi gave her a mock glare and then left Lexa alone in Elise's office with Kiley.

Lexa turned to Kiley, who was now sobbing into a tissue. "I'm proud of you. Money isn't everything."

"I know," Kiley wailed. "But I'm sad to be leaving New York. And giving up my dream of marrying a rich husband." She turned terrified eyes at Lexa. "What if he can't support us with his art? How are we going to have a family?"

"Well, I'm sure you'll find a job out there. Restaurants always need waitresses and bartenders." Kiley had been working in a restaurant around the corner from the gym.

Kiley sniffed, and Lexa handed her tissues. After blowing her nose loudly, Kiley looked up. "I know. I'm not afraid of work. I was going to break up with him, but when I pictured my life without him, I just couldn't bear it. I'd rather have him be in my life and not be rich than not have him in my life."

"That's good, Kiley." Lexa looked at her with new respect. If she'd had to bet, she would have thought Kiley would break up with John. If Kiley could stand up to her fears of being poor, then maybe Lexa could face her own fears and go back to Taiwan and confront Pin-Yen. And maybe she could allow herself to fall in love with Jake.

Kiley's eyes filled again. "I'm going to miss you. You've done so much for me this year. You've listened to me and helped me out so many times when I didn't understand things."

Lexa nodded absently and handed Kiley more tissues, her mind on her own problems. Was she really thinking of accepting Pong's conditions and going back and confronting Pin-Yen?

Kiley dabbed her eyes. "We're leaving in a few days. That's why I can't work out today. I have to pack. I'm going to find a trainer when I get to California, but I know I won't find anyone like you who'll listen to me the way you do."

Lexa patted Kiley's back, still distracted by the thought of actually returning to Taiwan. And what about Jake? Could they possibly make things work, given how different their views on children were? "That's good."

Kiley looked at her with curiosity. "Are you okay? You seem . . . out of sorts. Is something wrong?"

Before she could answer, Elise's office door opened, and a male voice said, "Hi, El. Ready to go to lunch?"

Lexa looked up, and her eyes widened. Greg stood in the doorway. His mouth opened as he registered that Lexa was in Elise's office with Kiley. They stared at each other, and no one spoke until Kiley asked, "Who're you?"

Lexa found her voice. "Kiley, this is my dad." She turned to him. "What are you doing here? I can't go to lunch. I have a client." She glanced back at Kiley. "Or I did." Then she turned to Greg again. "When have you ever called me 'L'? And how did you know I was in Elise's office?"

He turned bright red and backed out of the office. "Sorry, I'll catch you later." He slammed the door shut.

Lexa's brows furrowed, and she looked at the closed door. What had all that been about?

Kiley stood. "I've got to go. Can we stay in touch?"

"Of course." Lexa gave Kiley a smile, realizing she was going to miss her.

They left Elise's office, and Lexa walked Kiley to the front door of the gym, where she gave Lexa one last hug before saying good-bye.

Now that she had an hour free, Lexa decided to work out by herself to take her mind off Jake. On the way back from the front door, Lexa glanced into the gym's café. And there, sitting at a table together, were her dad and Elise. He raised a hand in greeting, and Elise gave Lexa a small smile, reaching up to touch the lotus necklace she was wearing around her neck.

And just like that, it clicked. The last time Lexa had seen a necklace like that was on her dad's coffee table in his apartment. She walked over to them.

"You," she said, gesturing between the two of them. They both looked guilty, like she'd caught them cheating on their diets with bacon cheeseburgers dripping with Russian dressing. "The two of you? Together?"

And Greg nodded and gave a weak smile. "Surprise?"

35

◦—

I don't know if I can walk any more." Hsu-Ling stopped in the middle of the Sunday crowd outside the Metropolitan Museum of Art. She'd been in New York for five days, but since Lexa had had to work all day on Thursday and Friday to make up for canceling on her clients earlier in the week, she had dragged Hsu-Ling all over Manhattan that weekend. She wanted to fit in as many sights and attractions that Hsu-Ling wanted to see as possible.

"I'm so sorry. I totally forgot about your leg." Lexa reached out to take Hsu-Ling by the arm.

"I'm glad you forgot. But I'm not used to all this walking. No wonder you're in such good shape."

"That's one of the perks of working out for a living. If I didn't teach classes, I don't think I would ever get to the gym. People always assume I work out for hours, but the truth is, I don't." Her text alert dinged, and she looked at the phone and smiled when she saw it was from Jake.

"Jake again?" Hsu-Ling gave her a knowing look.

"Yes." He'd been texting her every day since he'd gone home on Thursday morning. She sent a reply and then gestured to the museum. "Do you want to go home and forget about this?"

Hsu-Ling thought for a moment and then shook her head. "No. I've come all this way. I have to be able to say I at least set foot inside the Metropolitan Museum."

"There's a rooftop bar and a few cafés inside. We could get something to eat and sit for a bit?"

"If I sit now, I'll probably never get up again." Hsu-Ling grimaced as she shifted her weight to her left leg. "Why don't we at least walk through the French exhibit you were talking about, then we can get something to eat? I want to see the roof garden commission too."

They headed toward the museum, and Lexa stepped off the curb to avoid a large group of tourists planted smack in the middle of the sidewalk. Hsu-Ling grabbed her arm and pulled her back next to her. "You step into the street like that in Taiwan and you'll get run over."

Lexa turned to Hsu-Ling. "Sorry. I do that all the time. But I remember the traffic in Taiwan. It's a hundred times worse than New York."

"You'll have to be careful when you come over. You're so used to New York City streets and crossing against the lights. You can't do that in Taiwan."

Lexa didn't answer, but they exchanged a meaningful glance. Hsu-Ling knew very well Lexa was torn about whether to go back to Taiwan. They walked to the museum entrance in silence and got in line. Once they were in the museum, they followed signs to the French exhibit.

"Hey, so I've been wondering," Hsu-Ling said as they walked. "Do you get Alexa jokes a lot? You know, like, 'Alexa, what's the weather?' Or 'Alexa, turn on the heat.'"

Lexa scrunched up her face. "Yeah. I don't know why Amazon had to name their virtual assistant Alexa. But that's why I'm glad I go by Lexa."

"Can you imagine a virtual assistant named Hsu-Ling?" She snorted. "Non-Chinese people would have so much trouble pronouncing it. 'H-Su-Ling,' they'd probably say." She exaggerated the "h" sound at the beginning of her name.

Lexa smiled, and they stopped to look at a painting by Matisse. While Hsu-Ling studied the Impressionist scene of outdoor leisure, Lexa asked in a casual voice, "Have you talked to your mother?"

Hsu-Ling didn't turn from the painting, but her body tensed. "Yes."

"When?"

"I called her on Wednesday night, the day we read Pong's letter. After I got back to the hotel from dinner with you and Jake. It was Thursday morning in Taiwan, and I knew I'd catch her at home."

"Why didn't you tell me?" Lexa looked at Hsu-Ling in confusion. They hadn't talked about the will and Hsu-Ling's mother in the past few days, and Lexa had been waiting for Hsu-Ling to bring up the subject.

"I didn't want to upset you further." Hsu-Ling shuffled her good leg on the ground. "I was waiting for you to ask me."

"And *I* was waiting for *you* to bring up the subject." Lexa poked Hsu-Ling in the arm, making her sister smile.

"I'm so angry with her. You have no idea." Hsu-Ling's smile fell from her face.

"All these years, I was afraid to have you find out what really happened, because I thought you would take her side."

Hsu-Ling let out a dry laugh. "What? You really believe I'd side with my mother after finding out what she did to you? She kept us apart."

"I know. But she's your mother. I'm very protective of my mother."

Hsu-Ling cocked her head to one side. "If your mother did to me what my mother did to you, would you protect her?"

"No."

They looked at each other before Hsu-Ling turned away. Her hands opened and closed as she spoke. "I told her I knew everything. What she did to you. How Pong lied for her. Do you know what she did?"

Lexa shook her head.

"She laughed, like she was humoring a child. Said I had no idea what she'd sacrificed to make sure I got everything I deserved from Baba." Hsu-Ling squeezed her hands together. "ChiChi, she wasn't sorry at all. That's what I'm most mad about. If she'd apologized, said she was wrong, maybe I could have forgiven her and asked you to forgive her. But she's not sorry."

"I didn't figure she would be sorry."

"Oh, it gets worse." Hsu-Ling slanted a look at Lexa. "She told me not to believe everything you told me. Said you have psychological problems from having to grow up not knowing your father. That you were damaged in the head, not right, and jealous of me."

Lexa's hand flew to her mouth. *She* was the one with psychological problems?

"I shut her up. I told her about Pong's letter. How he left you money and the apartment, and if you accepted it, the building would come back to Baba, and in turn, to you and me equally." Before Lexa could open her mouth to ask about the legalities of that, Hsu-Ling jumped in. "I spoke to the lawyer too. He said he'd work out the issues. All you have to do is accept Pong's gifts, and he'll make sure we own the building."

"Your mother must have died when she heard that."

"I think so. She didn't say anything. She hung up on me." Hsu-Ling walked to the next painting, and Lexa followed her.

"I'm sorry."

"Don't be. Ah-Ma and the rest of the family are going to freak out when they hear about this. And about my mother's part in it." Hsu-Ling paused and looked at Lexa. "Did I say that right? Freak?"

Lexa laughed and nodded. She had just taught Hsu-Ling the word "freak" that weekend. "So the family doesn't know yet?" Lexa stepped close to her sister when a group of tourists speaking French came up behind them.

"No. I'll tell them in person when I get back to Taiwan."

Lexa took Hsu-Ling's arm and guided her away from the big tour group. They walked into another room, stopping now and then to study the paintings.

"Are you going to accept Pong's will?" Hsu-Ling broke the silence.

"I don't know. I'm thinking about it." Lexa walked to a free bench and sat, because she could see Hsu-Ling was trying not to limp.

"It says you have to come back to Taiwan by a hundred days after his death." Hsu-Ling sat next to her.

"It's not enough he's dictating what I have to do. Now he wants me to do it on his timeline."

"I hate how he went about it. But you know, it's Baba's final prayer ceremony too. It might be a good thing. You could come say good-bye to Baba."

Lexa looked at her sister with a frown. "Are you defending Pong?"

"No!" Hsu-Ling said, sitting up straight. "I'm just trying to see the good in all this. If Baba were still alive, then it would have meant a chance for you to go back to Taiwan and see each other again."

"But now I'll never get to know him, will I?" Lexa was surprised at the bitter tone in her voice. "In a way, it was Pong's fault. He finally told Baba the truth, and the truth sent our father to his death."

Lexa looked up when Hsu-Ling made a noise. She reached over and touched Hsu-Ling's arm. "Are you okay?"

Hsu-Ling's face was pale, and she took in a shuddering breath. "Yes. None of this was either of our faults. We just got caught in the mess made by our parents."

Lexa stared at her. "I know it's not our faults."

Hsu-Ling shook her head. "Never mind. You want to head to the café? I'm starving."

Lexa nodded. "It's way past lunchtime."

Once they'd gotten food and found a table, Lexa said, "Tell me about him."

Hsu-Ling looked up from her ham and Gruyère cheese sandwich. "Who? Baba?"

At Lexa's nod, Hsu-Ling gave a small smile. "He was the best. You know he always believed there was nothing wrong with me."

"I want to know everything. The good things as well as the bad."

"My mother was so upset about me being born with only one leg that she decided I had to be perfect in everything else to make up for it. She was always pushing me to do better, be better, be the best. But Baba always believed I was already the best. He never treated me as if I had a disability." Hsu-Ling smiled as a memory came to her. "One time, I had a temper tantrum and threw a whole bag of my cousin's marbles down the stairs in our building from the third floor. Baba was so mad. He made me crawl down the stairs and pick up every single one of those marbles by myself. He wouldn't let Mama help me. He told her I had two good hands, and if I could throw them, then I could pick them up by myself."

Lexa made a sound to indicate she was listening.

"He was always on my side," Hsu-Ling said, and then took a sip of her water. "When I was a teenager, there was an English speech and drama contest. Twelve winners were chosen as diplomat envoys and got to travel to several countries to help teens interact, but also to promote Taiwan and everything it had to offer. I'd been studying English since I was little because of you, so I won one of the spots."

"Your mother must have been so proud," Lexa said.

"Yes. We were going to Malaysia that year. But one of the parents of a student who didn't win was upset. She went to the Ministry of Education and presented a case that I shouldn't go because of my leg. She argued that I wasn't the best representation of the top teens from Taiwan, because of my disability."

"What a bitch."

"Bitch." Hsu-Ling turned the word over in her mouth. "Yes, that sounds exactly like what she was. Baba was so mad. He said she was just jealous because her daughter is a *lan yatou*. A lazy head. He accused her of discrimination. Said they should be proud to have me on the trip, to show what courage and strength in the face of stupid people like that mother was like."

Lexa laughed. "I wish I could have seen him in action."

Hsu-Ling nodded. "I can still remember how that mother came up to me at school the next week and apologized. Baba made such a big stink that her daughter wouldn't speak to her for weeks."

Lexa smiled, but her heart ached. She hadn't known that father.

"What about Uncle Pong?" Lexa asked. "Were you close to him? Was he a big part of your life?"

"Yes," Hsu-Ling said. "I trusted him. He was like a second father to me." Her face closed up, and she pressed her lips together. "I have to go to the bathroom." She stood abruptly, almost tipping herself over. Without another word, she left the table, leaving Lexa to wonder what she'd said to upset Hsu-Ling.

36

The next night, Lexa and Maddie hurried down Lexington Avenue on their way to meet Hsu-Ling for dinner.

"Dad's seeing Elise," Maddie said. "Did you know? And why are you walking so fast?"

"Sorry." Lexa slowed her pace, allowing Maddie to catch up. She'd been trying to time it to catch all the green lights, which sometimes meant running across the street before the lights changed. "Dad told you?"

Maddie nodded. "Did you know?" she asked again.

"I just found out. I saw them at the gym together last Thursday."

"Our family is turning into the United Nations," Maddie said as they dodged around a large group of tourists who'd stopped in the middle of the sidewalk to study a map and gape up at a building. "Even you're dating someone who's a quarter Asian."

Lexa shot her a look. "I'm not dating him," Lexa said. "We're just having fun together."

"Whatever. What do you think of Dad and Elise?"

"I don't know. I can't believe he's dating one of my friends. She's only eleven years younger than Dad. It's probably good for him. He's been so sad since Mom left him."

"How long has he been seeing Elise?"

"Since my birthday party."

"Really?" Lexa heard the surprise in Maddie's voice. "I didn't even see them together."

"You were too busy avoiding Mom and being rude to Phoenix."

"Oh." Maddie was lagging behind again. "Doesn't Elise have a kid or something?"

"Yes, a son who just graduated from college."

"Are we going to end up with a stepbrother? That's all you need, a stepbrother to add to your half sisters."

"They just started seeing each other. I don't think they're thinking marriage."

Maddie grabbed her elbow from behind. "Slow down! Why are you walking so fast?"

"Sorry."

"It's bad enough I have to have dinner with Hsu-Ling. Are you trying to kill me too?"

Lexa pointed to the four-inch heels Maddie was wearing. "If you weren't wearing those shoes, you'd be able to keep up."

"Whatever."

. . .

Dinner was awkward and stilted. Her two sisters sat, one on each side of her, like two stone lions flanking her. Neither had been enthused when Lexa had suggested this dinner. But it was Hsu-Ling's last night in New York, and Lexa desperately wanted them to like each other.

Lexa talked, and Maddie and Hsu-Ling answered in monosyllables. She'd chosen this Italian restaurant in the low Sixties because it was close to Hsu-Ling's hotel, and one of Maddie's favorites. Hsu-Ling had wanted food she couldn't get in Taiwan, and Lexa thought she'd be able to please both sisters.

But neither sister was happy. Maddie drummed her fingers on the table as if bored, and Hsu-Ling made a point of ignoring her, focusing her attention on Lexa. They hadn't even gotten their entrees yet and Lexa was already wishing dinner were over.

"What are you wearing?" Lexa looked up to find Maddie staring at the necklace around her neck. "Is that a Lifesaver candy?"

Lexa reached up to finger the flat jade disc with a circular hole in the center hanging from a silver chain around her neck. She shot Maddie a look. "This is the *bi* necklace Hsu-Ling sent me for my high school graduation. Remember, Hsu-Ling?"

Her Taiwanese sister nodded. "Yes. Mama didn't want me to send you a gift. But Baba helped me pick it out. The jade *bi* disc indicates someone of moral quality. It's considered a lucky charm and was supposed to bring Lexa a happy life and protection again harm."

Maddie wrinkled her nose. "Still looks like a green Lifesaver to me."

"Maddie, grow up. You said the same thing all those years ago. I loved your present too."

"What did she give you?" Hsu-Ling asked.

Lexa wondered if she'd imagined the competitive edge in Hsu-Ling's voice.

"Maddie gave me a wooden jewelry box. She handpainted a Chinese Zodiac dog on the lid. Because I was born in the year of the dog."

"Hmm," Hsu-Ling said.

Silence fell at the table again, and Lexa looked desperately between her two sisters as they picked at the platter of fried calamari on the table. She could hear laughter coming from neighboring tables, mixed with the clink of silverware against plates and the wonderful aroma of Italian spices and pizza baking in the stone oven, which had made her mouth water when they first walked in. But now her stomach was in knots, and she fished in her mind for some common ground between her sisters.

"Maddie was obsessed with Britney Spears that year. I found her listening to 'Oops! . . . I Did It Again' when I went to thank her for my gift." Maddie had placed the small wrapped box in Lexa's hand after making fun of the *bi* necklace and run off to their room.

"I was not obsessed with Britney Spears."

"Yes you were. I remember finding you in our room listening to Britney sing about how she's not that innocent. Hsu-Ling liked her too. I sent her all the Britney Spears CDs."

"You did?" Hsu-Ling's brows furrowed together. "I never got them."

"Your bitch of a mother strikes again." Maddie waved the calamari on her fork.

"Don't call my mother a bitch."

"I just call it like it is." Maddie shrugged. "She's a bitch and a Tiger Mom."

Hsu-Ling didn't answer, but Lexa could see by the way her eyes darkened that she was getting mad.

"She really was a Tiger Mom." Lexa jumped in. "The way she used to make you practice the piano when you were so bad, and she always wanted you to study."

Hsu-Ling's mouth twitched. "I was pretty bad at the piano. She only let me stop because the piano teacher told her he'd pay my mother if only she would stop bringing me."

Lexa laughed. "And you were born in the year of the tiger, so she really is a Tiger Mom."

"Wait, you're a tiger too?" Maddie asked. "I thought you were a year older than me."

"She's only six months older than you. She was born in February and you in August of the same year," Lexa said. She turned back to Hsu-Ling. "Your mom was so hard on you."

"I know. She had her heart set on me going to Taiwan University, the best university in Taiwan. She made me do so much *buxi*, cram school, and private tutors, to prepare. But I didn't want to go to school in Taipei. I wanted to stay in Taichung and go to Chung Hsing University, which was ranked number one in Taichung."

"But you ended up at Taiwan University?" Lexa asked.

"Yes." Hsu-Ling nodded. "I begged and pleaded, and Baba tried too, but she wouldn't budge. I got into Taiwan University and I was going." Hsu-Ling shrugged. "In hindsight, I'm glad I did, but still, it was horrible at first."

"What happened to you being a doctor?" Maddie looked interested, and Lexa held her breath, afraid to believe her sisters were actually having a conversation.

"I couldn't cut it in medical school. I was fine with the books and studying, but the actual hands-on stuff . . ." Hsu-Ling shuddered. "After my first semester, I told her I wasn't going back. I'd had enough. I'd done what she wanted all my life, but I didn't want to be a doctor." Hsu-Ling gave a small smile and picked up another piece of calamari. "She didn't talk to me for three months."

Lexa was starting to feel hopeful about her sisters getting along when Maddie spoke.

"You want to know what I think? I think you should say

screw it to your Taiwanese family. You can't let Pong dictate what you should do. Don't take his money."

Hsu-Ling stopped eating. "You're right, Maddie. It's not fair what Pong is asking of Lexa. And part of me even agrees with you. Maybe my mother deserves to lose her home. But not Ah-Ma and the rest of the family. They didn't do anything."

"You don't care how it makes Lexa feel, after being shunned by your mother and father all these years? You just want her to go back and fix your family's problem?" Maddie asked.

"I don't expect her to fix anything. I think she should go back for herself."

"You know what I find so sad?" Maddie turned to Lexa. "After that summer, you wanted nothing to do with your Taiwanese heritage. You threw yourself into being an American, except for two things. You kept going to Chinese school, and you started Kung Fu. As if you wanted to try to stay connected to your father somehow."

"He missed her too. I'd find him looking at pictures of her."

"And who put her in the position to not know her family?" Maddie asked.

Hsu-Ling flung up her hands, almost knocking over her glass of wine. "It was my mother, okay? My mother is responsible for every terrible thing that happened to Lexa." Hsu-Ling's voice rose, and Lexa could see people turning to look at them. "But I had no idea."

Lexa broke in. "Guys, stop. Please. There's no point rehashing the past. I just want to move forward and decide what to do."

"She's being such a *laowai*," Hsu-Ling muttered. "She doesn't understand our Taiwanese ways."

"What did you call me?" Maddie glared.

"Calm down, Maddie." Lexa held up a hand. "She just called you a foreigner."

"Foreigner! She's the foreign one here. You . . . you overachiever."

Hsu-Ling gave her a look. "That's your best comeback?"

Two waiters approached and placed their entrees in front of them, effectively shutting up both sisters. Lexa inhaled the garlicky aroma of the clams in white sauce and longed to dive into the food, forgetting about the tension that hung as thick as fog between her sisters.

After the waiter had grated fresh cheese over Maddie's and Hsu-Ling's chicken parmigiana (Lexa found it interesting that they'd both ordered the same thing), Maddie said, "Whatever you decide to do, I'm here for you."

Hsu-Ling raised her wineglass to Lexa. "On that, I actually agree with Maddie. I'm here for you too. Even if you decide not to accept Pong's conditions, we will always be sisters. I finally found you again, and I'm not going to lose you."

Lexa didn't say anything, but she smiled into her linguine. For the rest of the meal, they stuck to light comments about the people around them and the time of Hsu-Ling's flight the next day. When their dishes were taken, Lexa cleared her throat.

"What do you say we have a drink at the bar? To new beginnings?"

She waited, looking from Maddie to Hsu-Ling.

"Fine," Maddie said. "We might as well. Mike has the kids. He can see how hard it is to do bedtime by himself."

Hsu-Ling nodded, and after paying the bill, Lexa led the way to the bar. Maddie walked forward and grabbed two free stools. "You can have one of the seats, Hsu-Ling. Lexa and I can take turns on the other."

"What, you think because of my leg I need to sit down?"

Lexa turned at the belligerent tone of Hsu-Ling's voice. Maddie held up a hand. "Sheesh, calm down. I was just trying to be polite to our guest. It wasn't anything about your leg."

They glared at each other, and Lexa's heart sank. She'd thought her sisters were starting to soften, but there they were at each other's throats again.

"You both sit. I need to stretch my legs." Lexa reached for the drinks menu and stood on Hsu-Ling's right, with Maddie sitting on Hsu-Ling's other side.

The waiter had just set down their drinks when she felt someone hovering behind her. She turned around to find a man of average height with light brown hair staring at her. There was nothing extraordinary about him except for his thick neck and beefy arms. They were enormous. Lexa knew the type—she saw them at the gym all the time. The gym rats who spent hours pumping iron together, bragging about how much they could bench and talking about the latest protein drink that jacked them up.

"Hey, little ladies. You sure are beautiful. Can my friend and I join you?" He jerked a thumb back at a man who was the exact opposite of him. Slight, leaning toward scrawny, and wearing wire-rimmed glasses, his friend raised his glass of beer at them. The big guy inserted himself between Lexa and Hsu-Ling's chair. "Are you two sisters?" He gestured between Lexa and Hsu-Ling.

"Actually, they're both my sisters." Lexa's voice was cold, leaving no room for doubt that his attention wasn't wanted.

He either didn't get the message or chose to ignore it, and leaned in closer to Hsu-Ling.

"Can I buy you all a round?"

"Um, hello? Can't you see we just got our drinks?" Maddie's voice was sugar-sweet, but Lexa could hear the daggers in her tone.

The guy draped an arm around the back of Hsu-Ling's stool, causing Hsu-Ling to shrink away from him toward Maddie. "You're so beautiful," he said, staring into Hsu-Ling's eyes. "Where are you from?"

"Um." Hsu-Ling's forehead wrinkled. "Taiwan?" It came out sounding like a question.

Lexa was about to jump to Hsu-Ling's rescue when Maddie took the guy's hand from behind Hsu-Ling's stool and tried to lift it off the back. When she couldn't budge his arm, she said, "Hey. You need to remove your arm. I don't think she's comfortable having you draped over her like that."

The guy leaned across Hsu-Ling and said to Maddie, "Listen, I was talking to these two exotic beauties here. But you know, I've never had three sisters before. You can join us if you'd like." And he turned and gave an exaggerated wink at Lexa and Hsu-Ling.

Lexa would have laughed at the look of horror on Hsu-Ling's face if she weren't so incensed by this idiot's words. Exotic? What were they, birds?

Maddie started pushing on his arms, trying to loosen his grip on the stool as he leaned even closer to Hsu-Ling, trapping her against him.

"Listen. I'm serious. You need to let her go." Maddie's voice rose and attracted the bartender's attention. Lexa glanced at the guy's friend and saw that he was enjoying the show.

A rush of energy propelled through her when she noticed the terrified expression on Hsu-Ling's face. The bartender was coming around the bar, but Lexa didn't wait for him. A buzzing sounded in her ears, and her Kung Fu training took over. *Believe in yourself*, she could hear Shifu saying to her. *Trust yourself. Use your training to defend yourself. In a real fight, there is no style. You just try to knock down your opponent before they get you.*

She didn't think. There was no form, no style. She had the element of surprise on her side since the guy had his back to her, and she used it to her advantage. She found his weak points and broke his hold on Hsu-Ling and the stool, and in the next instant, he was lying flat on his back on the ground. She stood over him as he gasped for breath. She brushed herself off in the stunned silence that had fallen over the bar.

"Whoa." Maddie's voice was hushed with awe, and Lexa saw her exchange a look with Hsu-Ling. "That was awesome. I haven't seen you practice Kung Fu in so long. Remember I used to watch your classes sometimes?"

"Yes." Lexa deliberately turned her back on the guy, who had struggled to his feet.

"You're crazy, woman. Batshit crazy!" he shouted as he limped toward his friend, who had the audacity to be laughing at him. "Shut up, idiot," he said to his friend, and brushed past the bartender, who was telling them to go.

Hsu-Ling watched them leave and turned to Maddie. "Thanks for trying to get him off me."

Maddie shrugged. "I didn't. Lexa was the one who did. He was freaking strong. I couldn't move his arm."

Hsu-Ling smiled at Maddie. "But you tried. I appreciate it."

Maddie didn't answer, but when she smiled back at Hsu-Ling, Lexa's heart jumped with hope.

37

⁓

January, Nineteen Years Ago
Manhattan, New York

Maddie sat with her back against the wall, watching the end of Lexa's Kung Fu class. Their dad was taking them to lunch and then a Knicks game after. He had some work to do in his office, and Maddie had opted to stay and watch Lexa's class. She was curious about what Lexa actually did in Kung Fu. Her mom used to drag her with them when Lexa was younger, but ever since Lexa was old enough to take the subway by herself, Maddie had no idea what she was doing. All her sister talked about lately was Kung Fu and Shifu, especially since Shifu had asked her to move to the adult classes a few months earlier.

She'd thought she'd be bored for the two-hour class since she got bored easily, but instead she couldn't take her eyes off her sister. Lexa was the smallest and youngest in the class at only sixteen—everyone else was an adult. But she was the fastest and the lightest on her feet. Some of the men were clumsy and heavy footed when they did their kicks and jumps across the floor. Lexa seemed to skim across, at once grounded yet also kicking and jumping so high Maddie felt her mouth drop. When Lexa did her cartwheels across the floor, Maddie got dizzy trying to track the ball of motion that was her sister.

And the power! Maddie had never seen so much attack and power before. Shifu had it—Maddie could see when he demonstrated. Most of the adults didn't. They tried hard, but they were weighted down and didn't have the oomph behind their kicks. They were sluggish and struggled to kick their hands in the extended roundhouse kicks. Maddie heard someone call them *bian tui*.

Bian tui, she said to herself, loving the way the foreign word rolled off her tongue. Lexa's *bian tuis* were lightning fast. She hit her hands every time, striking them with a smacking sound, never missing a beat and with more energy than Maddie knew she had.

Ever since Lexa had come back from Taiwan two and a half years earlier, she'd been withdrawn. She spent a lot of time with their mom, the two of them whispering together. Every time Maddie tried to join in, they'd stop, and their mom would change the subject. Maddie was hurt. She wanted to know the secret too.

Lexa started losing herself in books. She never wanted to go to the playground anymore, or do crafts with Maddie, or play their own made-up game where they each had a family (their stuffed animals) and they'd act out the adventures the families had. Maddie had found her crying more than once, but Lexa always wiped her eyes and told her to go away.

So to see her now, so completely different from the quiet and withdrawn Lexa, Maddie could finally understand why Lexa spent so much time here. Under Shifu's guidance, she came alive. She was a star. The other people in the class asked her for advice. They watched her with admiration and spoke to her with respect, even though she was only a teenager. She was flexible and unbreakable, strong yet light on her feet, fast but controlled, and Maddie was sad when the class ended and they were stretching. She could have watched Lexa all day.

When Lexa came out of the dressing area changed and showered, she walked over to Maddie. "Let's go find Dad." She was trying to stuff her sweaty uniform into her pink Hello Kitty backpack and dropped her wallet on the ground.

Maddie reached to pick it up and saw the wallet had fallen open on a picture of Lexa's Taiwanese father. She studied the photo, thinking again how much Lexa looked like him. Lexa reached out a hand for her wallet and paused when she saw what Maddie was looking at.

"I didn't know you kept a picture of him in your wallet," Maddie said.

"Yeah." Maddie heard Lexa's sharp intake of breath and looked over at her. Lexa was biting her lips, like she always did when she was trying not to cry. Alarmed, she laid a hand on Lexa's arm.

"I'm sorry. I didn't mean to make you sad."

"You didn't." Lexa stared at the ground, not moving.

"Do you miss him?" Maddie asked in a small voice. Lexa usually bit her head off when she asked about her father or Taiwan.

"Yes."

"Why don't you go see him, then?" It made no sense to Maddie why Lexa had stopped visiting her father. And he hadn't been back to New York to see Lexa either.

Her sister looked away and didn't answer. When Shifu called to her, she ran to him without another look at Maddie.

38

Maddie came over to Lexa's apartment unannounced two weeks after Hsu-Ling went back to Taiwan. It was nine o'clock, and Lexa was pooped from another long day with her clients and classes. Ever since her father had died, she'd felt restless at work. Days that used to fly by now crawled, and she found herself checking the clock constantly.

She opened the bottle of wine Maddie had brought and poured them each a glass. "So, what's new with Mike?"

"Ugh. He wants us to see someone together. A therapist. Not something I want to do at all." Maddie took a big gulp of her pinot noir. "But I don't want to talk about him."

"Okay." Lexa sat on the couch next to Maddie. "Then why are you here?"

"I came over because I've been thinking."

"Uh-oh." Lexa made an exaggerated face. "Maddie's been thinking."

"Shut up." Maddie punched Lexa in the leg, causing Zeus to growl low in his throat. Maddie reached out to stroke Zeus's head. "That was a love tap, Zeus." He wagged his tail.

"So what were you thinking about?"

"I think you need to go to Taiwan. Not because of saving your family or any such bullshit like that. I think you need to do this, for yourself." At Maddie's words, Lexa hunched deeper into her couch cushion. She'd been avoiding making a decision, giving herself the excuse that she still had plenty of time.

Maddie shifted so that she was facing Lexa. "Listen, I've watched you struggle all your life with who you are. I know it wasn't easy for you to grow up in our family. And now that I know what happened all those years ago, I think you need to go back and resolve it for yourself once and for all."

"Why does everyone keep saying that?"

"Maybe because they're right?" Maddie turned up her hands. "You're so much stronger now. You need to go back and show that woman she didn't succeed in chasing you away forever. You're a rightful member of the Chang family, and she's kept you away long enough."

"I know. But every time I think about Hsu-Ling's mother, it makes me so mad that there was nothing I could do when I was younger to stop her lies. It was easier to push it aside and not think about it." Lexa played with her wineglass, swirling her wine around and staring at it as if hypnotized. "I don't know. I think I've already kind of decided I have to go. And truthfully, the money would help. But then I think about seeing her again . . . and what it means to take Pong's money. He caused Baba's death, even if it was inadvertently."

"Lexa." Maddie put her wineglass on the coffee table and took one of Lexa's hands. Lexa couldn't believe how gentle Maddie sounded, so unlike her usual brash self. "I don't have to remind you that's a lot of money he's leaving you. You'd be a fool to turn it down. But money aside—this is your heritage you've turned your back on your whole life. As awful as Pong's letter was, he's offering you a chance to go back and see your family and learn about your father. Don't you want that? It might help heal that hole in your heart. And make you see family in a different way."

Lexa stared into her younger sister's eyes, her face showing her surprise at Maddie's words. Too often, Maddie spoke without thinking, and Lexa was used to her lashing out or sulking and giving people the silent treatment instead of talking. But for once, she was being the adult here. She was actually being rational and mature.

"You're right," Lexa said, wondering if she'd ever said that to Maddie before. "But I want to wait to see what my Taiwanese family is going to do first. Hsu-Ling told me earlier this week that they're trying to figure out their finances, to see if maybe, all together, the family could buy back the building. They're supposed to have a family meeting in the next few weeks, as soon as they can gather all the cousins who've moved out of Taichung."

"But you're considering going back, whether or not they need you to save the building?"

Lexa paused and then nodded. "Yes, I am."

39

Three weeks later, Lexa sat in Mediterraneo restaurant on Second Avenue with Andi over plates of pasta.

"How's dating going? You haven't told me any stories lately."

Andi smiled and wiggled her eyebrows at Lexa. "I met someone. He works in finance and doesn't watch the Food Network so has no idea who I am. I really like him."

"Oh my God! Why didn't you tell me?" Lexa squealed. "That's fantastic."

"Things are great so far. We'll see." Andi's eyes glowed.

"What's his name?"

"Manos." Andi sighed. "He's Greek. Isn't that just the most romantic name?"

"Oh, my. You have it bad."

Andi let her eyes roll back in her head in a fake swoon, and then she grinned and turned to look at Lexa. "What about you? Are you still talking to Jake?"

Lexa nodded. "He texts or calls me every day."

"Is it getting serious?" Andi wagged her eyebrows at her.

Lexa heaved out a breath. "How can it be serious when he lives in California?"

"People have long-distance relationships all the time."

"It's not just the distance. It's . . ." Lexa didn't feel like explaining, so she shoved a giant forkful of gnocchi into her mouth.

"Oh my gawd! Is that Lexa eating gnocchi?"

Lexa looked up to find Carla, the woman who had accosted her on the street weeks earlier and who had just taken Lexa's barre class along with Andi not even an hour earlier, gawking at her.

"That was an awesome class, Lexa. Loved the burn. But I can't believe you're eating gnocchi. Isn't that fattening?"

Andi caught Lexa's eye, but before either of them could say anything, Carla launched on. "Hey, I saw you in the grocery store the other day. I tried to catch you, but you didn't hear me calling." Lexa looked away. She had heard Carla but had been in a rush and wanted to get home. "Anyways, next time you go to the store, let me know? I want to buy everything you get, and I'm going to eat everything you eat so I can look just like you. I love your body. You're so toned and lean."

Andi eyed Carla up and down. "Girl, I don't think eating any amount of any food that Lexa eats is going to turn you into a petite Asian woman." Carla was about five eight, with short brown hair cut in a shaggy style and light blue eyes. When Carla only stared, Andi shrugged and said, "Just saying."

Lexa hid a smile and was about to answer when her phone rang. Saved by the bell. She picked up without thinking, forgetting that she was having dinner with Andi.

"Hi, Lexa."

"Oh, Hsu-Ling. Hold on a minute, okay?" Lexa turned

to Carla, who was still hovering over their table, eyeing Lexa's plate of gnocchi in cream sauce. "Sorry, Carla, I have to take this. It's my sister in Taiwan."

"Oh, okay. I'm going to order the gnocchi too." Carla finally took her eyes off Lexa's plate. "I'll see you in class. Let me know when you're going to the grocery store."

Lexa waited until Carla had walked away before saying to Andi, "Sorry, I didn't mean to pick up the phone. Let me just tell Hsu-Ling I'll call her back later."

Andi waved a hand at her. "Talk to her. It's fine. You said you were waiting for her to call about the family meeting. And I can eat my pasta in peace. That's the problem with having a trainer as a friend—I always feel guilty when I eat with you. I need my carbs."

"Hey, I'm eating carbs." Lexa gestured at her own plate before turning back to the phone. "How was the meeting?"

"Not good. Have you decided if you're coming to Taiwan? Ah-Ma keeps asking. You know she's so upset with my mother."

Lexa played with her fork. "She's still not talking to your mother?"

"No. Everyone is angry with her. No one is really talking to her right now."

"Hmm." Lexa took a sip of her water. "So? The meeting?"

Hsu-Ling's sigh echoed down the phone line. "The price Pong set on the building is so high we can't afford it. None of us make that much money, and even if we combined incomes, we don't come anywhere close to the asking price."

"Why would he set a price that high? Is it above market value?"

"No, it's just at the higher end. That building is worth a lot of money. He knew none of us would be able to afford it.

It seems my uncles and aunts have made some bad investments recently."

"Ugh. It makes me sick." Lexa looked up and found Andi looking at her in concern. "And I'm the one who has to decide whether your family loses their home." Lexa wiped her mouth with a napkin, suddenly not hungry anymore.

"They're your family too." Hsu-Ling's voice was quiet yet strong. "But I want you to know you should do what's right for you. Don't accept Pong's conditions if it goes against everything in you. If you don't do it, our family will be okay. Our aunts, uncles, and cousins can rent cheaper apartments, and my mother can fend for herself. The only one I'm worried about is Ah-Ma. She's lived there most of her life."

Hearing that pierced Lexa's heart. How could she be responsible for making an old woman leave her beloved home, the home she'd built for her family all these years?

"But whether or not you accept Pong's conditions, I think you should come back for Baba. He was so sorry, ChiChi. His last thought was getting to you. And I think it'd help you too."

"I know."

"Come back and make your peace with Baba. Help him rest."

There was silence as Lexa tried to imagine her father's spirit floating around, waiting for her to return to Taiwan. Even though she didn't believe in ghosts, her spine tingled and goose bumps suddenly broke out along her arms. Andi reached out and laid a hand on Lexa's arm.

"Okay." Lexa stopped and took a breath. "I'm going to accept Pong's conditions and come back to Taiwan." Immediately she felt lighter, relief coursing through her at finally voicing her decision out loud.

Lexa heard Hsu-Ling's sharp intake of breath at the same time that Andi took her hand back and pumped her fist in the air.

"You will? You mean it? You're coming to Taiwan?"

"Yes. I want to say good-bye to Baba, to see Taiwan again, and Ah-Ma. It's also time I faced your mother." She suddenly felt weak-kneed and was glad she was sitting down. "I'm not afraid of her," she lied.

Yeah, right, Andi mouthed at her, causing Lexa to glare at her.

"I'm so glad!" Hsu-Ling's voice rose in excitement. "And I will back you one hundred percent. I won't let my mother push you around this time. That building is your legacy and should have been your second home."

Lexa let out a breath of relief when she heard Hsu-Ling say that. "Thanks. I'll look into plane tickets tonight. The final prayer ceremony is in a month, right?"

"Yes. I'm so glad you're coming. I'll arrange everything for you on this end. I can't wait to see you again. Ah-Ma is going to be so happy. She's missed you so much all these years."

"It'll be great to see her again, and the rest of the family."

They hung up, and Lexa sank back against her chair. "I'm going to Taiwan."

"I'm so glad you are. You think your mom will go with you?"

"Yes. I saw her yesterday when she taught her yoga practicum class in order to graduate from her yoga teacher training. She said she'd go with me."

"Your mom graduated already?"

"Yeah, she did great. Phoenix and I both took her class."

Andi raised her eyebrows in question. "And . . . ? How are things with Phoenix?"

Lexa started eating again. "Better. We actually have a lot in common. We talked some yesterday. Her father died before they could make peace about her telling him she's gay. She gets it, my feelings and regrets about my father."

"That's great, Lexa. I'm happy things are working out for your family."

Lexa nodded, and they resumed eating. For some reason, something Kiley had said to her weeks earlier popped into her head. *You have to face the past in order to confront your future.*

Lexa thought she knew what she wanted in life. But the past couple of months had made her question how happy she really was being single and alone, with only her career to sustain her. Maybe it was finally time to put the past behind her to see what her future could hold. Just like Kiley's fortune cookie had said.

40

⌒

"Shifu?"

Lexa stood at the entrance of the temple. It was after the Level One class, and the room was empty. She looked at the giant dragon painted on one of the red walls, the green training floor, and the statues of gods and goddesses scattered around. This room was as familiar to her as the house she'd grown up in. Yet she hadn't been here in years. Maybe it was time to come back, find room in her busy schedule to practice for herself again.

He came out of his office in a T-shirt and jeans. "Chi."

Out of habit, her right hand automatically went up to a prayer at heart center, with her left hand below it, her palms turned up. "*Amituofo.*"

"*Amituofo.*" He gestured with a hand. "Come. Sit." It was always like this with them. She wouldn't see him for years, but whenever she showed up, he always treated her as if he'd just seen her the day before.

He sat and studied her. He was a man of few words, but when he did speak, everyone listened. Lexa was leaving for Taiwan in a week, and her impending departure was making her so nervous she hadn't slept much in the past few days. And when she felt out of sorts and uncertain, she always came to the one place she'd felt safe and in control: the temple and Shifu.

"I'm going to Taiwan," she finally said, knowing he wouldn't speak until she did. "Next Friday." She was going to stop in San Francisco first to see Jake for two days before flying on to Taiwan.

"Ah. Going back for the first time."

She'd missed his voice. His English was surprisingly good, and the way he tended to overpronounce certain words always made her smile.

She nodded. "My father died. I'm going back for his hundredth-day prayer ceremony."

He leaned back on the wooden stump he was perched on. Anyone else, she'd be afraid they'd topple over, but Shifu had incredible strength and balance. He stayed upright, even as his body reached out at an impossible angle.

"Why did you come here to study?"

She was taken aback by his question. "What?" She'd expected him to say he was sorry about her father, or maybe offer encouragement, knowing how difficult it was for her to return to Taiwan after all these years. But she should have known Shifu wouldn't follow script. His mind didn't work that way.

"When you were child." He righted himself on the stump. "Why did you choose to come here?"

"I don't know. Something drew me." She thought back. "From my first class with you, I knew this was the right place for me."

"Yes." He nodded. "I watch you grow up. I watch you become strong, in mind and body. Kung Fu gave you confidence. You believe in yourself, trust yourself."

She stared at her hands. Yes, Shifu had done that. Or, he would say, Kung Fu had. She knew his mission was to spread the philosophy of Kung Fu and Chan Buddhism to as many people as he could. But he had no idea what Kung Fu had done for her.

She looked up and met his eyes. Or maybe he did know. The wisdom shining from his eyes was what had drawn her in that first class.

"I have to confront the woman whose lies have kept me away." She was surprised when those words left her lips. She hadn't meant to say them out loud.

"Your stepmother."

Lexa went still, and then lifted her gaze to his face. Her stepmother. In all these years, she'd never once thought of Hsu-Ling's mother as her stepmother. But he was right. Pin-Yen was her stepmother. Just like Greg was her stepfather.

She told Shifu all that had happened, and about Pong's will and letter. Her hands clenched at her sides, and she looked down. "He killed my father. He told him the truth, and my father ran out and died. I hate Pong for that."

"Chi." He said her name quietly, but with an authority that made her look up. "Peace is the most powerful weapon on Earth."

She stared at him, not answering. She didn't even know if he understood half of what she was saying, since it sounded so convoluted to her ears.

When she remained silent, he said, "Peace is the highest level of Kung Fu. You find peace here." He thumped his chest. "Then nothing can touch you."

She wanted to ask him how. How did she find peace in her heart to accept what she couldn't change? And why was she suddenly having second thoughts about going back to Taiwan when she was no longer that scared little girl? Pin-Yen couldn't hurt her anymore. She'd succeeded in driving Lexa away and out of her life for twenty-two years, but no more. Lexa was going back to claim her inheritance and her place in the Chang family. Nothing Pin-Yen could do could stop her. So then why did dread fill her heart and mind? This was what had driven her to the temple. She'd always found solace here.

Shifu stood and came to her side. "You remember when you told me you no longer wanted to study Kung Fu?"

Her mouth opened and she gaped at him because that hadn't been exactly what she'd said. She'd told him she was going away to college. Before she could respond, he laughed. "Kidding," he said. "But remember what I said?"

She smiled at him. No one ever expected him to crack a joke, so when he did, it always took people by surprise. "You told me that life is precious. I had to follow my heart. Open my mind and heart. Kung Fu will always be with me."

"Yes." He nodded. "Be honest with yourself. You will be fine in Taiwan, Chi. *Ni shi zhongguo ren.*" You are Chinese.

"*Shi,*" Lexa answered in Mandarin. "*Wo shi zhongguo ren.*" I am Chinese.

"Then you have nothing to worry about." He stood up straight, and just like when he started and ended a class, he shouted out, "*Amituofo!*"

Lexa stood, copied his stance, and repeated, "*Amituofo!*"

"More chi!"

"Train harder!" she shouted in response, even as she felt her eyes water.

"Merry Christmas!" Shifu yelled back with a straight face.

"Happy New Year!" she responded, and couldn't stop the lone tear that fell from her eye and trailed its way down her cheek, even as Shifu and Lexa grinned at each other over his little joke. She'd learned in her first class that "*amituofo*" was a greeting, for saying hello or good-bye, or literally, Buddha bless you, or even Merry Christmas and Happy New Year. Shifu always ended his class this way.

She had a sudden urge to hug him, but one didn't throw one's arms around a Shaolin Temple monk. He might pull a sword on her and slice off her head. Instead, she just grinned at him, willing him to understand how much he'd helped her over the years.

He looked at her with a gleam in his eyes, and before she knew what he was doing, he reached out and pulled her into a tight hug. "What? No hug for all I've done for you?"

He let her go, and she looked at his face, at the smile lighting him up, so different from the stern, serious face he usually showed in class. She laughed, and Shifu joined in, their laughter filling the air and lifting the cloud around her heart.

41

exa. Phoenix fell down the stairs and broke her leg."

"Oh, no, Mom. Is she okay?"

"She's fine. A bit bruised and banged up, but the broken leg is the worst of it. I'm at the hospital with her now."

"What can I do?"

"I have Corey and Connor with me. They spent the night last night."

"That's right. Their first sleepover at Phoenix's place." Her mom had been so happy when Maddie had allowed the kids to stay over.

"I can't get ahold of Maddie." Her mom's voice was rushed, the words running together. "Could you possibly come and get them so they don't have to sit in the hospital?"

It was Sunday, five days before she was leaving for Taiwan, and Lexa had the day off. But all she could think was, *Does this mean Mom won't be able to go to Taiwan with me?* She immediately felt bad for her selfish thought and said aloud, "I'll come right now."

. . .

"So, you know Phoenix is laid up with her broken leg."

"Yes, Maddie. I know. I was at the hospital yesterday with

them." Lexa had the phone on speaker so she could finish her makeup. She rolled her eyes, which was a mistake when trying to put on mascara. She poked herself in the eyeball and yelped in pain.

"What are you doing?" Maddie asked.

"Trying to put mascara on."

"Where're you going? Hot date on a Monday night?"

"No, just dinner with Andi and Elise. It's Andi's night off. Why are you calling? I'm running late."

Maddie huffed on the phone. "Well, sorry. I was calling to do you a favor, but if you don't have time for me . . ."

"Come on, Maddie. Just spit it out."

Maddie sniffed. "Mom feels bad leaving Phoenix by herself while she goes to Taiwan with you. You know Phoenix can't even take a shower by herself? Mom has to help her. God, have you ever thought of Mom and her together? Like, having sex? What do you think they do?"

"Maddie, I really don't want to talk about Mom's sex life with Phoenix. And I know all about Phoenix's broken leg. I've been helping."

"Well, I feel bad, since it's kind of the kids' fault. And I didn't answer when Mom called." Maddie had gone to the movies and turned off her ringer.

"It's not the kids' fault. I hope you didn't tell them that." Lexa capped the mascara and searched in her makeup bag for her lip gloss. "She was chasing them up the stairs and slipped."

"Well, I still feel responsible because they're my kids. Mom doesn't know what to do. She doesn't want to leave Phoenix alone. But she doesn't want to let you down either. She knows how hard it is for you to go back to Taiwan after all these years."

"Are you turning into a softie? And you actually care about how Phoenix is doing?" Lexa couldn't resist teasing Maddie.

"Maybe."

"I'm glad you're giving Phoenix a chance."

"Well, we'll see. But it looks like she's a part of Mom's life now, so I guess I'm going to have to try to get along with her."

"How very mature of you." Lexa smiled. "She's growing on me too." She found her lip gloss and leaned toward the mirror to apply it. "Anyways, what did you want to tell me?"

"Well . . ." Maddie paused for dramatic measure. "I told Mom I'd go to Taiwan with you instead of her."

"You?" Lexa's voice squeaked in surprise.

"Yes, me. Why do you sound so shocked?"

"Aren't you trying to work things out with Mike? You told me he was against getting divorced, that he wanted to go to therapy."

"Yes, but I don't want to go to therapy. I need a break from him. I can't think when he's always hovering over me, asking me what I'm feeling. He must have read a self-help book about how to fix a marriage. I don't want to discuss how I'm feeling. All I want is to be left alone."

"Oh, Maddie."

"Anyways, I had a long talk with him last night. We both agreed we need a break. It would be good for us if I went to Taiwan with you. It'd give me some space, and I would help you and make sure someone is on your side."

"But I'm leaving this week. And you hate Hsu-Ling."

"She's not my favorite person. But I want to be there to keep an eye on her mother."

"You'd do that for me?"

"Of course." Maddie's voice softened. "You're my sister."

"Oh wow. You really are going soft."

"Yeah, yeah. Whatever." But there was a smile in Maddie's voice. "I'll call the airline and take care of the name change."

"You know I'm going to San Francisco first to see Jake for two days, right? Mom was going to meet me in San Francisco so that we could be on the same flight to Taiwan."

"I know, she told me. So, no future potential with Jake, huh?"

"No. But I like him."

"Uh-huh." Maddie drew out the words. "So looks like you're stuck with me for Taiwan."

"Thank you. I mean it, Maddie." She paused, filled with a warm glow at the fact that her sister was being so supportive. Then she glanced at the time. "Listen, I have to go. I want to call Hsu-Ling and tell her you're coming with me."

"I bet she'll be so happy."

"Yeah, I bet." Lexa smirked as they said good-bye, and then she dialed Hsu-Ling.

Her sister picked up right away, almost as if she'd been waiting for Lexa's call. Lexa told her about Phoenix's fall and that Maddie would be coming with her instead.

"Oh, joy." The sarcasm dripped off Hsu-Ling's voice.

Lexa laughed. "Don't sound too happy."

"I'm sorry. I think it's nice of her to come with you." Hsu-Ling cleared her throat. "I was actually about to call you. I just talked to the lawyer. I made an appointment for the day you get in to meet in his office for you to sign the paperwork. Then you'll get access to the bank account where Pong put your money and also take possession of the apartment he left you."

"This is real, isn't it?" Lexa pursed her lips together and

then blew out a breath. "Pong really left me money and an apartment, and I'm going back to Taiwan." Lexa checked her reflection in the mirror one last time and then stood up. "Well, I'll be there soon. I can't wait to see you again."

"Me too, *jie jie*. Me too."

42

"You're here!"

"I am." Lexa stood at Jake's front door, not quite believing she was in San Francisco, on her way to Taiwan. She'd said good-bye to Zeus hours earlier when her dad had come to pick him up. Greg had hugged her hard and said, "Good luck in Taiwan. I'm so proud of you."

Lexa and Jake grinned at each other for a moment without speaking. Then Jake pulled her close, and she threw her arms around his neck. Her eyes closed when he buried his face in her hair, and just for a moment, she forgot her nervousness over her trip.

When his mouth finally settled over hers, every inch of Lexa's body remembered his touch, and she gave herself over to his kiss. She'd missed him and his kisses so much, and the way his touch awakened her body.

He pulled away first. "Welcome to my home." He grabbed her suitcase, and she followed him inside. He lived on the first floor of an Edwardian condo, and Lexa couldn't believe how big it was, compared to what she was used to in New York City. He left her luggage in the living room and gave her a tour.

"It's beautiful," she said, once they were back in the all-white kitchen with a gray quartz countertop and stainless steel appliances.

"I was lucky to find it. It's only five minutes from Sophia's mom's place." He pulled out a bottle of wine from the fridge and handed it to Lexa. "I saw this and thought of you. I had to get it."

She read the label and laughed. Kung Fu Girl Riesling. "Where did you find this?"

"Someone had it at a party I went to. I know you don't usually drink Riesling, but this is dry and crisp. I think you'll like it."

"With that name, I'm sure I will." Lexa handed the bottle back to him, and he opened it and poured two glasses.

"Let's sit outside." He gestured to the back patio, which overlooked a small yard.

Taking her glass from him, she slipped through the sliding glass door and settled into a chair. It was so peaceful here, compared to her New York City apartment with the loud traffic roaring below her window.

"I'm so glad I'm here."

"Me too. I thought we could go out to dinner, just us, tonight. I want you all to myself." He leered at her, making her laugh.

"Sounds good."

"And then tomorrow, you're still okay with meeting Sophia?"

Lexa shot him a look. Didn't single parents only want their children to meet someone if it was serious? Were they serious? But how could they be, being on opposite sides of the country and with opposing views on how they wanted to live their lives?

"Yes," she said, even though the thought set off butterflies in her stomach. "But are you sure you want me to meet her?"

"I told her you're a friend visiting from New York."

"Oh, okay." She nodded. That made sense.

"And we can play tomorrow night by ear, see how we feel. We don't have to go to Dave's if you don't want."

"You really want to introduce me to your friends?" She gave a nervous laugh. "You didn't meet my friends when you were in New York." Maybe she should have invited him to her birthday dinner?

"I met one of your sisters."

Lexa's mouth quirked. "Maddie is still mad that Hsu-Ling met you and she didn't."

Jake laughed and then leaned in toward her. "So. You're going to Taiwan."

"Yes. I really am. I couldn't let my Taiwanese family lose their home." She looked at him over the rim of her wineglass. "And if I'm being honest, I want to go back for myself. Not only to say good-bye to my father but also to see it again. I've let Hsu-Ling's mother . . ." Her voice trailed off as she realized she still hadn't told Jake what had happened with her father all those years earlier.

"What about Hsu-Ling's mother?" He sent her a questioning look.

She gazed at him as the warm San Francisco sun beamed down on them, although the temperature was cooler than it had been in New York City when she left that morning. She took a sip of her wine and realized she wanted to tell him.

"You really want to know?"

"Yes."

So she told him everything, in slow stops and starts and

in a voice so low that Jake had to lean forward to catch her words. Starting with what Hsu-Ling's mother had accused her of and her father's betrayal the summer she was fourteen, and ending with Pong's will and the reason she was going back to Taiwan. As she spoke, her voice got stronger, and by the time she'd finished the story, Jake no longer had to struggle to hear her.

"I'm sorry for what you went through," he said. "I can't imagine what that was like, to have your stepmother accuse you of things you didn't do and to have your father not believe you."

Lexa stared at him. "This is the second time I've heard her referred to as my stepmother. I've always thought of her as my father's wife."

"Lexa." Jake pulled his chair closer so he could take her hand in his. "As a father, I can't imagine not believing my child. But I've known Sophia all her life. Your father didn't get a chance to really know you. If he did, he would never have believed you were capable of hurting your sister. Or of coming on to Pong." Jake's eyes darkened, and his mouth twisted.

Lexa stayed quiet. She was glad she'd told him the truth, but she didn't want to rehash it again, especially since she'd be in Taiwan soon and have to face Pin-Yen in person. As if sensing her reluctance, Jake gave her hand a squeeze and let go. "I just want to say one more thing, and then we can put it aside if you don't want to talk about it. I'm sorry you never got a chance to reconcile with your father after he was finally told the truth. That must be so hard."

"I think that's the hardest part. He finally believed me, knew the truth, but then he died before I could hear him say he was sorry. I was mad at him. For getting into that stupid accident and dying." She let out a short laugh. "Ha. I'm mad at a dead person."

He looked at her without speaking and then said, "It takes a lot of courage to go back and face your past, to confront Hsu-Ling's mother and to admit you want to know your Taiwanese heritage. I think you're really brave, Lexa."

The side of her mouth lifted. "Thanks. I don't feel so brave."

"I knew you were special the moment I saw you."

"What, when I was sprawled on the floor with the massage table on top of me?" She gave him a doubtful look.

"Actually, yes. You looked so adorable all crumbled up like that. And you were so stunned, as if that table had done it on purpose and attacked you."

"It did."

He laughed and then jumped up and went into the kitchen, leaving Lexa to stare after him. She heard him say, "Alexa, play 'Perfect' on the patio." She rolled her eyes and smiled. Great. He already had an Alexa in his life.

Suddenly, Ed Sheeran's voice filled the air, and Jake came back. He held out his arms, and she stood, slipping into them as if she belonged. He sang along as he held her in his arms, and they swayed together to the music. Closing her eyes, she leaned her head against his chest and allowed Jake's voice to fill her heart.

. . .

Lexa wasn't prepared for the smiley, happy little girl who greeted her when Jake came back to his place the next day after picking up his three-year-old daughter.

"Sophia, this is Daddy's friend Lexa. She's visiting from New York."

The little girl had dark brown hair caught up in two pigtails with yellow ribbons on the ends, and Jake's eyes. She looked at Lexa and burst into such a happy smile, Lexa found herself smiling back at her. Sophia threw her arms around Lexa. "Moana!"

Lexa looked at Jake, who laughed helplessly.

"Sophia, honey, this is Lexa. Not Moana."

"No," Sophia said. "Moana!" She slipped her little hand into Lexa's and started to sing. Lexa had seen enough of the movie trailer to kind of recognize the song "How Far I'll Go" from the Disney movie.

"Sorry." Jake tried to compose himself. "She's kind of obsessed with *Moana* right now." He reached out and touched Lexa's hair, which she'd let loose down her back. "I guess with your long hair, you kind of look like the Polynesian girl from the movie."

"And I'm tanned from the summer," she said, looking down at her skin. "It's fine, I'm not offended." She squatted down to Sophia's level. "I'm happy to meet you, Sophia. I love your dress." Sophia spun around in her yellow dress sprinkled with daisies to show Lexa how the skirt spun out when she twirled.

"My dress is bee-yoo-tiful."

"Yes it is." Lexa looked up at Jake. "I have a niece about her age. I don't mind being compared to Moana. At least she didn't think I look like Ursula from *The Little Mermaid*."

Jake took them to lunch at his favorite taco and burrito place, and Sophia stuck to Lexa like glue. She wanted to sit next to her and reached out a few times to stroke Lexa's hair.

She chattered on in her toddler way, and even though Lexa didn't understand most of what she said, Sophia didn't seem to mind.

The restaurant was small and crowded, with the tables close together and people packed in. While Jake cut up Sophia's food, Lexa leaned back in her chair, sipping the iced tea she'd ordered, and looked around. She wondered what people thought when they saw the three of them together. Did they think she was the nanny? Or did they assume she was Sophia's mother, despite being Asian? Lexa narrowed her eyes at Sophia and decided that she could pass for being part Asian. Her hair was dark, and she had a slight tilt to her eyes. Lexa knew some children who were half-Asian looked more like their white parent, while she'd tended toward the Asian side.

She was jostled out of her daydreaming by Jake's voice. "Everything okay?"

She gave him a quick smile. She was glad he couldn't see what she was thinking about. "Yes." She shook her head to clear it. Why had she been imagining them as a family?

The rest of the day passed quickly, and Sophia was in tears when Jake had to drive her back to her mother.

"I want to stay with Moana!"

"Mommy's waiting for you at home. I'm glad you had fun with my friend Lexa."

Lexa gave the little girl a hug. "Thanks for spending the day with me. I had so much fun."

Sophia wound her little arms around Lexa's neck and gave Lexa a kiss on the cheek. "Me too. See you tomorrow?"

"I'm leaving on an airplane tomorrow. I'm going to Taiwan to see my family."

"Airplane?" Sophia's eyes widened. She thought, and then said, "You come back soon?"

Lexa glanced at Jake. "Maybe. Hopefully soon."

"Okay." Sophia gave Lexa one more hug and then took her father's hand.

"I'll be right back." Jake waved to her and led Sophia out to the car.

Lexa drifted through the house, her thoughts wandering as she waited for Jake. Her fingers touched the signs of Jake's life: framed photos of him and Sophia, Sophia's artwork on the fridge, a jacket thrown over the back of a chair, a stuffed pig forgotten on the couch. Jake found her sitting on the back deck when he returned.

"Hey." He said it softly, but Lexa still jolted. She'd been deep in thought and hadn't heard him come in.

"Jake." She put a hand on her chest, feeling her heartbeat quicken.

"Did you like Sophia?" There was a hopeful, almost boyish look in his eyes as he waited for her answer.

"Of course! She's so adorable, such a sweet little girl. And I'm not just saying that because she's your daughter. Or thinks I'm a Disney princess."

"I'm glad you two got along so well." Jake sat on the glider bench on the patio and patted the seat next to him. She sat, tucking her feet up under her, and he slid an arm around her waist. "I have to ask you something." She stilled at the serious tone in his voice. "Can you see yourself being a mother after meeting Sophia?"

"You mean a mother in general, or Sophia's mother?" Her pulse skipped and danced, because she knew they were about to have a conversation she didn't know if she was ready for.

He played with her hair, twirling a strand around his finger. "Either. Both." He blew out a breath. "I really care about you. You make me smile every time I see you, and I'm so attracted to you. I know it's kind of early to be talking about this, but I . . ." He trailed off without finishing his sentence.

"I know. I feel it too. But . . ." Now it was her turn to search for words. How did she tell him she really liked him but she couldn't see them together?

"But?"

"I just don't see how it would work. You live here, and I'm in New York. My whole family is there, my friends, my job, and my clients. Plus, I don't think I can be a mother. I just can't."

"Why?"

She shook her head. She'd waited all her life to feel like this for a man, yet when it happened, it was with someone who wanted a different life.

He stroked his thumb up and down the back of her hand. "Is it because of what happened with your father? That he didn't believe you?"

Lexa squeezed her eyes shut. "It sounds so stupid when you say it. My father didn't believe me and basically severed our relationship, and now I'm so damaged by it that I don't want kids."

Jake pulled away slightly to look down at her. "Lexa, I don't think what you're feeling is stupid at all." She could hear the hurt in his voice. "I'm just trying to understand where you're coming from."

"I'm sorry. I didn't mean to jump down your throat. I guess I think it's stupid. My mom loves me and has stood by me my entire life, and Greg has never treated me as anything less than his biological daughter. And yet, there's this . . . this hole in me because my father didn't believe me." Tears sprang to her eyes, and she blinked rapidly to keep them away. "I loved him so much. I thought he loved me too. But he . . .

he shattered my trust, and I just can't imagine being responsible for a child. What if I did the same thing to a child that he did to me?" She sat up straight so that she was no longer leaning on Jake. "My mom and dad would lay down their lives for me, yet they couldn't keep my father from breaking my heart."

She stopped and gulped air into lungs that suddenly felt too big for her chest. Not until then had she ever voiced to herself why she didn't want children. With her friends, she'd always been flip. *I just don't want them.* Or, *Not everyone wants kids.* But at that moment, the truth shook her. The breath she took in trembled, and she willed herself to get a grip and back in control.

Jake didn't say anything, only put a hand on her shoulder. They stayed like that for a long time, until Lexa's breathing evened and the tears no longer threatened.

Jake spoke. "I understand why you don't want to have children. But I need to ask you this because I'm in love with you." He held up a hand when she opened her mouth. "Don't say anything yet. Hear me out." She closed her mouth, her heart hammering in her chest so loud she was surprised he couldn't hear it. "I want to see where this goes with you. I want to see if we can find a way to be together. Sophia is a part of my life. If you can't accept her, then it'll never work. But I saw the way you were with her today."

"But how?" Lexa asked. "I can't imagine uprooting my whole life to move here."

"I'll fly to New York when I can; you'll come here when you can. And if our relationship does grow and we take the next step, who's to say you'd have to be the one to move? I could ask my company for a transfer to the New York office."

Lexa stared at him. Was he for real? "But what about Sophia? I don't think your ex will like it if you take her out of the state."

"Sophia's mom is from New York originally. She only moved here because of my job. I don't think she'd be opposed to moving back to New York if it really came to that."

Lexa sat and gaped at him. It was all too much. The realization of why she didn't want children, meeting Sophia, Jake telling her he loved her.

Jake reached out a hand and said, "I know. It's too much to throw at you right now. Especially because you're leaving for Taiwan tomorrow and confronting a past that you haven't resolved."

"Too much," she echoed.

"Maddie's meeting up with you tomorrow?"

"Yes. We're on the same flight to Taiwan from San Francisco."

He gazed at her with such a tender look on his face that it made her want to cry. She was about to speak when he said, "I'm not letting you go so easily. I'll give you time and space, but I'm not going anywhere. Go to Taiwan and figure out your past. I'll be waiting for you when you do." He turned her head toward him and stared deep into her eyes, and the look he sent her undid her.

"I'm scared," she whispered. "I don't know how to do this. I don't know how to let go and just be."

He reached out and placed a finger over her lips. And when he replaced his finger with his lips, she felt something loosen in her chest. Letting the feel of Jake's kiss take over her senses, she wondered if maybe it would be possible to keep him in her life somehow.

43

Lexa stood in the baggage claim area of the Taiwan Taoyuan International Airport, waiting for her suitcase to show up on the carousel. Maddie stood next to her, busy checking her phone to see what she'd missed while they were in the air.

The airport was loud, people talking in Mandarin and Taiwanese, some yelling, some waving their arms with wild gestures. Carts and suitcases rolled by, children ran around, and people struggled to pull their suitcases off the carousel. Lexa stood and took it all in, noting the Asian people with black hair and feeling that sense of belonging she'd felt when she'd been here the last three times.

Someone bumped into her, and she automatically excused herself in Mandarin. A woman asked if she knew where the bathroom was, and Lexa pointed in the right direction. Lexa smiled. She was back. She understood the language.

Lexa's phone dinged with a text message, and Maddie looked up. "Is that Jake?" Maddie asked.

Lexa looked at her phone. "No, it's Hsu-Ling. She's here."

"I still think you're being an idiot." Lexa had told Maddie about Jake on the flight over. "This hot guy who's totally into you and who you're totally into tells you he loves you and wants to have a relationship with you. And you turn him down 'cause you don't want kids." Maddie shoved Lexa lightly on the shoulder. "You are such an idiot."

Lexa shrugged, because part of her agreed with Maddie. Before she could reply, Maddie spied her bag. "That's mine. Lexa, grab it!"

Lexa reached over and hefted Maddie's suitcase off the carousel. "Why can't you get it yourself?"

"It's too heavy. You're the trainer."

Lexa pulled her own bag off and then squared her shoulders. "Okay. Let's go. Hsu-Ling should be out there somewhere."

She walked forward, going through the last checkpoint with Maddie trailing behind. Lexa couldn't keep the smile off her face as they walked through the doors into the terminal where people waited, some holding up signs written in Chinese. She was really here. She was back in her father's land.

.   .   .

"Sign here." The lawyer pointed to the paper. "And here and here."

Lexa picked up the pen he offered and paused before putting her signature to the paper. It was all in Chinese, and though she couldn't read most of it, she didn't mind. It made it less real that she was about to receive the equivalent of a hundred thousand dollars from Pong as well as an apartment. It still felt like blood money to her. And once this paperwork was done, she and Hsu-Ling would take over ownership of the Chang family building.

Hsu-Ling had hired a car and driver and met them at the airport in Taipei. They'd driven straight to the hotel in Taichung, about a two-and-a-half-hour ride. She'd booked them into a hotel by the old train station in the central district of

Taichung, less than a ten-minute drive from the family build-ing. "There's more to do around that area than where my par-ents live," she'd said. "You can walk to a lot of places."

After breakfast at a noodle cart on the street, Hsu-Ling had brought them here to the lawyer's office to take care of the paperwork involved with Pong and their father's wills.

"Having second thoughts?" Lexa looked up at Maddie's question and found both her sisters looking at her. She quickly shook her head. She scrawled her name on the first document and reached for the next until all the papers that required her signature were done. Hsu-Ling had already signed her part when Lexa had decided to come back to Taiwan, so it made that day's appointment easier.

They shook hands with the lawyer, and Lexa walked out of the building with her copies of the documents and the bank information, as well as the keys to her new apartment. She stood on the crowded sidewalk and faced her sisters. "It's done."

"It is." Hsu-Ling nodded. "Thank you."

Lexa shook her head. "Don't thank me."

The three stood there for a moment until Hsu-Ling asked, "Ready to face my mama? She's home right now. I told her we'd be over once we finished the paperwork with the lawyer."

Lexa took a big breath and nodded. "Let's go."

. . .

Lexa sat in the back of the taxi with Maddie at her side and Hsu-Ling up front next to the driver. She smiled, thinking this taxi was just as beat-up and smelly as the taxis in New York City. She listened to Hsu-Ling giving the driver direc-tions to her parents' place from the lawyer's office in a mixture of Mandarin and Taiwanese. Lexa had never learned Taiwanese because they didn't teach that at Chinese school, but now she regretted never having learned.

"It's not far," Hsu-Ling said from the front. "I live just over there to the north"—she pointed out the window—"about a five-minute walk from your new apartment, Lexa. And the Chang building is just south of here, about fifteen minutes by car. You can probably walk to your hotel from our family building, but it would take you over twenty minutes."

Lexa pressed a hand to her stomach as the busy streets of Taichung sped by. She was having a hard time following Hsu-Ling's directions of where everything was and would have to look at a map later. Right at that moment, she was more focused on the butterflies in her stomach. She felt like she was going to throw up.

When the taxi pulled up in front of the building with the red metal gate in the front, Lexa felt a jolt of recognition. This was it. This was her baba's building, hers and Hsu-Ling's now.

Maddie was silent as they waited on the sidewalk for Hsu-Ling to pay the driver. Lexa knew she felt out of place. It still wasn't that common to see a Caucasian in Taichung. For the first time in their lives, Maddie was the one who stuck out, not Lexa.

"Ready?" Hsu-Ling asked. Lexa took a breath and nodded. Hsu-Ling opened the gate with a key, and they walked into the courtyard.

For Lexa, it was like stepping back in time. Nothing much had changed in the courtyard. The same gray concrete steps leading up to the hallway to their baba's apartment. The paint on the white walls looked new, and the bricks on the outside of the building that Lexa had remembered as green had been painted white, but everything else was the same. Even the tree growing on the side of the courtyard, though bigger now, was just like she remembered.

Hsu-Ling pointed to the tree. "I used to climb it all the time, driving my mother crazy." She laughed. "She thought I was going to kill myself."

"You're lucky you didn't."

At the strange voice, all three of them turned toward the hallway. And there, standing at the top of the steps, was Hsu-Ling's mother. Her mouth was pinched exactly the way Lexa remembered, as if she'd swallowed something sour. Her hair was pulled back in a severe bun, streaked with more gray than black now. Wrinkles furrowed her forehead, and because of the way her mouth was drawn together, Lexa could see the lines radiating from it. Hsu-Ling had said her mother had taken their father's death badly, barely getting out of bed for two months after the accident. Lexa was sure that hearing Lexa had inherited the building as well as an apartment and money from Pong hadn't helped.

"Mama. You remember ChiChi."

Pin-Yen nodded at Lexa and then looked away.

Hsu-Ling gestured to Maddie. "And this is her sister Maddie."

Pin-Yen regarded Maddie, letting her eyes roam from Maddie's blond curls to the hot pink sundress with spaghetti straps she wore and down her bare legs to her wedge sandals. She didn't say anything.

Without acknowledging Maddie, Pin-Yen turned to Lexa. "You came back. I didn't think you would. Not after the way you shamed this family and the Chang name." She spoke in Mandarin, even though Lexa knew Pin-Yen spoke English well enough.

"Me?" Lexa stared at Pin-Yen and understood immediately how things were. Nothing had changed in twenty-two years. Pin-Yen still hated her, probably even more so now that Lexa had the very thing Pin-Yen had done everything she could to keep from her.

"Mama." Hsu-Ling's voice held a warning, and Pin-Yen turned to her.

"I only speak the truth. This, this bastard daughter of your father's, somehow managed to manipulate her way into his will, despite my best efforts to show Jing Tao her true colors. She even got Pong to include her in his will. She is despicable. I don't want her under my roof."

"Are you out of your mind?" Rage exploded in Lexa's chest, and she realized the woman was deranged.

At the same time, Hsu-Ling said, "Your roof! It's technically Lexa's roof, and you're lucky she's letting you stay here."

Maddie looked back and forth between the three of them. "What's she saying?"

"She's just as vicious as I remembered. She called me a bastard daughter and said I manipulated my father and Pong."

Maddie turned and aimed a glare at Pin-Yen that was filled with so much vitriol that the older woman recoiled visibly. *Don't say something you'll regret*, Lexa pleaded with her silently. Too often, Maddie lashed out and criticized people or said something mean when she felt threatened. As much rage as Lexa felt toward Pin-Yen, she knew it wouldn't help if Maddie said something scathing.

Knowing Pin-Yen understood English, Maddie said, "Lexa was right. You are a such a bi . . ." She trailed off when Lexa placed a warning hand on her arm. Shooting a glance at Lexa, Maddie huffed out a breath and planted her hands on her hips. She waited a moment and then said in a soft voice, "Lexa owns this building now, along with your daughter. Her father knew the truth about you in the end. Pong even said in his letter that he saw you for who you really are. Why don't you just give up, okay? You lost."

Pin-Yen's jaw dropped, and her entire body shook. She stood speechless, her eyes darting from Maddie to Lexa. Hsu-Ling made a sound, but her mother ignored her. Instead, she focused her wrath on Maddie. "What do you know about Pong? You know nothing about what was between us."

"Why don't you tell us, then?" Maddie challenged.

"You, you . . . ," Pin-Yen sputtered before she turned on her heels and stalked down the hallway back to her apartment, letting the door slam hard behind her.

Lexa and Hsu-Ling looked at each other. Lexa was suddenly curious about the man who had been her father's best friend. "Pong said he saw through your mother's act years ago. I wonder what happened."

"I have no idea." Hsu-Ling shook her head. "The only one who's still alive to tell us is my mother. But I don't think she ever will."

44

September, Seventeen Years Ago
Taichung, Taiwan

Did you see? Did you see what's happening in New York?"
Pong burst through the front door of their apartment
without knocking. Jing Tao had given him a key to their front
gate and apartment years earlier, yet he'd never used it without asking first.

Pin-Yen regarded Pong from her seat at the dining table,
where she was going over Hsu-Ling's homework with her. It
was late, but Hsu-Ling wasn't allowed to go to bed until everything was done perfectly. Pong was red-faced and panting for
breath, as if he'd run here all the way from his apartment,
which was fifteen minutes away by scooter.

"Jing Tao, turn on the TV," Uncle Pong ordered, and Jing
Tao immediately reached for the remote from his spot on the
couch.

"What happened?" Pin-Yen asked.

"There's been a terrorist attack in New York," Uncle Pong
said.

"*Aiyo!*" Jing Tao's eyes were glued to the TV.

Pin-Yen rushed to the couch, all thoughts of homework forgotten. Hsu-Ling slammed her math book shut and went to sit by her mother's side.

"The Twin Towers," Uncle Pong said. "Someone drove two planes into them."

Pin-Yen watched, fascinated, as the news showed the first tower collapsing, only moments before. It looked like a TV stunt, something she would see in a movie.

"ChiChi," Hsu-Ling said, turning to Jing Tao with wide eyes. "Chi lives in New York!"

He had already gotten to his feet and run to the phone, dialing Susan's home phone number. He hung up right away and said, "It's busy. Hsu-Ling, where's her cell phone number?"

She gave it to her father. "I think she's back at school. I hope she's not in New York City." Lexa was a sophomore at Middlebury College that year. They'd just reconnected the year before, when Hsu-Ling had found that letter from Lexa on Pin-Yen's desk. Pin-Yen still cursed herself for being so careless that day. She should have thrown out that letter as soon as she found it in their mail. But she'd been distracted by the Chinese soap opera she was watching and hadn't thought Hsu-Ling would come home from school so early. Ever since Hsu-Ling had read that letter, she'd been emailing that girl, even though Pin-Yen disapproved.

"*Wei?*" Jing Tao said into the phone. "Chi-ah, is that you?"

He listened, and Pin-Yen could hear Lexa's voice, loud and hysterical. Jing Tao said something, and then he hung up.

"She's okay. She's at college. But she can't find her dad."

Their eyes were drawn back to the TV, where a reporter announced that the second tower had just collapsed.

Three hours later, at one thirty in the morning, Jing Tao

finally retired to their bedroom with a book, and Pin-Yen and Hsu-Ling walked Pong out of the apartment. As soon as they stepped outside the front door, Pong reached into his front pocket for a cigarette and lit up.

"Uncle Pong," Hsu-Ling scolded in her sternest voice, "what did I tell you about smoking? It's going to kill you."

He inhaled deeply and blew out a perfect smoke ring. Catching the disapproving look in Hsu-Ling's eyes, he stubbed out the cigarette. "Ah, my smoking police." He chuckled. "Still after me, eh?"

"Yes. Especially today, with all those people dead." Hsu-Ling stood at the top of the stairs and shivered. "I can't stop thinking about ChiChi. I'm so glad she and her family are okay."

"I know. Crazy day." Pong and Pin-Yen walked down the stairs and stopped in the middle of the courtyard.

"The whole world's going crazy," Pin-Yen said.

"Poor ChiChi." Pong patted his front pocket, and Pin-Yen could tell he was itching for another cigarette. "I'm glad she was finally able to get through to her dad. It must have been terrifying knowing he was in the city at the time of the attack."

Pin-Yen frowned. "Too bad she wasn't in one of the towers at the time."

Pong's hand stilled, and he drew back sharply, as if Pin-Yen had slapped him. "What did you say?"

"I said I wish she'd—" Pin-Yen started, but Pong cut her off.

"Hsu-Ling, go to bed," he ordered.

Pin-Yen could see the startled look on Hsu-Ling's face at Pong's unusual order. Hsu-Ling opened her mouth to argue, but Pin-Yen shook her head at her daughter. "Yes, Uncle Pong. Good night, Mama." And she turned and went back into the apartment, closing the door softly behind her.

Pong came to Pin-Yen's side, so close she could smell the cigarette he'd just smoked mixing with the menthol drops he liked to chew. "What did you just say?" he repeated. "In front of your daughter, no less?"

Pin-Yen took a step back and crossed her arms over her chest. "You heard me. She's done nothing but cause trouble for us since Jing Tao learned of her existence." She laughed, a hollow sound that was too loud in the still night. "It would make life so simple if she'd just disappear."

Pong's mouth dropped open, and he stared at Pin-Yen as if he'd never seen her before. "You would wish your husband's child to perish in a tragedy like what happened today in New York, just to satisfy your own needs?"

She was quiet, studying him, and felt the first trickle of uncertainty run down her back. "You know what I mean." Pin-Yen softened her voice in the hopes of bringing Pong back on her side. "I was just kidding. Jing Tao was supposed to change his will so that Hsu-Ling is the only daughter to inherit, but I don't know if he did. Every time I ask him, he changes the subject. That girl doesn't deserve anything from the Chang family after what she did. I just thought it would make things easier if she'd . . ."

". . . if she'd die." Pong completed her sentence for her. "She didn't do anything. You were the one who set her up. Are you starting to believe your own lies?" His eyes bore into hers. "Are you really this cold-blooded? What happened to the courageous, dream-filled girl I knew from years ago, who cared about making a difference in the world?"

Pin-Yen didn't answer. She stared back at him, waiting to see what he'd do.

"I've been so blinded by my feelings for you that I made excuses for your behavior and your lies. Even though I knew it was wrong, I did it for you. But to wish your husband's flesh and blood to die in a terrorist attack . . . who are you?"

"Pong." She put a hand on his chest to placate him, but he grabbed her wrist and held her hand away from his body. She winced from his strong grip. They stared at each other, and she saw something shift in his eyes. "Don't do anything stupid," she said in a soft voice. "Don't go telling Jing Tao the truth. You think he'll thank you?" She shook her head, narrowing her eyes. "All you'll do is lose face in front of the man you respect so much." Her voice lowered even more. "Is that what you want? For Jing Tao to know what a coward and traitor you are? In love with his wife all these years, lying to him, causing his daughter to go away? Because we all know the truth. He'd never have believed me if you hadn't backed me up."

They stared at each other for what felt like hours, Pong's breath a harsh rasp in the quiet night while Pin-Yen held hers. Finally, Pong flung her arm away from him, and she rubbed her wrist. He turned his back on her and brought a hand to his forehead. She knew she'd won.

She raised her chin. "I knew you didn't have it in you to lose face with your best friend."

He turned, and the look he shot her was filled with so much hatred it made her take a step back. Before she could react, he stalked to the gate and left, slamming it on his way out.

She stood alone in the middle of the courtyard and knew the young boy who had fallen in love with her all those years earlier was no more. She gave a shake of her head and turned to return to her husband and daughter, safe inside their home. She may have lost Pong's love and devotion, but she knew he'd never betray her. Because to do so, he'd lose the respect of the only person in the world he could call family.

45

Lexa and her sisters stood in the courtyard and stared at one another, not sure what to do after Pin-Yen's dramatic departure.

Hsu-Ling turned to Maddie. "Nice going. You just made my mother so mad she probably won't let us into the apartment."

"It's your apartment, yours and Lexa's. Don't you have the key?" Maddie crossed her arms over her chest, not looking sorry at all that she'd pissed off Pin-Yen.

"I'm not sure if I want to go in now if she's there. I knew things weren't going to be easy, but I didn't think they were going to be that bad. She hasn't changed at all. I think she's gotten worse." Lexa stood rooted to the spot, unable to believe that woman still harbored so much hatred toward her.

"You've come all this way. You said you wanted to see Baba's things, to see pictures. I'm sorry for my mother." Hsu-Ling turned to her, apology written all over her face.

"Don't apologize for her. Maybe we can come back later, when she's not home," Lexa said.

Before the others could answer, the door to the apartment suddenly opened again and Pin-Yen strode out, carrying a large tote bag. She swept by the trio and addressed Hsu-Ling only.

"I'm going out. Let me know when they leave." And with that, she marched to the gate and walked out, letting the gate slam behind her.

Maddie raised her eyebrows. "She likes to slam doors. But I guess the coast is clear."

They walked to the apartment, and as they crossed the threshold, Lexa found herself holding her breath. She almost expected her father to come striding out to greet them like he had the very first time she'd come to visit. But the apartment was silent, and she went through the foyer into the living room and stood in the center, looking around.

Like the courtyard, everything was so familiar, yet with slight differences and updates. If she squinted, she could almost imagine it was the last time she'd been here and her father was in the next room, getting ready to take her and Hsu-Ling on an adventure around Taichung. She could almost smell the *dua mee gee* noodle soup that Pin-Yen was known for, and hear her fourteen-year-old self and Hsu-Ling giggling together on the blue couch, huddled over a photo album of their father and Pin-Yen's wedding.

"Is that the same blue couch you had all those years ago?" Lexa turned to Hsu-Ling, who was still standing in the foyer.

"No. But Baba loved that couch so much he found one almost like it to replace it."

Lexa walked over to the living room wall and reached out to touch the velvety texture of the tan damask-print wallpaper. "But this is the same wallpaper, isn't it?"

Hsu-Ling nodded. "Mama hates that wallpaper. She was always after Baba to replace it or to rip it down and paint the room white. But Baba said it was home to him and didn't want to take it down. And now that he's dead, she wants to keep it exactly the way it was when he was alive."

"I can't believe it's still here after all these years."

Lexa turned around in a circle, taking in the shrine with the statues of gods and goddesses, and noticed that a recent picture of her father had been hung next to a picture of their ah-gong, as well as her father's grandparents. She stood in front of the shrine and brought her hands up in prayer, bowing her head and closing her eyes. She wasn't sure if she should say something, so she remained silent, trying to absorb that she was really standing here in her father's home after all these years.

When she opened her eyes, she found Maddie looking at her. For once, Maddie kept her mouth shut, and for that Lexa was grateful. She needed time to allow her mind to catch up to the fact that she was back in her father's home. Lexa wandered around the apartment, walking into her old room, staring at the bamboo bed, and wondering if it was the same one she'd slept on. She went from room to room, only pausing briefly at Pin-Yen and her father's door out of respect for Pin-Yen's privacy, although she wished she could look in her father's closet and see his belongings, touch his clothes.

When she got back to the living room, Hsu-Ling asked her, "Are you okay?"

Lexa smiled and nodded. "It's just so strange to be back here without him."

Hsu-Ling's expression turned sober. "I know. It's hard for me to come home now, knowing he'll never be here again." She darted a glance at Lexa and then said, "Are you ready to go see Ah-Ma? She's waiting for us upstairs."

Lexa took in a breath. "Yes. I don't know why I'm so nervous to see her."

"Don't be nervous. She's been waiting impatiently for you to come back." Hsu-Ling led the way out of the apartment and up the concrete steps to the second floor, with Lexa behind her and Maddie trailing silently at the tail. Hsu-Ling knocked lightly on the door and then opened it.

"Ah-Ma?" she called into the apartment. "We're here!"

Lexa had only a moment to register the strong smell of incense that wafted out of the apartment before a small figure unfolded itself from a chair in the main room and rushed toward Lexa, her arms outstretched.

"Chi-ah! You're finally home." Ah-Ma spoke in Taiwanese, but for some reason, Lexa understood. She found herself enveloped in Ah-Ma's arms, her face buried in her grandmother's shoulder, and breathed in a combination of mothballs, tiger balm, and an herby scent that emanated from Ah-Ma.

Lexa held still, listening to Ah-Ma speaking in Taiwanese and wishing again she could understand. When Ah-Ma finally pulled back, she studied Lexa's face intently.

Hsu-Ling translated for her. "She's saying you still have an auspicious nose. It's nice and rounded at the bottom, like the Taiwan wax apple. She's happy you didn't lose your nose when you grew up." Lexa heard Maddie stifle a snort of laughter behind her and felt her own lips twitch in response.

Ah-Ma next focused on Lexa's ears and continued speaking in Taiwanese. "And your earlobes are still big and fat, signifying good fortune and a good life."

"I always thought big earlobes just meant you could have multiple earrings," Maddie said. Lexa smiled at her words, even as she glowed inside from Ah-Ma's attention.

Ah-Ma finally let go of Lexa, and Lexa pulled Maddie next to her.

"Ah-Ma, this is my American sister, Maddie."

"Welcome, welcome." Ah-Ma spoke one of the few English words she knew, smiling widely and patting Maddie on the arm.

"Thanks for having me, Ah-Ma," Maddie said, her voice at a reverent pitch.

They smiled at each other, and then Ah-Ma clapped her hands and spoke in Mandarin. "*Lai, lai, chi fan.*"

Lexa turned to Maddie. "Are you hungry? She wants us to eat."

"She's been making dumplings in anticipation of your visit," Hsu-Ling said. "Ah-Ma makes the best dumplings. When we were younger, we'd have these big dumpling-making parties. All the cousins and aunts would gather here in Ah-Ma's kitchen, and we'd make huge batches of dumplings to freeze so we could have them anytime. We'd create an assembly line—one person rolled out the disc, someone else would put the filling on the wrapper, another would pinch it shut. We'd fight over who got to mix the meat and vegetable mixture." Hsu-Ling smiled. "The boy cousins always got into dough fights, throwing bits of dough at each other until Ah-Ma scolded them and made them make tea for the rest of us."

"That sounds like so much fun." Lexa bit her bottom lip, feeling a swell of emotion at all she'd missed over the years with her grandmother and the rest of the family.

"She can teach you how to make them. She makes different kinds, with pork or chicken with chives and leeks, or even all vegetarian ones."

"That would be amazing." Lexa turned to Maddie. "We could make them at home with Mom."

Maddie nodded. "I can't wait to taste Ah-Ma's dumplings."

Ah-Ma bustled into the kitchen, still a spry figure despite her age. Lexa stared after her and felt a lump in her throat as she watched this tiny woman, who was her father's mother, turn on a big pot of water for the dumplings. Her hair was now snow white, caught back in a low bun, and her hands were slightly gnarled from arthritis and riddled with blue veins. But her grip was strong and sure as she pulled out soy sauce, Chinese barbecue sauce, and a pot of homemade hot sauce. Lexa walked into the cluttered kitchen, crowded with a variety of jars, tins, and containers filled with all sorts of mysterious items on the countertops and on the open shelves. She remembered the day Ah-Ma had taught them how to make tea eggs. She leaned over and kissed Ah-Ma on the cheek, marveling at her surprisingly smooth skin.

"I'm so happy to see you again, Ah-Ma. Thank you for having us here," she said in Mandarin.

"*Aiya!*" Ah-Ma clucked her tongue. "You are my grand-daughter. You are always welcome in my home." She set the sauces on the counter and turned to cup a hand around Lexa's cheek. "Took you long enough to come back, huh?"

Lexa dropped her gaze, embarrassed. Standing in front of her grandmother, it did seem foolish that she hadn't been back in all these years.

"Never mind," Ah-Ma said. "You're here now. And hope-fully, it will help your father to rest." She gave a shiver and bowed her head for a moment. "His ghost lingers because he is greatly upset by the rift in his family. He died trying to get to you, to make right what his wife did wrong." She gave Lexa's cheek a pat and then dropped her hand, turning back to the sauces lined up on the counter. "He's unable to go in peace to the afterlife. I know he would be so happy that you are finally back where you belong."

"Thank you, Ah-Ma," Lexa said softly.

Lexa stood next to her grandmother and watched her drop the dumplings into the boiling water, stirring them briefly so they wouldn't stick together. And she listened as Ah-Ma showed her how to make a dumpling sauce, adding soy sauce, sesame oil, a big heaping spoonful of the Chinese barbecue sauce, and hot sauce, and stirring it around until it became a fragrant mixture that had Maddie leaning forward to get a better whiff.

They sat at Ah-Ma's table when the dumplings were done, and for a few moments, the only sounds in the kitchen were of them picking up the dumplings with chopsticks (even Maddie managed to spear one without it flying across the room), dipping them into the sauce, and bringing them to their waiting mouths. Maddie moaned out loud in pleasure at her first bite, causing Ah-Ma to smile widely at her.

Lexa couldn't speak. Her mouth was full, the delicately seasoned pork mixing with the strong flavor of the chives and brought together by the slightly spicy, tangy sauce, and she swore it was the best thing she'd ever had. Dumplings in America couldn't even compare. The wrapper was just chewy enough to offer a contrast to the flavorful filling, and she couldn't stop eating.

By the time they pushed back their plates and leaned back in their chairs, Ah-Ma had already placed a dish of the Taiwanese wax apples that she'd mentioned earlier in front of them. Maddie picked up one of the pink and white fruits and studied it.

"I've never seen such a pretty fruit," she said. "So this is what your nose looks like, huh?" She held up the wax apple next to Lexa's nose and peered at both.

"Very funny." Lexa swatted away Maddie's hand while

Ah-Ma laughed, seeming not to have any problems with the language barrier.

They each picked up a piece of the fruit that Ah-Ma sliced right at the table with a small paring knife, and when Lexa bit into the dense, juicy body, a memory of her father giving her this fruit the first time she was in Taiwan flashed before her eyes. It was a fleeting memory of them in a produce market, brought back only by the flavor in her mouth. Before she could focus on it, it disappeared.

"What's the matter?" Hsu-Ling asked. Ah-Ma was also looking at her in concern.

Lexa swallowed her bite. "I was just thinking of Baba, of how I don't have many memories of him. I keep thinking I remember something, but it slips away before I can bring it all back."

Ah-Ma looked at her for a moment. "Do you want to know about your baba?"

"Yes. I really do."

Ah-Ma stood and said, "I'll be right back."

She shuffled into the bedroom and returned in a moment with a large photo album. "Hsu-Ling, can you get the rest from the shelf? You know where they are."

Hsu-Ling walked out of the kitchen, and Ah-Ma settled back at the table and opened the album in front of Lexa. The album was old, the photos all black-and-white, but Lexa could see they'd been well taken care of and preserved.

Ah-Ma pointed to a picture of a little baby lying on his stomach with a hand propped under his chin. The baby had an enormous head. "That's your baba."

"I had a giant head too when I was a baby." Lexa smiled to see the resemblance to her own baby pictures.

Hsu-Ling came back with a few albums stacked in her

arms, and Maddie helped her put them on the table. Ah-Ma sat back in her own chair as Lexa continued to stare at her father's baby pictures.

"Your father was my firstborn child. A male, which is cause for much celebration. It had been a difficult birth—I mean, just look at that head! But the moment I held him in my arms, he placed a hand right over my heart as if reassuring me he was there. I knew this boy would always take care of me and his family . . ."

46

Lexa stood in the foyer of her father's apartment and greeted her father's family as they came in. She knew some of her cousins from Facebook, but really, they were all strangers. They came up to her, one or two at a time, and exchanged a few awkward words. Hsu-Ling stood next to her, explaining who everyone was and how he or she was related to Lexa. One of the last guests to arrive was a man about their age with broad shoulders and dark-rimmed glasses that gave him an air of intelligence. Hsu-Ling introduced him simply as Kuan-Yu, and Lexa looked at her with curiosity, especially when the man placed his hand at Hsu-Ling's waist and leaned down to give her a kiss on the cheek.

Lexa was distracted by the arrival of the nun who would be reading sutras for their father and Pong's final prayer ceremony. After Hsu-Ling introduced her, Lexa went into the apartment to find Maddie. Pin-Yen rushed over to greet the nun. Lexa did her best to ignore the older woman. This was a day to honor her father and to remember him, and she wasn't going to let anyone distract her.

Ah-Ma came to Lexa's side and, with a hand on her arm, walked her over to the shrine where more pictures of her father and Pong were hung. Lexa stared at a recent photo of her baba, his face so much older than she remembered in her mind. She reached out and grasped Ah-Ma's hands carefully in her own, feeling her grandmother's papery-thin skin. While Ah-Ma's face was relatively unlined, her hands and arms were covered in wrinkles, with age spots dotting her skin.

"His ghost mourns for you, his lost daughter. But you are back, and maybe now he can finally cross over and be at peace." Ah-Ma closed her eyes and began to pray, her lips moving soundlessly.

Lexa turned away to give her privacy and focused on the offerings laid out at the shrine. Oranges, Chinese apples, melons, and other fruits she didn't recognize; bowls of rice with meat; plates of vegetables and tofu; and cookies and numerous desserts were set out for her father and Pong. There was incense burning in urns, and when Ah-Ma was done with her prayer, she let go of Lexa's hand to retrieve fresh sticks.

She handed Hsu-Ling three incense sticks and then gave Lexa the same. The two sisters stood in front of their father's picture. Lexa held up the incense in front of her chest, knowing she was supposed to pray to him or offer a blessing. But all she could think was, *I miss you. I wish you hadn't died before we could have seen each other again.* She bowed three times before placing the sticks in the urn with her left hand. Bringing her hands together, she bowed one last time.

Ah-Ma handed three sticks to Maddie and gestured toward the shrine. Maddie didn't hesitate and followed Hsu-Ling's and Lexa's lead. The nun handed out books, and Hsu-Ling said, "Don't worry that you can't read it. Just listen." And when the nun started chanting sutras and her relatives joined in, following along in the books, Lexa stood with her head bowed, letting the singsong chants wash over her. She closed her eyes and brought a picture of her father into her mind.

. . .

"I've never seen so much food in my life," Maddie moaned, holding her stomach. "How do you people stay so thin? You eat so much but are so skinny." She slumped back in her chair at the restaurant down the street from the apartment. Jing Tao's brother was hosting this late lunch for the entire family following the ceremony.

Hsu-Ling laughed. "I guess it's an Asian thing."

They'd eaten course after course of food: soups and platters of chicken, Chinese vegetables, tofu, oysters fried and also in soups, whole fish, bamboo shoots, noodles, and a whole bunch of stuff she'd never seen before. Bottles of beer had been passed around, and everyone had eaten until they were full.

"Where's Kuan-Yu?" Lexa asked.

"He had to go back to work."

"Who is he? Another relative?"

"No." Hsu-Ling looked down at her food with a small smile. "He's a . . . friend."

Lexa looked at her in question. "A boyfriend? Why didn't you tell me about him?"

Before she could answer, Maddie leaned in close to them. "Why is everyone so red?"

Lexa looked around at her relatives and realized Maddie was right. Most of them were bright red, as if they'd just run a marathon or had been caught in the sun without sunscreen.

"It's the Asian glow." Lexa grinned.

"Right, the Asian glow." Hsu-Ling giggled.

"What's that?" Maddie looked baffled.

"Asians are often missing an enzyme that processes alcohol, so they tend to turn bright red after only one drink," Hsu-Ling said.

Maddie turned to Lexa. "But you don't get like that."

"No." Lexa shook her head. "I guess Mom's genes won out over my father's in this."

They were still laughing when Hsu-Ling and Lexa's uncle walked up to them. He drew a chair and sat behind them, causing them to turn in their seats so that they could see him.

"Hsu-Ling." They stopped laughing at the serious tone in his voice. "Your mother is causing trouble." They all looked across the large table with the lazy Susan in the middle, which they'd used to pass the dishes around. Pin-Yen sat at the far end between two of their female cousins, her arms crossed over her chest. "She's telling us that ChiChi manipulated your father into changing his will to include her. She wants the whole family to contest the will."

Hsu-Ling put her hands to her cheeks, which were flushed red from the beer she'd drunk. "He didn't change his will." She blew out an exasperated breath. "The lawyer told me he'd always included Lexa in the will. Mama's out of her mind."

Their uncle nodded. "I know. None of us believe her. I've had many conversations with Jing Tao, especially recently, about ChiChi. It weighed heavy on his mind that he had allowed her to walk away all those years ago without putting up a fight."

Lexa spoke up. "Then why didn't Baba try to make things right with me?"

Her uncle answered before Hsu-Ling could. "Your baba tried. When you first went home, he called often, wanting to work it out. But your mother wouldn't let him speak to you at first. And then she said you didn't want to talk to him. Over the years, he eventually thought it was better to leave you alone. You made it clear you wanted nothing to do with him beyond the occasional emails."

Lexa felt her face flush with heat. "It was horrible, what happened. I wanted to forget it." She sighed. "I guess it was my fault."

Her uncle held up a hand. "No. It wasn't your fault. I just wish you'd had a chance to know him before he died. I speak for the whole family when I say we're glad you came back. And not just because you saved our home."

"There's one person who's not happy I came back." Lexa turned to Hsu-Ling, who was translating for Maddie. "Your mother looks like she wants me to drop dead."

Maddie caught Pin-Yen's eyes. "Hey," she called across the table. "I hear you're trying to get everyone to contest the will. Well, you're out of luck. The lawyer told us the will is solid."

Lexa laid a hand on Maddie's arm. "Maddie, stop. Don't provoke her."

Maddie turned to Lexa, her eyes blazing. "I'm not going to sit here and have her saying nasty things about you to your family." At the look on Lexa's face, Maddie's expression softened. "I'm sorry. I'm not trying to make things difficult for you. But I can't let her get away with what she's doing to you."

"Let it go, Maddie. She's never going to change her mind about me."

But Maddie turned back to Pin-Yen. "Lexa owns the building you live in. She saved the family and that building, and from where I'm sitting, it looks like everyone is grateful. Except you." Maddie paused and looked around the table. Most everyone who could understand English had stopped talking, looking back and forth between Maddie and Pin-Yen. "You should be groveling at Lexa's feet that she allowed you to stay. I heard everyone else wanted to boot you out on your ass, but Lexa said no."

Pin-Yen stood with a sharp scrape of her chair. Without a word, she stormed out.

"Oh, geez." Hsu-Ling rolled her eyes. "Not again, Maddie." Their uncle stood and gave both Hsu-Ling and Lexa a pat on the shoulder before returning to his seat.

"I just said what everyone else here is thinking." Maddie raised her eyebrows at Hsu-Ling.

"Stop poking at her," Lexa said. "She already lost. Do you have to keep rubbing her face in it? You're just making her angrier."

"Well, she's making me angry at the way she's treating you." Maddie pushed away her bowl.

Lexa's shoulders slumped forward. "I don't understand why she hates me so much. I should just go home. Stop causing trouble for your family."

"What?" Maddie looked at Lexa, her face screwed up with indignation. "Don't let her drive you away. This is your family too. You're not that fourteen-year-old girl anymore."

Hsu-Ling put a hand on Lexa's arm. "Maddie's right. Don't leave because of her. I'll stand by you."

The waitresses began clearing away the dishes. "Are we done here?" Maddie asked.

"Almost. They're serving a dessert soup, with red beans." Hsu-Ling gestured to the large bowl a waitress was setting on the lazy Susan. "We don't have to stay. Most of them will linger for another hour or so, drinking and catching up."

Lexa pushed away from the table. "I can't eat another bite. I want to save room for the FengJia Night Market later."

"Where's that again?" Maddie asked. She pulled up the map of Taichung on her phone.

Lexa pointed. "It's to the north and west of where we are now."

"Is that all you do here? Eat?" Maddie asked.

"Pretty much." Hsu-Ling laughed. "Taiwanese people love to eat."

They said good-bye to the relatives and headed back to the apartment. On the way, they passed open food stalls lining both sides of the street. "These used to be food carts," Hsu-Ling explained. "Now most of them are part of the building and branch out onto the sidewalk with no door. Except when it's really hot; then they close it off for the air-conditioning."

"It's good to be back." Lexa looked at the busy street full of scooters and cars, and the sidewalks crowded from where stores and food stalls spilled out. They were forced to dodge around racks of clothing, shoes and accessories, or rickety tables and stools where people huddled over bowls of noodle soup or oyster omelets. "I've missed this."

"Then don't let my mother drive you away." Hsu-Ling and Lexa exchanged a look.

"You're right. I won't," Lexa said. "I am glad to be back."

"I wish you were staying longer."

"I'm here for eight days. I think that's long enough to be away from my clients."

"All you think about are your clients." Maddie shot Lexa a disdainful look.

"I do not."

"Hey, look. Sesame balls. Your favorite." Maddie pointed at the window of a bakery.

"That's right," Hsu-Ling said. "You loved them from the

first time Baba bought you one. Let's get some." And Hsu-Ling rushed into the bakery before Lexa could stop her.

Hsu-Ling had already ordered three sesame balls by the time Lexa caught up with her. "Um . . ." Lexa started to tell her she didn't like them anymore but then stopped. She didn't believe in bad luck and ghosts. She couldn't let her superstition ruin one of her fondest memories of her father.

"Thanks," she said when Hsu-Ling handed her one. Taking a bite, she closed her eyes, enjoying the chewy texture and the memories the treat brought back to her. She just hoped she didn't get run over by a bus or something once she finished the sesame ball.

"You still want to go furniture shopping tomorrow after we go visit Baba's ashes?" Hsu-Ling's voice broke into Lexa's thought. She'd taken them to see Lexa's new apartment that morning. It was a one-bedroom and bigger than Lexa's apartment in New York City.

"Yes."

"I wish someone would leave me an apartment." Maddie stopped to let a toddling little boy cross in front of her. "That was actually a pretty nice thing Pong did."

Lexa snorted. "Yeah."

"You know, it's so strange that he just happened to die on the same day as your father," Maddie said. "I mean, I know he was sick, and you said he suffered a stroke after he told your father, but still. It's almost like he died of a broken heart or something."

Lexa watched as the color drained from Hsu-Ling's face. "What's the matter?"

Hsu-Ling paused in front of a 7-Eleven and leaned against the wall.

47

Three Months Ago
Taichung, Taiwan

The ambulance carrying her father's body was ready to pull away. Hsu-Ling sank down onto the curb of the road, her legs too weak to hold her up.

"Ride back with us." Kuan-Yu, one of the paramedics, stood in front of her. Her father was one of them, having worked at the hospital for over thirty years. Kuan-Yu was the one who told her Uncle Pong had suffered a stroke when her father had run out of the hospital.

"No." She shook her head. She couldn't get into the back of that ambulance with her father's body. She refused to believe he was gone. He couldn't be. Not her baba. He was supposed to give her a ride home on his scooter after visiting Pong. They were going to take Mama to her favorite soup dumpling place tonight, for *xiao long bao* and noodle soup. He wasn't supposed to be lying so still and broken and so dead in the back of that ambulance.

"We can't just leave you here." Kuan-Yu took her by the elbow and tried to pull her up.

"No!" she screamed. "I can't."

He dropped his hand and stared at her as if she were a feral animal. She couldn't control her breathing, which was coming in loud, jagged breaths.

"Hsu-Ling, breathe. I'm so sorry."

"No," she gasped. "Don't say that. If you say it, it means he's gone."

Kuan-Yu gave her an uncertain look. She knew what he was thinking. He thought she'd lost her mind. Maybe she had. Kuan-Yu put a hand on her shoulder.

"Hsu-Ling. Please. Your baba wouldn't want us to leave you here. Please come . . ."

She looked away from him, from the sympathy shining in his eyes. She couldn't take it and looked at the scene of the accident instead. Her heart clenched as she stared at the mangled mess that was her father's scooter and the car he'd crashed into. The driver of the car had been unharmed, minus a few cuts and bruises, and was near hysterical. She'd kept repeating, "I didn't see him. I didn't see him. He came out of nowhere." Hsu-Ling had been relieved when they'd taken her away in another ambulance.

"Just go," she said. "I'll walk back."

He was reluctant to leave. He lingered, hovering over her, making her want to scream and yell. His colleague stepped forward. "We have to go."

Kuan-Yun looked at Hsu-Ling. "Are you sure?"

"I need to be alone. I'll walk back."

With one last lingering look, they left. She sat on the curb for a few more minutes, gathering the strength to stand. Why hadn't she gotten into the ambulance? She could have sat in the front. She didn't know if she'd make it back to the hospital with the way her body was shaking.

How was she going to tell her mama? Tell her that Baba, the light of both their lives, was dead? Dead because of what Pong had told him? Hsu-Ling sobbed, burying her face in her hands, her shoulders hunched as she huddled on the curb. Someone touched her on the back, but she shook the hand off so violently they withdrew immediately. No one else approached her.

Pong. He was responsible for all this sadness. Baba was dead because whatever Pong had said to him had upset him so much that he'd run out and gone the wrong way and died.

A sudden ball of anger gathered in Hsu-Ling's chest, and she stopped shaking. She stood, the fury taking over her body and giving her a strength she didn't know she had. Turning toward the hospital, she started running, her gait unsteady because she didn't have her running leg on. But her pace was fast when moments before, she'd thought she couldn't possibly make it to the hospital. She didn't need her running leg. She used her whole body to will her prosthetic leg forward, and each time it hit the pavement, Pong's name echoed in her mind and her fury grew. Step, Pong, step, Pong, step, Pong. It became a chant, and she ran faster and faster back to the hospital.

By the time she made it to the ICU, sweat was pouring down her back, making her shirt stick to her skin. An ICU nurse saw her and laid a hand on her shoulder. "I'm sorry about your father." Her eyes flashed sympathy, but then she rushed toward a patient whose husband was calling out to her. The ICU was busy, a hub of disease and serious injuries, where people hung on the cusp between living and dying. Nurses and doctors rushed around, issuing orders and asking questions, some not related to their patients; machines beeped and droned, and alarms went off with increasing frequency. No one noticed when Hsu-Ling slipped into the room where Pong lay sleeping.

She stood at his bedside, watching him, the fire burning in her chest taking over her entire body. She needed someone to blame for her father's death, and she directed all her anger at this man whom she'd loved as an uncle, who'd been a part of her life for as long as she could remember.

As if sensing her presence, his eyes fluttered open. There was a moment of confusion, but they cleared when they focused on Hsu-Ling. She could see the question in his eyes. *Where is Jing Tao?*

"He's gone, Uncle Pong." Hsu-Ling didn't recognize her own voice. "You killed him. Whatever you said made him so upset, he ran out of the hospital and crashed his scooter into a car. He's gone, and it's your fault."

Pong's eyes widened, and though he couldn't speak because of the breathing tube, she understood the questions he was shooting at her. Tears dripped down her face, and before she could say another word, Pong let out a terrible sound, like the moan of an animal in great pain. His eyes rolled back in his head, and Hsu-Ling slowly backed out of his room. She turned and walked toward the entrance to the ICU, melting into the chaos as alarms went off in Pong's room and staff responded by running toward him. She kept walking, never once turning around to see what she'd done.

48

Lexa traced the small plaque bearing her father's name with her fingers. She was in the pagoda-shaped columbarium on the grounds of the temple where her father's ashes were kept. Hsu-Ling had tried to explain the complicated funeral rituals in Taiwan to her and Maddie. The family had consulted with a geomancer to find a good day for burial, which would be months after the passing. In the meantime, his ashes were stored in this pagoda, inside what looked very much like small metal lockers found at a train or bus station. Lexa couldn't get over how many compartments there were stacked on top of one another, spanning all the way to the ceiling and all around the room, each labeled with a number and a name if the family had decided on a plaque.

They'd brought offerings, and Lexa had laid them before the gods and goddesses who protected the souls of the deceased outside the pagoda. Now she stood inside on the yellow tiles and bowed her head. She felt more connected to him there than she had at his final prayer ceremony the day before. Her sisters stood slightly behind her, giving her space.

Clasping her hands together, Lexa thought of all the things she'd wanted to say to her father. She'd stored them in her head over the years, waiting for that moment when they'd finally see each other again. She'd dreamed about this moment so many times, of finally coming back to Taiwan and confronting him. But she never dreamed she'd be doing so to his ashes. She'd blamed their estrangement on him, but the truth was she had as much to do with it as he did. As her uncle had pointed out the day before, her father had reached out to her, especially in the early years, but Lexa had rebuked him.

Her eyes downcast, she brought up an image of him in her mind, as he was the last time she had seen him in person. She began to speak.

"Baba, it's me, Chi. I've finally come back to Taiwan. I wish the reason I'm back wasn't because you're dead. All these years, I dreamed about the day when I'd finally hear you tell me you believe me."

She squeezed her eyes shut tightly and dropped her voice to a whisper, not loud enough for Hsu-Ling and Maddie to hear but, she hoped, loud enough for her father's soul to hear.

"Baba, Hsu-Ling thinks she killed Pong. Help her to see that Pong was basically on his deathbed. She didn't cause his death." Although there was a part of her, one she wouldn't admit to out loud and certainly not to Hsu-Ling, that wondered if Hsu-Ling's accusations had caused Pong's body to give out.

Lexa paused, waiting to see if she'd feel anything, if she could sense her father's spirit. When nothing happened, she opened her eyes and continued, this time speaking out loud. "I know I'm supposed to forgive you, Baba. But the truth is, I don't know if I can." Her fingers sought out his name again. "My head understands why you chose to believe Pong and your wife over me. But my heart can't get past it." She dropped her hands to her sides. "Shifu tells me peace is the most powerful weapon in the world. And I know I'll never get any peace unless I let it go." Her voice dropped to a whisper again. "I'm trying."

She paused for breath, and Maddie stepped forward, slipping her hand into Lexa's. Hsu-Ling grabbed her other hand, and Lexa gave both a squeeze. "I miss you, Baba. I wish I could have heard you say you believed me before you passed away."

She fell silent and took her hands back from her sisters to bring them together in front of her heart. She bowed her head and felt Hsu-Ling step close on her one side. She didn't have to turn her head to know Hsu-Ling was praying to their father too.

A sudden wind blew through the pagoda, lifting Lexa's hair away from her neck and swirling the light blue skirt she was wearing around her legs. She looked up when the scent of sandalwood, a smell that always made her think of her father, filled her nose. She expected to see the door open, bringing in the wind, and sandalwood incense sticks burning. But the door was closed, and no incense burned. Lexa stood still. A strange calm settled over her, like a warm blanket on a cold winter night.

Believe, a voice said in her mind. *Believe in yourself.* For a moment, she thought it was Shifu. But as the words repeated in her mind, she wondered if it was her father. She hadn't really believed Ah-Ma when she said their father's soul was stuck, unable to move on to the heavens with the gods because he had unresolved issues. But standing there in front of his ashes with the unexplained breeze lifting her hair and the smell of sandalwood teasing her nose, she believed. For one moment, she believed.

49

〜

"Why are we back here?" Maddie stood on the sidewalk staring at the red gate. She'd been busy texting with Mike and the kids in the taxi ride from the temple and had missed the conversation between Lexa and Hsu-Ling.

"We're picking up Ah-Ma to take her for coffee, before going furniture shopping. She doesn't get out much these days. She loves the bread at this coffee shop we go to." Hsu-Ling unlocked the gate, and they headed down the hallway toward the stairs leading up to the second floor, where Ah-Ma lived.

The door to Pin-Yen's apartment opened before they could round the corner up the stairs. Pin-Yen stood in the doorway with her purse in hand but stopped when she saw the three of them.

"Mama. We're taking Ah-Ma to coffee." Hsu-Ling spoke in English.

Pin-Yen didn't say anything and turned around as if to go back into the apartment.

"Mama," Hsu-Ling said again, louder. She walked to her mother and put her prosthetic leg in the door before her mother could slam it shut. "You're not talking to me now?"

Pin-Yen held still.

"Stop this." Hsu-Ling pushed past her mother and went into the apartment. "You can't stop talking to me just because Lexa is here. I'm still your daughter."

Lexa and Maddie glanced at each other, and then Maddie shrugged and went in after Hsu-Ling, with Lexa trailing behind.

"As long as that girl is here and you continue to bring her around, we have nothing to say to each other." Pin-Yen spoke in English and stood stiffly in the foyer with her arms crossed over her chest, glaring at the trio, who had made their way into the living room.

"That girl is my sister," Hsu-Ling said between gritted teeth. "She is welcome here whenever she wants, because she owns the building. She's family."

"She'll never be my family."

Maddie laughed. "Well thank goodness for that. I wouldn't want you in my family."

Lexa turned and glared at Maddie. "Shut up," she hissed.

"No, I won't shut up. I've had enough of her attitude." Maddie walked up to Pin-Yen. "You've done nothing but make us feel unwelcome from the moment we met you. You put Lexa down and won't admit what you did to her all those years ago was wrong. I think it's time *you* shut up. Your husband acknowledged that Lexa was his daughter. And there's nothing you can do about it."

"Get out of my house." Pin-Yen stabbed a finger at Maddie, and Lexa could literally see the steam coming out of her ears.

"No." Maddie said the word deliberately and crossed her arms over her chest.

"I said get out!" Pin-Yen screamed. She pointed to the

door, and when no one moved, she walked over to Lexa and grabbed her arm. "You will never be Jing Tao's daughter. Get out of my home."

Lexa tried to shake off Pin-Yen, but the older woman had a tight grip. "Get your hands off me."

Maddie cocked her head. "Lexa knows Kung Fu. I'd let go of her arm if I were you."

"Fook you." Her face red with rage, Pin-Yen let go of Lexa's arm and turned to Maddie. Lexa went back to Hsu-Ling's side.

"Fook? What the heck is that?" Maddie pretended to scratch her head and let out a laugh. "Oh, you mean 'fuck.' If you're going to curse me out, at least pronounce it properly."

Pin-Yen's face turned so red that Lexa almost wondered if she'd been drinking. The older woman stared at Maddie with loathing.

"Maddie, stop," Lexa said, hoping to shut Maddie up. Lexa could see the distress in Hsu-Ling's eyes as she fixed on the duo standing in the foyer. But there was no stopping Maddie.

"Just admit you lost. Lexa is back. She's claiming her Taiwanese heritage, getting to know her family again. And what do you have? Nothing. Your husband died knowing the truth about you." Maddie leaned in so close to Pin-Yen that the older woman shrank back. "He died knowing what a liar and bitch you are. So go ahead, stop talking to Hsu-Ling. She's the only one still on your side, but if you want to alienate her . . ." Maddie threw up her hands and shrugged. "You're going to die a lonely, bitter old woman because your precious daughter, who you did all this for, is going to end up hating you."

Time stopped. Hsu-Ling stood with a hand over her mouth while Lexa held still at her side. She was about to move, to say something, anything, to dispel the terrible tension in the air, when Pin-Yen suddenly sprang to life. Reaching for the big blue-and-white vase that had stood in the foyer for as long as Lexa could remember, Pin-Yen picked it up and swung it over her head.

Lexa had time to marvel at how Pin-Yen was able to lift the heavy vase before reality crashed in and she realized with horror that Pin-Yen was aiming for Maddie's head. Before Lexa could react, she heard a cry and, out of the corners of her eyes, saw Hsu-Ling leap forward.

As if in slow motion, her eyes tracked Hsu-Ling's form as she sprang between her mother and Maddie, pushing Maddie aside. Pin-Yen's eyes widened as she realized her daughter was directly in line with the downward arc of the vase in her hand. But by then, it was too late. The vase crashed down hard over Hsu-Ling, who fell against Maddie, causing Maddie to stumble and sprawl to the floor. Hsu-Ling crumbled backward out of the apartment in a shower of broken glass, her head making a sickening crack as it connected with the concrete floor. Then the only sound was the harsh breathing coming from Pin-Yen as she stared down at the still form of her daughter, the broken vase still in her hand.

50

Someone was screaming. Over and over again, a loud, piercing scream that made Lexa want to put her hands over her ears. She stared at the still form of her sister. It reminded her of all the times Hsu-Ling used to trip when they were younger and Lexa had stared, horrified, at her sister sprawled out on the floor. Except this time there was blood, so much blood, seeping into the concrete floor. Lexa glanced at Maddie, also on the ground, but she was sitting up. Maddie looked dazed but seemed otherwise okay. Realizing the severity of Hsu-Ling's situation, Lexa finally got her body to move, going to her sister's side and grabbing her phone to call 911. But wait, was it 911 in Taiwan? Or something else? Oh, God, she didn't know. Frantic, she jabbed at her phone as if the answer would magically appear.

Footsteps pounded down the stairs, and suddenly Li-Chung, one of her cousins, appeared on the landing. She ran to Pin-Yen, who was screaming her head off, and slapped her hard. Pin-Yen collapsed to the ground and crawled to Hsu-Ling, and Li-Chung pulled out her phone and dialed for help. Her voice was calm as she asked for an ambulance and gave their address.

Lexa dropped to the other side of Hsu-Ling, not sure if

she should touch her but wanting to stop the blood. She could hear Maddie behind her saying something to her, asking questions, but her attention was on Hsu-Ling. *Oh, God, please hurry. She needs help.* Lexa knew CPR but not basic first aid, and she crouched helplessly over the still form of her sister.

. . .

Lexa sat as far away from Pin-Yen as she could in the waiting room. They'd just taken Hsu-Ling into surgery to relieve the pressure on her brain. She called her mom.

"Mom." Lexa tried to keep the hysteria from her voice as she told her mom what happened.

"It's my fault. I should have been there with you and not sent Maddie. I'm so selfish!" Her mom's voice rose with each word.

"It's not your fault, Mom." Somehow, her mom's panic calmed Lexa's own hysteria.

"I'll get on the first plane. Poor Hsu-Ling. She saved Maddie's life. Is Maddie with you?"

"No, she's still at the building with my cousin. I came in the ambulance with Hsu-Ling."

"I could kill her mother!"

It took Lexa a few minutes to calm her mom. She only hung up after Lexa promised to call as soon as they had news. Lexa paced the waiting area, unable to sit still. She prayed, not sure who she was praying to; the gods, her father, anyone who would listen. *Please don't take my sister away when I've finally found her again. I just lost my father. I don't want to lose her too.*

Without thinking, she pulled out her phone again. And it wasn't until he answered that she realized she'd called him.

"Lexa, what's wrong?"

She sank with relief into a hard plastic chair and closed

her eyes as the sound of Jake's voice washed over her. Her heart calmed as his comforting voice soothed the raw edges of her nerves.

. . .

The doctor was speaking in Mandarin, and Lexa struggled to understand.

Brain injury . . . first forty-eight hours . . . critical . . . bruising on the brain. And then a whole bunch of medical terms before more words seeped in. *Lacerations . . . relieved the pressure . . . hole in skull.*

Pin-Yen nodded at whatever the doctor said, tears running down her face. Lexa looked back and forth between them, trying to gauge if the news was good or bad. She was about to speak when the doctor turned to her and spoke in English. Lexa let out her breath when he said they'd done what they could for now and it was up to Hsu-Ling to wake up.

. . .

Something beeped, and Lexa looked up, her eyes anxiously scanning the monitor above Hsu-Ling's hospital bed. The machines hooked up to Hsu-Ling were terrifying, and every noise made Lexa jump, sure that something was wrong and she should call for a nurse. But after two days of sitting by her sister's side, she'd learned which beeps signaled an emergency and which were routine. She learned to look at the numbers and graphs that appeared on the display panels and trust that they were doing their job to inform the medical staff of Hsu-Ling's condition. She dropped her gaze back on her sister, lying so still and pale, with large white bandages wrapped around her head.

Lexa fidgeted in her chair, trying to get comfortable on

the hard wooden surface. Her cell phone was clutched in one hand, since her Taiwanese family was constantly reaching out to see if there was any change. Her mom and Greg had been calling and texting from New York too. Hsu-Ling's friend Kuan-Yu had stopped by many times, and even though it was supposed to be family only, the nurses had let him in to see Hsu-Ling briefly.

Lexa was dying of thirst but didn't want to get up. Too soon, Pin-Yen would be back, and Lexa wanted to stay by Hsu-Ling's side as long as she could.

Her phone dinged. It was from Jake.

Any change in HL?

No.

I'm sorry. Wish I could be there with you.

Her mouth curved, even as sadness weighed in her heart. Her phone dinged again, this time from Maddie.

You need anything? Want me to come to the hospital and keep you company?

Yes, come, if you can get Li-Chung to drive you over. Maybe bring me a bubble tea?

Ok. Be there in half an hour.

Maddie had wanted to be with Lexa at the hospital right after the accident. But in the chaos that ensued, Lexa had been glad that Li-Chung had taken over. She had calmed Maddie down, herding her upstairs so Lexa could ride with Hsu-Ling to the hospital. Her husband had driven Pin-Yen to the hospital on his scooter.

Lexa leaned her arms on the side of the hospital bed and dropped her head on top. She was so tired and so scared. Pin-Yen had insisted on staying overnight with Hsu-Ling both nights, so Lexa had gone back to the hotel, but she hadn't slept. She'd spent as much time in this room as she could, keeping watch over Hsu-Ling when Pin-Yen needed a break, and willing her to wake up. Hsu-Ling's face was bruised and swollen, and she'd needed many stitches to close the cuts caused by the broken glass. But it was the blows to her head, one from the vase and one when her head hit the floor, that the doctor had been most concerned about. Her head had been shaved for the surgery. They'd hoped she'd wake on her own after the surgery, but she'd remained still and silent for two days.

Hsu-Ling made a noise, a soft sigh, and Lexa picked up her head. The first time her sister had done that, Lexa had called the nurse, sure it meant Hsu-Ling was waking up. Now she knew it was an involuntary sound, and after scanning Hsu-Ling's face for movement, Lexa sighed herself. She picked up one of her sister's limp hands.

"Hey there, sleepyhead. Wake up." They'd told her it couldn't hurt to talk to Hsu-Ling. "That's what my dad used to say to Maddie and me when we were little." Lexa smiled, thinking about Greg trying to wake them when they were young.

Lexa used her other hand to adjust the blanket from where she'd pulled it loose when she'd leaned on it. "We still have so much to see and do, Hsu-Ling. You can't just sleep my entire visit away. There's only three and a half days left before I go back to New York. You promised to take me to the Yizhong Shopping Street. We were supposed to take Maddie to Sun Moon Lake today. You promised to take me to the original bubble teahouse in Taichung. What's it called again?" Lexa took her hand back to scroll through her phone, where she'd bookmarked the website for the teahouse. "Oh, yeah. Chun Shui Tang. You said you loved their turnip cakes and cuttle-fish balls. And the handmade noodles with the minced meat sauce."

Lexa stopped when her stomach growled. All this talk of

food was making her hungry. She couldn't remember the last time she'd eaten. Maybe she should have asked Maddie to bring food along with the bubble tea.

She picked up Hsu-Ling's hand again and continued her monologue. "I can't lose you now, Hsu-Ling, not when we've finally found each other again. You're my only real link to Baba. You said you'd teach me Taiwanese. Our cousins are nice, but it's awkward when you're not around. I need you. I need you to help me get to know our family, our history and culture."

Her phone dinged, and Lexa looked at the message.

I got steamed buns for you. Thought they'd be easy to eat at the hospital. Li-Chung also picked up tian bu la for Hsu-Ling. Maybe if she smells her favorite food, it will wake her up?

Lexa held up her phone. "Look, Maddie's on her way. She's bringing *tian bu la* for you. How does that sound?" Not really expecting an answer, Lexa let the phone drop to the side of the bed. "That was a brave and selfless thing you did. Maddie and I will never forget it."

Hsu-Ling's mouth moved, and Lexa grabbed the cup of ice chips from the table beside the bed and ran some over Hsu-Ling's lips.

"Okay, I'll make you a deal. If you wake up now, I'll stay in Taiwan for a whole month. Longer if necessary, until you're back on your feet. I'll stay in my apartment. You'll teach me Taiwanese, and we'll eat so much my clients won't recognize me when I go home. I want to spend lots of time with Ah-Ma, hear more stories about our family. I want to visit the temples and the graves of our ancestors. I want to know who I am, Hsu-Ling." Lexa looked down when a large tear plopped on the sheet and watched as the cotton absorbed it immediately, leaving a round wet spot.

A noise at the door made Lexa looked up. Pin-Yen hovered just inside the room, and Lexa stood as soon as she saw her. They'd worked out a silent agreement where if one wanted time with Hsu-Ling, the other would leave. They'd yet to say a word to each other since the incident.

Pin-Yen looked awful. Her salt-and-pepper hair was hanging around her face in greasy strings, and her face had aged ten years in the past two days. Lines pulled at her mouth, drawing it down, and dark shadows darkened the skin beneath her eyes.

They stared at each other for a moment, and then Lexa walked to the door, trying to pass Pin-Yen without touching her. She stopped when Pin-Yen laid a hand on her arm. Lexa stilled and looked at it.

Pin-Yen cleared her throat. "Stay. Just for a minute."

Lexa raised her eyebrows, her face stony.

"Please."

With reluctance, Lexa backed into the room, keeping her eyes on Pin-Yen. The older woman looked like she'd lost everything dear to her in the world, which she almost had. She dropped her eyes to the floor, as if the sight of Lexa hurt her eyes.

Impatience brewing inside her, Lexa spoke first. "What is it?"

"I . . ." Pin-Yen's mouth opened and closed, but no other words came out.

"Fine. I'm leaving."

"You're going to stay? For a month or more?" Pin-Yen's voice was hoarse, as if she'd lost her voice and was just getting it back.

Lexa's chin came up, and she said in a steely voice, "Yes. Don't even think of getting in my way. Whether you like it or not, I'm part of the Chang family. You can't chase me away. I'm not that fourteen-year-old girl anymore."

"No, you're not." Pin-Yen lowered her gaze again, her eyes stopping to rest on her daughter.

"I will stay for as long as it takes Hsu-Ling to wake up and get better. If it takes longer than a month, then so be it."

"Yes." Pin-Yen's head dipped once.

"You can spread all the lies you want about me, but this time, I'm not going to run home crying. I missed out on getting to know my father because of you. You tried to keep Hsu-Ling and me apart, but our bond is stronger than your manipulations. I am a Chang, my father's eldest daughter, and I'm back."

"Yes."

Lexa realized the other woman wasn't fighting her. Pin-Yen had her head bowed, her hands clasped in front of her, as if praying for forgiveness. "Yes?"

Pin-Yen raised her head and met Lexa's gaze. "Yes. I'm sorry." Her voice trembled with emotion, but she took a breath and continued. "I was wrong."

That was the last thing Lexa expected. What was she supposed to say to that? "It's okay"? No, it wasn't okay. Pin-Yen was responsible for keeping Lexa away from her father. And it wasn't okay that Hsu-Ling now lay in the hospital because this crazy woman had tried to kill Lexa's other sister, only to injure her daughter instead.

Pin-Yen was openly weeping now. She took one of Hsu-Ling's hands and laid it against her cheek. "I'm so sorry. I almost killed my own daughter."

"You're only sorry because Hsu-Ling got hurt?"

"No. I don't know." Pin-Yen shook her head vehemently. "I'm sorry for all of it. But almost losing my daughter . . .

that's what finally made me see what I did to you was wrong." She dropped Hsu-Ling's hand and reached into her purse for a tissue. Dabbing at her eyes, she said, "I don't even know how to apologize to you. You were a threat to my daughter. You could have taken everything away from Hsu-Ling."

"I wouldn't have. I didn't want Baba's money or the building. I only wanted to know Baba. And my sister." Lexa sank into the chair she'd vacated only moments before.

"I know that now." There were still tears in Pin-Yen's eyes, but her voice was steadier. "I . . . all my life, I've been told women are worthless. My father ruled our house, and my mother and I couldn't do anything without his permission." She looked up. "When Hsu-Ling was born, I vowed she would never feel the way my father made me feel. I would make sure she could be whatever she wanted, to have the best, be the best." She caught Lexa's eyes and held her gaze. "I knew Pong since I was a teenager. My father took him in as a foster child for a few months. He treated Pong better than he did me in the short time he lived with us."

Lexa blinked in surprise. "You knew Pong before you met Baba?"

Pin-Yen nodded. "Pong was the one who introduced me to your baba. I always knew Pong wanted to be more than friends with me, but I never saw him like that. But your father . . ." Pin-Yen stopped and ran a hand down Hsu-Ling's arm. She brought her daughter's hand to her lips before placing it on the bed gently. "He was so handsome and so kind. He said I was the bravest woman he'd ever met and that he admired me for my grit and backbone when I said I'd defy my baba to go out with him. So of course I married him." She gave a bitter laugh. "Turns out my father approved the marriage because the Chang family had a good name."

"And Pong?" Lexa leaned forward.

"Pong." Pin-Yen shook her head. "I loved him like a brother. I knew he was in love with me, and I used that love for my own gain."

"Why do you hate me so much? What did I ever do to you?"

"ChiChi . . ." Pin-Yen looked across the bed at her, and Lexa realized that was the first time she'd ever heard Pin-Yen refer to her by her Chinese nickname. "It wasn't you personally. It was the threat you posed to Hsu-Ling. If you'd been a boy, I would have hated you more. Having been told I was nothing all my life, I vowed to give my daughter everything I didn't have. And when she was born with that leg . . . I was so filled with guilt. I thought it was my fault. I knew I had to secure her future for her. I pushed her so hard all her life . . ." She gave a slight shrug. "You stood in the way. I had to get rid of you."

"And yet Baba still left the building to both of us."

Pin-Yen slowly let out her breath. She closed her eyes briefly and then opened them to look straight at Lexa. "I won't get in your way. If you want me out of that building, I'll go."

Lexa gazed at her, pity mixed with anger warring within her. In the end, she shook her head. "No. You're my sister's mother. I'd never do that to you."

Pin-Yen nodded, tears welling in her eyes again. "*Xie xie.*"

"Mama?"

Lexa and Pin-Yen swiveled their heads toward Hsu-Ling. They'd been so engrossed in their conversation they hadn't realized Hsu-Ling's eyes were open. They stared at her until Hsu-Ling said again, "Mama."

The cry that came out of Pin-Yen was filled with so much relief and joy that Lexa lifted her face upward. Her insides melted with relief, and she brought her hands up in front of her chest in a prayer of thanks.

When the smell of sandalwood filled her nose, Lexa smiled. "Thank you," she whispered. A gentle breeze stirred the hair around her face like a kiss against her cheek. "Baba, thank you."

51

While Hsu-Ling recovered in the hospital, Lexa roamed Taichung by herself. Hsu-Ling had shown her the little sidewalk stall that their father liked, a ten-minute walk from the hotel Lexa and Maddie were staying in. Every morning, Lexa slipped out of their room early, leaving Maddie still asleep. She'd sit on a rickety stool on the uneven sidewalk, imagining meeting her father here for breakfast. She ordered bowls of *rou geng* soup and oyster noodles, two of her father's favorites. Surrounded by strangers, she'd eat her soup and absorb the day-to-day life of Taichung, from the loud traffic noises to the rapid spoken Taiwanese that flew around her.

She'd take a taxi to the Chang building and spend time with Ah-Ma, listening to her stories about her father when he was a boy. Sometimes Maddie would come with her, and one day, Ah-Ma showed them how to make dumplings. Lexa would never forget sitting at Ah-Ma's kitchen table sprinkled with flour, watching Ah-Ma roll out the dumpling disc with a wooden rolling pin while Lexa and Maddie scooped the pork, cabbage, and chive filling into the middle. Ah-Ma taught them how to wet their fingers in a bowl of water and run them around the rim of the wrapper before pinching the dumpling shut. Maddie caught Lexa's eye, and they smiled at each other.

Another day, Lexa explored the neighborhood around the building alone after her visit with Ah-Ma. Every step she took, she wondered if her father had walked this same path, stopped to buy fruit from that fruit stand, or a bubble tea from that teashop, or fixed his phone in that phone store. She couldn't stop thinking of her father and of all the years she'd missed with him. He was there in every step she took, every corner she turned, and every meal she ate.

On the fourth day after Hsu-Ling woke up, Maddie was flying back to New York, and Hsu-Ling was going to be released later that same day. Lexa and Maddie went to the hospital so Maddie could say good-bye to Hsu-Ling. Kuan-Yu was sitting at Hsu-Ling's bedside, holding her hand. He greeted them and then rose to give Hsu-Ling a kiss before walking out the door.

"So . . ." Lexa pointed after Kuan-Yu. "How long has this been going on?"

Hsu-Ling looked down, a small smile on her lips. "He started checking up on me after Baba's accident. Then we were spending more time together. I've known him for a long time. Just never thought of him like that."

"And now?" Maddie asked.

"We'll see." Hsu-Ling smiled again.

"Good for you." Maddie leaned over the hospital bed and gave Hsu-Ling a hug. "Thank you again for getting between your mother and me."

"You would have done the same for me."

Maddie tilted her head. "I don't know if I would have done the same."

Hsu-Ling nodded her head emphatically. "You would have. You tried to save me from that asshole in New York even when you didn't like me."

They smiled at each other, and Lexa bit her lip to keep from laughing out loud.

Maddie reached out and gently touched Hsu-Ling's head. "You're going to look like a badass with your shaved head."

"Badass." Hsu-Ling rolled the word in her mouth.

"Take care of my sister, okay?" Maddie picked up one of Hsu-Ling's hands.

Hsu-Ling nodded. "I'm so happy she's staying for an extended visit." She turned to Lexa. "Are you sure it's okay? What about your clients?"

Lexa shook her head. "You're more important."

Maddie's eyes widened in disbelief. "I can't believe you're saying that."

Lexa took Hsu-Ling's other hand in hers so that the three of them were linked. "Me either. It was hard telling them I'm not coming home for a while. Well, not all of them. Some of them, I was glad to get a break from." Like Mrs. Lockwood. But she felt bad for leaving Christy Sung, who'd come to depend on her, even though Christy had gained so much confidence in the past months and continued to stand up to her father. And come to think of it, Andi was fine too, as good as engaged to her new boyfriend. She'd been emailing updates to Lexa, sending pictures of the two of them. And Kiley, thriving in California with John, who'd been a success at his first art show and sold many paintings. Even Beth Shapiro, who claimed she couldn't live without Lexa, was doing okay with the substitute trainer Lexa had found for her and her husband, David.

Lexa turned back to her sisters. "I need to do this for myself. I think I was burning out at work. My clients are fine without me. They can't be my whole life." She looked at Hsu-Ling. "Are you and your mother going to be okay?"

Hsu-Ling shook her head. "I don't know. I don't remember much. But knowing she tried to hurt Maddie on purpose . . . I don't know if I can forgive her for that."

"Oh, Hsu-Ling. Don't hold on to your anger. She's your mother. No matter her intentions, everything she did was for you."

"I know, but she went too far. She'll always be my mother, and I won't press charges against her, but other than that . . ." Hsu-Ling shrugged. The police had come by to question her, and Hsu-Ling had insisted it was all an accident.

They were silent for a moment, still linked by their hands until Maddie pulled away. "I should go. I have to finish packing."

"What are you going to do about Mike?" Hsu-Ling asked.

"We're going to counseling when I get back." Maddie gave a small smile. "Like you, I don't know how I feel, but I'm not ready to completely cut him out of my life. I want to see if we can work it out. And to see if I can learn to hold my tongue and not let everything I'm thinking fly out of my mouth." She and Hsu-Ling exchanged a wry glance. "That might be partly what was wrong in our marriage. I don't know." She shrugged and then gave Hsu-Ling one last hug. "Come see us again in New York soon."

"I will," Hsu-Ling promised.

Lexa smiled. Her sisters were finally getting along.

· · ·

A few hours later, after seeing Maddie off in the car Li-Chung had hired to take Maddie to the airport in Taipei, Lexa walked through Taichung Park. She remembered when her father and Uncle Pong had first brought her here. She walked over the curved bridge, running her hand over the giant white stone railing. She saw herself as an eight-year-old, running over the bridge and down the other side, crying, "Baba, look at me" in Mandarin.

She walked along the lake and watched families in kayaks and canoes floating by. Her father had taken her in one canoe, with Uncle Pong and Hsu-Ling in another. They'd had a race, and Lexa could still remember the screams of laughter that had trailed behind them as Baba and Uncle Pong pumped their arms, trying to outdo each other.

She went north to a quiet area of the park. She stopped at the end of a walkway lined with stone pillars and stared at the set of stairs leading up to two bronze horses and the statue of Confucius. She remembered coming here, and how Baba had led her to the statue and they'd sat at a bench on the side. He'd told her about Confucius, the philosopher and teacher who tried to create ethical models of family and public interactions.

Walking up the stairs, she noted the pavilion was empty. She chose a bench in the shade and sat gazing at the statue. She let her thoughts go, for once not worrying about anything: her clients and how they were doing back home without her, if Maddie had gotten to the airport okay, Hsu-Ling coming home from the hospital later, and Lexa's decision to stay in Taiwan for at least a month. The wind blew gently, lifting her hair off her neck, a welcome relief from the heat.

Her phone dinged, and she looked down at the screen. It was a picture of Greg and Elise with Zeus in between them, his tongue out and a smile on his face.

Zeus misses you. We do too. Elise says hi.

Lexa smiled to see her dad and Elise looking so happy together and taking such good care of her dog. Before she could respond, her dad texted again.

I'm so proud of you, Lexa. You are my brave, courageous girl. Love you.

She smiled again and sent him a reply. **Love you too, my father.**

"*Ni hao*," someone said from near the statue.

Lexa started and looked up, putting down her phone next to her. She'd thought the pavilion was empty. A shape moved, and an old man emerged from the shadows of the statue. She raised a hand in greeting.

He walked toward her, dressed all in black. "*Ni shi zhong-guo ren?*"

She nodded. "*Wo shi zhongguo ren.*" I am Chinese. "But I live in America." She spoke in Mandarin.

"Ah." He crossed his arms behind his back and regarded her. "*Ni xinqing chenzhong.*"

Lexa's eyes widened. How did he know she had a heavy heart? And he hadn't phrased it as a question, rather as a statement. She nodded at him. Despite her decision to stay, her father's death and all that had happened still weighed on her. And at the back of her mind was Jake. Should she take a chance, allow him into her life, or was she better off by herself?

"*Mei guanxi.*" The old man looked at her as he told her it didn't matter. He gestured toward the statue and switched to accented English. "Confucius says, 'Life is really simple, but we insist on making it complicated.'" The old man thumped a hand to his heart and switched back to Mandarin. "You will find your way. Believe in yourself."

He turned and walked down the steps, away from the statue, before Lexa recovered. She wanted to ask him what he meant, but by the time she stood up, he'd disappeared from her view. She looked right and left but didn't see him. He couldn't have gone very far in the few seconds it took for her to stand and turn around. Where was he?

She turned back and faced the statue of Confucius, sitting high on a pedestal with Chinese writing on it. She couldn't read the characters, but the old man's words rang in her head. Could it be that easy? That life was in fact simple, and she was the one who made it complicated?

What did she really want? What was important to her? She stared at Confucius, at his long beard and his hands clasped in front of him, and suddenly, all sounds from the park faded away. She no longer heard the kids yelling and laughing, or their parents calling to them to "come here" or "stop that." She didn't hear the conversations as people walked by below or the sound of traffic outside the perimeter of the park. She stood and stared at the statue.

Family. Family was what was important. She was being offered a second chance to get to know her Taiwanese family. Baba was gone, but Ah-Ma was still here, along with her aunts, uncles, and cousins and, of course, Hsu-Ling. She was going to learn Taiwanese and practice her Mandarin, spoken as well as written. She realized then that Pong had done her a favor. She didn't know if she'd have had the courage to come back by herself, without his prompting.

She brushed dirt off her shorts as plans formed in her head. In April, she'd come back for another month for Qingming Festival, or Tomb Sweeping Day. Her father would be buried by then, and she wanted to be here to honor him and all the ancestors she hadn't had a chance to know.

And maybe when she returned to New York, she'd be ready for Jake's love. Who knew if they'd work out? Maybe the distance would prove too great or they'd find they weren't as compatible as they thought. But she'd never know if she didn't try. And she did want to try. Maddie was right. Lexa was being an idiot where Jake was concerned. She'd let the estrangement with her father dictate the path of her life for too long. It was time to break free and listen to her heart.

Her heart pounding, Lexa picked up her phone and texted Jake.

I want to try.

A few seconds later, he answered. **I'm so happy. I love you, my Kung Fu Girl.**

Lexa exhaled, the air releasing out of her mouth. Without fear, she texted back, **I love you too.**

A smile breaking over her face, she turned and headed down the stairs and across the bridge. She wanted to get back to the hospital to help bring Hsu-Ling home. She stopped in the middle of the bridge at the very top of the arc and looked down at the water. A movement to her right caught her eye. Turning her head, she saw the old man who'd spoken to her at the Confucius statue. He lifted a hand and winked at her. She waved back, and when she blinked, he literally disappeared. Gripping the railing, Lexa stared hard at the place where she'd just seen him.

Believe in yourself. The words formed clearly in her mind. Pushing away from the edge, she crossed the bridge wondering if she was seeing things, or if she'd just witnessed one of the ghosts that Ah-Ma was so adamant roamed among them. The wind stirred her hair, and she thought she could hear her father talking to her. With each step she took, she felt her baba's spirit, and when the scent of sandalwood drifted around her, she knew she was right. He was there with her, in her heart and in the air around her.

A last breeze brushed her cheek, and then the air went still. She laughed, a joyful sound that was carried away across the water and merged with the echoes of the shrieks of two little girls from years earlier. She turned and exited the park, blending into the crowd of Taiwanese people on the sidewalk.

Acknowledgments

I never dared to dream I would get to write my acknowledgments, and yet, here I am.

Thank you, Rachel Brooks, for pulling me out of the slush pile and being the perfect agent. From your speedy editorial feedback and wise advice to your grumpiness when people didn't get my book, you have championed me 100 percent. Here's to our flying meatball anniversary! Thank you also to all the agents at BookEnds: I'm with the best and most supportive literary agency.

To the entire team at Berkley, thank you. Cindy Hwang, my brilliant editor who made my dream of being published by Berkley come true: I am so honored to be one of your authors. Jin Yu (my first fan!), your enthusiasm for my book helped make it a reality, and I am so grateful for your support. To Angela Kim for answering all my questions and being such a fount of information, Vikki Chu for the stunning cover, Elke Sigal for the beautiful book design, and Andrea Monagle for her eagle eye and witty comments. A big thank-you to Danielle Keir and Erin Galloway in publicity, and to Megha Jain, the unsung hero of publishing and who kept everyone on track.

To Christine Adler, who has been such a supporter and champion from the moment we met online and realized we live in the same town. My writing buddy, brainstormer, eater of all things, cheerer of all news, peed on by Lokie: thank you for your friendship and belief in me.

To David Geshwind and Peter van Buren, my earliest readers of the original version of this book, you saw something in that crappy first draft and helped improve my writing.

Thank you to the members of the New York City Writers Critique Group, especially Christopher Keelty, Steven Tate, Sheryl Presser, Hector Acosta, C. Correa, Letitia Edghill, Sara Lord, Whitney Trilling, Beatrice Indursky, Jeffrey Baer, Robert Turley, and Ken Chanko, who have either critiqued portions of my work or cheered me on.

To my critique partner, Delise Torres, who gave such insightful feedback and helped to shape my writing and stories. We will meet in person one day!

To my agent sister and critique partner, Jessica Armstrong, your writing inspires me. I can't wait for the world to meet your books.

To Farah Heron, Kristin Rockaway, Kristin Button, and Suzanne Park, authors who believed in me when I was querying for the third time and gave me feedback, encouragement, and courage.

To Denise Williams, Anita Kushwaha, Saumya Dave, Samantha Vérant, Devon Daniels, Kate Lansing, and Allison Ashley for keeping me sane during the LONG wait for this book to be published.

To Charles Salzberg and Tim Tomlinson, whose New York Writers Workshop taught me how to write a pitch. Because of them, I got my first full request ever, from Amanda Ng, then Tom Colgan's assistant, on the first version of this book. It was so bad, but Tom was kind enough to pass it along at Berkley. Thank goodness none of the editors remembered that unformed disaster when Rachel pitched the new, shiny version. Sometimes, life does come full circle.

To Allie Larkin, an author who helped me out when she had no idea who I was (except a big fan of hers). Allie, you were so kind from the first, and then we found out I live in the town where you grew up. Thank you for your willingness to answer questions and champion me.

To Alison Hammer, who called me when I got my offer and gave me wise advice. Thank you also for talking me down about all things publishing related.

To Em Shotwell, who I've never met, but whose Pitch Wars entry inspired me when I was about to give up. Because of her, I soldiered on, rewrote my first book, and signed with my agent.

To my beta and earliest readers, especially Lori Myers, Jeremy Marshall, and Jodi Lew-Smith. You helped me so much when I was just starting out.

To my friend Lauren Gleicher, thank you for ramening with me, reading my book, and always believing in me. And to her parents, Susan and Len Gleicher, and her kids, Leah and Zach Goldstein, for being my earliest (non-writer) readers.

To Linna Heck, who inspired the character of Hsu-Ling, and the entire Heck family, Allison, Maren, Abigail, and Carey, who are like family.

To my cousin Leslie Shei, thank you for helping me with the Taiwanese parts and fixing the wording of how our Taiwanese family would say things. Any mistakes are my own.

To my sister, C. J. Liao, for reading a draft of this book and pointing out things that didn't make sense or things about Taiwan that I'd forgotten.

To my mother, Hsiang-Fang Liao, and my father, Yaw-Ting Liao, who have supported every endeavor I've ever pursued (and some of them to spectacular failure). Thank you for not being Tiger Parents. Thank you also for taking care of Lakon so I could write.

And to my husband, Jim, thank you for putting up with crotchety old me and for reading all of my books. You never once thought that I was wasting my time. Thank you to Lakon, the happiest little boy in the world, who shows me every day how life should be lived. And to Pinot and Lokie, who were right next to me for every word written, every rejection, every accomplishment, always at my side, ready to listen or lick away tears. Pinot, my heart is still broken that you are no longer with me. You will live forever in my heart.

THE TIGER
MOM'S TALE

Lyn Liao Butler

Discussion Questions

1. Lexa tells Maddie at the beginning of the book that Greg is her real father because he's the one who raised her. Do you agree? Or do you think blood and biology makes someone the real parent?

2. Lexa struggles to fit in. She feels like she sticks out in her all-blond family, but when she's in Taiwan, people tell her she isn't really Taiwanese, since she's half white. Have you ever felt that you don't fit in because of your background?

3. Taiwanese food is mentioned throughout the book. Do the descriptions make you want to try it, if you're not already familiar with it?

4. Do you think Pong's method to try to reconcile Lexa with her father was cowardly and manipulative? Or do you think he did the right thing? Would you have agreed to his conditions?

5. Lexa equates sesame balls with bad luck after her mother tells her about Phoenix and her father dies. Have you ever associated things with bad luck because you were using/doing something when you got bad news?

6. Do you think Lexa's estranged relationship with her father is why she is still single and doesn't want children? Why or why not?

7. Susan thinks Lexa has buried herself in her work to avoid dealing with her past. Do you agree? Have you ever used work to ignore emotional feelings?

8. Maddie made it clear she didn't like Hsu-Ling even before meeting her. Why do you think she was so jealous of Hsu-Ling?

9. Was Pin-Yen a sympathetic character at all? Can you understand how someone could do something like what she did to Lexa, all to protect her own daughter?

10. Lexa is reluctant to let Jake in because they live on opposite coasts and differ in their views of children. Do you think she really feels that way, or is it just an excuse? Do you think Lexa and Jake can overcome their differences and have a healthy relationship?

11. Lexa finds solace and strength in kung fu, relying on it throughout her life when dealing with difficult situations and people. Do you have something similar in your own life that helps you get through difficult times?

Keep reading for an excerpt from
Lyn Liao Butler's next novel,

Red Thread of Fate

coming soon from Berkley.

S he was on the phone with her husband when he died.

Tamlei Kwan leaned against a wall outside the elementary school during her lunch break, phone tucked between her ear and shoulder. She balanced on one foot and slipped her other foot out of her taupe pumps. Ah, much better. The shoes felt like prison after a summer of flip-flops.

"Did we get it?" Tony's brusque voice greeted her. They were anxiously awaiting their letter of acceptance for the little boy they were adopting from China. But still. He couldn't bother to say hello first?

Tam stuck her tongue out at the phone. "No, I haven't heard anything. Will you be home for dinner?" Two days back at school and she was already acting like her young charges. "I could cook." But seriously, why was she even offering? He sounded so distant, as if he had better things to do than take her call.

"Sure, that sounds good. I shouldn't be home late. Thanks, Tam." Tony's voice softened on her name and just like that, she was glad she had made the effort. She knew she wasn't being fair. He *had* been doing a lot lately and she shouldn't be so prickly.

A sudden cacophony of traffic noises made her hold the phone away from her ear.

"What's going on?"

"Nothing . . . a lot of traffic." She could barely hear his voice.

"You're going to the deli on Amsterdam?" she yelled.

"Yes . . . hang on a sec." She could hear Tony's muffled voice before he came back on the line. "I'm grabbing lunch before my afternoon class. Let me know if you hear from Sandra, okay?" Their caseworker, Sandra, had told them their dossier had gone through review and was in match mode, which meant they should be getting that letter any day now.

"Okay." Tam chewed on her bottom lip. "Um, what should I make?" She wished she didn't sound so wishy-washy. Why was she so confident in her mind, but the moment she opened her mouth, she sounded like a meek mouse?

"I don't care, whatever you . . . HOLY SHIT!" Tony's voice was cut off in the midst of a loud roaring sound that made Tam think of the old wooden roller coaster at Coney Island that Tony had dragged her on once. Then, nothing. Silence.

"Tony? Tony! Hello?" Tam shouted. What the heck? She straightened off the wall, jamming her foot back in her shoe, all thoughts of her aching feet and wishy-washiness forgotten. She immediately redialed him, only to get his voice mail. His phone didn't even ring. She dialed again and again, her heart jumping into her throat. She finally decided to try his department at Columbia University, hoping someone could find him.

Her hands were shaking and she touched the wrong contact, dialing Tony's Pizzeria instead of Tony's office. "Darn it," she muttered, stabbing her finger at the phone. "I don't want a freaking pizza." This time, she hit the right number and a colleague of Tony's in the Department of East Asian Languages and Cultures picked up, informing Tam that Tony had left for the day.

"What do you mean he left for the day?" Tam's voice rose

with each word. "I just spoke to him and he said he was going to the deli on Amsterdam."

The woman on the phone was silent for a moment. "Uh, I saw Tony an hour ago and he was definitely leaving. He has a half day on Thursdays."

A half day? What was the daft woman talking about? Tony taught an afternoon class on Thursdays at Columbia this semester and then had office hours to meet with students, which was why he was sometimes late coming home. She started to explain but realized she was wasting her time. She hung up after making the woman promise to have Tony call her if she saw him.

Looking at the time, Tam knew she had to get back to her own class of first graders. She tried Tony one more time but still couldn't get through. She returned to her classroom, tamping down the panic that threatened to erupt.

Where was Tony? What had happened? Should she call the police? But if he had only dropped his phone and broke it, he wouldn't appreciate a police hunt for him. She had a bad feeling in the pit of her stomach and left her phone on her desk.

"Mrs. Kwan. Mrs. Kwan! I have a question about hot and cold." Tam looked up to see Steven Abrams waving his arm frantically. It was only the second day of school and already she knew this precocious little boy with the floppy brown hair would be a handful.

"Yes, Steven. What is it?"

"I heard my daddy talking to his friends about you. He said if you got rid of your glasses and unbuttoned your shirt, you'd be hot. But if you took off your shirt, wouldn't you be cold, not hot?" Steven tilted his head and looked up at her. His father was a single dad and so good-looking he had all the female teachers (and some of the male ones) fluttering about him.

"Oh, my." Tam knew she sounded like an eighteenth century schoolmarm, but she was at a loss. Normally, she was quick on her feet with the children and could come up with a clever answer to the questions her students asked. But now she could only stare, her mouth open "like a nincompoop" as Steven had so blithely called a fellow student yesterday, while the six-year-olds debated her hot and coldness.

She tugged at the white shirtwaist dress she wore. When she pulled the dress out this morning, she'd debated against wearing it since it was a few days after Labor Day. But it was such a warm, sunny day and she wanted to wear the dress one more time, despite the fact it would probably get dirty from the children. It was buttoned to the top and a size too big. She hated clothes that dug into her skin. She dressed that way for school, but if she had to be honest, she dressed that way outside of school too. She'd much rather be comfortable even if it made her look like a shapeless blob.

When the bell finally rang and she saw her charges safely to the bus and pick-up area, she huffed out a breath and rushed to her car. Tony hadn't called and she still couldn't get through. She threw her phone on the passenger seat in frustration. Driving the short distance to their home in Dobbs Ferry, she decided she would call the police when she got home. Maybe they could trace his cell.

But as she pulled into the dead-end street that led to their townhouse at the bottom of the hill, her heart sank. Sitting in front of their unit was a Dobbs Ferry police car. She knew then—something bad had happened.

She pulled into her parking spot and gripped the steering wheel hard to stop the tingling in her fingers. When her vision blackened, she squeezed her eyes shut and rested her head on the cool leather between her hands. She forced herself to breathe slower to stop the panic from taking over her body, not wanting to leave the safety of her car. She knew the minute she got out, her life would change forever, and she wanted to hold onto her old life for as long as she could.

What happened next passed in a blur. Facing the sympathetic-looking officers as her legs turned to jelly, she heard only bits and pieces of what they said.

"Flushing police . . . accident . . ."

The officers' radios buzzed to life in a burst of static and Tam turned toward the noise, her eyes glazed.

"Your husband . . . terrible . . ."

She turned back to the officers and they swam in front of her eyes. She swayed and would have fallen if one of them hadn't reached out to steady her, helping her inside and onto a chair. They continued to speak but they might as well be speaking Russian for all that she understood.

She looked down at her lap to avoid their gaze, grabbing fistfuls of her dress in her hands to keep from screaming. Then her eyes widened as she realized with dawning horror that she was wearing the symbolic color of death in China. Tony was more traditionally Chinese than she was and had commented this morning that she was dressed for a funeral. *Had she killed her husband by wearing white today?*

". . . call your family to come?"

She looked up, eyes wide with shock and shook her head. The officers kept talking and she scrambled to understand but her body refused to cooperate. She was frozen in her chair. Suddenly, something they said penetrated the fog that had descended over her brain.

"Flushing police? What do you mean? He was in Manhattan, at Columbia University where he teaches."

The officers looked at each other and then at her. "Uh,

no ma'am. He was on the corner of Main and Roosevelt in Flushing, Queens."

Ma'am? She was a ma'am now? How'd that happen? She had an absurd urge to laugh and had to choke it down. "You're wrong. I was on the phone with him. He said he was going to the deli on Amsterdam Avenue." Tam pulled her phone out to show the officers, as if that would prove he had been in Manhattan at the time of the accident. Maybe they had the wrong man since her Tony was at Columbia where he belonged, and not miles away in Flushing, Queens?

The officers exchanged a look. The younger one asked if they could call a friend for her. Tam closed her eyes. She put her hands over her ears knowing she was being childish but she couldn't help it. She didn't want to hear anymore. They were mistaken. They had the wrong man. She needed to make them stop, stop trying to ruin her life when she knew Tony was fine.

"His cousin was with him."

Her eyes flew open. She'd heard, even through her hands. Tony only had one cousin. "Mia? He was with Mia?"

One of the officers looked at his pad and said, "Mei Guo. She didn't survive either."

"Oh, no. That's her. She goes by Mia." Her head began to ache and she could feel every heartbeat in a vein in her temple. What was going on? Mia was dead too? Why would Tony tell her he was at work if he'd been with Mia? Hysterical laughter bubbled out of her and she was suddenly laughing even as tears streamed down her face and soaked her dress.

She gave in and let the police call her friend Abby Goldman. She was grateful to see her friend's familiar pouf of curly blonde hair and sank into Abby's arms, the tears falling fast. She could finally let go and stop trying to piece together the events of the day, which made no sense.

Tam didn't remember driving with Abby to Flushing from their town in the suburbs of New York City or identifying the body. She didn't understand a word anyone said to her in the noisy police station except that one young officer thought it was incredible she had been on the phone with Tony when he died. She kept hearing him say, "That's so weird. She was on the phone with him!" until an older officer hit him on the side of the head and told him to shut up.

She let Abby take care of everything. All Tam wanted was to curl up in her warm familiar bed with the blankets over her head, the smell of Tony lingering in the sheets. Her eyes were red and gritty and she was so tired, yet every time she closed her eyes, she heard again the last words he ever said to her ringing like a giant gong echoing in a temple, "HOLY SHIT!" They rarely cursed, so for that to be his last word to her made her feel like . . . well, shit.

When they finally, finally got home, Abby helped her upstairs to her bed.

"Here, take this." Abby handed her a round pill. "It'll help you sleep."

Tam took it and gulped it down with the water Abby handed her, eager for the pill to work and take her away from this nightmare. She pulled off her clothes and put on one of Tony's T-shirts. Crawling into bed, she longed for sleep to stop the spinning of her mind and the questions she refused to acknowledge. But before the darkness finally took her, one thought broke through her defenses. What was Tony doing with Mia in Flushing when she knew they were no longer speaking?

Dave Cross Photography

Lyn Liao Butler was born in Taiwan and moved to the States when she was seven. In her past and present lives, she has been: a concert pianist, a professional ballet and modern dancer, a business owner, a personal trainer and instructor, an RYT 200 yoga instructor, a purse designer, and, most recently, author of multicultural fiction. Lyn did not have a Tiger Mom. She came about her overachieving all on her own.

When she is not torturing clients or talking to imaginary characters, Lyn enjoys spending time with her FDNY husband, their son (the happiest little boy in the world), and their two stubborn dachshunds, and trying crazy yoga poses on a stand-up paddleboard. So far, she has not fallen into the water yet.

CONNECT ONLINE

LynLiaoButler.com
 LynLiaoButlerAuthor
 LynLiaoButler
 LynLiaoButler

Ready to find
your next great read?

Let us help.

Visit prh.com/nextread

Penguin
Random
House